The Thriller of Two Continents!

SAM 7

"Tension-packed . . . drama all the way."
—*Publishers Weekly*

"Riveting."
—*Vogue*

"A disaster novel . . . far superior to Hailey's AIRPORT."
—*Delaware News Journal*

"Every aspect of calamity—rescue, fire-fighting, body recovery, accident investigation, insurance binds, plus grief and panic—triggers an explosion of detail."
—*Kirkus Reviews*

SAM 7

Richard Cox

BALLANTINE BOOKS • NEW YORK

Library of Congress Catalog Card Number: 76-51429

ISBN 0-345-27112-2

This edition published by arrangement with
Reader's Digest Press

Manufactured in the United States of America

First Ballantine Books Edition: May 1978

Author's Acknowledgments

Although this story is fictional, I owe a great debt of gratitude to many officers who assisted me with details on the way in which their organizations plan for emergencies. In particular I wish to thank Commander L.F.J. Walker of the Metropolitan Police; Chief Superintendent T.W.A. Lucas of the British Transport Investigation Branch, Department of Trade; Mr. L. Singleton of British Rail; Mr. C. Kenyon; Station Officer M. Keevash of the London Fire Brigade; Mr. M. Barsby of the Westminster Hospital; Captain O.S. Evans of British Airways, and Mrs. D.I. Moss of the W.R.V.S.

Finally, this book could never have been completed without the efforts of Vanessa Baber and Juliet Searle who typed its many versions and revisions.

Chapter One

The restaurant was like a thousand others in Paris, with the faded red awning stretched across its front bearing a brewer's slogan "Meuse Pils Bière d'Alsace." Permanently dusty from the heavy traffic that ground past the front door in this industrial suburb called Argenteuil, a scattering of chairs and tables stood empty on the pavement.

Two hundred yards down the street from the restaurant, almost out of sight, two men and a woman sat in a Citroën saloon car. The two men, one in the passenger's seat in the front and the other in the rear, were surly and unsmiling. Their driver was an attractive young girl with almond skin and dark eyes, wearing slacks and a white cotton shirt. A passerby might have thought she was one of those emancipated Arab girls who had broken away from the veil, and the discipline of her grandmothers, to study at the Sorbonne. A closer look would have revealed the small transistor radio she held in her hand, a short, thick aerial sticking up from it. But passersby in Argenteuil usually have the sense not to stare at the girlfriends of Arab roughnecks in the *bidonville*.

The Arab *bidonville* is a shantytown where some three thousand Algerian migrant factory workers live. The name derives from old gasoline cans—*bidons*—that are hammered flat and used for the roofs and sides

1

of the shanties. Together with sheets of cardboard and any fragments of rubbish scrounged from construction sites, the *bidonville* looks like the worst of the refugee camps in the Middle East. If it had been such a camp it would have attracted worldwide condemnation. Because it was in France, and local factories needed workers, it remained unnoticed—a slum Casbah that few save the Algerians themselves dared enter.

In the saloon car, the two men and the girl listened intently to the little radio. Someone was transmitting in short bursts. And in Hebrew. The radio crackled slightly before the last words were received.

"Nothing changes inside."

The girl peered through the windshield and looked in the rear and side mirrors before raising the little radio to her lips. The two men surreptitiously checked their pistols. Both carried .22 caliber Beretta automatics, the short barrel of each lengthened by the thick sleeve of a silencer. The Beretta is accurate, reliable, and has all the punch needed for close-quarter work. It is the standard weapon for Israeli commandos.

"Let's go," the girl said in Hebrew into the radio. Putting the radio down in her lap, she let in the clutch. The Citroën glided forward.

She braked to a gentle stop a full five yards short of the restaurant. The two men swung open their doors, slid out and paused to join up on the pavement, then strolled casually under the awning and into the restaurant. Swarthy, unshaven, wearing the blue denims beloved of French workingmen for decades, they appeared to be typical immigrant laborers in their mid-twenties. Nodding to the group of men seated at a table just inside the door, they muttered the traditional Arab greeting: *"Salaam Alaykum."*

As the Algerians seated at the table glanced up, incuriously replying, both newcomers fired simultaneously. Two of the five went down, collapsing in their chairs. A third drew his gun, but was impeded by the table and shot through the head before he could aim. Another dived sideways. The fifth twisted out of the bench seat and with gun in hand broke past the gun-

2

men to the door. The girl, leaning casually out of the car window as though waiting for a friend, shot him in the stomach. He clutched at his belly, staggered, tried to aim at her, fired and missed. As the bullet slammed into the car's bodywork she shot him again and he fell among the chairs on the pavement, screaming. Inside, the barman stood trembling with his hands raised. Disregarding him, the gunmen swiftly gathered up the papers and snatched a briefcase lying on the bench seat, interrupted briefly by the Arab under the table. He only had a knife, and they shot him too before making for the car. As the girl drove off, she clicked the stop on her large masculine wristwatch.

"Seventy-three seconds. Not bad."

She accelerated down the avenue, then turned left into a boulevard that led through to a trunk road before speaking again.

"Did you find much?"

"A lot of papers," answered one, "and the briefcase."

"At least three must be dead," said the other.

"Mine wasn't," remarked the girl coolly. "But I think we have scored. Give them the code word."

One of the men reached for the little radio, flicked the transmit switch.

"Naharia."

"Ma'alot," came the answer.

One of the few self-indulgences of Naomi, the girl who led this killer team, was using the names of Israeli villages that had suffered fedayeen raids as code words for the success of her own. Naharia, a small seaside resort, had been the target of a raid by Al Fatah. Ma'alot was where schoolchildren were murdered in 1974. One of them was her niece.

Abruptly the fuzz of static ceased as the spotter in the rented room opposite the restaurant switched off. With his fresh complexion and his Belgian passport it was unlikely that anyone would suspect him when he checked out and left Argenteuil. He and the others in the spotter team had spent nearly a month tracking the group, learning their habits. Far away from the Middle East, operating from the superb cover of the *bidon-*

3

ville, the Arabs had forgotten the dangers of a routine, of either eating or sleeping to a pattern. They ate regularly at the restaurant. Naomi and companion commandos had needed to be in Paris only two days. The date of their raid was May 1.

In both Paris and London May Day had heralded summer with unusual exactitude. This year London was basking in unexpected warmth. In St. James's Park the tulips marched proudly along the flower beds, their colors rivaling the scarlet tunics of the guardsmen outside Buckingham Palace. At midday on May 2, two mounted policemen rode slowly along Birdcage Walk toward the palace, the deep brown leather of their saddles and harness glowing softly, their horses' hooves clopping on the tarmac. Both men wore regulation uniforms and peaked hats with the black and white checkered band of the Metropolitan Police around them, but the older of the two also had distinctive silver braided georgettes on his tunic lapels and a band of silver on the visor of his hat. The older man was Robert Thompson, and he was the commander in charge of this district of London, known as "A" Division. More colloquially it was his "patch," his being one of London's twenty-five police areas.

His patch was the London of the tourist brochures, Thompson reflected, the absolute heart of it. From his vantage point on the horse, he could see the St. James's Park lake shimmering through the trees, their leaves fresh green flakes of sunlight. Half a mile away Big Ben was sonorously striking one. People were sitting in their shirt sleeves on the grass, making the most of the warmth. Out of sight beyond them he knew that workmen were erecting flagpoles along the Mall for a state visit. Next Monday a visiting foreign president would drive to the palace in an open carriage, escorted by troopers of the Household Cavalry, their burnished steel breastplates and plumed helmets glistening, while thousands of spectators lined the route. This was the traditional Britain that drew the tourists. By God it was succeeding, too. As the horses

4

reached the end of Birdcage Walk, Thompson could see lines of tour coaches parked up Constitution Hill and huge groups of visitors eddying around the palace railings.

For the policemen of "A" Division, summer spelled work: royal processions and the Queen's birthday parade, the Trooping the Colors, political rallies in Trafalgar Square and Hyde Park, all kinds of demonstrations. It spelled traffic jams and diversions and countless hours of extra duty because the division, like the whole force, was seriously understrength. This was why Thompson was taking an unobtrusive look at the preparations for next week's state occasions. He liked riding, and he liked seeing things for himself. There were more than thirty horses stabled in the division, including one called Banner, given to the police by the Queen. His own mount was a gray, sixteen and a half hands high and spirited enough to react well when confronted with a crowd.

The two mounted policemen came around in front of the palace as the Changing of the Guard in the forecourt was being completed. In a minute the outgoing troops, resplendent in their bearskins, would march out of the great wrought-iron gates. As Thompson crossed the road a throng of tourists was pressing hard up against the constables on foot who were trying to keep the road clear for the soldiers. As he watched, Thompson realized that the constables near him had a problem. A jostling party of youngsters, forty or fifty of them, were disregarding the constables and surging out across the carriageway. Letting visitors get their money's worth was one thing; letting them get out of hand was another. Pressing his knees into the horse's sides, Thompson urged the gray into a trot, then wheeled around in front of the group, the mounted constable close behind him.

"Get back," he ordered loudly, "back on the pavement."

The leader, a lanky man in torn jeans, yelled out what sounded like an insult and ran straight out past him. For a second the horse reared; then Thompson

5

nudged it into a sideways movement, so that its flank came parallel to the crowd. Pawing the tarmac and tossing its head, the horse edged firmly toward the people. A girl shrieked. Suddenly they all drew back, frightened, leaving their leader stranded.

"Come back, you," shouted Thompson, "and stay off the road."

Reluctantly they all obeyed, alarmed by the physical size of the horses.

"We'll stay here until the guard has marched off," said Thompson to his companion.

He steadied his horse, surveying the packed throng outside the palace. There was always potential conflict in a crowd: conflict between what spectators wanted and what the requirements of order made possible. From the horse you could see way over everyone's heads, while the animal itself was a powerful ally. A mounted policeman was as effective as ten men in dealing with a crowd.

An hour and a half later Commander Thompson was concluding his regular Thursday afternoon conference with his staff on the coming week's activity at his office in Cannon Row Police Station, tucked away down a narrow lane off Whitehall, close to Westminster Bridge. Up to fifty thousand protesters were expected on Sunday from all over the country, demonstrating against changes in the abortion laws. They would swell the normal incursions of tourists and trippers. Then there was the three-day state visit starting on Monday. The following Saturday there would be yet another demonstration. The inspector from Thompson's Ceremonials' Office, Colin Sturgess, explained what he knew about it.

"This General Union of Palestinian Workers had been advertising the march pretty widely, sir. There are about six thousand Arabs in London."

"What's their program?"

"It's standard enough. Assemble Trafalgar Square three P.M. Speeches—"

Thompson interrupted.

"Is it Israel's removal from the UN that they're on about?"

Sturgess nodded.

"Apparently there's a UN debate starting the day before on the tenth. Demos are being staged in every European capital."

"Well, they've been given permission for this one," said Thompson bluntly. "So long as they comply with the terms of the permit, Trafalgar Square's all theirs."

"We've had private warning that they're going to march to the House of Commons."

"It's a Saturday. Parliament won't be sitting. They'd do better to march on Downing Street. Whose bright idea is that anyway?" Thompson held up his hand. "No, let me guess."

Although Parliament would not be in session and so the presentation of a petition there would not require permission, there was always a chance that it might provoke a newsworthy confrontation with police. Thus it was almost certain that it would get whoever received the deputation onto television.

"I know," said Thompson. "Andrews. That bloody man from Mid-Fife." Some of the six hundred and thirty-five Members of Parliament would do almost anything for publicity.

"Got it in one, sir. As before, he's promised he will personally present their petition to the prime minister. Doesn't want the PM stealing the limelight from him, I suppose."

"Well," said Thompson, "if he decides to divert them into Downing Street instead, we'll let the normal number of representatives through the barrier. Democracy must be seen to be working."

The peculiar characteristics of "A" Division required that its commander be much more than simply a policeman. He needed to be diplomat, courtier and politician as well. The division not only included St. James's Park and the whole of the far larger Hyde Park, but ran from the celebrated Trafalgar Square, in the east, down to the Houses of Parliament and the river, then went west to include Victoria Station, the commuter's gateway to southeast England, and the whole of the residential districts of Pimlico and

7

Belgravia, the latter studded with foreign embassies. Protecting these buildings and dealing with other diplomatic requests were part of Thompson's business. So was the protection of the residences of the royal family, notably Buckingham Palace and the smaller red brick Tudor Palace of St. James, and he retained a small detachment of police at each. The security of the royal family was a permanent headache, and the attempted kidnapping of Princess Anne in the Mall had shocked Thompson more than most people. Nonetheless, the royal palace that gave him the most trouble was the Palace of Westminster, more familiar to the world as the Houses of Parliament.

The original royal palace at Westminster was built by Edward the Confessor in 1340. Later on King Richard II had ordained that "Parliament shall be holden or kepid wheresoever it pleaseth the King." It had become established at Westminster, but the sovereign still summoned it to meet with an official opening at the start of each session, and a sessional order prohibited processions within one mile when members were sitting. Short of an international crisis, they would be away next Saturday in their constituencies as they were every weekend. Except, apparently, for Mr. Enoch Andrews.

Thompson decided that the MP could hardly be much of a nuisance and pondered what else might happen.

"Presumably there will be counterdemonstrating?"

"We've had a preliminary phone call from the League of Jewish ex-Servicemen," said Sturgess.

"They don't usually get violent." Thompson studied a map, though he knew the area so well that he scarcely needed to. "Work out where they can assemble— Speaker's Corner maybe—and make out the control plan for both groups. Keep them well apart, Colin, I don't want any trouble."

There were two other men at the meeting, both chief superintendents, which was the administrative rank immediately below Thompson's. One was his deputy, whose interest in the coming week was polite but academic as he was going on leave. The other, David Chance, ran the Criminal Investigation Department within "A" Division. Like all CID officers, he wore plain clothes. He was a well-built man with thick dark hair and looked like a rugger player, which for many years he had been.

"We've had a Special Branch assessment on this demo," said Chance. "They don't rate it much of a risk. They've given us a rundown on the local representatives of the Palestinian General Workers Union and of Palestine Liberation Organization leaders known to be in Britain, men like Salah Khalaf down at Chobham in Surrey. Standard stuff really. However, they have tacked on an Interpol report. Our friends across the Channel believe a new wave of Palestinian guerrilla attacks may be starting in Europe."

Thompson listened attentively. He had spent four years in the CID himself and learned the hard way that it was a mistake to discount Special Branch information, irrelevant though it might seem.

"What's the evidence?"

"It's more the lack of it! A gang of Arab guerrillas were ambushed and badly shot up in a Paris café yesterday, on the first. No one knows who by. The barman was unhurt and says a lot of documents were taken from them."

"Is there any reason for thinking this could spread to London?"

"No," said Chance. "Not concretely. I just know that the French have an acute sense of smell, and maybe they smell more than they can actually say."

"We'll bear it in mind then," said Thompson. He turned back to Sturgess. "Now, Colin, buzz off and work out those crowd controls." For a moment he lapsed into the formal police jargon that he used only when he wanted to underline a point. "I want the necessary action to guarantee there's no trouble. The necessary action, no more, no less."

The conference was ended. The three others rose, leaving Thompson sitting behind his leather-topped desk with its photographs of his family. This talk about

Arabs jerked him into thinking back to what he had been doing at Sturgess' age. Ironically he'd nearly joined the Palestine Police, the British force that existed before Israel was born. "£20 a month and all found" the advertisements had offered back in 1948, when he was twenty and just finishing his conscript service in the Royal Marines. It was good money, more than a second lieutenant took home. And he was a private. Then someone suggested that if he wanted adventure he should train as a commando. So he signed on for a further three years and gained his coveted green beret. At the ripe old age of twenty-three he became a policeman. He spent seven years on the beat in the East End of London, where robbery with violence, stabbings and gang warfare were commonplaces of his working life. There was none of the accelerated promotion which had taken Colin Sturgess from constable to sergeant in two years. Thompson was thirty by the time he got the three silver stripes on his sleeve and was transferred to the totally different environment of Epping, full of open grass and trees on the fringe of the Metropolitan Police's eight-hundred-and-twenty-mile area. That was when he married Carol.

Life at Epping had nearly made Thompson opt for a transfer to a truly country police force, like Hampshire or Gloucester. Carol's verdict against such a move was coincidentally rewarded by further promotion, back to the East End, as an inspector. Finally, a year ago, at forty-seven, he had reached the appointment that placed silver georgettes on his tunic, next below the assistant and deputy commissioners who ran the force under its ultimate arbiter, the commissioner of the Metropolitan Police. But like every single policeman, from the commissioner downwards, Thompson remained a constable. That was the basic rank. All the grades above that were appointments, earned on merit and able to be taken away for lack of it, just as the primary task remained as it had been laid down in 1829—the protection of life and property. Furthermore, the overwhelming majority of constables still preferred, as did Thompson himself, to carry out their task without resort to firearms if possible. Of late the activities of both armed robbers and of terrorists had made more skill at arms training necessary, but the principle held.

Thompson's reverie ended abruptly as he remembered that May 12 was his wedding anniversary. He and Carol had always joked about avoiding the unlucky thirteenth. This year May 12 would be a Sunday. Last year he had been involved in the control of a demo and the year before that with the siege of some gunmen, holed up in a tenement flat. This year he would damned well be at home. Having, as it were, filed and docketed this intention, his thoughts turned back to the Palestinians. He picked up the phone and called Colin Sturgess.

"I'd like you to do a bit of deviling for me. Drop in at the library at the Commissioner's Office and see what you can find out about these Arab guerrilla organizations. I'd like to know who we're up against."

He put down the receiver. Quite often he dealt face to face with rally leaders, and for no better reason than that he was a seasoned policeman, he had an inkling that this knowledge might come in useful. Colin would enjoy a bit of ferreting, too. He was a bright lad, the college-educated copper the force had been trying to attract. Not yet thirty, he'd be promoted again in a year or two.

Downstairs in the Ceremonials Office, which handled arrangements for all public occasions, Sturgess spoke to the sergeant who was helping him plot the marches.

"Well, skipper, I'm off to do a little digging at the Commissioner's Office."

"Let's hope she's pretty, sir."

Sturgess smiled. He was a bachelor and, unusually for a policeman, shared a flat with two outsiders, an accountant and a lawyer. Ever since he moved there he had suffered inevitable jokes about his sex life. In fact, the reason he had left the officially provided police quarters was the sense of being a race apart which living on the job produced. Of course, you could

11

never pretend you were not a policeman. Whether you were in uniform and so were automatically singled out from ordinary citizens, or in civilian clothes as both he and Commander Thompson normally were, whether you were on duty or off, the commitment was unchanged. Both literally and metaphorically your uniform was always hanging in the cupboard ready to be put on. But at least by living as most other young professional men in London did, he could retain a feeling for what was going on in the community.

It was barely ten minutes' walk to the Commissioner's Office, as the headquarters of the Metropolitan Police in New Scotland Yard was known. Sturgess went past the Houses of Parliament, a flag flying on one of the Gothic towers to denote that Parliament was sitting, past the ancient bulk of Westminster Abbey, and down Victoria Street. It was a curious street this, a busy thoroughfare leading to Victoria Station which not so long ago had been rundown and dowdy, familiar to Londoners mainly for the station and the army and navy stores. In the 1960s the developers had moved in, tearing down the small shops and erecting great concrete office blocks in their place. The Department of Trade and Industry occupied one, Monsanto Chemicals another and New Scotland Yard a third. The building stood roughly halfway down Victoria Street, close to the St. James's Park underground station. A slowly revolving triangular sign in the forecourt announced the name, successor to the famous Scotland Yard adjacent to Cannon Row, which had featured in countless detective novels and films. On March 8, 1967, everything had been transferred, including the Black Museum of murder weapons. But what New Scotland Yard lacked in tradition, it more than made up for with efficiency. It was a far better place to work in.

Reaching the library, Colin Sturgess made his inquiry.

"What have you got on the Palestine Liberation Organization?"

"It's a complicated subject," the librarian answered. "Let's have a look."

He went off and returned quickly with a handful of books and pamphlets.

"Christ alive!" said Sturgess. "I'm only briefing myself, not writing a thesis!"

"In either case," remarked the librarian dryly, "the relevant deity is Allah." He picked out a thick pamphlet bearing the imprint of the Institute for the Study of Conflict. "This is a little out of date, but short and comprehensible. Try it first and come back for more if necessary."

Sturgess took it to a table and started to read. A sentence caught his eye. "The threat and practice of selective terrorism have increased to a level where a wide range of Western interests have become targets." This was what he was after. Sturgess recalled photos of Yasir Arafat, leader of the PLO addressing the UN General Assembly, a round, fleshy face under an Arab headdress. He had held a gun in one hand and an olive branch in the other. Evidently at the moment Arafat favored the olive branch—he was achieving more and more diplomatic recognition thereby. But the five main fedayeen organizations that sheltered beneath the PLO's umbrella often preferred the gun. The most notorious was Black September. "Arafat and the Central Committee appear powerless to control it," stated the pamphlet. Black September was created to avenge King Hussein's clearing the fedayeen out of Jordan in September 1970. One of their first actions was to assassinate the Jordanian prime minister, Wasfi Tal, in Cairo. One of their failures was attempting to shoot the Jordanian ambassador in London in 1971. Sturgess remembered that. The gunman had fired on the ambassador's car as it slowed down at a street intersection in Kensington.

The style of Black September's operations was exceptionally violent. On September 5, 1972, the Israeli team at the Munich Olympic Games had been attacked. Eleven Israeli athletes and one West German policeman were killed. So were five of the Black September's commandos. That did not seem to have worried the organization. Nor, curiously, did the publicity. Quite the reverse. It was done for publicity, just as was the massacre at Athens Airport when gunmen had fired on a crowd in a passenger lounge.

Sturgess wondered about the psychology of this terrorism. Such cold-blooded ruthlessness ought to have produced international revulsion against the Palestinian cause. In fact, the upshot had been a wider international recognition of it. Furthermore, there had been a great many lesser attacks. Oil installations in West Germany and the Netherlands had been sabotaged. There had been explosions in Trieste, a murder in Madrid. He began to see why the French had passed that message through Interpol. The sponsor of the coming demo, the General Union of Palestine Workers, was one of the most militant Palestinian organizations in Western Europe, where some sixty thousand Arabs resided. Reading on, he became uncomfortably aware that a twilight war was being waged against Israeli interests and that not surprisingly the Israelis had begun fighting back. In a daring nocturnal raid on Beirut operatives of the Israeli intelligence organization, Mossad, had attacked members of the Black September, tracking down the Palestinian leaders to their homes. One, Mohammed Youssouf Najjar, had been so confident of his own security that he actually had a visiting card of his alias ABU YOUSSOUF pinned to the front door of his apartment. The Israeli commandos had shot him and his wife in bed.

After an hour and half's further research, Sturgess went home on the underground to Gloucester Road. He found himself more than usually conscious of the number of Arabs going in and out of the hotels and shops. Any one of them could be a terrorist for all he knew; any one of the countless small flats and bedsitters in the neighborhood could be a safe house for a guerrilla gang, just as similar ones in south London had been for the IRA. If the French were right and an extension of terrorist operation was about to take place, then London might indeed be in the front line.

Unknown to Sturgess, this same afternoon had seen a meeting not far from where he lived that could have added considerably to his knowledge. A well-known journalist, Sam Eckhardt of the *Sunday Post,* had been lunching with a Libyan diplomat. Eckhardt was a special breed of writer, a foreign correspondent, whose reputation rested on his skilled interpretation and reporting of events in the Middle East and Africa. His retentive memory held all that Sturgess had learned in the New Scotland Yard library, plus a great deal more besides, while his files at the newspaper's offices had yielded the material for two books. Eckhardt was an established veteran, albeit beginning to be affected by the self-indulgence that success in journalism often breeds. The Libyan's motive in offering him lunch was simple: to set in motion a story which, if printed in the respected *Sunday Post,* would be widely repeated around the world. It was a story that not every journalist could persuade an editor to accept. Though it had the incalculable merit of being true, it sounded more like fiction.

"My friend," the Libyan had insisted, "you did not believe when I told you how many Israeli killers are operating in Europe."

Eckhardt had smiled across the wineglasses. Thinking to himself, "This man becomes more stupid by the minute," what he had said was: "Journalists need facts, Ahmed. No bricks without straw."

The Libyan gazed across the table. They went through the ritual of these lunches at regular intervals, and since he very seldom possessed any worthwhile knowledge that his government wanted published, their conversations were often restricted to a "tour d'horizon," wherein each attempted to pick the other's brains. But the Libyan knew that Eckhardt, despite his German Jewish name, would be basically favorable to anything that gave him an exclusive story. And today, like diamonds concealed in the palm of his hand, Ahmed had brought some facts. To amuse himself, he proposed to make Eckhardt sit up and beg for them. The temptation was understandable. Eckhardt looked misleadingly like the sort of glutton who might easily beg for tidbits. Nearly fifty, he was putting on weight. His face, with its prominent nose and full mouth, would have been perfect in an advertisement for gourmet dinners. One could imagine him holding up his manicured hands in horror at the idea of eating army food or sleeping in a tent. The fact was he had spent a quarter of a century knocking around the world, sleeping in everything from deserts to bordellos as he reported on wars, famines, revolutions and disasters. Even if he was well fed now, he remained physically resilient and mentally tough. He waited for the Libyan to tell him more.

"You receive the Agence France Presse?"

"We do."

The *Sunday Post* was one of very few British papers that subscribed to the French wire services.

"Then you have read about the assassinations at Argenteuil."

Eckhardt had not. However, he had let his host continue.

"It is reported as an attack by one Algerian gang on another in a café *compte rendu,* a settling of accounts."

"And what makes you think Israelis are involved?" Eckhardt was intrigued. The diplomat paused. One day he, or whoever succeeded him as intelligence officer at the embassy, would find out whether it was only journalistic greed that made this kind of political story strike such sparks in Eckhardt. In the meantime, Allah be praised that the man was so strongly motivated.

The diplomat pushed aside his plate and leaned forward to speak confidentially across the table. "Firstly, my friend, those killed were *not* Algerians. Between ourselves, they were Palestinian representatives among the Algerian workers in France. Algerian workers there contribute generously to the cause."

Eckhardt had to applaud such an ingenuous description of what must have been a terrorist group. "So to paraphrase Chairman Mao, the Algerian settlements were the sea in which these Palestinian fish swam?"

"The Argenteuil *bidonville* is impenetrable by outsiders, impenetrable." The Libyan spoke emphatically. "Believe me, I have been there. It should have been safe, yet somehow it was penetrated by the Israelis, by Mossad."

Eckhardt eyed the diplomat warily. He knew that the *bidonville* was an unhealthy place for strangers. By chance he had been there, because it was close to a wood that housed secret French radar installations on which he had once written a story. The *bidonville* was unquestionably a law unto itself, and normally only colored gendarmes, Arabs or Africans were sent on inquiries there.

"Every camp has its traitors," suggested Eckhardt.

"There was a girl with the assassins," the Libyan diplomat continued. "Two people who passed their car in the street saw her. They swear she was not an Arab. She and the men with her were Israelis. Even the French do not know this yet. The fact is, my friend, that Israel commandos are now operating in Europe. In France, in Germany, even in Britain."

Eckhardt had sipped a little more wine, rolling the liquid around his tongue, savoring it, while he pondered. "It might make a story. But you'll have to tell me more, Ahmed. Names particularly."

He put down the glass sharply in a gesture of decision. A little wine spilled on the tablecloth, making a spreading red stain. "Ring your friends in Argenteuil and tell them I shall be there this evening. Tell them a man with the good old Arab name of Eckhardt is coming to penetrate the *bidonville*."

From the restaurant Eckhardt had telephoned warning the *Sunday Post* to hold space for a major news piece and asked for a reporter to research all that could be found on the Israeli intelligence agency, Mossad.

"The Paris office won't like this much, Sam," the foreign editor had complained.

"Stuff the Paris office. Why haven't they got the story themselves, the layabouts?"

When he was on to something Eckhardt became cutthroat and ruthless. This was how he had been in

Vietnam, in Ulster, in the long-ago fighting in the Congo when he first made his name. The foreign editor had hesitated, but only for a moment. If the paper was going to pay highly for talent—and it did—it was common sense to give that talent rein. "Champagne living on beer incomes" was how one *Sunday Post* staffer delighted in describing journalism. Eckhardt's income was at least on the whisky level.

"OK, Sam," said the foreign editor, "go ahead. You know we need early copy. If you can file on Friday night, please do."

Three hours later Eckhardt was in Paris.

At much the same moment, though it was evening there, a clutch of Israeli officers were in conference in Tel Aviv, out at the Hakirya, the army headquarters. Israel's modest equivalent to the Pentagon is a sprawl of low-built modern office buildings inside a high-fenced compound. Like the whole of Israel's armed forces, the Hakirya operates with an informal camaraderie that would be unthinkable in Britain or America or indeed in most countries. But then, Israel is a close-knit community on permanent alert. There are plenty of women soldiers around at the Hakirya, too, and usually they are better turned out than the men. One such was the lieutenant called Naomi, as crisp as lettuce in a freshly pressed uniform, who had arrived in advance of the conference. The sentry at the gate to the compound greeted her with cordiality but no salute.

"I heard you've been abroad," he remarked as she passed.

"You'll hear too much one day," she replied good-humoredly.

Abashed, the sentry grinned. "Some people have all the fun," he remarked.

"Just keep the flag flying here," said Naomi tartly. "And we'll win the war."

The sentry watched her go with curiosity, noticing the large businesslike sportsman's watch on her wrist. When she was out of sight he relaxed again. The Israeli soldier wins battles, yes. But in other respects he is a sergeant major's bad dream. His most characteristic pose is slouching with his hat back on his head, a loaded Uzi submachine gun in one hand, a bottle of pop in the other. Having both hands full seriously impedes such minor military activities as saluting officers.

The soldiers at the Hakirya did salute one man, however. This was the stocky director of Military Intelligence. In his late forties, spectacles adding a false air of sleepy benevolence to his broad sunburned face, the general was respected for his energy and directness of speech. The soldiers liked his humor, too. With him, as he returned to the Military Intelligence block on this evening of May 3, was a man less often recognized, though much more discussed, one whose identity the Israeli government was always anxious to conceal: the director of Mossad, which is Israel's equivalent to America's CIA, Britain's MI6, and France's Deuxieme Bureau. In 1972 Mossad had organized a special department to conduct antiterrorist operations against the Palestinian guerrillas. The information given Eckhardt had been correct. It had indeed been one of Mossad's squads in the *bidonville* that Naomi had led. She had returned safely late on Wednesday. The documents she had seized had been in the hands of the staff at the Hakirya less than an hour after El Al's direct Paris-Tel Aviv plane had landed. Now their analysis was complete, and Naomi herself had come to join the experts evaluating their signficance.

The general realized as he entered the room that they must have unearthed information of real importance. It radiated from their faces and the excitement of their greetings.

"*Shalom,*" he replied coolly. "Do I smell good news?"

A swarthy hook-nosed colonel in shirt sleeves answered. "Whether it is good, that is questionable. It is certainly important news. Used correctly, it might be good."

"Trust an Iraqi to talk in riddles," said the general

cordially. "Come on, explain. Like the American senator asking about the Cubans, I want to know: were these good guys or bad guys?"

The colonel flushed. He was an Iraqi born in the old Jewish quarter of Baghdad, who had come with his family to Israel at the age of twelve in 1947 when the state was founded. He still looked, thought and spoke like an Arab, which made him a valuable officer.

"They were bad guys," said Naomi, interrupting.

"So it's good news!" The general beamed. "Let's have it then."

"We hit a new organization, they're called Abu Youssouf 73." Naomi hesitated, noticing the discomfort of the Iraqi colonel, and let him resume.

"As you know, General, we believed the cell was part of Black September. But it appears to be a breakaway faction, named for Mohammed Youssouf Najjar, whom Mossad"—here the colonel smiled acknowledgment to the director—"settled scores with in the Beirut operation of April 10, 1973. Najjar's alias was Abu Youssouf."

Both men nodded. They needed little reminding of that spectacularly successful raid. It had been followed by the similar Operation Caesarea in June 1975, and it had gone a long way to convincing the Palestinian terrorists that Lebanon was not necessarily a safe resting place. Golda Meir, then still prime minister, had been in ecstasy afterward at such revenge for the countless fedayeen attacks on Israeli border farms. "Very marvelous shining pages will be written about this," she exclaimed. That the Palestinians had been hurt was confirmed when the Voice of Palestine radio in Algiers tried to link it to American activities in an hysterical broadcast: "The American-Zionist alliance is like a dog going for the Arab nation . . . for this reason Arab masses are required to strike everywhere at American interests and embassies and kill and assassinate everyone who is American."

"It would be logical to honor Abu Youssouf," the Iraqi colonel continued. "A founder of Black Septem-

20

ber, responsible for the elimination of Wasfi Tal and the hijack of the Sabena Boeing 707. He was a fedayeen hero."

The Mossad director reflected. "What evidence is there that this Abu Youssouf 73 is something more than the one cell we have destroyed?"

It was a valid question. Originally Black September itself had been a state of mind more than an organization. Its existence had lain dormant in the desire of various PLO supporters to take more extreme action than the PLO itself was doing. Many felt that the PLO had not reacted strongly enough against King Hussein. But it was more than a year before their first recorded action, the murder of Wasfi Tal, in November 1971. Even when they began turning ideas into deeds, Black September's order of battle was so informal that in Western terms it would barely have counted as an "organization." An "intrigue" would have seemed a more apt word.

"Are you sure that Abu Youssouf 73 exists?" repeated the Mossad director.

The Iraqi's dark eyes glittered. He had been in no hurry to reveal what had electrified his team of analysts.

"They have an address in East Berlin. And they used to have one in Beirut. In Mazraa Street."

Everyone laughed. At least twenty Palestinian "organizations" had offices there until fighting in the city dislodged them.

"No names of terrorists either. Only code words. But there are other names, an amazing list. I still ask myself, is this a plant or is it real? On balance I think it is real."

He passed copies of a long list of names to the general and the director.

The general glanced at the list of names on the paper, checked himself, then muttered, "This is crazy."

"Remember we thought we were tracking an ordinary Black September cell," interjected Naomi, incensed at the suggestion that she might have fallen for a trick.

The director waved the list she had captured. "You are convinced that this was not a plant?"

"I am. They might have been willing to sacrifice a few immigrant workers to deceive us. But these were not Algerian workers. One was a Syrian, two were Palestinians."

"There is confirmation of this from Paris," interjected the Iraqi colonel. "At first the French assumed this was part of a local immigrant power struggle, another reckoning in the gang warfare they so much enjoy. Our sources inform us that one man recovered sufficiently to talk. He was the Syrian."

"So, Colonel," said the director, "you yourself believe this list is the heart of a plan to assassinate political and business leaders in Europe and America who are sympathetic to our country, whether they are Jews themselves or not."

"Yes, I do. It may be only an embryo plan. It may even be no more than a dream, a fantasy. But all the working papers we captured refer to the list and I conclude the overall plan is seriously intended." The colonel spoke with quiet intensity. "Consider the guerrillas' past operations: blowing up civilian airliners, letter bombs, assassinations in crowded cities. Extreme forms of violence against targets connected with Israel overseas. What has been the result? Colossal publicity for the guerrillas at trifling cost to them!" The group listened intently. The Iraqi was an expert on the motivation behind PLO operations. "Have these gross examples of violence alienated world opinion? Hardly at all. Why not?" He glanced questioningly around his small audience. "First, the guerrillas can always count on the support of some Arab states. They can always find sanctuary afterward. Only occasionally can we invent an operation like Uganda. Secondly, the European countries where the atrocities are committed are too dependent on Arab oil to risk punishing the guerrillas if they do catch them. The rationale of these operations," concluded the colonel firmly, "is that violence pays. The older PLO members may worry about its image. But to the breakaway factions, no attack can be self-defeating. That is why I believe Naomi's list is genuine."

The director was impressed. "You have a sharp nose for realities, Colonel," he said. "I think you are right. Except on one point. The world will react defensively against these plans if we reveal them before they can be activated. We must inform the prime minister at once."

The general nodded. "It could be very useful ammunition in the UN debate on the tenth. Real political dynamite." He smiled at the Iraqi. "Colonel, you may classify this officially as good news."

Later that night the prime minister gave orders for the Foreign Ministry to prepare a brief based on the documents. The brief and the captured papers would be sent to the UN for the use of the Israeli delegate in the debate on the tenth.

"The Arabs will deny everything, of course," remarked his private secretary.

"But the documents will be indisputably genuine. There is no way they can be discredited. What better proof could we have that, in spite of the PLO's observer status at the UN, the Palestinians remain murderously irresponsible?" The prime minister paused. "Didn't I hear that one of our UN delegation is home at the moment?"

"That would be the first secretary, Ben Maier. He leaves again early tomorrow."

"He can work on this then and take it back with him. Tell him his visit is extended for a few more days."

Chapter Two

Connie Maier woke early in her New York apartment, as she did habitually. Being a pathologist at Bellevue Hospital, she was expected to be in her laboratory before 9 A.M., which meant leaving home in Tudor City on Forty-second Street by 8:10 A.M. at the latest.

As a first-class doctor and also a conscientious one Connie had continued working after her marriage to Ben, even though she knew that she would have to resign her position when he was posted away from the UN, as eventually he would be. The huge hospital is in the heart of the city, on First Avenue and Twenty-seventh Street, and it receives as great a variety of cases as any doctor could hope to see outside a war. From attempted suicides, stabbings and shotgun wounds to incipient peritonitis or a child stung in the throat by a wasp—the emergencies come to Bellevue, and just like every morning, there would be a huge amount of work waiting for her. This was why she usually gulped down a glass of juice and a cup of coffee at the apartment in the mornings, in order not to delay herself, and waited to eat something more substantial when the midmorning cart came round with its welcome burden of Danish pastries and, of course, more coffee. Coffee and Danish is a ritual at Bellevue.

However, there was one thing that made this Friday

morning, May 3, special. Ben was due back from Tel Aviv in the afternoon. In two years of married life they had never been separated so long, and she had missed Ben a lot. She had not married until she was thirty-one and established in her medical career. Though her many friends and acquaintances had assumed Connie would make a highly competent job of marriage, most of them had wondered if such a self-possessed, well-educated, lavishly reared and by no means plain a young woman would give all of herself to her husband. Their worries had been groundless. Even Connie had been surprised at how wrong they were. During this past week of Ben's absence she had felt just as though part of her had been physically taken away. She missed his jokes in the morning about her running off in a hurry to cure the sick while he, only having to find a remedy for the whole world's ills, could safely sleep late. But UN debates often did not start until 4 P.M. and then wrangled on long into the evening. So Ben was frequently late to bed. . . . Connie rolled over luxuriously, reflected that she missed him like hell both in and out of it and then sprang up. He might easily be home before she was today, and she wanted to make sure the apartment looked welcoming.

Tudor City is what passes in New York for an ancient building. Constructed around 1929, its apartments are solid and comfortable, with leaded light windows giving them a spuriously old English appearance. It is conveniently close to the towering block of the UN Building, and the Maiers were pleased to be there. The L-shaped living room was a full twenty-seven feet long, big enough for the cocktail party entertaining that is an inseparable part of every diplomat's career, and its windows overlooked the East River. Connie had bought an armful of flowers the day before and distributed them in vases around the room. Now she darted round, rearranged the roses a fraction, checked that drinks were ready on the tray, removed a dirty glass, then caught sight of herself in the gilt mirror that hung over the fireplace. "What a mess," she thought. "Thank heaven he can't see me now."

Most unusually, Dr. Connie Maier did not reach Bellevue this morning until ten past nine.

The telephone call from the Israeli UN delegation came just after the midmorning cart had been round. Connie was examining a blood sample under a microscope.

"Hey, Connie," someone called out, "the Tower of Babel's on the line."

She smiled. Her colleagues were always dreaming up new names for the United Nations, never complimentary ones. New Yorkers had little respect for the embryo world government in their midst. But a sudden shiver of fear killed her smile. As she took the phone she had that sick, empty feeling in the gut that you get when you know something is going wrong, though you don't know what.

"Mrs. Maier?" queried a thick, almost sleepy-sounding man's voice. Connie recognized it as Saul Horovitz's, the counselor at the delegation and Ben's immediate boss.

"What is it, Saul?" She could hardly keep her voice steady.

"Nothing serious, nothing to worry." He had picked up the fear in her tone immediately. "We have a telegram from Tel Aviv. They want Ben to stay on some more days. There is something important—" The counselor hesitated. On the assumption that every telephone line from the UN was being taped, he wanted to reveal only what was essential.

"Yes?"

"The prime minister wishes him to bring back a personal brief for the ambassador. You understand I cannot tell you more now."

"Oh." Connie felt a little relieved, but only a little. "When will he be back then?"

"Probably next Thursday."

"Nearly another whole week. Oh, Saul."

"I am so sorry." Horovitz, for all his apparent sleepiness, was a perceptive man. These were good young people, not so long married. He understood. "My dear, it is an honor for Ben. He is highly valued."

"I was so looking forward to the weekend." Connie checked herself.

"If you would like to pass the Sabbath with us, please come over. We will be delighted."

Connie considered rapidly, then, her voice completely under control again, declined politely.

"That's sweet of you, Saul. But I think I'll go to Rye and visit my family."

After accepting further commiserations, she rang off. You couldn't be angry with Saul. Anway, it wasn't his fault. She was just disappointed and unaccountably apprehensive. She picked up the phone again and dialed her father's Wall Street office. Connie was only half Jewish, on her mother's side. Her father was a successful stockbroker, a Protestant who had not been overwhelmingly keen on his only daughter marrying an Israeli, even a Harvard man with a Ph.D. and as much charm as Ben. However, it certainly had not affected his adoration of Connie, which in days gone by had amounted to outrageous indulgence. There wasn't much that money could buy, and that Connie had wanted, or her father thought she ought to have, that she had not been given. She rode her own horses, sailed her own Lightning and at sixteen had been presented with a dashing red Triumph convertible. During vacations from the exclusive Rye Country Day School and later from college at Radcliffe, she had visited Europe many times with her mother. Some girls might have been ruined by this generosity. Connie had not been. If her tastes were expensive they were also sophisticated. Nor did she allow them to interfere with the pursuit of her chosen career as a doctor. She had done well in medical school at New York University and emerged from it a mature and capable woman. All that remained of her privileged childhood now was a tiny, diamond-hard, ineradicable knowledge that if she ever wanted something badly enough, she would damned well get it.

When her father heard what had happened he was

all sympathy. "Of course, honey, wonderful to have you. Will you come with me on the train?" Her father was a regular commuter on the fifty-minute ride from Grand Central Station to Rye.

"No, I'll drive. I have to pick up some clothes from the apartment. If the traffic isn't too heavy I'll be home in time for drinks at seven."

"Good. Your mother will be delighted. We'll have some tennis in the morning. I'll fix up a court at the club."

When her hospital stint was over Connie wasted no time. Back at her apartment one rueful glance at the roses in the living room was enough. She felt if she stayed a moment longer she would burst into tears. She packed hurriedly and was headed out along the river on the East Side Drive in her Volvo station wagon just ahead of the heavy Friday evening traffic. With the windows open and the warm May wind blowing her black hair, she began to feel better.

That Friday evening an obscure English officer was also heading for Westchester County, and another wife was cursing the fact that work had kept her husband on the wrong side of the Atlantic at the weekend. Jim Donaldson was one of a little publicized breed of civil servant. In his mid-forties, of average height, dressed in a sober gray suit, he was the sort of person who does not stand out in a crowd. You could see men like him every day on a commuter train into London, in New York, in Frankfurt, and take him completely for granted. Unless you chanced to look into his cool blue eyes, deepset in the way that airline pilots' or navy captains' often seem to be. Then you would notice a lot more determination in his face than a middle-run civil servant might ordinarily need. But Jim Donaldson did need it. His job was investigating aircraft accidents, and the accidents were never pretty sights. Wherever a British registered aircraft crashed, Donaldson or one of his fellow inspectors went. For the past three weeks he had been sifting the wreckage of a 707 jet that had descended too low on a night approach to Wash-

29

ington's National Airport and had impacted a mere hundred feet below the top of Round Hill, killing all on board. The news had reached him at home in Surrey on a Sunday morning. He had packed, apologized to his wife, Jane, kissed his two young daughters and told them to look after Mummy, caught the British Airways afternoon flight to New York and was alongside officials of the Federal Aviation Administration at the crash site only thirteen hours after the disaster occurred. Now he had been compelled to apologize to Jane again. His cable had read:

JANE DONALDSON, 121 DRIFTBRIDGE DRIVE, EPSOM, SURREY, ENGLAND. TERRIBLY SORRY DARLING CRASH PAPERWORK STILL UNFINISHED STOP HOPE RETURN TUESDAY ALL MY LOVE JIM.

He sent it via Western Union to make sure it arrived the same day. Cables that passed through the hands of the British post office were frequently delivered with the ordinary letter post, which in this case might be Monday morning, allowing that the time in Britain was five hours ahead of New York. Rightly, Jim Donaldson reckoned his wife would be upset. It was the end of his daughters' school holidays, and he had promised to be at home.

Jim Donaldson was not a man who broke promises lightly, and it was true that his draft report on the 707 disaster was incomplete. But there was another reason for his wanting to stay on a few days. During the three weeks he had spent in and around Washington one of the FAA accident investigation team had introduced him to Hugh Johnson, the president of Atlantic Airlines, a New York-based carrier founded by Johnson himself, an energetic former pilot, who was known as one of the most dedicated leaders of American aviation. Johnson drove men hard. This, coupled with the contacts he had made during a lifetime in the business, had enabled him to jockey Atlantic up level with older established airlines like Delta and National to the point that Atlantic was now operating internationally. Johnson had invited Donaldson to stay this weekend, and although there was no hint of anything more than kindness to a visiting Britisher in the suggestion, Donaldson's FAA friends had told him he would be a fool to decline.

"At least you'll see how a legend gets born," commented one. "Johnson's one of those guys we'll never see the like of again."

They had met on the 707 crash site in the wood where a hundred and twelve people, all members of a British Rotary Club, had died. Jim Donaldson could never inure himself to inspecting the wreck of an aircraft. This one must have been flying almost straight and level, having pulled out of its descent, when it hit. The tail had come off first and now lay at an angle to one side of the path that the body of the plane had gouged through the trees. The wing had broken next, twisted and shredded by the tree trunks as the ninety-four-ton weight plowed down through the upper branches which at first had cushioned the impact slightly. After that the disintegration had been swift. Standing on a tarmac at an airport or cruising majestically among the clouds, a big airliner looks solid and indestructible. The reality is different. The only solid conglomerations of metal in it are the engines. Its thin aluminum skin can be punctured by hitting a bird. In the days when stiletto heels were fashionable, air hostesses were forbidden to wear them because the weight of an ordinary girl, concentrated on two such thin points, could punch straight through the lightweight floor of an airliner's cabin. True, the aircraft's wings are constructed around immensely strong main spars, its landing gear can take punishment, but the basic airframe is beautifully designed to push its way only through air. Anything more substantial destroys it. Not that the human frame is in much better shape. A deceleration from two-hundred mph or more to nothing in a few seconds would kill people no matter what vehicle they were in, and there were no survivors of this crash. As always, Donaldson had needed to take a firm grip on himself not to be sick as he surveyed it.

With him was another British expert, Peter Denman of Hanson's, an old family firm of undertakers who had specialized in the identification of air crash victims since the early days of commercial flying. Denman was retained by several airlines to perform this slow and gruesome task and then to carry through the complicated process of embalming the remains and returning them to the relatives of the dead in a decent and proper manner. Denman had flown out on the same plane as Donaldson, not for the first time. They had worked together before.

Johnson had come up to them, introduced himself briefly and explained he had special permission to be there from the FAA. His interest was due to his own airline's having suffered two major crashes in as many years, plus three near misses. One of the near misses had been in circumstances similar to this disaster, on a night approach to Washington National over the Round Hill market beacon.

"What caused it, do you reckon?" Johnson had asked brusquely.

"To judge by the cockpit voice recordings, the crew must have descended to the approach altitude before they'd passed the beacon," Donaldson had said. "The question is why, when the approach charts clearly show that thirty-three hundred feet is the minimum until Round Hill has been passed. This 707 was below seventeen hundred feet."

"If any man in the world *can* find that out," the FAA official had chipped in, "it'll be Jim Donaldson here." He had gestured at the scarred path through the wood where the twisted shards of metal that were all that remained of the 707 lay scattered. "We're all experts at making this kind of chaos tell its story. But Jim has some kind of extra feeling for it."

"I've had the fortune—the misfortune I should say—to investigate a variety of accidents," Donaldson had remarked.

"Is that so?" Johnson had said, then changed the subject. But the next day he called Donaldson at his hotel.

"Donaldson," he had said, "I heard you may have to stay on another week. Too bad. If you've nothing better, why not come up to Westchester with me for the weekend. You play golf? We can shoot a few holes."

Donaldson hesitated. He'd heard of Westchester County but did not really want to go so far. He spent enough of his life traveling as it was. Johnson misinterpreted the silence on the phone. He suspected that British officials were poorly paid.

"Catch the Eastern shuttle and I'll have a helicopter pick you up at LaGuardia. Your tickets will be at the FAA in the morning."

So it was that, as Connie Maier was driving out up the East Side trying to beat the Friday night traffic out of Manhattan, a four-place Bell helicopter was ferrying Donaldson overhead to land him at Westchester Airport. Donaldson was not alone. There were two other passengers. One was Hugh Johnson's conventionally pretty, blond, long-legged daughter, Sharon, who was attending a school of interior decorating and could have stepped straight out of *Vogue*. The other was Atlantic Airlines' chief pilot, still wearing a well-cut dark gray uniform, distinctive because the captain's four rings on the sleeve were in black braid, not the usual gold. In the highly competitive business of flying passengers, Johnson aimed to make everything about Atlantic distinctive, including its profit ratio. "Trust the old man not to leave a seat empty," joked the chief pilot when they had all met on the tarmac at La Guardia. He had shaken hands warmly with Donaldson, introducing Sharon and then himself.

"Bill Curtis. I've heard about you."

By the time the brief flight was over Donaldson had guessed that more organization had been devoted to this weekend than Johnson's casual invitation had suggested. Sharon had broken a date to come along, and Curtis, whose wife was waiting for them with a car, had brought Atlantic's Blue Ribbon Paris–London–New York flight into Kennedy Airport only an hour earlier. Later on Curtis admitted that "some pretty fancy scheduling" had been involved, but the objective remained a mystery through Friday evening and the whole of Saturday. Partnered by Sharon at tennis, sipping cocktails on the terrace of the Johnsons' twenty-four room house overlooking lawns and paddocks, Donaldson found the time passing agreeably enough. As often as he had been to the United States, this was his first sustained experience of upper-crust living. He was genuinely sorry his wife, Jane, was not there to enjoy it with him. Nor could he resist a twinge of envy when he discovered that Curtis also lived nearby. But then, airline captains in the States were in the seventy-thousand-dollar-a-year bracket now. By Sunday morning Donaldson was in precisely the frame of mind that his host intended.

The paneled dining room of the Westchester Country Club with its comfortable leather upholstered chairs and windows overlooking a well-tended golf course was where Johnson gave them lunch on Sunday. It was the same club at which Connie Maier had been playing tennis with her father. Donaldson, used to observing things around him closely, noticed the pair across the room. Connie Maier's dark good looks, inherited from her mother, were in such contrast to her father's broad, open Anglo-Saxon face that people found it hard to believe they were father and daughter. Sharon intercepted Donaldson's gaze. "That's Connie Maier. She's terrific, isn't she? Everyone adores Connie. She's married to an Israeli diplomat. It's a shame, but I guess her mother must have encouraged it."

Johnson broke in. "No gossip, please. I want to talk with Jim, Sharon." He gazed firmly at Donaldson across the table. "Mind if I ask you a direct question?"

"Go ahead." So at last the point of this weekend was emerging. There was a ruthlessness about the way Johnson had silenced his daughter that did not surprise Donaldson. During his stay he had noticed several such pointers to the airline president's character. Johnson was a man who allowed the small events of life to flow on until he himself wanted something that mattered. Then he could be abrupt to the point of rudeness, both with his own family and subordinates. That they obeyed instead of objecting was a tribute to their faith in him. Sharon was now watching the two men with interest.

"Do you earn enough in England?" Johnson demanded. "Are you satisfied? I mean, I always heard the pay in aviation there's about half what it is here, and even worse in government. Is it buying you what you want out of life?"

The bluntness of the question rocked Donaldson. It wasn't the sort of thing Englishmen were asked, least of all civil servants, where personnel departments and top brass alike seemed to assume that by definition government employees must be contented. He sipped his drink and thought of Jane in their four-bedroom "executive style" house in Epsom with its "American Kitchen," the tennis club down the road, the local pub, children's holidays in the Isle of Wight. They lived well by his standards, but her ambition was to move into one of the more spacious houses actually overlooking Epsom Downs, a move he would never be able to afford.

"Our pay's improved a lot lately," he countered.

"That's not what I meant."

"I would be happy, except for one thing. The children's school. The local comprehensive—that's the state school—is frankly bloody awful. Rather than risk it, I've got my two daughters in private schools. But the fees are going up much, much faster than my pay is. Thirty percent a year at least. It's all right for Foreign Service men, they get special allowances. So does the army. We home civil servants don't."

"How old are your daughters?"

"Ten and twelve."

"You've a long haul ahead," commented Johnson, not unkindly. Then his voice gained a tougher edge. "Listen, Jim," he said, "I've had two bad crashes, plus several near misses the public doesn't know about. That's more than any airline can afford."

"Right," remarked Curtis.

"I've some top-class pilots, like Bill here. But I need a man who's fresh to the airline, who can go through its every procedure, check out every last cause of potential accidents in the air and on the ground because, whatever the price, that's going to be cheaper than another crash. Jim, from what I hear, you could be that man. I'll give you a five-year initial contract at the same salary he gets"—Johnson nodded towards the pilot—"or damn near it. Seventy-five thousand bucks. Plus all your transfer expenses and help with housing." He waved his hand as if putting the dining room on private display. "Our life-style's pretty good around here. I'm not saying you'll afford a place like the Rockefellers' up the road." Johnson laughed genially. The Rockefeller family compound in the Pocantico Hills was legendary. "But we can find you a good house with an acre or so."

Donaldson nodded. One of Jane's discontents was the scrap of garden around their home—scarcely one-sixth of an acre. She often commented on the established lawns and flower beds of larger, older houses.

"And"—Johnson paused to emphasize the point—"we have one of the best school systems on the East Coast. People move out here just because of it. So there'll be no school fees in your budget—you'll be pretty well set up. You won't regret it."

"When Dad says that, he means it," added Sharon loyally. "And it's a lovely place for children to grow up in."

Donaldson looked straight back at Johnson. "I believe you knew I had two school-age daughters before you invited me here," he said good-humoredly.

"And your wife is taking an art course afternoons, and you had over two thousand jet hours in command before you left the RAF, and you drink tea and never coffee. So what? Should you respect me more if I hadn't done my homework?"

"It's a generous offer, Mr. Johnson, very generous. But I'll have to talk to Jane about it."

"I'll fly her out," said Johnson shortly. "Go call her now."

Donaldson nearly gave way, then he remembered it was the last weekend of the holidays, with all the packing and preparing that it entailed. He knew well how Jane would react to being disturbed in the middle of this ritual. It was odd how much fuss women managed to make over every aspect of the school holidays. Better to leave the possibility of moving to America until he was home and could explain it in detail. Anyway, he was far from certain that she would welcome the idea, in which case a sudden summons to cross the Atlantic might prove counterproductive.

"Unfortunately the girls go back to school on Monday. Jane will be terribly busy. And I can't stay away any longer than I have to. Give me a week." He pulled out his diary and flipped through it. "I'll cable you not later than the thirteenth."

"I'm superstitious. Make it the twelfth. Yes or no. And if you want to bring her out, just call our London office. They'll have instructions to issue you tickets."

Leaving the club after lunch, they paused to glance at the ticker tape machine in the hall, tapping out the world news, with the earlier lengths of printout pinned up on a board alongside the machine. One item caught Donaldson's eyes. The opening slug read:

0509000 ISRAELI COMMANDOS
LONDON MAY 5 AP
A SQUAD OF ISRAELI COMMANDOS KILLED FIVE PAL-
ESTINIAN GUERILLAS IN LAST WEEK'S PARIS CAFE
SHOOTOUT ACCORDING TO A REPORT IN THIS MORNING'S
LONDON SUNDAY POST. HITHERTO FRENCH POLICE
BELIEVED A RIVAL ARAB FACTION RESPONSIBLE. THE
POST CLAIMS OTHER ISRAELI KILLER SQUADS ARE
OPERATING ELSEWHERE IN EUROPE AGAINST PALES-
TINIAN GROUPS THAT HAVE QUIT LEBANON WHERE
FIGHTING MADE THEIR BASE UNSAFE. THIS MORNING
ISRAELI DIPLOMATS IN LONDON DENIED THERE WERE
ISRAELI COMMANDOS IN BRITAIN AND CALLED POST
STORY QUOTE A COMPLETE FABRICATION UNQUOTE.

"That should stir things up a bit at home," thought

Donaldson, reluctantly leaving the tape as his host moved away down the hall. He was a regular reader of the *Sunday Post*. With luck Jane would keep their copy until he got back.

The *Sunday Post* boasted a readership of one and a quarter million, the best book page in Britain, short of the *Times Literary Supplement;* and a titled owner who had recently raised a hefty loan in order to promote the circulation to the magic figure of a million and a half copies an issue. Although the owner had averred frequently in television interviews that he never interfered with editorial policy, he normally had "a little chat" with his senior staff before the regular Tuesday afternoon editorial conference. The book page had done all it could for the circulation. Nudes were out of the question. Two weeks ago, after picking the brains of the news editor in his avuncular, yet menacing way, the owner had made it clear that "fearless investigative journalism" was the path to salvation for the *Sunday Post*. He had also given the news editor a spectacular pay raise, and the news editor took the point at once. If salvation were not achieved he would rapidly be looking for another job. Hence Sam Eckhardt's story about the Israelis could not have come at a more fortunate moment. The news editor had spread it across four columns of the front page and would have made the headline slug ISRAELI KILLER SQUADS IN BRITAIN, in order to bring it harder home, had someone not pointed out that Sam Eckhardt had produced no evidence to support this and the *Sunday Post* had a reputation for accuracy to maintain. Total factual accuracy was often hard to square with the news editor's simple motto "Give the public a good read and they'll buy the paper." But even he had no inkling of the size of the story that would develop from Eckhardt's article.

The effects had begun twelve hours before the *Sunday Post* was on sale, and a full twenty-four hours before Donaldson saw the ticker tape at the Westchester Country Club. They hit the Israeli Embassy's

38

press counselor first, just before dinner on Saturday evening.

One of the accepted tricks of Fleet Street is that every newspaper obtains copies of its rivals' first edition as soon as they are printed. With luck and hard work any editor can carry a version of another one's scoop in his own final editions. On Sunday papers, which put their first editions "to bed" by 5 P.M., this scramble happens in the early evening. The *Sunday Post*'s news editor could comfortably expect to have the next day's *Sunday Times, Observer, Sunday Express* and the rest in front of him around 7 P.M. on Saturday. And vice versa. None allowed their reporters home until the competition had been scanned. So the telephone had started ringing at the press counselor's Hampstead flat as he was changing for dinner. From then on he had been besieged by reporters' calls. Completely taken by surprise and having no brief, he could only stonewall the queries. To the journalists he knew and trusted, he pointed out that there unquestionably were Palestinian groups operating all over Europe, but dealing with them was strictly a matter for the police of the country in question. At 9 P.M., unable to get through on the telephone, he had driven to the ambassador's residence, where a number of photographers were hanging about outside the gate. For want of anything better they had photographed him going in.

The ambassador had been equally at a loss. Intelligence services of most countries inform their own embassies in advance of any major operations they are planning because if things go wrong it is the envoy who has to face the ensuing political storm. But Mossad's operation had been in France with no British connection, even though Eckhardt's story had implied one.

"We shall have to telegraph Tel Aviv for guidance," remarked the ambassador, "and also send the full text of this press story as soon as you can obtain it. Meanwhile, the line you have taken is correct. Do you know this writer Eckhardt?"

"Curiously, he has never come to us for information."

"Find out what you can about him." The ambassador smiled. "You have a busy time ahead of you, my friend. Console youself with the thought that old Arik will be having a much worse time in Paris."

When the press counselor reached the embassy building in Kensington Palace Gardens, the broad, treelined street that used to be known as Millionaires Row before all the rich men's houses became embassies, he did indeed find an urgent message from Paris asking for the full text of the article. Resignedly, he drove down to Fleet Street to buy an advance copy of the *Sunday Post*.

The mass of the *Sunday Post*'s readers were middle class, or professional people or men on their way up in the world, not tolerant of either hippies or hijackers. As the news editor had rightly expected, they were delighted to read of someone giving the Palestinians a pasting. The more subtle international political implications of the story, which were Eckhardt's real target, were less interesting; the subeditors had cut them.

Station Officer Mick Melville of the London Fire Brigade lapped up the article. For a change he was having a Sunday off duty. Instead of being at the Westminster Fire Station, as the shift system often dictated at weekends, he was sitting contentedly in the kitchen of his three-bedroomed semidetached house in the commuter suburb of Purley, drinking strong tea and regaling his pretty wife, Patsy, with extracts from the paper. This habit of his always infuriated her because it spoiled all her fun when she settled down to it herself later. But as she was glad to have him home and it kept him happy, she did not complain.

"These Israelis are a switched-on bunch, whether you like them or not," he was saying. "Listen to this. 'Eyewitnesses swear the killings were over in a minute and a half at the most. Many weeks of planning must have gone into the operation.' That," said Melville enthusiastically, "is the way to work."

"I still don't think it's right, though," said Patsy equably. "What if they start doing it here?"

"They are, love. I mean, the IRA are. It would be no bad thing if someone sorted *them* out."

These sentiments were not as strange coming from a fireman as an outsider might have thought. Before he had joined the Fire Service, Mick Melville had been a sergeant in the Special Air Service, a near legendary regiment that carried out cloak-and-dagger military operations. Indeed, he had killed several Arab guerrillas himself during a battle that had fully lived up to the regimental motto of "Who Dares, Wins." A mere three hundred soldiers had destroyed a rebel force on top of a mountain plateau—the Jebel Akhdar in the British-protected Sultanate of Muscat and Oman—which had successfully held against every previous attack in history. Genghis Khan himself had assaulted it with ten thousand men and failed. The SAS soldiers did the trick by scaling a thousand-foot mountainside which the Arabs considered impregnable. They climbed it at night, carrying a variety of weapons that would have shocked any conventional commander: sawed-off shotguns, Berettas, commando knives, Sterling submachine guns, even some ordinary rifles. Any weapon a man particularly liked he could use. Melville's choice was the Sterling, backed up by a vicious long-bladed hunting knife that he'd acquired on a visit to the Green Berets at Fort Bragg, North Carolina. The elderly storeowner in the dreary local town of Fayetteville had cautioned him, "Be careful, son. You could easy kill a man with that."

"Just what I plan to do," Melville had answered cheerfully.

After three weeks on the Jebel Akhdar the colonel reckoned they had cleared out every hideout the rocky landscape offered. So they left, pursued only by the thanks of the sultan and a ration of medals, one of which went to Sergeant Melville.

Six months later he had met Patsy when he was on leave in Singapore. She was working as a secretary in the Far East Land Forces Headquarters, so she had a fair idea of what the SAS did. Nonetheless, he had never talked to her about it, then or since. They had married as soon as his army engagement was over and he had joined the Fire Service. It sounded as though it offered the same kind of comradeship as the army, plenty of action, the element of danger that stimulated him and good pay. All that and none of the constant moving around so unattractive to army wives.

Three days after saying good-bye to the SAS, Mick Melville started his twelve-week basic training. After four years he was fully qualified and made leading fireman. Another five saw him promoted through to station officer, with two silver pips on his shoulder. He was happy, and since the Fire Service is one that promotes only from the ranks, he stood as good a chance as anyone of reaching the top. He kept up both the physical fitness training and the unarmed combat techniques that the SAS had taught him. "Train hard, fight easy" was his watchword. Firemen needed to be as fit as front-line soldiers, and Melville made his men train incessantly: ladder work, pump work, rescue work. Whenever they were not out on an emergency they trained and exercised. One incidental result was that Melville himself, though now nearing forty, stayed lean, hard and good-looking. He could pass for thirty any time, and Patsy derived great pleasure just watching him. Her worst fear was that he might be injured in a fire, maimed or burned. She thought that for a man like him it would be worse than dying. As far as she could tell, he did not think about that at all, and she never raised the subject but tried successfully to hide her anxieties.

"Not that it means he's going to get his own way all the time," she told herself frequently. And that was how she felt about his admiration for the Israeli commandos on this Sunday morning. He was out of that game now, and she didn't want to hear about it. The subject developed into quite a row.

Commander Thompson of the Metropolitan Police read the *Sunday Post,* too, and clipped the article. He was in his quiet office at Cannon Row this Sunday morning because he would be supervising the control of the abortion protest march during the afternoon. Much as he disliked leaving home earlier than he had to, it gave him a chance to reflect without any normal weekday disturbance. He read the clipping again. He was beginning to be anxious about the Palestinian demonstration next weekend. Technically, a mere two or three people can act in such a way as to commit the offense of riotous assembly. More practically, two or three people can incite a large crowd into behavior that all the rest of its members never intended. From information reaching the Special Branch this could be the plan for Saturday, May 11.

Thompson called Colin Sturgess up from the Ceremonials Office downstairs.

"Anything more to report on the Palestinian demo?" he asked.

Sturgess shook his head.

"Not really, sir. I had one call from the General Workers Union organizer insisting that all they want to do is follow the program they're publicizing."

Thompson frowned. Strictly speaking, the police had no power to demand information from demo organizers once the Department of the Environment had given permission for a march. In fact, if they were not carrying banners or stopping to make speeches they did not require permission at all.

"Have you spoken to the Zionists?"

"Not yet," Sturgess confessed. "This afternoon's demo and the state visit have had to come first."

"It's not one of our easiest weeks," Thompson acknowledged.

"The Commissioner's Office have had two more threats to assassinate the president if the state visit isn't canceled. Some of these South Americans are not too popular in their own countries."

"Maybe," said Thompson, "our job is to stop them being knocked off while they're here."

This week was indeed going to be a bastard. The rigid timetable of a state visit, well publicized beforehand, made good security even more difficult. Inevitably there would be bomb alarms too. Scotland Yard received upwards of ninety a day. Almost all were hoaxes. But a few were not, and "A" Division had its share of both. Thompson was used to them. It was, for instance, standard procedure to search the sewers under Whitehall before a royal occasion. But every precaution stretched his manpower further. "A" Division had only eight hundred men instead of the one thousand officially allowed for. Even with hundreds of constables drafted in from other divisions Thompson's manpower was going to be stretched to the limit this week. Policemen were human. They needed a break like anyone else. Indeed if they were called in for extra duty at short notice the regulations allowed them either extra pay or extra days off in compensation.

"With luck Thursday and Friday will be quieter, sir," said Sturgess skillfully interpreting Thompson's thoughts.

"It's the best we can hope for," said Thompson. "Now, about this afternoon. . . ."

In fact, the Palestinians' plans were shifting hourly toward a more concrete demonstration of power than a simple march to the Houses of Parliament. Both the Palestine Liberation Organization and the surviving adherents of the Abu Youssouf 73 faction had known within hours that the assassinations at the café in Argenteuil had been carried out by an Israeli team. Other possibilities, including the raid's having been an action by the French secret police, had been quickly ruled out. But it took longer to establish what the commandos had taken away. The system of operating in small cells for security reasons had many advantages. It also had the snag that if a whole cell were wiped out it could be difficult to check on what equipment or documents had been lost with them. That the plan for the series of assassinations of prominent pro-Israeli business and political leaders had been captured was not realized until late on Sunday. When it was, a number of leading Palestinian guerillas met at a villa in

Tripoli. Some were supporters of Abu Youssouf 73. Others were from the Black September, one of whom dominated the discussion. He was a wiry, small man, with grizzled hair and visionary depths in his dark eyes. He spoke with energy, talking fast in a Syrian dialect.

"Brothers. By this stupidity we may lose much. To allow such plans to be captured is criminal, a treachery to the Palestinian cause." His voice rose in pitch. "It is a gift to the runnning dogs of Zionist imperialism, a valuable gift, brothers. If any of those responsible are still alive, they must be disciplined in the harshest manner."

Mutterings of assent came from around the table. The Syrian went on relentlessly.

"That is for the future. First we must stop the use of these documents against our cause." His eyes darted around, fixing each man in turn, compelling attention.

"If it is revealed now, this plan will not only make the vote go against our cause in the United Nations next Friday. It will do worse. It will reveal that we have been defeated again by the Israelis."

He paused to let his audience absorb this thought.

"In the past hijackings have failed at Lydda and again in Uganda. Brothers, never forget this. An out-cry from the Western world when an operation suc-ceeds always helps us. It forces both the world and Arab governments to recognize that the fight for our cause is serious. Success demonstrates our power, and the West is frightened to retaliate. The only bad public-ity for us is for a failure which may make those who back our efforts have doubts about us. Above all, we must not be defeated by the Israelis."

There was a murmur of assent from the others.

"Brothers, we have suffered a defeat in Paris. But we can still stop Israel from proving it. We can recover the documents. We must assume they are now in Tel Aviv. We must assume they will be taken to the United Nations. They must not reach New York. Whoever carries them must be identified and killed. And if our plans cannot be recovered, they must be destroyed."

He turned to the three Abu Youssouf 73 men present.

"The responsibility is yours. We will all help. But the work is in your hands. If you fail, it is you who will pay the price."

Chapter Three

When the United Nations granted observer status to the PLO in 1975, Joseph Flaherty had scented mutual profit. An employee of the New York Telephone Company, Flaherty worked at night raising funds for the Irish Republican Army, and his efforts had purchased variety of armaments for terrorist squads throughout Ireland. What Flaherty knew was that the IRA always needed money and the PLO had it. What the PLO did not have was a power base in New York City. On the other hand, the Irish in generations past had established themselves in every municipal agency in the metropolitan area, and Flaherty had been quick to let the PLO know that he was establishing a clandestine group of IRA sympathizers in these departments.

"Call me any time you have a problem," was how Flaherty had put it. Problems there had been, and with his help, they had been solved. Now, on the afternoon of Monday, May 6, the PLO called again.

What had prompted the PLO to call was Abu Youssouf 73's failure to identify how and when the Israelis would take the stolen documents to New York. Could the information be obtained in New York? If so, the guerrillas would do the rest. The PLO representative at the UN agreed to assist, and, by midday, helped by an African diplomat whose country

47

still maintained relations with Israel, he had established that one member of the Israeli delegation was believed to be in Tel Aviv. The diplomat's wife was not with him, so presumably he was on business, not a vacation. His name was Ben Maier, and an inquiry made by the supposedly friendly African to the Israelis elicited the guarded reply that Maier was "expected back later this week." The obvious presumption was that he might be bringing the documents with him. Furthermore, someone would inform his wife of how and when he was returning. After making these deductions, the PLO representative had telephoned Flaherty, who in turn contacted an Irish American employee of the telephone company.

Late that same Monday afternoon the telephone employee called at Tudor City, presented his company pass to the back door elevator man and was allowed in through the service entrance. Carrying a huge toolbox, he descended to the basement, where the building's telephone junction boxes were housed, and set to work. All the wires were color-coded. Eventually he identified the Maiers' pair and neatly connected another pair to them inside the junction box. Next he joined the spares, using neutral-colored wires, to a radio bug, which he concealed a few feet away. The bug would transmit every word or noise on the Maiers' line to a tape recorder located in a listening post established in a rented room close by. By professional standards it was not a sophisticated arrangement. For a long-term intercept Flaherty would have fixed a tap in the telephone exhange itself. But this was needed for a few days at most, and the risk of the bug's being found accidentally was negligible. The only thing that worried the telephone employee was to be completely certain that he had tapped the correct phone.

He took the handset slung on his belt, tapped into the Maiers' line and called the exchange, asking them to check back and giving the Maiers' number. Twenty seconds later the operator did so. He had the right line. That, he reflected, was three hundred bucks easily earned. Upstairs in the apartment the cleaning woman heard the phone ring and wondered if she could be bothered to take a message. Before she could decide the ringing stopped. She shrugged and thought no more of it.

When Connie Maier returned to her apartment that evening she was still feeling refreshed by the lazy weekend in Westchester. Even a savage day at Bellevue could not sour her mood, and she was hopeful that the evening might bring a call from Ben in Tel Aviv. Half an hour later, impatient, she decided to check with the operator whether there was any delay on calls to or from Israel. There was not. Slightly mollified, she went and poured herself a drink, then puttered around the apartment, restoring ornaments to their proper places. Presumably cleaning women deliberately moved everything to prove they had done their job.

A block away the tape recorder had successfully taken its first transmission from the bug; twelve hours later it received the information the PLO wanted. They would have had it sooner if Ben Maier had been able to tell Connie anything definite. He was concerned to let his wife know what he was doing. The problem had been that he did not know himself. Consultations had been continuing nonstop for nearly five days. Both Mossad and the Military Intelligence staff out at the Kadirya had mobilized every resource they possessed to locate further proof of the plot outlined in the documents captured by Naomi at the café. In London, Paris, Munich, Amsterdam, among fringe revolutionaries, student leaders, hippie drug addicts, among anarchists and arm dealers alike, Israeli agents had determinedly sought for futher clues to where the Abu Youssouf 73 might have other terrorist cells. Every fragment of information already on file about the Palestinian movements was analyzed afresh. The evidence to be presented to the UN General Assembly on the following Friday, May 10, had to be as damning as possible.

By Tuesday afternoon, Tel Aviv time, some results had come in from both Paris and London. It was decided that rather than send them separately to New York, Ben Maier should collect them and receive further briefings in Europe on his way back. Therefore, instead of taking the direct El Al Boeing 747 flight from Tel Aviv, he was to travel via London on the Thursday 707 and be briefed during the one and a half hour transit stop at Heathrow Airport. It is a firm rule that Israeli diplomats and couriers fly on the national airline, whose security measures against hijacking are extremely tough. Armed guards are aboard every flight, prepared to shoot it out with any terrorist. So Ben Maier was booked on Thursday's 707 flight number LY 255. He knew this definitely on the Tuesday afternoon and booked a call to Connie, which would catch her before she left for the hospital. She was unashamedly overjoyed to hear him.

"Darling, it is good to hear you! I was so disappointed on Friday, and then last night the phone went wrong. When are you coming home?"

"I'll be back Thursday evening on the plane from London."

"London?"

"Only a transit stop so I can collect some things they need at the delegation." His voice was reassuring. "I only knew when I was coming a few moments ago myself. Things have been"—he hesitated—"shall we say a little busy here. It couldn't be helped. I'll explain when I see you."

"You won't be delayed again?"

"No!" Although Ben was speaking slowly to offset the fractional time lag on the line, his tone was emphatic. "I promise you, darling, I have to be back before Friday morning. That's official."

Less than two hours later, in a jabber of Arabic, the gist of the Maiers' conversation was being relayed back to the southern shores of the Mediterranean. Then the guerrillas at the villa in Tripoli held a brief, but fiery, conference.

The Syrian, the visionary to whom every handful of Arab soil was sacred, in whose eyes the blood shed by a Jew regenerated Islam as surely as water makes the desert flower, gave the orders. He could be practical.

"Brothers," he declared incisively. "We must recognize facts. To hijack the aircraft will be difficult, in all probability impossible. The security on El Al is too good. Perhaps a marksman could kill this Israeli at either London or New York. But that would neither recover nor destroy the documents. Therefore, both the man and the aircraft must be destroyed."

"Can we plant a bomb on the plane at London Airport?" queried one of the men.

"Possibly," said the Syrian. "Mohammed Khadir in London could attempt it. But I have a better plan. Can we not shoot down the aircraft when it is approaching or leaving the airport?"

There was a moment's silence; then a younger man spoke up hesitantly. "You mean with a missile?"

The Syrian exploded, his gaunt face angry. "Listen, Kamal, my friend," he hissed. "We have possessed these weapons several years. We have sent men like Mohammed Khadir to Odessa to train with them. Now is the time to use one. Are you afraid of killing Europeans?"

The young man flushed.

"I myself faced the Israel fighters with such missiles in the October war," he exclaimed indignantly. "I am not afraid. However, there could be technical problems." Being an engineer, he understood more of these than the Syrian would. "In war," he went on, "the sky is full of enemies. If you aim at one and hit another, what does it matter? For this we must hit only the right plane."

The Syrian did not understand. His response was acid.

"It has El Al painted in large letters on the side surely?"

"If the English weather is bad," explained Kamal carefully, "it may not be so easy to see the markings.

51

Especially because we must shoot at it when it is high enough to be destroyed and catch fire in the crash. If it is hit when it is close to the airport and low down there is a possibility that the pilot could make some kind of landing."

"I am glad you say 'we' when you speak of this task," said the Syrian. "You, Kamal, must go to London and help Mohammed Khadir. You must make sure of success. 'Technical problems' are no excuse for failure. Tell me, what happened to the Israeli aircraft you saw shot down in the October war?"

"They went out of control, hit the ground and disintegrated. The pilot was killed, and the wreck immediately caught fire. The one I myself claimed was on fire even before it crashed."

"Nothing survived?"

"Only fragments of metal. Not maps or papers. His own mother could not have recognized the pilot's body."

"It is as I thought," said the Syrian. "You will go to London tonight."

The SAM 7 is a small weapon. The launcher tube, missile and high explosive warhead weigh only ten kilos complete. As the whole thing is only a meter and a half long and no thicker than a drainpipe, it is easily carried. "Manportable" is what the military calls it, and its manufacturers, the Russian State Factories, obligingly provide a canvas carrying sling. Its designation, SAM 7, is military jargon, too, though the jargon of the West. Surface to Air Missile 7 was introduced in 1966 as one of a family of Russian defensive missiles, the rest of which are monsters of various sizes, mounted on tracked chassis like tanks or on long trailers. It was a SAM 2, capable of reaching fifteen miles above the earth, that so surprised and embarrassed America by bringing down Gary Powers' U-2 spyplane over Russia in 1960. The SAM 7 is not in this class at all. Its effective range is three thousand five hundred meters, roughly eleven thousand five hundred feet either vertically or horizontally, and it is designed for hitting low-flying aircraft. The Russians appropriately call it *Strela,* which means arrow. They equipped the Vietcong with SAM 7s, and the Americans lost a number of planes in Vietnam as a result. The Russians also shipped a considerable quantity to Egypt, and it was one of these that Kamal had used on the battlefields of the Yom Kippur War in October 1973.

The pair of SAM 7s that Mohammed Khadir kept in his two rented rooms in London's seedy, cosmopolitan Earls Court district originated from the Egyptian consignment. Early in 1973 Libya's fanatically Muslim president, Colonel Qaddafi, had been deep in negotiations with Anwar Sadat, successor to Nasser as president of Egypt, over a union between the two states. When Qaddafi asked Sadat if he could spare a few SAM 7s, the answer was affirmative. In turn Qaddafi gave some to the PLO, and they found their way to various European and African countries. The Belgian police got wind of a couple late in 1973, and the first full-scale army alert at London's Heathrow Airport on January 6, 1974, was occasioned by a message that SAM 7s were believed to have been transferred to Britain. But it was impossible to stop them since they were sent in the diplomatic bags of countries friendly to the Palestinian cause.

Earls Court was an ideal place for a foreigner to keep arms. An area of once prosperous houses now fallen into the decay of what Londoners call "bedsitterland"—a genteel word for rooming houses—this part of the Royal Borough of Kensington was polluted by cheap tourism. More than a hundred small hotels disgorge their package-tour visitors into its streets each day in search of entertainment—Dutch, Germans, Jamaicans, Indians, Americans, Japanese. Immigrant Irish workmen drank and fought in the public house bars. Australians lived in motor caravans, smoking pot with their hippie girlfriends. Arab women, veiled and shrouded in black as if at home, humped their washing bundles to the launderettes while their children played on the pavements. Earls Court was one of the cross-roads of the world, and Mohammed Khadir passed unremarked among its transients.

The message to prepare for action reached Khadir on Tuesday evening, London time. In spite of the thoughtfulness of the Russians in providing a carrying strap, Khadir felt that to use it might arouse comment even in Earls Court. So he had brought the five constituent parts of each missile to his room in parcels, the two long launcher tubes being disguised inside a roll of vinyl flooring material and a package of architect's drawings. They stayed parceled in his bedroom cupboard. When the message came, he took them out and began carefully stripping off the protective wrappings, his own first and then the factory's. Taking each part in turn, he methodically checked the pistol grip firing mechanism which would attach beneath the launcher tube, the thermal battery that would ignite the missile's rocket when he pressed the trigger, the stubby round caseful of propellant, the tube itself and finally the warhead with its guidance vanes, which he would erect before firing. The instructors at the Odessa training school had taught him how to assemble a SAM 7 quickly and accurately. On this occasion he took his time, only dismantling the missiles again after he was completely satisfied.

The doorbell rang after midnight. Khadir descended the three flights of linoleumed stairs and tried to identify his visitor through the Victorian stained glass panels at the side of the entrance. He failed.

"Who is it?" he called softly in Arabic.

"Kamal, the friend of Abu Youssouf."

Khadir opened the door. Outside stood Kamal, the engineer. He had walked from the West London Air Terminal, a mere four hundred yards, but was nonetheless shivering in the chilly night air.

"Welcome," said Khadir and led him upstairs to the two-room apartment, with its scratched and worn furniture, where they talked and planned until dawn. They had only a day and a half and much to arrange.

At 0850 Eastern Standard Time on Wednesday, May 8, Captain Bill Curtis lined up the 208-ton bulk of his DC-10 jet for takeoff at New York's Kennedy Airport. He had been lucky. Although Atlantic Airlines' Blue Ribbon transatlantic flight usually boarded its passengers on schedule, there was often a procession of other departing aircraft ahead of it, delaying the actual departure for as much as half an hour. The timetable allowed for such delay, but it wasted fuel and frayed the passengers' nerves. This morning Atlantic's flight to London and Paris had received its startup, taxi and lineup clearances with no waiting.

Strapped into the jump seat behind Curtis, the spare place kept for such occasional visitors as pilots learning the procedures on a route before flying it themselves, was Jim Donaldson. He had been planning to fly home via British Airways, until Johnson and Curtis jointly persuaded him to accept their hospitality.

"Whether you join us or not, it would be plain stupid to throw up a chance to see Atlantic in action," Johnson had remarked, adding wryly, "Besides, you'll be saving your government an airfare. From what I hear it could use the money."

"Except that the government makes up British Airways' losses," responded Donaldson sourly. There was a streak of puritanism in him, and he admired Johnson for building up a transatlantic route in the face of subsidized competition from other countries' state-owned airlines. So although he would have preferred to fly undisturbed and be able to concentrate on the pros and cons of moving to America, he had accepted Johnson's suggestion and was watching the crew go through their routines with interest. Later he would go aft to his first-class seat and breakfast.

"Atlantic two five nine, take off" came the controller's voice on the radio. The second pilot acknowledged the instruction, and Curtis firmly pushed the throttle levers to full power, held the brakes until the three giant engines were beginning to make the whole aircraft tremble and then released her to gather speed down the runway. The second pilot called "VI," the speed beyond which takeoff could not be aborted, followed two seconds later by the cry "Rotate." Curtis hauled back gently on the control column, the nose came up, and Atlantic's flight 259 lifted off for Europe, the green and gold motifs of its livery glittering in the morning sun. Six hours and forty minutes later the DC-10 would touch down at London Heathrow and two hours and fifteen minutes after that at Paris' new Charles de Gaulle Airport, where by then it would be evening.

Donaldson enjoyed his flight. The wide body of the airplane gave one room to move around. It held many fewer seats than the maximum possible, and the designer had utilized this uncrowded layout to full advantage. In the forward cabin there was a neat little bar where first-class passengers could gather to talk if they felt like it or flirt with the perky hostess in her green and gold uniform serving the drinks. The chief steward, whom Atlantic somewhat grandiosely called the maître d'hôtel and who wore an elegant gray tailcoat, had clearly been briefed to look after the Englishman. But Donaldson reckoned the staff gave as much pleasant, good-humored attention to everyone. At his own request he was taken on a conducted tour of the aircraft, seeing the three galleys—one for first class, two for economy—that provided for up to two hundred seventy-eight passengers. He even poked his nose into the lavatories at the extreme rear. Back here you noticed the deep, dull roar from the DC-10's third CF6 turbofan jet, which was mounted in the rudder fin just above the body.

"There's a damn great lot of power up there," he commented to the girl, thinking aloud. She smiled back blandly at him, uncertain what to say. The engines were not her department. Equally Donaldson refrained from remarking that it was just here that the cabin floor of a Turkish Airlines DC-10 had collapsed after a door in the pressurized cargo hold below had blown out. That aircraft had been at nineteen thousand feet, climbing away from Paris en route for London when the pilot lost control. It hit the ground at four hundred mph, and all three hundred forty-six on board lost their lives. To date it was the world's worst air crash, though subsequent modifications to the cargo door latch made any repetition of the accident unlikely.

Donaldson spent most of the journey in first class, eating a five-course luncheon, sipping complimentary drinks and cogitating whether or not he really did want to work for Johnson. He only returned to the flight deck for the descent, admiring the unhurried professionalism with which Curtis went through the procedures of the approach to Heathrow Airport. The two pilots had a great deal to do accurately in very little time, guiding if things went wrong what was effectively just a heavy, fast-moving projectile. For all crews the two crucial phases of the takeoff and the approach to land were minutes of extreme concentration. Bill Curtis and his second pilot handled both with skilled assurance. Donaldson left them with regret after they had gently nosed the DC-10 up to the arrival bay at Heathrow. Tomorrow they would pass through here again in the late afternoon, having night-stopped in Paris, on their way back to New York as Atlantic Airlines' flight 260. And he would simply be "flying a desk" again, in the old RAF phrase. Meanwhile, there was Jane.

Jane Donaldson stood in the crowded arrivals hall of Heathrow's Terminal 3 waiting for her husband to emerge from the customs area. Forty minutes after the "landed" time shown on the indicator board she was still fidgeting by the barrier, irritated at having this final delay added to his extra five days away. Her dislike of aviation had intensified as she grew older. She even found herself jealous of the way its demands stimulated her husband. She wished he could be promoted, both for the money that would bring and because he might then investigate fewer accidents in person. She loathed his unpredictable comings and goings.

At last Jim Donaldson came through, a raincoat over his arm, suitcase in hand, not in the least frazzled by the forty-eight minutes that customs clearance had taken. He lowered the case carefully, then embraced his wife.

"Darling, what do they do in there, I've been waiting an age?" she complained.

"Never mind. It's worth it in the end and lovely to see you."

He kissed her again. He was a sincere rather than a passionate man and felt awkward at public shows of emotion. Now, sensing that an immediate gesture was needed, he fumbled in his raincoat pocket and pulled out a package.

"A little present for you," he said. He had intended keeping it for later.

Jane began to recover herself. She gave him a kiss of thanks. "I'll open it in the car," she said and led him away through the crowd to the parking garage. As they walked she asked, "Why did you change flights? I thought you had to fly British."

"It's a long story. I was the guest of the airline."

He was determined not to say more until they were back home, comfortably settled down in the sitting room, and he could explain Atlantic Airlines' proposition unhurriedly. If possible, he would hold back until the weekend. But despite her pleasure at opening the neatly wrapped half-ounce bottle of Ma Griffe, her favorite scent, Jane was not prepared to wait. As she threaded her way along the roads past Kingston and so to the A217, she insisted.

"Something has been going on and I want to know what it is."

"There has," he admitted, "but it needs thinking about. Couldn't I tell you later?"

"No, Jim Donaldson, you could not."

Her tone suggested that tears were close. So he related the events of the weekend with Johnson, describing Westchester County, mentioning the salary as casually as he could.

"What's that in pounds?" she asked sharply.

"Over forty thousand a year. Depending on the exchange rate."

"But I don't want to leave England. I might hate America."

He had a sick feeling that the conversation was moving out of his control.

"The children's friends are all here, my friends are here, I've only just hung the new curtains. We'd have to start all over again!"

She drove on automatically, images racing through her mind. The morning coffee parties, tennis at the Ebbisham Club, crowded swimming pools all through a long, warm summer. By the time she swung the Ford into their driveway at home her emotions had reached one single, surging peak. She pulled on the hand brake, switched off the ignition and sobbed, "I don't want to go. I just don't want to leave here. Not even for so much money."

From then on things definitely were out of control. Donaldson had little appetite for the cold supper she had ready—he had eaten too well on the plane. That annoyed her, and when he revealed that he would have to go to the ministry the next day she flared up.

"You might as well live in an hotel for all the time you spend with me," she cried angrily, and burst into tears afresh.

Meanwhile, Wednesday, May 8, had been an active day for Mohammed Khadir in London. The orders brought by Kamal from Tripoli were simple.

"We must destroy the Israeli Boeing 707 flight LY 255 on Thursday either as it comes in from Tel Aviv or as it leaves again for New York."

"What are the times?"

"It lands at twelve fifteen and departs at thirteen thirty-five."

"I have studied the airport closely," said Khadir. "Usually there is a westerly wind and the aircraft come over London. They are flying slowly and almost in a straight line, but they turn onto the line at different places. When they take off, they climb quickly and turn soon, and each aircraft follows its own course."

Kamal nodded. "They climb fast and turn for noise abatement," he commented. "So the best place is near the airport when they are approaching and only three or four hundred feet above the ground. It is low enough for us to see the markings and high enough for all on board to be killed."

"It is also patrolled by the police and often by the army," said Khadir sourly.

"Are you afraid?"

"No. But do you want to fail?"

Kamal remembered the Syrian in Tripoli. No, he did not want to fail.

"I believe," Khadir went on, well satisfied at the dismay in his companion's face, "that it would be possible to fire from the top of a high building in the city. I have found such a building, containing offices, that can be entered easily. It is close to the river by the Southwark Bridge, and it has a flat roof. Many of the airliners pass overhead. I do not think they fly higher than about one thousand meters. The roof is at least one hundred meters high, so the range would be only nine hundred, and the missile is effective up to thirty-five hundred meters."

Kamal took a pencil and paper. On it he drew a tower and the outline of an aircraft passing overhead, then a curving line from the tower to the tail of the aircraft.

"It has enough range," he decided, "even when the missile must fly in a slight curve if it is to come from behind and guide itself toward the heat of the engines."

"The problem," explained Khadir, "is to know which is the right airliner. How can we be sure?"

Kamal reflected. It must be a matter of plotting the airliner's course. At that stage it would be obeying directions from the ground.

"If we could listen to its radio and follow its progress on a map, we could do it," he decided. "But you say they do not always turn at the same place."

"Some turn far away beyond the City of London, others closer over Battersea and Fulham." Khadir had watched them.

"Then we must be prepared for two attempts. If firing from the tower fails we must go near Heathrow and shoot it down after takeoff. There is a road that runs near the west side of the airport, past some big reservoirs. The road is busy, and the position would be very exposed. The risks of being seen will be high."

"Yes, I understand this plan is not so good. But it will be easy listening to the takeoff orders and easy to recognize the airliner. The team can wait in the car until the last moment. The police will realize exactly what has happened. The first way, from the tower, is better. It may look like an accident or sabotage, especially if the aircraft falls in the Thames."

Kamal paused, then in a harder tone went on. "We must mobilize all our resources. We must find an airline pilot to help us."

At lunchtime, in the safety of a back room at the Libyan Embassy in fashionable Prince's Gate, the two terrorists met an Arab airline pilot. On a table he had laid out a series of aeronautical radio charts. One covered northern France, much of Belgium and southern England, showing the main airways with their tracks and the radio beacons along them. The beacons were marked as circles.

"Coming from Israel, he will fly up the coast of Italy, over Nice, then Paris and follow either Amber Two or Amber Two West across the Channel. Most probably Amber Two West," the pilot explained. "You can pick him up when he first calls London with a time for passing the Abbeville beacon near the French coast. Then he will fly over the beacon at Biggin. From there if there is a lot of traffic he will go into the stack over Ockham and circle until they direct him out of the stack and bring him over south London in a wide turn to intersect the final approach direction. Often when I come from Paris myself we pass over Tower Bridge on the way to lining up with the runway. London is one of the very few cities in the world where the approach passes over the city center."

"Fortunately for us," remarked Kamal crisply. "And how do we know which frequency to listen on?"

The pilot handed him a thick book bound in gray paper and titled *Europe Supplement to AERAD Flight Guide*.

"It is all here. Recently the authorities made a change that will help you. All aircraft coming from the southeast call on the same channel."

"Channel?" queried Mohammed, who was finding this difficult to follow.

"Radio frequency. You will need an aircraft-type radio to be certain of tuning to the correct channel. But do not worry, the air traffic controller always states the frequency clearly when he tells the aircraft to change on to another one."

Kamal looked at the pilot and at the Libyan diplomat.

"My brothers," he said gravely, "this is a technical business. I am an engineer. If you want to blow up a bridge or a building, I can tell you where to place the charge. Mohammed and I are both trained in firing missiles. We can do that. But for this operation we also need an airline technician. We need a pilot or a navigator."

"It would be an honor," said the pilot quickly. "Alas, I am scheduled to take a 727 to Paris and Casablanca tomorrow morning."

"Passengers can wait," said Kamal brutally.

"I am sure a relief pilot can be found," interjected the diplomat suavely, "and it is always an honor for any Arab to serve the cause of the oppressed Palestinians."

The pilot saw he was trapped. The idea of shooting down an aircraft full of passengers appalled him. It was even worse than the possibility of being caught and spending years in a British jail. But the immediate reality consisted of these two determined killers.

Kamal, watching him closely, read his thoughts. "May I remind you," he said, "that armed violence must destroy the military, political, economic and financial institutions of the occupying Zionist society? That is our mission." Then, softening his voice, he added, "In any case the British are weak. When we put pressure on them they released Leila Khaled. You have nothing to fear."

The pilot remembered the woman hijacker, Leila, a heroine to all Arabs. He smiled tightly at Ahmed.

"What do you want me to do?"

"First, find a suitable radio receiver. Then plot the probable course of the aircraft on a map of London. Meet us this evening in Earls Court. Longridge Gardens is a street near the underground station."

The pilot wasted more than an hour searching hi-fi shops in the Tottenham Court Road for an airband receiver. None that were on sale could be tuned to a preselected frequency. Then it occurred to him that aircraft radios might be advertised in aviation magazines. He walked to a newsstand, bought three current issues and studied them on the spot. In *Flight* he found what he was hoping for. The short advertisement read: "360 channel portable VHF transceiver for hire."

The address and telephone number of a firm dealing in aircraft spares followed. The pilot went to a call box and rang the number.

"Yes," said a cultured English voice, "the set is available. It's a Dynair Sky 515A. It works off its own battery and weighs nine pounds."

"What is the cost?"

"Twenty pounds a week. The battery is a rechargeable Nikad, by the way, and we can loan you the battery charger."

"I will come at once," said the pilot. "I will need the set today for one week."

He reached the firm's office in Chiswick just before they closed. The young manager eyed him curiously but relaxed when it became clear that the pilot knew about radios. The set was ideal. Compact, it had a pair of strong carrying handles on the top, along which were ranged the controls. Two large black knobs operated the crystal controlled tuning, the left-hand one the coarse MHz, the right-hand one the fine selectivity down to 50 KHz. In fact, it could work three hundred and eighty channels, from 117.00 to 135.95. The young man slid out the slim black rod aerial, switched the set on and turned the knobs to 128.60. Clear as a bell, although they were indoors, came the monotonous voice of the London Volmet, broadcasting its continuous weather report for aircraft.

"Excellent," said the pilot. "May I pay you now?" He slipped a twenty-pound note from his wallet.

"Out of curiosity, what are you going to use it for?" asked the young man.

The pilot had prepared himself for this during the taxi ride to Chiswick. "A rich friend of mine is trying a field near his house as an airstrip. I have told him I shall take a Cessna into it, but that I must have radio contact with him on the ground."

The young man seemed satisfied.

"We hired it out for a month recently for some demonstration flights in the Far East. Same sort of problem. By the way, what's your address for the receipt?"

The pilot gave a fictitious hotel in Kensington, shook hands and carried the set and the charger gear out to the waiting taxi. Twenty minutes later he was with Mohammed Khadir in Earls Court.

At much the same moment, though local time was an hour later in Jerusalem, Ben Maier was preparing to leave the Israeli Foreign Ministry, go home to his parents house, pack and have an early night before his breakfast time departure next morning. He was clearing the desk in his borrowed office when the internal phone rang. It was the head of the department that deals with France.

"The cipher room has just told me there is an urgent telegram in from Paris. You had better stay until they've unbuttoned it. Would you come along to my office please?"

Half an hour later the decoded telegram came through. It said simply that more important information about the Abu Youssouf 73 group had come to light during the day. It would be desirable for Maier to travel via Paris in order to collect it and receive further briefing. To transfer the material to London in the time available was impossible.

"Decisions and revisions which a moment will reverse," commented the head of the department, who was an admirer of T. S. Eliot. "You will have to take the seven ten flight to Paris instead. I think it is seven ten on Thursdays, arriving about midday." El Al's schedules changed often.

He pulled an airline timetable out of his desk drawer and consulted it.

"Almost right. Twelve fifteen it arrives."

"How do I go on from there? Surely there we do not have a Paris to New York flight."

The head of the department perused the folder.

"Correct. It is essential that the documents are with the delegation by Thursday evening. The ambassador must have time to study them before the debate on Friday. This is explosive stuff. We don't want it to misfire. Best we ask the El Al manager in Paris to make the arrangements. There is certainly an Air France flight, and the security will be greater if your booking is a last-minute one. We'll warn New York to expect a message from El Al tomorrow."

In New York it was early afternoon when the Foreign Ministry telegram from Jerusalem reached the Israeli delegation. The counselor failed to catch Connie at the hospital and finally spoke to her when she was back home in Tudor City.

"There's nothing to worry about, Connie," he assured her. "Ben has to visit our Paris embassy on the way back, so he'll be on a different flight. We shall know which tomorrow, and I'll call you straightaway."

Yet when Connie put the phone down she felt a pang of fear that something was going wrong, that sick feeling in the pit of the stomach for which there is no medicine. She told herself not to be a fool, that an educated woman, a qualified doctor like herself, should not succumb to irrational emotions. It was no good. The uneasiness persisted.

News of these changed Israeli plans reached Mohammed Khadir in London at 3:45 A.M. on Thursday morning. The telephone shrilled on the landing outside his two rooms in Longridge Gardens. Khadir slept lightly and was half expecting a communication from Tripoli anyway. He ran out and answered it before the other tenants could wake or complain. Then, knowing he could do nothing until daytime about the problem, he sensibly returned to his bed.

At Cannon Row on Thursday morning Commander Thompson was discussing the remainder of the week with Sturgess and Chance. So far it had gone smoothly. Sunday afternoon's demo had attracted huge support —at least forty thousand people—without any worse disturbance than a minor scuffle when counterdemonstrators tried to break through a police cordon. Equally, the three-day state visit, one of the major events of the year, had passed without incident. There had been threats, but no actual bombs. Not that the hoax demanded less police effort than the real thing; it could easily take more. Any search for explosives in Buckingham Palace had to be exhaustive since the Queen resolutely refused to leave the building merely on account of a threat. She would leave only if a bomb had been positively identified. Nonetheless, a hoax could still cause a disturbance to exactingly timed schedules. If the price of liberty was eternal vigilance, it was the police who paid the price on these public occasions. Cumulatively Sunday, Monday, Tuesday and Wednesday had been exhausting days. Thompson was keeping his fingers crossed that he would not need many constables to control the Palestinian demo on Saturday.

"How many marchers are you expecting?" he asked.

"They're hoping for fifteen hundred. I reckon if half that show up they'll be lucky," said Sturgess. "We'll just have one control van at King Charles' island."

At the top of Whitehall, in the center of the road, stands an equestrian statue of King Charles I, gazing proudly down the wide street toward the Banqueting

Hall outside of which the "Royal Martyr" was executed on January 30, 1648. Each anniversary costumed "royalists" lay wreaths there in his memory. More prosaically it is a favorite spot for the police to park their vans during Trafalgar Square meetings.

Thompson indicated approval. "How many serials?" he asked.

"Seven," said Sturgess.

A serial was a busload of police comprising one inspector, three sergeants and twenty-one constables. They arrived in the bus, then walked as escorts to the marchers.

"Have another two in reserve down here. I want a tight rein kept in this demo, Colin. Now, what about the Jews?"

"I've persuaded the Zionist General Council to meet at Hyde Park Corner. It should be no sweat keeping the two demos separate."

Thompson nodded. Hyde Park Corner and Trafalgar Square are a full mile apart. Things could only go wrong if the young Jewish right wingers of the Heerut were allowed in sight of the Palestinians. That was unlikely.

"Any more Interpol messages?" he asked Chance.

The burly CID chief superintendent consulted a notebook. "No. But the Special Branch report that a suspected Black September leader flew in from Algiers last night. His name is Kamal al-Khulaifi. He gave the immigration officer a nonexistent hotel in Kensington as his address."

"No grounds for stopping him?"

"He had a valid visa," said Chance. "He's not a known terrorist. His kind are too smart to carry arms on an aircraft unless they're actually hijacking it."

"They'll pick up weapons here, though," Sturgess commented.

"Let's stick to the point." Thompson's rebuke was mild. "And the point is, has he come for the demo, or just for a beer, or what?"

"The demo's the only reason we can think of," commented Chance.

"That is exactly what puzzles me," said Thompson reflectively. "It's not in their interest to turn the demo into a riot. Not when they are trying to present themselves at the United Nations as responsible Arab politicians, or at least the PLO are. And talking of politicians, any news of Andrews?"

"As far as we know, he's still encouraging the organizers to believe the prime minister will be thrilled to receive their petition."

"He's a cunning so-and-so, that. I wish I knew what he was really up to."

Had either the police or his fellow Members of Parliament known what Enoch Andrews, the Honorable Member for Mid-Fife, was doing on this fine morning of Thursday, May 9, they would have been deeply surprised. Even the rest of the thirty or so MPs reckoned by the Security Service to be in the pocket of one foreign power or another might have wondered at the way Andrew was earning his retainer from the Arabs. At 10:45 A.M. he was leaning on the counter of the El Al office in Regent Street, talking with earnest sincerity to one of the ticket sales girls. She was obviously English, and he had taken care to join the short queue of inquirers at her position. She would be more likely to give information away than an Israeli would.

"I have an old friend passing through London on your flight today," he was saying in his Lowland burr, "and I particularly wanted to see him while he's in transit." He made a show of consulting a notebook.

"It's your flight two five five from Tel Aviv, and his name is Maier."

"I'm afraid we're not allowed to give details of passenger lists," said the girl firmly, and then to soften her refusal to this friendly plea for help, she added, "Anyway, you wouldn't be able to meet him when he's in transit. They don't come through customs."

"As a matter of fact, that's where you're wrong, lassie," he declared unhurriedly. "I have the happy privilege of being a Member of Parliament, and arrangements will be made for us to use one of the VIP

68

rooms at the airport." Less pompously, he explained, "But I dinna want to go all that way if for some reason he's not on the flight at all. Luckily I was passing, so I came in."

The girl hesitated. She realized she had seen the name Maier somewhere today. Perhaps she ought to be more helpful to an MP.

"Can you identify yourself, please?" she said cautiously.

"Indeed I can that," said Andrews unhesitatingly, and drew a House of Commons pass from his wallet.

She examined it and then asked, "What did you say your Mr. Maier's initial was?"

"B. B for Benjamin."

"Would you mind waiting a moment?"

She disappeared into the office behind. Andrews stood, hoping she had not merely gone to fetch another official. He had no idea why the Libyan wanted this information. He merely knew from the diplomat's tone on the telephone at breakfast time that this was not a request he could refuse. One reason was that if he did then his two-hundred-pound-a-month cash retainer would cease, which he could ill afford on a parliamentary salary after tax of less than four hundred pounds a month. The second was that even then he would remain open to the threat of exposure. They had said as much during a quarrel six months ago. It had not been necessary to repeat the threat this morning. The harsh urgency in the Libyan's voice was enough. Now he prayed the El Al salesgirl would not ask more questions because he knew instinctively that in performing this service he was sinking a whole stratum lower in the underworld of international politics, and it frightened him.

After a very long four minutes the girl returned, smiling.

"I thought I remembered the name," she said, as pleased as a kitten that had found the cream. "Your friend isn't on the two five five after all. We had a telex from our Paris office. He's booked on Atlantic Airlines' two sixty flight from Paris to New York instead. It lands at Heathrow en route at sixteen twenty-five."

Andrews thanked her profusely and stepped out into Regent Street. He walked down to Piccadilly Circus and telephoned from one of the call boxes in the underground station. His hand was trembling, and the Libyan's sly congratulations did nothing to lighten his growing depression.

Ben Maier's sojourn in Paris was brief. During lunch at the embassy the significance of the new evidence about the Abu Youssouf 73 group's plans was explained to him, and the additional documents handed over. Then he was driven back to Orly just in time for the Atlantic Airlines' flight 260, on which El Al's Paris manager had booked him in the economy class with no mention of his diplomatic status. He was the last of the two hundred and sixty-four passengers to check in and he showed his boarding card at the departure gate only twenty minutes before the Blue Ribbon's scheduled takeoff time. Had he arrived two minutes later he would have been left behind.

Few if any of those two hundred and sixty-four passengers realized the preparations and effort devoted to making their departure punctual. During its brief stay in Paris the DC-10 had been cleaned, carefully inspected by maintenance engineers and fueled with thirty tons of aviation kerosene. The galleys had received the appropriate number of meals, plus a few spare, and the holds in the aircraft's belly had been loaded with twenty-one tons of containerized freight. At 1400 Bill Curtis and his crew had taken over. Two pilots, a systems engineer, the maître d'hôtel and nine stewardesses. Thirteen in all. The second pilot, Joe Walther, a comparative youngster of twenty-eight, had completed the load sheets, calculating the total weight as one hundred and seventy-nine tons. As usual the tanks were only partly full; otherwise the landing weight after the short Paris-London hop would be above limits, so the DC-10 was comparatively light. Joe then worked out the exact speeds for lift-off, for climb to the altitude of twenty-seven thousand feet which they had been assigned when they filed their flight plan with air traffic, and for their brief cruise along the Amber Two West airway. Finally, the two pilots had made their own external and internal checks of the aircraft. They and the systems engineer were completing the long list as the passengers boarded. The DC-10 was pushed gently back from her dock at the terminal at 1520. At 1526 she was airborne. The way she left the ground, you would hardly have thought she weighed so much.

Ben Maier loathed the takeoff. He loathed it whatever the aircraft, and he loathed it equally at Ben Gurion, Orly, Heathrow, Kennedy or anywhere else. That thudding roaring rush along the tarmac and then the sudden steep angle of the climb always alarmed him. If he had known what pilots think about the dangers of the noise abatement procedures that demand this climb plus an early reduction of power, he would probably have refused to fly again. As it was, he gripped the armrests of his seat and tried not to look out of the window beside him. He hated the way the whole world tilted crazily when the aircraft was turning. This time they passed quickly above the few clouds and continued ascending straight.

"Ladies and gentlemen, you may now smoke if you wish and unfasten your seat belts, though we recommend you keep them loosely fastened when seated. In a moment we shall be serving drinks from the bar." The familiar stewardess' announcement over the loudspeaker eased Maier's tension a little. Even as the voice clicked off a blonde in a crisp green and gold uniform was asking him what he would like.

"We have a pretty wide selection, sir, starting with champagne."

She looked disappointed when he ordered an orange juice.

Now the DC-10 was passing over the Pontoise radio beacon north of Paris, joining the Amber Two West airway for Abbeville and the French coast. On the flight deck Bill Curtis was handling the controls in the left-hand seat while Joe Walther worked the radios. Both were in their shirt sleeves. Behind them the systems engineer regulated banks of dials and switches. On the Paris to London route you scarcely reach the cruising altitude before you start to think about the descent. By the time the autopilot had taken the aircraft up to twenty-seven thousand feet, the distance measuring equipment was showing that they had only twenty-one miles to run before they would be over Abbeville. At four hundred and eighty knots that would take less than three minutes. Curtis glanced down at the French countryside, the scattered clouds casting shadows which he saw as dark patches on the sunlit woods and fields below.

In front of them through the windows above the crowded instrument panels the streamlined nose sloped away sharply. No other part of the aircraft's body could they see. Were it not for the stewardess coming through the partition door and unobtrusively placing cups of coffee beside them, they might have been perched by themselves in space.

"Everything OK back there?" asked Curtis.

"There's one woman at the rear has a baby crying. That's our total of problems right now. Except meeting all the drink orders."

"There's never enough time on this sector, honey, never was, never will be. Well, I guess I'll give them the spiel."

Curtis flipped the intercom switch that would put his voice through to the cabin.

"Ladies and gentlemen, this is Captain Curtis speaking. We are now cruising at twenty-seven thousand feet with a ground speed of five hundred and fifty miles per hour. Very shortly we shall be passing near Le Tréport. Le Touquet will be over to the right side of the aircraft and Dieppe away to the left. We expect to arrive at London Heathrow on schedule at four twenty-five P.M. local time. The weather there is fine and sunny with a temperature of twenty degrees Centigrade, that's sixty-nine degrees Fahrenheit. Thank you."

He had hardly switched off before the voice of the French air traffic controller came over, his English heavily accented, addressing them by their flight number.

"Atlantic two six zero, call London now please on one one seven decimal five. Good day."

Joe Walther reached out to the communications console, adjusted two knobs to the frequency 117.5 and spoke quietly into the microphone of his headset. The time was 1553, but he gave only the minutes past the hour, not the hour itself.

"Good afternoon, London, this is Atlantic two six zero at Abbeville five three, estimating London two four."

Immediately, clear and calm, the reply of the controller in the huge room at the West London Air Traffic Center out at West Drayton came back.

"Good afternoon, Atlantic two six zero. Thank you. Your routing is via Cliff and Biggin to London airport. Landing runway two eight right. Maintain two seven zero. Steer three two zero."

These directions told Curtis to maintain his height and follow the heading of the airway across the Channel. On his circular screen at West Drayton the controller watched the yellow dot which was the DC-10's radar reflection move slowly across the outline of the French coast. From other directions many dots were converging on southern England. His job was to direct them toward their destinations with an orderly, safe separation of height and distance. When the DC-10 was fifty miles or less from London and below fifteen thousand feet on its descent, he would hand it over to the Heathrow Approach. Now he wanted to be absolutely sure that his dot over the Channel was the Atlantic Airlines DC-10.

"Atlantic two six zero," he ordered in the curious international English of aviation, "squawk indent."

On the flight deck Walther leaned foward and pressed the button that activated the transponder that a second later would cause the four-figure identification code for this flight—6612—to flash up on the controller's radar screen below the yellow dot. In another couple of seconds the Control Center's computer decoded the signal and 6612 was replaced on the circular screen by the flight number, AL 260, in tiny figures of yellow light that faithfully followed the radar "blip" of the aircraft. The DC-10 was positively identified.

On the roof of the tower block in Southwark the two terrorists and the Arab pilot squatted behind a parapet designed to hide water tanks and elevator machinery from the eyes of the public below. There had been no problem gaining entrance. With the missile disguised as a large bundle of drawings, the first two said they were going to the design office and excited no comment. The pilot had come separately. Well dressed, he had simply nodded to the doorman and walked to the elevator, as though he worked here. In a large briefcase he carried both the Dynair transceiver and a powerful pair of binoculars. Even with its battery attached, the radio was less than seventeen inches long.

Now the pilot had the radio's thin black aerial extended and was listening through a pair of headphones plugged into the set. In front of him were spread out two maps. An ordinary map of London and the Home Counties, with big rings inked around Biggin Hill in Kent, Ockham in Surrey and their own location on this tower a thousand yards south of the Thames. The other map was the Radio Navigation Chart, showing the airways and reporting points. Mohammed had assembled the missile and was checking it, while Kamal covered the rooftop doorway to the building, a small 9mm Makarov pistol in his hand. They had agreed to carry a minimum of arms and rely on surprise if they were discovered.

The view from the roof was superb. A strong wind had blown away the smoke and dust that often lie over London, and the morning's puffs of cloud had developed into majestic galleons of cumulus, sailing in rows across the sky. The visibility beneath them must, the

Libyan pilot reckoned, have been at least twenty miles. Orienting the map in relation to their position, he had no difficulty identifying the Houses of Parliament and Big Ben to the west, the Surrey Hills to the south and, nearer, the high ground around Crystal Palace with its TV pylon. A mile to the northeast lay the famous shape of Tower Bridge, while beyond the widening River Thames wound away through mile upon mile of dockland. Overhead, comfortably beneath the clouds, came a procession of aircraft, all turning slowly over south London and the docks to line up at what seemed to be one-minute intervals for the airport, fourteen miles distant. It was obviously a busy time.

Silently the Arab pilot thanked Allah for the weather. In low clouds this operation would have been impossible, and he would have been forced to go out later to the airport itself. Although there could be no error in identifying the airliner at takeoff, and shooting it down as it climbed would ensure its destruction, he was convinced that such a task would be suicidal. The two men he was with were killers, and crazy killers at that. If he failed here, their only reason for letting him live would be to make a second attempt. He prayed that nothing would go wrong. Already it was 1555, five minutes to four, and although he could hear a succession of airliners calling London, he had not picked up Atlantic Airlines. He feared he might have somehow selected the wrong channel, even though he knew that all aircraft inbound from the southeast now called on a single frequency.

Mohammed was crouched beside him, listening and not comprehending. He was tense and agitated.

"Have you heard it yet?" he demanded in a whisper. "When is it coming?"

"The takeoff may have been delayed. A thousand things may happen."

Then to his immense relief he picked up a brief transmission. "Atlantic two six zero."

That must be the acknowledgement of a message from the London controller which he had somehow missed. The Arab pilot swore to himself. Evidently he had also missed the airliner's first call. Perhaps the buildings between him and London Airport were screening the air traffic controller's transmissions, preventing his hearing them. If so, he would have to rely on the airliner's reading back of instructions. He forced himself to smile at Mohammed and say in a cheerful undertone, "Contact."

Above the Channel Bill Curtis was starting his descent. A moment before London had authorized them to come down to flight level eight zero—eight thousand feet—by the time they reached Biggin Hill. That meant there would be no circling in the stack. The inertial navigation system and its associated computer, housed beneath the flight deck floor, could guide the ship the whole way down to the runway threshold. But Curtis enjoyed flying. He cut the autopilot out, adjusted the throttles manually, then took hold of the thick, curving branches of the control column and pushed the nose forward into a shallow dive, bringing the DC-10 down at four thousand and five hundred feet per minute. Far below he could see tiny flecks of white that were waves on the gray sea. Joe Walther spoke on the intercom to the passengers.

"Ladies and gentlemen, we are now starting our descent to London Heathrow, where we expect to land at four twenty-four local time. In about two minutes we shall be passing over the English coast to Hastings, which will be on the left side of the aircraft. The weather is fine and clear at London. Thank you."

In the economy class cabin Ben Maier stretched his legs and fidgeted. The irritating chain holding the briefcase to his wrist would soon have to be snapped on again. This was his first experience of acting as a diplomatic courier, and he was thankful that it was not his career. How could those men stand spending their lives strapped to an airliner seat? The plane lurched, and nervously he clipped the briefcase's chain around his wrist.

Curtis could feel the plane shivering gently in his hands as he nosed down among the clouds, catching glimpses of the fields and villages that create the patchwork countryside of southern England. The altimeter was unwinding fast, and the clouds made the air bumpy. London called again as the controller monitored the DC-10's progress.

"Atlantic two six zero, eleven miles on your run to Biggin."

Walther acknowledged with their call sign. They were passing through ten thousand feet now. Curtis eased back on the control column, cutting the rate of descent to bring the speed back to the two hundred and fifty knots he now wanted.

"Atlantic two six zero," came another order. "Leave Biggin on heading two eight zero and call Heathrow Approach on one one niner decimal five."

Walther repeated back these instructions, wished the West Drayton controller "Good day" and called up on the new frequency.

The high red-brick control tower at Heathrow, rearing up among the passenger terminals, has a conspicuous "glasshouse" on its top. But the radar controllers who bring aircraft down to within sight of the airfield work in a darkened room two floors lower. One deals with the stack of aircraft south of London, another with the north stack. These two collaborate to feed the aircraft to the final director, who assembles them into one steady stream, each aircraft four miles apart, although the air turbulence created by wide-bodied aircraft like the Boeing 747 or the DC-10 dictates a space of six miles behind them. The director's radar screen has a grid faintly imposed on it, marked off at two-mile intervals from the runway center line to help him judge the distances between the tiny "blips." It looks simple. In fact, it depends on the accumulated experience of many years, passed on from controller to controller, and even so, the longest a trained man can follow these blobs of light without losing concentration is a couple of hours. No one is more aware of the responsibility they carry than the controllers themselves, who invariably either hold, or have held, pilots' licenses.

When the Arab pilot heard Walther repeat the new frequency he hastily rotated the black knobs on his radio until 119.50 showed on their indicators. He just caught Walther's next transmission as the DC-10 made its first contact with the Heathrow radar controller.

"Atlantic two six zero. Biggin at zero nine, steering two eight zero at flight level eight zero."

But the Arab was unable to pick up Heathrow's relaxed reply. "Good afternoon, Atlantic two six zero. Descend to seven zero. Maintain heading two seven zero." Nor did he hear the new controller's demand for a "squawk indent." In any case he was fully occupied plotting a line on the map running at two hundred and eighty degrees from Biggin and making calculations with his stopwatch. The time was 1610. The aircraft must be flying along the outer suburbs, heading parallel to the runway but around twenty miles farther south. In the bare fifteen minutes between now and touchdown it would zigzag over London following a course shaped like a Z. Currently it was tracing the straight bottom line of the letter, going west. Soon, the Arab pilot knew, it must swing around to head northeast, making the slanting upward stroke, until a left turn would bring it ponderously around again toward the runway, as it were along the top line of the Z. The critical question was where that last turn would be carried out. Everything depended on how the controller planned to slot the DC-10 into the stream of planes approaching Heathrow. The pilot strained his ears unavailingly to catch Heathrow's directions.

"Where is it?" Mohammed asked him impatiently. "How soon shall we see it?"

"It is down there," said the pilot, pointing south and trying to sound confident, "many miles away. Please be silent." He pressed the earphones closer to his head with both hands and stared down at the map.

As the Atlantic 260 neared Epsom, the plane was ordered to turn right onto a course of seventy degrees along the slanting upright of the Z. It was also told to contact the Heathrow director on 120.4 and to descend to three thousand feet.

Curtis eased the DC-10 into a wide turn and began gently losing height. Beside him Joe Walther again changed the radio frequency to make contact with the final director in the Heathrow control tower, the man who unknowingly either would, or would not, guide the aircraft past the waiting terrorists with their SAM 7 missile.

This was one of the busiest hours of the day, with an average of sixty aircraft landing and thirty-one taking off between 1600 and 1659. There were a good thirty yellow blips at various places on the director's screen being channeled in from both north and south to slot into the approach stream. He decided to send flight 260 a considerable way northeast before swinging her around again to intersect the approach path out over the London docks. Eventually, when she was established on the instrument landing system—the ILS—he would hand her over to the man in the "glasshouse" two floors above. At that point she would be eight miles out, roughly over Chiswick, and would stay under the tower's control until touchdown. This mental picture of the DC-10's progress was already fully formed when the final director heard Joe Walther's voice for the first time.

"London Director, Atlantic two six zero steering zero seven zero. Five thousand feet descending to three thousand."

"Roger two six zero. Continue as cleared."

In the passenger cabin Ben Maier relaxed a little. At least they were beneath the clouds now.

On the rooftop in Southwark, the tension among the three Arabs was almost visible. As the pilot drew the new course on the map, Mohammed snapped impatiently, "Where is the plane? How can I tell which one it is?"

"It must be coming soon," said the pilot anxiously, trying to convince himself that it was. "It is heading east over the suburbs." He waved at the dull expanse of south London. "But it is still in the clouds. Soon it must come lower."

Mohammed glared back, angry that he could not understand what was happening and fearful of mistakes. The pilot disregarded him. The time was 1617. At any second another order must be transmitted. Straining his eyes through the binoculars, he thought he could distinguish the silhouette of a DC-10 over south London, just below the clouds. But he was not sure.

"Be ready," he warned.

From the flight deck Curtis could see the tall television transmitter mast at Crystal Palace passing beneath. Ahead lay an area of small terraced houses interspersed with high-rise flats and beyond them the river and the docks. The altimeter was reading three thousand feet.

In fact, the DC-10 was four and a half miles south of the terrorists as it flew over Crystal Palace. Next came the crucial order that would bring it around toward Heathrow on the final line of its Z-shaped track. The controller, watching the converging blips on his radar screen, had decided he must take Atlantic 260 slightly north of the exact direction to the runway; then, when it was near Tower Bridge, he would alter its course left again. Otherwise he could not establish the necessary four miles' separation between it and the British Airways Trident ahead of it.

"Atlantic two six zero," he ordered. "Now steer three two zero. Maintain three thousand feet and speed one seventy knots."

Walther repeated back the instruction, and Curtis heaved the DC-10 into a left turn. His speed was down to one hundred and seventy knots. The slower one flew, the less responsive that giant aircraft became. He selected twenty degrees of flap, one of the first preliminaries to landing, and flashed the stewardesses to make the routine announcements, while he and Walther went methodically but quickly through the flight deck approach checks.

"Ladies and gentlemen," came the girl's voice over the cabin loudspeaker, clear and relaxed. "We shall shortly be landing at London Heathrow. Will you please fasten your seat belts, extinguish cigarettes and bring your seats to the upright position? Thank you."

Ben Maier fumbled with the button that made the seat recline, tightened his belt and uncrossed his legs. He had a fear that if for some reason there were a crash, he would be more easily trapped if his legs were crossed. He sat straight, gazing out at the sunlit dreariness of south London. Other passengers joked. The stewardesses scurried up and down the aisles collecting empty glasses and cups. In the first class the maître d'hôtel in his dark gray tailcoat was unctuously asking each passenger individually if he had enjoyed the flight.

As the DC-10 completed its turn over the docks and headed for Tower Bridge, the Arab pilot on the rooftop knew that everything was going to be satisfactory. At least as far as he was concerned. A few hundred yards south of them a Trident was whining past at about three thousand feet. Curving in four miles behind came a DC-10. There could be no mistaking that high fin with the enormous engine set in it. No other airliner had the same configuration. It looked as though it, too, would pass slightly south of them. But if Mohammed failed to hit it, that was his affair.

"That's the target," the pilot pointed. "Don't fire until it's past!"

"I know when to fire," replied Mohammed curtly. He positioned himself close to the parapet, one knee on the black roofing, and hoisted the launcher onto his right shoulder. It looked like a drab painted length of drainpipe with the snub-nosed missile protruding from the front end, while the rear stuck out well behind his back. His left hand kept the assembly balanced; his right hand grasped the pistol grip. He

81

adjusted the launcher's position on his shoulder so that by leaning his hand slightly to the right, he could see clearly through the simple battle sight. So long as it was aimed near enough at the plane, the missile's infrared guidance system would home on the heat from the engines.

"Remember we want to hit the engine in the tail," cautioned Kamal, who was squatting to one side to avoid the blast. "To be certain of destroying the plane, we must hit the tail."

Mohammed did not reply. The DC-10 was already coming close.

From the DC-10's flight deck Curtis saw the whole of central London spread out before him and Tower Bridge coming up on his right at about two miles. The Thames glistened in the afternoon sun.

"Giving the passengers a grandstand view," he quipped.

"Sure are," agreed Walther.

The Heathrow final director's voice interrupted them.

"Atlantic two six zero. Further left heading two six zero to intercept localizer four two eight right. Range fourteen miles."

Curtis altered course again. He was now flying parallel to the river. Ahead of him it looped to the left with the Gothic bulk of the Houses of Parliament on the far bank. A few seconds before 1621 the DC-10 passed the tower block, still at three thousand feet.

Mohammed Khadir held on until the rear engine of the DC-10 was visible from behind, then squeezed the trigger in the pistol grip. A gout of flame shot back from under the launcher tube as the SAM 7 fired. The missile shot out. Twenty feet from the launcher, its rocket ignited, sending it streaking upward at a speed that would exceed one and a half times the speed of sound. Khadir watched it follow the DC-10 in a shallow arc and explode against the rear engine. He saw the flash and pieces of metal falling off the tail. Almost at once the aircraft nosed into a dive.

The explosion momentarily wrenched the control column out of Curtis' hands. He seized it again and pulled back, at the same time slamming all three throttles forward, striving to maintain height. The master fire warning light was flickering red in front of him. A warning hooter blared. The aircraft shook again and began to shudder appallingly. One set of engine instruments was going wild.

"Christ, the rear engine's blown," Curtis muttered, and hastily throttled it back.

Behind him the systems engineer responded to the warning lights on his annunciator panel. He rose to his feet and yanked down the rear-engine fire handle in the overhead panel between the two pilots. That would shut off the fuel and hydraulics and actuate the fire extinguishers. Next he stopped the warning hooter and began racing through other emergency drills.

Curtis was struggling to counteract the dive.

"Seems we have an emergency," he remarked coolly to Walther. As yet they were not losing much height. He reckoned he could bring the ship level.

Walther began the international distress call.

"Mayday, Mayday, Mayday. Atlantic two six zero rear-engine explosion."

After twelve seconds they had lost four hundred feet. Unknown to Curtis, whirling turbine blades from the disintegrating engine had severely damaged both the rudder and the tail plane's aluminum skin. With every second the slipstream tore off more, so with every second there was less tail plane intact to keep the aircraft in balanced flight. Deprived of its tail, any aircraft goes into a steepening dive. Abruptly Curtis realized he had lost something more than just an engine. The elevators were not responding, and the vertical speed indicator was showing over four thousand feet per minute descent.

"Help me, son," he shouted. "Let's get hold of this bastard."

Both men strained together on their control columns. The vertical speed indicator went past six thousand feet per minute.

"I can't move the son of a bitch," said Walther, suddenly frightened. He pressed the radio transmit.

"Two six zero going out of control."

In the tower at Heathrow the final director heard the calls, saw the radar blip disappearing and rang the alarm bells for the Fire Service and ambulances.

Ahead and to the right Curtis could see two patches of park; one was St. James's Park and the gardens of Buckingham Palace, the other the green expanse of Hyde Park. He must try to reach one.

"Right, right rudder, Joe."

"Can't . . . jammed."

"Pull. Pull."

The dive was steepening. They passed over the Houses of Parliament at sixteen hundred feet with the rate of descent off the clock. Only eighteen seconds had elapsed since the missile's warhead detonated. In the cabin passengers began to scream. Ben Maier held to his seat and prayed. One stewardess, brave and composed, clutching a bulkhead, managed to use the intercom.

"Please keep calm. Brace yourselves. Everything will be OK."

The noise from the rear was a roar they all could hear.

People on the ground heard it, too, and saw the giant plane with smoke pouring from its tail and shreds of metal falling from it like leaves.

Curtis realized he could not make even a controlled crash. The houses and streets were coming up at him too fast. Nevertheless, he opened the undamaged turbines to full throttle, still hoping that power would raise the nose. At 4:22 P.M. local time, Atlantic Airways flight 260, the Blue Ribbon Service, slammed on to the wide, arched glass roof of Victoria Railway Station, her one-hundred-and-eighty-two-foot-long fuselage breaking up as she tore into the girders. Just before the impact Curtis made his only radio call of the flight, still cool, still fighting to save his ship.

"We're hitting now," he said.

Two seconds later he and Joe Walther were

crushed as the DC-10's nose rammed into the thick brick wall of the Grosvenor Hotel, which forms the west side of the station buildings. Neither let out a cry.

On top of the Southwark block three Arabs packed up the SAM 7 launcher in the roll of architect's drawings and surveyed the condition of the roof. Only a faint mark betrayed the firing. Nothing else. There had been no reaction to the noise. They left as they had come, nodding to the doorman on the way out.

Chapter Four

The crash occurred just as the rush hour was beginning in Victoria Station and crowds of people were milling around the concourse and the platforms—wives returning to the suburbs from shopping expeditions in town, businessmen sneaking home early, workmen finished with the day shift. The DC-10 slithered across the sixty-foot-high roof spans of the station's western side, instantly fragmenting glass and wooden framing, sliced through the thin metal latticework that held the roof in place, then plunged down on to the stronger main girders thirty feet up, which twisted and broke beneath its weight. Finally, the airliner's nose slammed into the wall of the Grosvenor Hotel like a heart-stopping thunderclap. The plane disintegrated, its fuselage telescoping, its wings shearing off. A fraction of a second later the heavy cargo containers in the airliner's aft hold slammed down onto trains, platforms and people, crushing everything beneath. The two underwing engines impacted like six-ton bombs, while the rear engine, which the Arab's rocket had damaged, broke free from the tail fin and shot forward, ripping up the length of the airliner's white-painted roof and finally burying itself in the hotel wall alongside the remains of the flight deck. The third major weight in the plane, the twenty-six tons of human bodies and hand luggage, did the same.

Both seats and seat belts tore free from their anchorages. Passengers were flung forward in a grisly heap, though a few were catapulted out through the gaping rents in the fuselage, which broke in half behind the wings.

The central London air crash that the authorities had long feared, and hoped air safety regulations made impossible, had happened.

Victoria is actually two stations that were constructed alongside each other by competing nineteenth-century railway companies and only much later amalgamated. The eastern side, designed for the old Chatham and East Kent Railway, is the smaller. Its stone façade and two wide arched roof spans protected platforms 1 to 8 of what is now the southern region of British Railways. But in size it is eclipsed by the high brick edifice built for the former Brighton and South Coast Railway, into which most of the main line trains run. Railway staff still call them the "Chatham" and "Brighton" sides, not without affection for the old days. In its fatal dive, the DC-10 plummeted squarely into the Brighton side.

Seen from above, the roof over the Brighton side of Victoria Station looks like a row of four enormously long greenhouses, their glass dulled by accumulations of the city's grime. These four spans shelter platforms 9 to 15, while a shorter roof protects 16 and 17. To the south they are cut across by the broad carriageway of Ebury Bridge Road, running above the railway tracks. At the northern end they terminate in the lee of the high Victorian station offices, which make an L shape with the flanking bulk of the Grosvenor Hotel, rising a full six stories above them. The DC-10 straddled all four of the main spans, crushing them as a falling tree would crush a shed, smashing across their ridges and into the hotel.

The commuters crowding the platforms and the concourse barely had time to look up before they were overwhelmed. As girders bent and the cast-iron columns supporting them snapped with a noise like cannon fire, the heavier parts of the aircraft hammered into the stationary trains, killing passengers immediately beneath and maiming those close by. A hailstorm of debris spattered down; broken glass and whirling fragments of wood and metal made the bustling concourse a cavern of destruction; its air filled with choking dust. The impact was deafening. For five or six seconds after it time stood still. Then streams of kerosene began pouring down from the fuel tanks in the aircraft wings that were lodged in the broken rooftop girders. Those who survived the crash suddenly began to run. Then they panicked, quickly becoming a hysterical mob as people frantically jostled one another to escape, flailing a path with briefcases and handbags, trampling underfoot anyone who fell, disregarding the screams of the trapped and injured.

Among the first men to react calmly was the senior signalman in charge of the central signal tower. He heard the whining roar of the jet's engines as it came down and rushed from his desk to the long windows overlooking the tracks in time to glimpse the stricken airliner, trailing smoke. Then other buildings hid it. A second later the walls shook and the windows rattled.

"Stop everything," he shouted to his three colleagues, each of whom controlled one range of polished brass handles. "Replace the levers." That would stop all trains on the home signals. As they did so, he pushed a green alarm switch and picked up the direct telephone to the electrical substation eight and a half miles away at Selhurst. All the lines into Victoria are electrified.

"Discharge traction current," he ordered. "Crash at station."

By now the lines should have shorted automatically anyway, but he didn't want anyone restoring six hundred volts to the circuits. Next he rang the traffic control at Croydon.

"Victoria emergency. Stop all traffic at Clapham."

Finally, he tried the telephone to the station manager's office. It was dead. On the tracks outside train after train slowed to a halt, brakes grinding.

The British Transport police offices at Victoria are on the Chatham side, along by Platform 1 where the night ferry trains leave for Paris and Brussels. When he heard the crash the duty sergeant thought a monster terrorist bomb had exploded. Bomb scares were a frequent occurrence. Indeed, the main booking office on the Brighton side had been blown up on September 8, 1973, and since then its high-ceilinged marble-columned magnificence had been replaced with two floors of offices, as though by bees building new layers of cells inside a hive. One result was that the entrance to the station at that point had been drastically narrowed. Remembering 1973, the sergeant immediately sent alarm calls to the Fire Brigade, the Ambulance Service and Metropolitan Police.

The commander of the transport police, Chief Superintendent Peter Chisholm, was in the neighboring Customs Office. He dashed out onto the narrow Chatham side concourse. But the high arches that divide the two sides, all bricked in, prevented his seeing anything except a crowd of passengers surging through the one opening that joins the two stations. Clouds of dust billowed through. His immediate conclusion was that a train's brakes had failed, causing a pileup. He ran around to the police duty room.

" 'Serious explosion' we told them, sir," said the sergeant.

"Activate the crash drills," Chisholm ordered. Either way the set procedures for dealing with a crash would be appropriate. He glanced around his staff, jabbing a finger at them in turn.

"We must get the exits clear. You two take the booking hall, you two Wilton Road. Bill"—he spoke to his chief inspector—"you'll need at least six men round the other side. Drain the station of people; then stop sightseers coming in. John, you get up an incident post here and ask Force headquarters for reinforcements." The normal shift included only eight constables and two women police. More men could be sent from Waterloo.

Seizing a loudspeaker, Chisholm ran out again to the Chatham side concourse. Frightened passengers were streaming across it. At the biggest exit, a wide arch leading to Victoria street, there was a huge fan-shaped crowd. Fear had spread fast. People were jumping out of the undamaged trains and fighting their way past the ticket barriers. Chisholm knew that at this time of day there could be three thousand travelers on the station. In the peak sixty minutes of the rush hour more than twenty-two thousand six hundred commuters would pass through.

"Keep calm. Do not panic. Walk to the exits."

His voice booming through the loudspeaker had no effect. He realized it was impossible to cross the concourse. But he had to find out what had happened. He swung his legs over the railings at the end of Platform 3, jumped down on the gravel by the buffers, then up again on the inside of the ticket barriers. Chisholm was six feet four inches tall, broad-shouldered, altogether a great chunk of a man and conspicuous in his black uniform. In his day he had been a talented rugby football captain. Nonetheless, it took him a full minute to fight through the scrum in the archway between the two stations. Once there he understood. The whole roof had collapsed. Through swirling dust he could see twisted girders and long shreds of wreckage dangling down. He gazed at the scene in bewilderment. This was no train crash. It was destruction on a scale beyond anything he had ever contemplated. As the seething crowd began to clear he saw bodies lying everywhere around the tangled platform barriers. Survivors sat leaning against walls, faces streaming blood. Others stumbled about as though blind. A few dazed railwaymen were dragging the injured away. The sounds were pitiful: moans and cries for help; a crunching thud as more debris fell followed by a piercing scream. Chisholm struggled for a sense of reality and could find none. Had a monster bomb been placed in the roof? Was it an explosion? He looked up and in disbelief slowly recognized pieces of what could only have been an airliner, swaths of grotesquely shredded aluminum caught fast overhead, a long section of fuselage with windows in it. Liquid was splashing down in several places. Suddenly he understood that the parts in the roof must be the wings, while the body had fallen across the platforms and trains, tearing down the train indicator board that had stood above the platform barriers.

Chisholm absorbed all this in a few seconds. Instantly he began to make decisions. As police chief on the station it was his responsibility to bring order out of this chaos. He turned to one of the men who had followed him.

"Get back and tell Scotland Yard it's an air crash. Major Incident Procedure. Unknown number of dead and at least several hundred casualties. Clear the Wilton Road side for ambulances."

The constable doubled off. Chisholm noticed a woman with a small boy, both bleeding profusely. The woman was kneeling on the platform, sobbing and trying to stanch her son's wound with a handkerchief. Chisholm helped her to her feet, then lifted up the boy.

"Can you walk?"

"I think so," said the woman, stumbling.

Chisholm hoisted the boy in his arms and led her off, shielding her from the crowd with his body. As they passed through the arch an ambulanceman appeared.

"Here you are, dear," said Chisholm. "He'll look after you."

He returned to the main concourse. On the far side firemen were struggling in past the new building work dragging hoses. He doubled across to them.

The call from Chisholm's sergeant came into the Information Room on the first floor of New Scotland Yard at 4:23 P.M. All emergency calls to the Metropolitan Police are routed here whether it's an old lady who has lost her purse or a man claiming to have planted a bomb in the Hilton Hotel. It's a long room with two rows of twelve telephone consoles back to back down the middle. When a call comes in a red light flashes on every console. Whoever is free picks it up. The constable who took this one answered routinely.

"Police, New Scotland Yard."

"British Transport Police, Victoria here. Major explosion."

The constable calmly began writing on a large white form. With his other hand he pushed a button that would give him a computer readout of which patrol cars were available in "A" Division.

"Any more details?" he queried on the telephone.

"Not yet, we're calling the Fire and Ambulance services."

"We'll be with you," said the constable. He quickly finished completing the form, folded it and slipped it into the miniature conveyor belt that ran between the consoles and would take it to the radio operators. Then he left his seat and hurried along the room to the duty inspector.

"Major bomb explosion, Victoria Station, sir," he explained. As he stood there more red lights flashed as more calls came in.

"Air crash Victoria," called out another constable loudly. In an office block across from the station an eyewitness had dialed 999 and reported it. For a moment the inspector was puzzled. He had been on this job for four years now and had experienced most emergencies that London had to offer. He had been on duty when the bomb exploded in the Tower of London at lunchtime on July 17, 1974, when the underground train rammed into the buffers at Moorgate in May 1975, and when the Spaghetti House siege had started in Knightsbridge that October. He was not easily frazzled.

"The two must be the same thing, Jack," he concluded. "You and one of the drivers take a control van down." He did not need to add, "And take it fast." The constable was already off. All the telephonist constables in the Information Room were trained to operate the control van at an incident.

At his own console with its direct lines to the Fire Service, the Ambulance Service and the Bomb Squad, the inspector worked fast, too, systematically mobilizing police resources from all over London. Any moment now the switchboard would go mad as more members of the public, recovering from the initial shock, started calling for help.

Meanwhile, the constable and the duty driver grabbed a trolley in the corridor. It was ready laden with two megaphones, six radios, coats labeled "Incident Officer," "Collection Point Officer," "Mortuary Officer" and bundles of armbands marked "Official," "Press" and "Doctor." The two men ran with the trolley down the passageway skidding on the shiny black and white vinyl floor as they rushed it around the corner to the elevator. To an outsider this might have seemed a clumsy way of operating. In fact, they had the trolley inside a blue control van parked in the yard within a minute and seconds later were forcing their way into the heavy Victoria Street traffic, horn wailing and blue lights flashing. Their van, with its radios and other equipment, would be the mobile control center for whoever took charge on the spot. As they careered the quarter mile to the station, driving on the wrong side of the road to overtake what had already become a solid traffic jam, they reached the Victoria Station forecourt at 4:27 P.M. Two fire engines were there ahead of them. Meanwhile, the duty officer at Scotland Yard was informing Commander Thompson at Cannon Row.

Mick Melville, at the Westminister Fire Station in Greycoat Place, had exercised all his self-control in not reacting instantly when he heard the DC-10 come down. Greycoat Place lay directly below the crashing aircraft's path, and when Captain Curtis had put on full power in a last effort to avert disaster, the noise had been tremendous. Melville had been crossing the fire station courtyard, spick-and-span in a white shirt with black shoulder boards bearing the two silver pips of his station officer's rank. He had stopped short and craned his head upward. Although the view was largely obstructed by the high roof he did see the aircraft momentarily. That one glimpse told him it was doomed. An eternity later—maybe fifteen seconds—he heard the crunch of the impact. His men heard it, too.

"Christ," exclaimed one, "it's a goner." They began to run back into the garage where the station's two glossy red fire appliances stood ready.

"Hold it," yelled Melville after them. "Nothing moves until the bells go down."

He raced after them, into the building past the watch room with its teleprinter and along the short passage to the garage. It was an absolute rule that no appliance left the station for an emergency until a call came in. It might be direct from a member of the public. More often it was a teleprinter message from control which both gave them instructions and automatically activated the alarm bells in the garage, in the recreation room and by the window in his own office. The bells rang fit to wake the dead, and their first strident note set the adrenaline pumping in every fireman's stomach. No one ever grew accustomed to that moment. But even though Melville was privately certain that the plane had crashed, that one of the fiercest fires he would ever have to fight might already be blazing, he had to steel himself and the fifteen men with him on the white watch to wait. There were three shifts, or watches, all named by colors. He always commanded the white watch.

"Don't move until we get a call," he reiterated to a newly joined trainee.

Nonetheless, as he said it, he was swinging open the passenger's door of the huge Dennis dual-purpose fire tender that was his particular pride and reaching for his kit. His heavy boots stood on the cab floor, yellow oilskin trousers draped over them. In seconds he had them on. As he was reaching for his thick black tunic, and the rest of his four-man crew were following his example, the bells did "go down." Their shattering clangor made them jump even though they were expecting it.

Melville sprinted to the watch room, boots thudding on the floor. Out at Control at Wembley a teleprinter operator, listening to the Victoria railway police through his headphones, was simultaneously tapping the keys of the Visual Display Unit, starting with Greycoat Place's code number, A 25.

As Melville reached the teleprinter machine the red emergency light beside it was flashing and paper was curling out.

"VICTORIA STATION AIRCRAFT CRASHED ROUTE CARD KC40 KC41."

Melville did not have to be told the way. All the drivers knew their own ground, though other stations would need route cards. He pounded back to the pump tender. In London the station officer always rides the pump because it goes to all incidents in the station's area. The driver had started up; the crew were aboard struggling into tunics and buckling belts; others had opened the high doors. As Melville climbed in they shot off, horns blaring, lumbering around into Artillery Row and so to Victoria Street, jumping the lights, then swerving out onto the offside and overtaking cars and buses. A 25's second appliance, the pump escape, was close behind. When they came to the confusion of traffic lights and islands at the entrance to the railway station a pair of motorcycle police were already clearing a route. The police waved them straight in through a dense crowd of people. They halted by the taxi rank in the forecourt. Melville was out of the cab two and a half minutes after the bells had rung at Greycoat Place. It was 4:31 P.M.

"Never go in empty-handed," was Melville's motto. But this was obviously a major accident. As the first fireman on the scene his immediate task was to assess the emergency. Ordering his crew to bring first aid gear and the driver to get the tender's two-hundred-and-forty-foot rubber hose into a hydrant, he made for the station entrance. Merely getting through the narrow opening against the tide of people struggling to escape was hard. A few made way. Most did not. One bald-headed portly man cannoned into him head-on.

"Let me through." Melville heaved the man aside with his shoulder. But others piled up behind, and eventually he managed only by staying close to the wall. Once there he stood to one side, sweating in his heavy uniform. He had emerged in the extreme north-west corner of the station concourse, close to the hotel entrance, by a chemist's shop, its wide glass front broken. Rapidly he took stock of the situation. He could see that the aircraft's nose was embedded in the hotel and that the disintegrated wreck lay athwart the platforms.

"It's cut the whole bloody station in half," he muttered to himself. "We'll have to tackle it from the far side, too."

Anxiously he scanned the debris for signs of fire or smoke. There were none that he could see. Suddenly he noticed the bookstall, hardly fifteen yards away. It was all but flattened. Around were strewn magazines, books, fractured planks and at least two partly dismembered bodies. Even the fleeing passengers were skirting it. One of the engines must have hit it. Victoria was familiar ground to Melville. He commuted to and from Purley every day across this concourse. He remembered that underneath the bookstall was a men's lavatory. Kerosene was flowing in rivulets all round.

"Christ," he thought, "it must be filling up like a bath, and the jet engine down there must still be as hot as hell."

Maybe the kerosene would swamp the engine. Maybe it would ignite. The whole place was a potential inferno. Melville realized he had two priorities: to rescue the injured and to blanket that bookstall area with foam. He dashed back to his fire tender, orders forming in his mind as he ran.

"Foam," he called to his crews, "all we've got," then went around to the driver's door. The driver operated the radio, but to save time he took the microphone himself.

"Alpha two five two. Initiate Major Accident Procedure."

"Go ahead," came the answer.

"From Station Officer Melville at Victoria. Aircraft crash. Make pumps twenty-five, emergency tenders eight, foam tenders two, turntable ladders four, hose layers two. Fifty ambulances required."

When Control had read this back he transmitted again. "Airliner crashed on railway station. Approximately five hundred casualties. Many persons trapped. No fire apparent." Then, because whoever took command from him would have to work on both sides of the crash, he added, "All assisting pumps to park in Buckingham Palace Road."

That road formed the western boundary of the station. There were other entrances and plenty of fire hydrants along it, he knew. As he finished speaking two more fire engines roared in. They were from Fire Station A 26 in Knightsbridge. He pointed the drivers around the corner to Buckingham Palace Road, then snapped to his own, "Tell the next lot to take hoses in by the cartoon cinema."

His own crews had already unrolled most of the thousand feet of hoses that his two appliances carried and had the foam containers out. Once the foam compound mixed with water its expansion rate was fantastic. One five-gallon container of compound would produce eight hundred gallons of foam. Melville wanted hoses positioned all around the wreck. When that was done he could be sure that if a spark did set light to the fuel they could extinguish it almost instantly, in minutes, if not in seconds. But even so, in the present situation a fire was going to kill a hell of a number of trapped people. Melville knew how fast a fuel fire can spread. Even if all the aircraft passengers had already died, and Melville didn't think many could have survived, that left all the travelers in the trains. Images of the normal rush hour flickered in his mind, the press of commuters, people standing in carriage corridors. At least five platforms were affected. There could be a thousand injured. This was a colossal rescue task with further disaster threatening him all the time.

"Bring the first aid," he called to his subofficer. "We'll start on the wreckage."

This time there was no problem entering the station. Railway staff were starting to drag injured people away from immediate danger. Melville spotted one with a gold ring on his cuff and stopped him. "This lot could go up any second."

Suddenly Melville noticed that the official's uniform coat was drenched with kerosene.

"And you with it. Form your men up out of the way, and we'll call them forward when we need 'em." To his own surprise the official did as he was told. In a crisis Melville had the kind of instantly recognizable authority that men obey.

Three more fire crews came onto the concourse, trailing hoses, axes hanging from their leather belts. Melville seized on them.

"Lay those out here."

He pointed to the ends of platforms 13 and 14 where the plane had pinned and crushed the ends of trains. "I want complete foam coverage. Then follow me."

He reckoned no one could have survived inside the front section of the aircraft. They had to be dead from the deceleration alone. But from the look of it the aircraft's back had broken both between the wings and the nose and at the tail. Passengers there might have had a chance to survive. So might the rail travelers underneath. Two ambulancemen appeared at his side, carrying a stretcher.

"This way," he yelled.

At the barrier to Platform 13 they found the ticket collector lying beside the buckled wrought-iron gate, his knees doubled up, one arm still protecting his face. Blood was trickling from a gash in his head. Melville bent down.

"He's had it," he told his crew, straightening up again.

Beyond the barrier the tarmac of the platform was littered with a cascade of luggage and mailbags; in places it was pitted where falling roof girders had struck it while the girders themselves, their ends bent to the ground, held up a tangle of aircraft wreckage, a bramble thicket of torn metal the more distant part of which was hidden in a haze of dust. Two yards away a recognizable section of the plane with a row of windows still intact had sliced into a railway carriage roof, which farther along was totally crushed. The carriage was like a giant toothpaste tube that had been squeezed in the middle. The near end was twisted up and leaned away from the platform at an angle. Somehow the impact had flung two doors open. Melville headed for the first. Inside, an elderly woman was pinned facedown across the seat by a splintered wooden partition. Melville noticed her tweed skirt and the awkward way she was half lying, half sitting. He touched her shoulder. She moved.

"Keep still, love," he said. "I'll soon have you out."

He yanked the ax from his leather belt and began prizing away the wood that imprisoned her. It creaked, cracked and loosened. She rolled over slightly, enough to speak.

"Be careful, young man," she said in a clear, frail voice. "My leg is broken."

He tugged at the wood, severed it with two sharp chops and gently maneuvered her body out from underneath. She gasped with pain. Stooping, he carried her through the door. As he passed her to the ambulancemen she managed to say, "Thank you, young man. That was very kind."

"You'll be OK now," he said, thinking, "If it was all as simple as that!" He knew it would not be. Not by a long shot. His mouth was full of gritty dust. He spat, wiped his lips and turned back to the wreckage. Mounds of luggage had fallen off a platform trolley. Beyond he could recognize several aircraft seats, their upholstery ripped, still attached to sections of the floor. He counted at least twenty corpses. One was still strapped in a seat, which had ended up propped

100

against some mailbags in an almost normal attitude. The corpse was a man in a blue suit, who lolled sideways. The bile rose in Melville's stomach as he realized that the man had no feet. His ankles were gory stumps with bone protruding from them. Suddenly one leg stirred. Melville leaped forward, shouting for help. Between them he and another fireman freed the man and bore him away.

"There may be more alive there," he shouted to the others. "Leave the aircraft bits as much as you can. Only shift what you have to."

He knew that after aircraft accidents an inspector came to examine the wreck and find the cause of the accident.

Back on the concourse parties of ambulancemen were scurrying to and fro. As they took away the blue-suited man the unmistakable figure of Chisholm loomed up. Melville had met him before.

"Glad to see you," said Chisholm as casually as though they were at a picnic.

"We must clear the station. This lot could go up any minute."

"We're doing that. Where are your fire appliances?"

"Buckingham Palace Road."

"Good. Then we'll put all the dead and injured over our side. In the Continental Booking Hall."

"The railwaymen would be more use out of the way," said Melville.

"Agreed."

Chisholm raised his loudspeaker and began shepherding the anxious railway staff away. Suddenly across the concourse he spotted a man carrying two suitcases, making for the exit. Chisholm lumbered after him, catching up with him under the arch. The man dropped the cases and tried to run. Chisholm gripped his arm, swung him around and marched him to the police offices. One thing that really got his goat were the looters at accidents. He'd heard that at the Staines air crash passersby had even been in the wreck disregarding the dead and injured before the first ambulances arrived. He wondered how much had been stolen here at Victoria in the past few minutes. As he handed the man over to a constable he glanced at his watch. 4:34 P.M. Twelve minutes since the crash. A hell of a lot could happen in twelve minutes: hundreds of people die, much of central London be brought to a halt, firemen risk their lives, insurance companies lose many millions of pounds in liability for claims. And a handful of sordid little opportunists could try to profit by quick-fingered lifting of the dead's possessions.

Chisholm's momentary thought was interrupted by an ambulanceman.

"We're overflowing Hudson's Place, Chief. We need more space."

Chisholm followed him through the Continental Booking Hall and out into Hudson's Place, the cul-de-sac on the station's eastern side. Nine white ambulances were queuing nose to tail to load casualties from the pavement. A tall officer wearing a bright red jacket over his gray-blue uniform was having a hard time of it.

"Pretty tricky for the loading officer," commented the ambulanceman.

"Who's in charge?" asked Chisholm.

The man pointed to another officer, whose red jacket was emblazoned with the words "Ambulance Incident Officer" on its back. He was speaking into a walkie-talkie set. Close to him, tucked up on the pavement, were a white car and a white Land Rover with a small trailer, its doors open revealing stacks of stretchers. Chisholm joined the incident officer. He could hear a stream of instructions coming over the radio.

"Red Base. Red Major One," the incident officer replied. "Chelsea Two now leaving scene to Westminster Hospital with two male recumbent, both serious head and back injuries."

"Red Major Red Base," came back the ambulance control at Waterloo, who used the call sign "Red Base." "Hospital are requesting estimate of casualties still at scene."

The incident officer looked at Chisholm.

"Any idea?"

"Could be five hundred. Minimum."

"Red Base Red Major One. Minimum five hundred. We're only just beginning to fetch the bad ones out."

"Red Major Roger."

"You'd better take over Wilton Road," offered Chisholm. "Keep this area for casualty handling. I'll have it cleared." Wilton Road was a long street that ran south from the station, down among the small hotels of Pimlico. Chisholm called one of his constables and gave him instructions.

"Make it one way running up toward Victoria Street," said the incident officer. "We need a traffic circuit to the Westminster Hospital."

"Any others?"

"We've designated the Westminster, St. George's and St. Thomas'. And alerted St. Stephen's, the Middlesex and Guy's as supporting hospitals. One problem is that St. George's closed their Accident and Emergency Department a few months ago. But they'll take some of these. They'll have to."

He hardly had to emphasize the necessity. A lengthening row of stretcher cases lay on the ground, waiting for ambulances because each vehicle could take only two. Already the crews had run out of blankets. Two doctors in ordinary clothes, one with a cut head himself, were helping ambulancemen splint fractures and bandage wounds. Both had been railway passengers themselves. A third was examining the less seriously hurt, sitting them up against walls, helping identify who needed hospital care and who could wait. Many had blood running down their faces from scalp or facial cuts and were in a state of shock.

"The first mobile medical team from the Westminster should be here any second," the incident officer told Chisholm. "A vehicle's been sent for them."

"As others arrive, you ought to send them round the far side. The crash has near enough cut the station in two."

"I saw it."

Chisholm grinned at the faint rebuke. He knew that

the average time it took the London Ambulance Service to attend an accident was six and a half minutes. Like the Police or the Fire Service, their first man on the spot surveyed the situation, then called for appropriate help. Just the same, the station was his ground.

"No one's faster than you boys," he replied. "I'll have space cleared for you to lead casualties from Eccleston Bridge, too. With luck the stairs up from the platforms to the road there aren't damaged."

Eccleston Bridge carried a wide road right across the tracks and platforms, as did Elizabeth Bridge and Ebury Bridge farther down. In days gone by passengers could reach trains from Eccleston Bridge, and the stairs and barriers were still there, though locked.

"Where's the police control point?" asked the incident officer.

"My office for the moment. But I'm just going to contact the Metropolitan Police's incident officer."

"Better take him with you," the incident officer jerked a finger at the ambulanceman who had fetched Chisholm. "Tell them this suits us fine for loading."

As Chisholm hurried off into Wilton Road to walk around the front of the station to the forecourt, three more ambulances slewed to a stop. The ambulanceman glanced at them.

"Fulham," he commented. "Not bad going in this traffic."

The Fulham Ambulance Station was a three-mile drive. Vehicles from all over the capital must be converging on Victoria now.

When Chisholm reached the forecourt he realized with shock that while he had been preoccupied inside the railway station, tremendous activity had developed outside. At least twenty police motorcycles were propped up on the pavements, radios crackling with a stream of orders while their riders, still with white crash helmets on, directed the last of the big red London Transport double-decker buses out of the area. The forecourt is largely taken up by a bus terminal. A line of his own men were holding back a gathering crowd of sightseers. There appeared to be a solid traffic jam in Victoria Street. Chisholm absorbed this scene in seconds, then made for the blue police control van parked on the taxi rank. An inspector was in charge, while inside, the two constables who had brought the van were busy logging events on white forms and making radio calls. Chisholm recognized the inspector, who was from the Rochester Row Police Station hardly five hundred yards away.

"We've asked for railway police reinforcements," said Chisholm. "It's a bloody dangerous situation inside.. Kerosene everywhere. Could go up any moment."

"You think we're a bit close here, sir?"

"I do," said Chisholm grimly. "You'll have to evacuate the hotel, too."

"That's being done."

"What I suggest," said Chisholm, remembering that in principle he himself took orders from the Metropolitan Police, "is that we keep all the ambulances around near my offices in Hudson's Place. I'll have space cleared for bodies and for property."

The ambulanceman listened and then chipped in.

"There are medical teams from the Westminster and St. Stephen's on the way. We'll take them to Hudson's Place. Our mobile control is there."

"It has to be alongside us." The inspector's tone was firm. Inwardly he was less sure. A situation of this magnitude was totally new to him.

"Wherever you are"—Chisholm interrupted impatiently—"you'll have to get the hell away from here."

He gestured at the squads of firemen now dragging more equipment into the station.

"You're too close in," he said. Whatever one service did in this kind of chaos, another was bound to want something different. The needs of firemen, police and ambulances were bound to conflict. Personally he was in no doubt that this time the police had to clear the field for the others and then hold the ring for them.

A minor quarrel was averted by the arrival of a black saloon car. Out of it stepped Commander Thompson, the silver oak leaves on the visor of his black peaked hat marking him out unmistakably. With him was Inspector Colin Sturgess. Thompson had been in civilian clothes in his office when the duty officer at Scotland Yard rang on his private line and told him about the air crash. That was at 4:25 P.M. It had taken him another few minutes to scramble into his uniform —it was pointless going to an incident unless you were instantly recognizable as a police officer—then to bolt through the outer office and down the stairs, shouting for the faithful Bert, his civilian driver and driver to five commanders before him. Avoiding the inevitable traffic jam in Victoria Street, they had raced through St. James's Park, where he had been riding again only this morning, and past Buckingham Palace. As they drove Sturgess made contact with Scotland Yard and was told that all the air crash transmissions were being allocated to Channel 6, which would be kept clear for this until further notice. Sturgess had switched over and then listened with one ear to what was going on while with the other he took in Thompson's preliminary requirements. Thompson did not need to consult a map to make a rough plan. He knew every street and alley of his division.

"When we get there," he had told Sturgess in the car, "work out inner and outer rings for traffic and put them into effect. As fast as you can. No vehicles at all to enter the inner ring and no pedestrians either. No one. Then I shall want everything except essential vehicles and residents on foot kept out of all Belgravia and most of Westminster. Roughly from Hyde Park corner in the north down to the river and from the Houses of Parliament in the east to Sloane Square in the west."

"We'll have problems with the embassies," Sturgess had suggested.

"They'll live. We have to get a grip on this area, a really tight grip. Quickly. Have all the special patrol group men and the solos you can lay your hands on sealing off streets and ask Scotland Yard to call on other divisions for help."

The Yard could allocate them up to two hundred

special patrol group men in cars and seventy-five "solo" motorcycle police. But Sturgess knew it would be a big job even in a city where a simple length of white tape strung across the street will keep most ordinary curious citizens out.

By the time they had reached the station forecourt at 4:38 P.M. Thompson had clarified a few other points in his mind. Now he joined the railway police chief superintendent at the control van. Chisholm saluted.

"What's the position?"

"Pretty bad."

Chisholm outlined what had happened. To his relief Thompson's orders tallied with his own thoughts.

"I'd like the control vehicles for all the services in Grosvenor Gardens. It's close enough but out of the way." To the ambulanceman he said crisply, "Send your control there, please. I presume you'll keep a deputy in Hudson's Place." The ambulanceman did not argue. As he left, Thompson turned to the inspector with the van, inside which Sturgess was already seated with a map spread out, marking street closures and relaying them over the radio.

"Inspector, you stay in charge here after we move the van. Have another one sent along and set yourself up in Hudson's Place."

"You can use my office meanwhile," said Chisholm.

Thompson nodded to them and looked around.

"Now where's the fire officer in charge?"

"All the fire appliances are lining up along the Buckingham Palace Road side of the station," said the inspector.

"OK. You go out and sort out communications from Hudson's Place. Oh, yes. Find a place we can use as a press center. Undercover. And whatever happens keep them and the bloody sightseers away from the crash."

As Chisholm and the inspector hurried off Thompson turned briefly back to his waiting car and driver.

"Take her around to Grosvenor Gardens, Bert. I'll be there in a moment."

Then he started to walk along the forecourt to the

fire engine. He had seen confusion before, but seldom like this. All along the station's entrance front injured people were being attended to until, one by one, ambulancemen escorted or carried them away. He noticed the gray uniforms of a St. John's Ambulance team of nurses. There was fire-fighting equipment everywhere. Reel after reel of hosepipe was being snaked out toward the concourse. There must have been a hundred firemen on the forecourt if there was one. And there were still crowds of ordinary travelers appearing on both sides, streaming out and being marshaled by his police with the familiar "Move along please, move along quickly please." Abruptly Thompson realized what had happened. The Victoria underground station must have been closed and now all the passengers from it, barred also from the main station, were emerging from the wide tunnel that connects the two systems. A colossal weight of both pedestrians and traffic converged on Victoria in the rush hour. Buses, taxis, cars, underground trains. The daily routine possessed a solid momentum not easily stopped.

"No matter," he said to himself, "stop it we bloody will. Stop it we have to." He returned briefly to the control van and gave more orders to the inspector, then made his way across the obstacle course of fire equipment to Buckingham Palace Road.

Despite his experience, he was amazed when he finally rounded the corner and saw a line of at least twenty fire appliances stretching down the road, which he realized must have been sealed off several hundred yards away, down near the high white bulk of the British Airways Terminal. The air was alive with the wailing of sirens from every direction and more red-painted fire tenders were roaring up all the time. Thompson strode over to the fire officer marshaling them.

"Who's in charge?" he demanded.

"The boss. Mr. Plowden," the fireman shouted above the din. "He's inside."

"Police control is back in Grosvenor Gardens. Ask him to send your mobile control there if you see him."

"Will do," said the fire officer and returned to waving in another appliance, thinking to himself, "Too many bloody chiefs in this game." OK, so the police had a job to do, but so did the Fire Brigade, and right now theirs was more urgent. At least, that was how he felt.

Thompson made his way to the station's side entrance by the news cinema, where the fire officer had pointed. The man's inward reaction would not have worried him much even if he had been aware of it. Some friction between the emergency services was inescapable, no matter how often collaboration was rehearsed in exercises. Thompson's time in the commandos had taught that you cannot train men to take the initiative and respond fast without also making them confident of their own superiority. But whereas you could smooth over disagreements with tact, you could not create supermen overnight. He reckoned firemen had to be supermen most of the time they were in action, and he understood their feelings, even though he had no illusions about who was in overall command here. He was.

The scene inside the station momentarily killed every other thought in his mind. He threaded his way through a gateway by the news cinema. A narrow road runs from the parking space between platforms 15 and 16, along to a ramp rising up to Eccleston Bridge used as an exit for taxis. Built over the road is the British Caledonian Air Terminal, a rectangular box of offices and ticket counters squeezed in below the main girders of the station roof. Now the roof had caved in on top of it, crushed by the DC-10's port wing. Over to the left, toward the main concourse, both the passenger walkway and the platforms were blocked by a jungle of metal: the remains of the plane's fuselage, broken spars, glass, luggage, twisted railings, derailed carriages. This was the other side to the chaos that Chisholm had seen and where Mick Melville was urgently hacking at the wreckage. The only difference was that, although he scarcely realized it, Thompson had arrived after the nearest bodies and the accessible injured had already been removed. Now the roadway was a jumble of fire-fighting equipment. The noise in here was deafening. Recognizing the chief fire officer, Thompson jumped over some hoses and accosted him.

"Mr. Plowden," he shouted.

The firemen swung around, saw Thompson and shouted back, "We'll have this under control soon. It's a bastard. Can't get at this side of the wreck properly because of the trains."

"What's the chance of a fire?"

"Odds on. It's a miracle it hasn't gone up already. Lucky we're spoilt for water. Plenty of hydrants, and I should have fifty appliances soon. And high-expansion foam. Give us a few minutes, and we'll have the gear to smother any fire." Plowden wiped his forehead with his hand. "But that wouldn't save the people trapped in there. Could be hundreds. Can't put down foam until we've got them out either."

"Would Eccleston Bridge be affected?"

"Shouldn't be. No, we could keep fire away from there."

"I'll have an ambulance loading point at the top of the ramp then," decided Thompson. "Who's in charge on the other side?"

"There's a senior divisional officer and Melville from Westminster. Useful lad, Melville. I'll be around there myself soon."

"I'll leave you to get on with it then," said Thompson. "I'm locating all the mobile controls in Grosvenor Gardens."

Plowden considered this briefly.

"All right. That'll do for us."

Then he indicated the Grosvenor Hotel, normally hidden, but now partially visible through the broken roof.

"It could collapse, the station side could. My men are checking it. None of the offices around this half of the station are safe from fire."

"The whole lot will have to be evacuated," Thompson agreed. "We'll handle that."

As Thompson retraced his steps among the teams of firemen, Plowden reviewed his hastily made plan. As chief of the six thousand strong London Fire Brigade, he took control only of the worst accidents. Command of this one had escalated from Melville through one of his senior divisional officers to himself with unusual rapidity. The process had worked fast because the brigade headquarters was a bare mile and a quarter away, just across the Thames on the Albert Embankment, much closer than the Paddington Division's headquarters, whose fireground this area was. In fact, Plowden had been on the spot before the divisional officers from Paddington, and he had very rapidly used his authority to increase the "attendance" of fire appliances. Melville's demand for twenty-five had been superseded by the senior divisional officer's for thirty, then by Plowden's own for fifty. Now his problem was organization: organizing protection for the buildings around the station, all of them old, all constructed with wooden joists and floors and roof timbers; covering the trains—some had steel-bodied coaches, others were older commuter carriages with wood-lined doors and partitions; covering the floods of kerosene that must now be running into the drains and sewers beneath the station. Plowden knew that kerosene in an aircraft fire burns at around eight hundred degrees Fahrenheit. This was a potential inferno, with the high buildings forming it into a monstrous brazier. His one chance lay in the newer formulas of aviation kerosene being slower to catch fire, having a higher flash point than gasoline, which vaporizes very quickly and so is more flammable. The snag was that because kerosene does not vaporize, and so disperse, it does the other thing. It hangs around, a lasting peril until it can be washed away. But that would take thousands of gallons of water, and Plowden could not turn on the hoses until he had rescued the survivors, at least not without condemning many who might have lived to a choking, gasping death by immersion. So his plan was to make covering the fireground against a conflagration an equal priority to rescuing the survivors.

By 4:45 P.M. Plowden reckoned he had enough hoses set into Victoria's trunk hydrants, enough foam canisters connected up, enough high turntable ladders out as water towers from which firemen could train their jets onto a fire from above. He could afford to divert more resources to rescue work. He had also decided where to concentrate the effort. On his walkie-talkie he called the divisional officers in the various parts of the station.

"All available men to rescue now. Use cold cutting equipment only. Don't use mobile lighting or any electrical gear unless you have to. Stand by the breathing apparatus tender."

When his orders had been acknowledged, he left a divisional officer in charge and began to make his way around the outside to the main station concourse. As he stepped onto the pavement, a flashbulb exploded in his face. Even in the full daylight it dazzled him. He blinked startled. Voices assailed him.

"What's going on in there, Chief?"

"How many dead? Can you make a statement?"

Two reporters and a photographer barred his way.

"How the hell did you. . . ." Plowden controlled himself. "Its a bad situation in there. Yes, the aircraft came down smack on the platforms. No, gentlemen, I'm sorry, you cannot. There are problems enough as it is. Yes, later I will talk to you. Now would you please clear off out of the way."

He thrust them aside and continued. Frightened guests clutching personal belongings were streaming out of the Grosvenor Hotel's street entrance, guided by policemen, while firemen ran up the steps carrying equipment. Across the road in Grosvenor Gardens stood a group of vehicles, the blue police van, a white ambulance Land Rover, his own staff car. Beyond, a chain of police, arms linked, were holding back a crowd of sightseers. Plowden dismissed all this from his mind and hurried around the corner to the forecourt.

While Thompson and Plowden were giving their respective orders, the ambulance bringing the mobile medical team from the Westminster Hospital had drawn up in Hudson's Place. Out had tumbled four nurses in white track suits. Red cloth crosses were sewn on their backs, and their armbands read "Site Medical Team." With them was a young male registrar, tousle-haired, identified by a white coat marked "Site Medical Officer." He and the nurses, helped by an ambulanceman, had swiftly offloaded a series of boxes and chests—dressings, resuscitation equipment, a basic surgical kit for on-the-spot amputations, saline drips, blood transfusion packs. The doctor himself was a registrar in anesthetics—the hospital would need all its surgeons in its own operating theaters. Aided by the other doctors already there, he started establishing a casualty clearing post in the Eastern Booking Hall on the Chatham side.

The registrar and the nurses had all been on duty in the Westminster Hospital's Accident and Emergency Department when the first warning from the ambulance control at Waterloo had reached the hospital switchboard down on the lower ground floor. It had come at 4:25 P.M. with a buzzer and a red light flashing on the special two lines kept free for major emergencies.

"London Ambulance Service Headquarters," the call had run. "Major accident—Aircraft crash Victoria Station. Request mobile medical team. You are the designated hospital."

The supervisor, sitting at his desk watching the four operators who tend the switchboard's fifty-eight lines and the bleep system for alerting staff, had leaned back and pulled a white form off a shelf. Then, using two telephones and somehow contriving to chain-smoke at the same time, he had started methodically calling different departments.

"Major accident request medical team." He had ticked off one space on his form.

"Major accident. Report to the main hall please." Another space ticked. While he did this, the bleep operator had been punching out numbers on a gray control box that would activate little plastic alarms

113

which each doctor and nursing officer carried in his or her pocket. There were one hundred fifty-five of them in use at the hospital, and the encoder could call six simultaneously. When the recipients answered, which meant going to a telephone, the standing orders were simple. Housemen report to their wards, anesthetists to the control center, senior doctors to the control center. The "surgical firm on take"—that is, the team on duty—had been stood by. Meanwhile, the other telephonists had interrupted ordinary conversations.

"Please clear the line. There is a major accident."

On the floors above the activity had heightened, nurses and doctors unashamedly running. By the time the young registrar had assembled his team, opened the major accident cupboards in the A and E Department, and the nurses had wriggled awkwardly into their track suits, too stiffly laundered to fit easily, the ambulance was waiting outside for them. A demented rush to Victoria had deposited them there fourteen minutes after the crash.

This was the registrar's first experience of a major incident, and he would never forget the first half hour. Barely had he begun to attend to his first casualty, telling a nurse how to bind a terrible gash in a railway porter's leg and scribbling details on the card that would accompany the man to the hospital, when a fireman, sweating in his heavy tunic, yellow oilskin trousers bloodied, tapped him on the shoulder.

"Can you come, sir? We've a man near cut in half. He's alive and conscious. He needs a shot while we cut him free."

"Would you come with me?" the registrar asked one of the nurses. "Bring morphine and a drip." Hastily gathering up morphine and dressings, they followed the fireman into the station. Thick canvas fire hoses lay limp and flat across the concourse. A procession of ambulancemen, firemen and police were carrying away the injured. The registrar reached Platform 13. The barrier had now been cut away. Station Officer Melville was leading a team here, slowly penetrating deeper into the one part of the aircraft where it

114

seemed certain there must still be survivors. Heavy jacks and lifting gear were gradually raising up spars and wreckage so that Melville's men could reach the passengers in the crushed railway carriages. Melville did not bother with introductions.

"Here, Doc," he said.

The registrar noticed Melville's taut, handsome face, grimy, streaked with sweat, then followed his gaze. The nurse gave a little gasp. Ahead of them, embedded in the roof of a carriage, was a piece of steel girder. It rose at an angle out of the carriage and then disappeared in a buckled section of aluminum, obviously part of the aircraft's body. Caught between the two was a man. Or rather the remains of a man, bent double across the edge of the sharp metal, which cut deep into his abdomen. The man's face, white and contorted, was almost level with the registrar's, though several feet away. He looked about forty years old and had dark hair.

"It's going to take ten minutes to cut that aluminum away and God knows what *it* isn't holding up," said Melville. "If we lift you forward you could reach him."

The registrar felt sick. He could see the man's stomach was fearfully wounded, gouged out by the jagged aluminum. Trying to steady his voice, he turned to the nurse.

"Morphine please."

She handed him the hypodermic capsule. Two firemen hoisted him forward, his shoes slipping on the debris below, until he could reach the man.

"They'll get you out in a tick," he said, trying to sound confident, searching for an arm. "They'll have you out of this in no time. You'll be OK."

He found one of the man's hands, managed to grasp the wrist and slid the needle into a vein. It was impossible to fix the drip.

The man murmured. "Helluva bang . . . everything shaking . . . she came down."

His whisper died as the morphine took him away. They helped the registrar back. Once on his feet he looked straight at Melville and shook his head. Melville's answer was curt.

"While he's alive, we go on. Did he say something?"

The registrar repeated it.

"Better remember that. Could be evidence. Write it down, Doc, before you forget."

"I must get on to someone else. I'll send an ambulanceman."

As the registrar and the nurse returned across the concourse they were stopped by a man in a suit, holding a notebook and a bulky camera.

"Excuse me, Doctor," said the man. "Are there any airline survivors in there?"

Sudden indignation overcame the registrar, the shock of what he had just seen finding a release in anger. "You flaming reporters," he shouted. "Why don't you get out of the way!"

The man stared at him coldly, then pointed to a red armband on his right sleeve.

"Donaldson is the name. AIB. Accidents Investigation Branch, Department of Trade, and I'll thank you to keep a civil tongue in your head. There's enough trouble here as it is without lost tempers."

"Sorry, sir. I thought—" The registrar caught Donaldson's eye, mumbled further apologies and recounted the few words of the dying passenger.

"If there are going to be survivors, they would be back there," remarked Donaldson, almost to himself, repeating, "'A helluva bang,'" with puzzlement. Leaving the registrar and the nurse without a word, he walked determinedly across to the senior divisional fire officer, whose insignia he had just spotted, explained himself and then asked, "If it's humanly possible, I need to see what's left of the flight deck."

"That's right up front in the aircraft?"

Donaldson nodded.

"There's not much left I should think," said the fire officer. "And there'll be less still if it burns."

"Can you spare someone to help me? The reason for this crash must be up there."

116

"I reckon we've three hundred firemen or more here. Even so we've none to spare."

The fire officer saw the determination in Donaldson's expression and relented.

"It's unusual. Rescue comes first."

"It's an unusual crash. It's the one we all pretended couldn't happen. Every busybody from the prime minister downwards is going to want to know why it did. If it's humanly possible we have to fish the pilot out for a postmortem. He could have had heart failure. The instrument panel should tell me a lot, too. Not that there'll be much left of that. But I have to see it."

"I'll give you Melville. He was first on the scene, too."

He called to another fireman.

"Fetch Mick Melville, will you? Quick."

Melville was not pleased. Under his leadership twelve people had been cut free, eleven of them miraculously alive. The American from the aircraft had died before they could release him, as the registrar predicted. But Melville's blood was up, he was emotionally committed to the rescue, tense, toiling with the strength of two men. He cursed at being stopped.

"Snap out of it, Mick," said the divisional officer. "This is important." Melville's discipline reasserted itself. A few seconds later he was considering how to reach the flight deck, while Donaldson calmly photographed more wreckage and made sketches in his notebook. By the time the firemen had completed searching for survivors much would inevitably have been moved, while a fire would be catastrophic. What was observed now would be irreplaceable evidence.

When the DC-10 crashed Donaldson had been in his office in Shellmex House, up on the fourth floor with a magnificent view across the Thames to the Festival Hall. He had been scribbling amendments to his report on the Round Hill accident near Washington. Had he been standing at the window he might actually have seen the Atlantic Airlines DC-10 shot down. As it was, a notification of the accident came to the branch's information officer: initially from the police and immediately afterward from the London Air Traffic Control Center. The news was relayed automatically to the principal inspector on duty—Jim Donaldson. Ironically he had asked to be on today, despite only just being back from America, in order to clear his desk and be certain of having a free weekend. Now, while members of the staff arranged the back up resources for him, he had simply gone to his cupboard, taken the briefcase that held his basic necessities— yellow overalls for outdoor work, red armband, notebooks, Polaroid camera—told his secretary to inform the Principal Inspector Engineering, bolted to the elevator and hailed a taxi on the Embankment. Later he kicked himself for not requesting a police car. Inevitably the taxi was caught in the traffic, and he had to run the last hundred yards, wasting more time identifying himself to the constables outside Victoria.

The mixup of wreckage, of roof girders and train carriages, coupled with the dust, made it difficult to identify the aircraft. It could be a Tristar or it could be a DC-10. That the plane was American registered he could tell from lettering on part of the underside of the wing. He noticed parts of a green-gold livery scheme, mere touches of paint on fragments of metal. A first shiver of apprehension assailed him. Wasn't the Blue Ribbon due back through London today? Was it only yesterday that he stepped off it at Heathrow? The row last night with Jane made it seem longer. Melville interrupted his speculations.

"I reckon the only way to it is through the hotel," said Melville, pointing up. Amid the confusion of wreckage it seemed the nose had impacted on the first floor, where a part of the hotel had been built out underneath the station roof, close to the women's lavatories. Donaldson agreed. Together they forced a way through fallen plaster and bricks, up the steps of the hotel access from the concourse and into the reception area of the hotel itself. It was in shattering disorder. Parts of the ceiling had fallen; the air was a fog of dust. Policemen were guiding out the last of the residents. An old lady, swathed in blankets, was being carried in a fireman's arms, like an outsized baby. The manager, disheveled, his black jacket white with particles of plaster, stood to one side watching.

"Where did it hit?" Donaldson demanded.

"The end of the gallery lounge," he replied in a dazed, unreal tone. "Thank God no one was there."

"Show us."

Melville had to take the manager's arm to steady him as they climbed the wide staircase. Ahead of them the room's double doors had swung open, half off their hinges. They found themselves in a seventy-foot-long room, whose windows overlooked the concourse. Or rather, had done so. They were now barricaded with a jumble of metal, and the wall they were set in was collapsing. To the right the room scarcely existed. The crumbled front section of the DC-10 completely filled it, like a monster in a dream. The tip of the nose, squashed by the impact, was buried in the inner wall of the room, clearly originally the solid outside wall of the hotel before this extension was constructed. The floor had collapsed so that the huge bulk of the plane, far higher than the room itself, was sunk among the joists. Although what remained of the body was buckled where it had not fractured and burst open, yet some windows and its general shape were distinguishable.

"Jesus," said Melville. "It's unbelievable."

Donaldson stood silent. He had a fair idea of what it was that had supported the inside of the fuselage so that it had retained a semblance of its shape. His attention was not focused on that. His eyes were on the thick horizontal green and gold line that ran, irregularly now, along what had been the cabin's side. Though deformed, the nose retained unmistakably the stubby shape that Douglas has given its designs since Donald Douglas built the prototype DC-1 in 1933 and the modern airliner was born. Donaldson knew exactly what, and who, they would find inside. He also knew, in the same shocked instant, that this was the worst accident he would ever have to investigate, both publicly and personally. The pressure on him to find a reason for it was going to be many-sided and intense.

"This was the front cabin," he said calmly. "When the wings caught the roof girders, everything inside must have been thrown forward."

He remembered the first-class cabin and its tiny bar where the pretty stewardess served drinks. Somewhere in front of him was the very seat he had sat in, somewhere among the compressed pile of men and women and hand luggage were the stewardess and her bar counter and the pretentious maître d'hôtel in his tailcoat. Somewhere there, but for the grace of God, could have been his own corpse. Donaldson shuddered and turned his attention to the practical question of reaching the wreck. Immediately in front of him the floor had vanished, leaving a gaping hole through which parts of the rooms below were visible.

"Can you put ladders across to it?" he asked Melville.

"We can try, sir. I'll fetch some more of the boys to help."

The skin of an aircraft is thin; the structural strength lies in the spars and formers to which it is riveted. Melville was able to cut through the aluminum easily with his ax, relatively unworried by the possibility of a spark, since there are no fuel pipes in the nose, and there was no trace of kerosene around. Nerving himself to the horror, feeling that somehow he owed it to Curtis and to Atlantic's owner to be the first to see how the crew had died, Donaldson motioned Melville aside and squeezed his head and shoulders in through the gap that the fireman had hewn. Although he knew what he would find, it still caught him like a punch in the belly. The copilot and Curtis were crushed in their seats, sandwiched between a dislodged bulkhead and the instrument panel. He could recognize neither. Their white shirts and dark gray trousers were soaked in bloody pulp. Donaldson had to presume that Curtis was flying in the left-hand seat, while any possible doubt about their identity was eliminated by the dark gray clothing. Only one airline dressed its crews in that gray.

"Poor bastards," Donaldson thought.

Resolutely he turned his attention to the controls. The simplest to find were the throttle levers, protected slightly by their position between the pilots' seats. He saw that one throttle was closed while the other two were fully open. In the flattened instrument panel, such as was visible beyond Walther's corpse, the instrument needles had been pressed into the dials indicating temperatures, pressures, speed, everything as it was at impact. Because the engine instruments were also centered between the two pilots, Donaldson could see that the rear engine had been far above normal heat limits, yet was showing very low turbine revs. In his mind he again heard those words, "a helluva bang . . . everything shaking." It could all be consistent with a turbine blade fracture, followed rapidly by the disintegration of the engine: the number two engine, in the rear. He backed out of the rough hole, clutching at a ladder.

"Melville," he said, "I have to locate the rear engine. Can you remember seeing it?"

Melville's face was taut and grim.

"It's solid corpses in there," he muttered, "solidly bloody human flesh."

"I know," said Donaldson brutally. "It always is. They're thrown forward by the impact, but they're dead in the same instant. Now, did you see the rear engine anywhere, the one in the tail?"

"No, sir."

"I'm going to look for it. Listen, Melville, at all costs salvage that instrument panel and the pilots' bodies. OK? It's very important."

Suddenly Melville's mind jumped eighteen years, back to soldiering in the Oman and a chopper pilot whom they had all thought a bit soft, a nonentity, a man with no swank to him. Then one day his helicopter had been forced down and they had to fight it out with a band of rebels. The pilot had been ice-cold efficient from the moment the first rifle fire hit them. He recognized the same quality in Donaldson.

"We'll get them out, sir," he said.

"Thank you," said Donaldson, "the captain was a friend of mine."

Calmly he retreated backward on all fours along the ladders that bridged the collapsed floor of the gallery lounge.

Outside, in Grosvenor Gardens, Commander Thompson reckoned a semblance of order was being established. The orders given by Colin Sturgess on his behalf had closed off the ends of seventy-six streets. His outer ring was firm. Steadily traffic within it was being drained out, while as far away as the City of London in the east and Fulham in the west policemen of other divisions were placing signs warning motorists to keep clear of the SW1 area. The inner ring had its problems, however. Residents of fashionable Chester Square on one side and visitors staying in cheap Pimlico hotels on the other were objecting with equal vehemence to being denied access. As a result of allowing some through, a hard core of sightseers had also penetrated the police cordon and was having to be restrained, in some cases forcibly, from approaching Victoria Station. The first TV and radio reports, clamorously piling on the drama, had brought the curious out in thousands. The legitimate press representatives and cameramen already numbered over a hundred. Thompson had ordained that a small street called Neathouse Place, running into Wilton Road, should be the press center. But the unhappy chief superintendent sent by Scotland Yard as press officer was under heavy pressure.

"He's on again," Colin announced after yet another radio message. "The TV news are demanding to film the wreckage."

"Tell him they emphatically, definitively cannot," said Thompson. "We'll be making a statement in a few minutes."

Colin passed the message.

"Has anyone found the city engineer?" Thompson demanded next.

"The Fire Brigade have, sir. He's having more street barriers brought, and he's sent me down to check on the kerosene in the sewers."

"What about London Transport?"

"Victoria underground's been closed. Neither District nor Victoria line trains are stopping here until we give the word."

"And the gas?"

"Both the Gas and Electricity Board have engineers standing by."

"That's something," said Thompson, relieved. "Before we see the press we'd better do some adding up. Has the stationmaster been traced yet?"

"Actually he's called the area manager. They don't have stationmasters anymore apparently. He's waiting over there."

Thompson noticed a railway official talking to the ambulance incident officer a few yards away and walked across.

"Thompson," he said, holding out his hand. "Sorry I didn't realize you were here."

The manager's face was scratched. The back of his coat was torn. He looked ill and haggard.

"You all right?"

The ambulance officer cut in.

"I should say he's suffering from shock and ought to rest for a bit."

"I think the wing tip must have hit my office," the manager explained unsteadily. "Something did. I had my back to it sitting at the desk. I was thrown forward and knocked unconscious for a moment."

"Tell me one thing, then, before we pack you off to bed," said Thompson kindly. "How many people would there have been on the station?"

"That's what's been worrying me. We have statistics. But they're only approximate. It could be weeks before everyone who might have been traveling is accounted for."

"Let's have what you've got."

"Two hundred thousand a day pass through on a weekday. About twenty-two thousand an hour in peak periods. This was before the peak. Could be anything between fifteen hundred and two thousand on the platforms and trains, perhaps six hundred on the concourse. You see," he went on, swaying so much on his feet that the ambulance officer had to support him, "a normal rush-hour train has about seven hundred seats, but with standing passengers there can be a thousand on just one train."

Thompson caught the ambulance officer's eye and said quietly, "He's done in."

From nowhere, seemingly, a blue uniformed Salvation Army captain appeared.

"If you'll allow me, gents," he said firmly, "our hostel is just up the road. We'll give him a cup of tea and a lie down." He turned to the ambulance officer. "Won't use up your precious beds, then, will he?"

The Salvation Army captain led the manager gently away.

"So that's the size of the problem," declared Thompson. "With several hundred in the aircraft as well."

"Almost all dead," said the ambulance officer.

"Find out how many casualties you've taken to hospital so far, would you?"

Thompson crossed to the Fire Brigade's control unit, a coach with a red and white checkered dome.

"How's it going? How long before you're reasonably certain all the living have been rescued?"

"Dawn tomorrow, they're estimating," said the control officer. "It's a slow job. They can only use cold cutting equipment because of the fire risk. Won't be able to use arc lamps tonight. It's like"—he fumbled for a comparison—"like trying to take a house down without damaging the bricks."

The ambulance officer came up.

"One hundred and fourteen casualties so far taken to hospital, Commander. Walking wounded mostly, but the less badly hurt always come out first. Another forty-one in the casualty clearing post. Nearly all serious injuries. We're just designating another six hospitals, making twelve all told. They doubt if a third of the survivors are out yet. Fifty-two ambulances in action."

Thompson consulted his watch.

"Thirteen minutes past five," he noted. "Fifty-one minutes since the crash."

"That won't impress the reporters," remarked Sturgess acidly. His brother-in-law was a reporter on a local London paper, whose cynicism about police work had made them blood enemies.

"There's no escape from the media. Let's get it over with."

Neathouse Place is barely sixty yards long, marginally protected from the weather by a new office block that spans it. Not that the glorious evening into which the day was now declining made protection from the elements necessary. Furthermore, the reporters loathed being cooped up there. Thompson met a rough reception. While cameras and arc lights were trained on him, he was floored by the second question.

"What aircraft was it?" someone shouted.

Abruptly Thompson realized that he had no idea. This was one fact that had been irrelevant to the immediate problems. A drawling Australian voice interrupted.

"Maybe the police would like to know it was Atlantic Airlines' flight two sixty from Paris to New York."

There was a titter of laughing among the journalists. Flashbulbs popped.

"Say, is there anything you *can* tell us?" It was an American accent this time. Thompson hesitated. He was no kind of expert at dealing with the press. Despite all the emergency services' efforts in the past fifty minutes, this bunch was obviously going to give him a roasting. To hell with it. He seized the microphone.

"Gentlemen," he roared, "one thing I can tell you. Approximately one-third of the injured have been saved and taken to hospital. The situation is coming under control."

Donaldson had reasoned that there must be a window in the hotel which overlooked the station. From there he would be able to obtain a panoramic view of the wreck. Once clear of the gallery lounge he ran upstairs as high as he could go. On the sixth floor, after trying several door handles in a passage, he hit lucky. He found a bedroom overlooking the platforms. He flung up the old-fashioned sash window and leaned out. As if by magic all was explained. There beneath him lay the outline of the DC-10, sunk deep into the roof. He saw how the wings had come off, how the fuselage had telescoped and then snapped open like a Christmas cracker. He could also see the tail plane, perched high up on the shattered roof and how the rear engine must have broken loose and shot forward from its mounting in the fin. It appeared to be buried in the hotel, somewhere beneath him. He began to photograph the scene. Looking insignificant and distant through the camera's viewfinder, he saw a sudden spiral of smoke float up from the debris, followed instantly by a spurt of flame. In a fraction of a second fire burst out in a dozen places, sweeping up into a huge inferno. Donaldson ducked back from the window, his face saved from the searing heat only by the bulky camera. Clutching it, he ran downstairs, while above Victoria a thick black column of smoke told the world of the blaze.

Chapter Five

Mick Melville was cutting his way further into the carnage where the DC-10 first-class compartment had telescoped into the flight deck and was close to freeing the crushed bodies of the crew when he heard the shout "We have fire."

In the same instant there was a great roaring whoosh of sound as the kerosene vapor hanging over the wreckage ignited and exploded, followed by the blaring of the Fire Brigade's warning horns.

Heedless of slipping, Melville ran back across the ladders that bridged the break in the lounge floor and raced toward the hotel stairs. A moment later he was out on the station concourse. Less than fifty yards away an incandescent caldron of flame was enveloping platforms, trains, debris, roof, and shielding his face with an arm, Melville bolted to rejoin his own men. From both sides jets of foam sprayed over the blaze, hissing and spluttering on the flames. The hoses trailing across the concourse had come alive as the mix of water and foam chemical pulsed through them. Others were supported on lightweight tripods which directed the jets on fixed arcs. Melville panted up to the divisional officer who had ordered him to help Donaldson. The officer gestured to the station buildings at their backs.

"We must push the fire out of the buildings."

For a few seconds they surveyed the rapidly spreading inferno. Through swirling black smoke they saw that the shattered timbers of the roof were catching fire. The heat was intensifying at a frightening rate. Melville guessed there could be thousands of gallons of kerosene lying on the tracks between the platforms, flowing in drains and gullies, dripping through damaged train carriages. The roof had prevented them from putting up any high turntable ladders so there were no hoses aiming down on the wreck, the tail end of which was not yet burning.

"Get foam on there, Mick," yelled the divisional officer above the din. "There may be survivors still."

That was the place where he had been toiling with the other rescuers before Donaldson had called him away. The thought of trapped people being choked and drowned in a blanket of foam was appalling.

"We must smother it," shouted the divisional officer again. Nearer them the cascade of tiny bubbles that make up the foam, spurting from hose jets at the rate of twenty-five hundred gallons a minute, was already suppressing the spread of the fire across the concourse. Foam that would smother the fire was the only answer, suffocating it by depriving the flames of air. Water would just carry the burning fuel along with it. This was the worst decision a fireman ever had to make—when to risk life in order to stop a conflagration spreading. But he barely hesitated.

"No choice, Mick," he shouted. "Get going."

Melville doubled across to the teams at the other end of the concourse, dodging other firemen and leaping over hoses. Already the tarmac was becoming slithery with the wet foam. Back with his own men he did not need to give spoken orders. The hoses kicked as they turned them on, and the jets of white froth arched over the broken barriers on to platforms 11 and 12, spewing over the crushed trains and twisted pieces of aircraft, still expanding as it poured down, enveloping everything like some monstrosity of science fiction. Even as it did so, flame was running along the remains of the wing overhead and igniting fuel from pipes that had once led beneath the cabin floor to the rear engine.

Then, as he scanned the wreckage, Melville saw what he had most feared to see. Movement. Over to the left, in a part not yet heavily coated with foam he was sure he saw something shift. Shouting to the men to keep their jets off that part, he ran forward, scrambling over debris, slipping and sliding, struggling to reach what he knew must be a living person.

"Never bloody gives up, does he?" said one of the others to no one in particular, and charged after him.

Somehow a man had crawled free from the carriage where he was trapped and had been painfully hauling himself across shards of metal and splintered wood when the fire broke out. That searing heat and the prospect of dying in it gave him the last spurt of energy to pull himself farther. He could actually see the firemen when the foam came down. The movement Melville spotted was his last despairing effort to raise his head above the soaking, choking spume. The two men pulled him clear and Melville swung him over his shoulder in the classic fireman's lift. Suddenly flame reared behind them. Kerosene that had seeped through had been lit by fire snaking along where the foam had not yet sealed it off from oxygen. To those watching it seemed as though the firemen and their limp burden were caught.

"Cover them," shouted the leading fireman.

Struggling to aim the heavy nozzles as accurately as possible, the rest of the crew shot jets of foam as close to Melville as they dared, almost knocking him over. It sizzled in the new blaze behind as he stumbled out.

Panting for breath, Melville eased the man he had saved off his shoulder and laid him on his back on the tarmac. The burst of flame had burned the man's legs, just as it had scorched Melville's yellow oilskin trousers and heavy boots. Melville's black ridged helmet and dark blue tunic were spattered with dirty white froth. He wiped the muck out of his eyes with the back of his hand.

"Fetch a doc, quick."

There were now five medical teams operating an improvised casualty clearing station on the concourse of the other half of Victoria. Ambulancemen were hurrying the victims out of the vehicles, while the ambulance control was alerting hospitals in outer London and Surrey to be ready to take patients. But the fire had forced both doctors and stretcher-bearers off the main concourse. Only one team and a couple of ambulancemen remained in the shelter of the wide arch between the two stations agonizedly watching and waiting in case by a miracle there were more survivors.

The doctor was the same young registrar from the Westminster Hospital who had helped Melville less than forty minutes earlier and then had sworn at Donaldson. In that brief interval of time he had consigned nineteen obvious corpses to the temporary mortuary which Chisholm had set up and with his team of nurses had given immediate first aid to fifteen seriously injured, swiftly stanching the worst wounds so that they would at least reach the hospital alive. An older doctor who had run in to help from Victoria Street, where he had been shopping, had told him, as they toiled together, that it was as bad as the advanced dressing station he had commanded during the bitter Battle of Cassino in 1944. Inside half an hour the registrar's white coat had become as bloody as a butcher's apron, while his manner and voice had acquired a terseness born of necessity. When he saw one of the firemen stumbling out of the burning wreck with a body on his back, he did not hesitate. Calling for a nurse to follow him, he ran across, clutching his bag of instruments.

The casualty was laid out flat on his back, apparently unconscious. The registrar felt his pulse. It was weak, but discernible. He quickly thrust a finger down the man's throat to clear his airway, flicking out a spattering of foam. That was all right. Then he swiftly checked the body. The right leg stuck out awkwardly. A moment's examination showed it was fractured and that both legs were burned. The trousers were charred and tattered. The man was shivering. He must be in deep shock. The registrar remembered the senior consultant's last words to him before he left for the crash. "No heroic doctoring on the spot unless it's life or death. Far better to get the casualities into hospitals."

This was a case in point.

"Come on," he said to the nurse. "Let's get him to an ambulance."

As they and the two ambulancemen lifted the body onto a stretcher the man came to, gazed at the faces looking down at him and then with a great effort, raised his head and spoke. The words came broken, almost incoherent.

"The wife and children are still"—he stopped, then gathered all his strength and hissed—"in the train."

Then his head fell back, and he lay gasping in pain.

Swiftly the doctor went through the routine of injecting morphine straight into a vein. As he and the nurse bent over the man, a young reporter in a black anorak, holding a tiny radio transmitter half concealed in his hand, joined the group unnoticed.

"Children still there," the man cried out suddenly, and as quickly collapsed again in a dead faint.

"You can take him off now," ordered the doctor. He rose to his feet and rejoined Melville, who was again directing his crews. The heat was so intense that firemen manning hoses nearest to the flames were having to be sprayed with water by others.

"We must get his children out," the doctor insisted. "If that man was alive they will be."

If there was one thing that tore Melville's soul apart, it was children being trapped and dying. At the same time going in again meant possibly breaking the foam cover and letting in the air that would enable the fire to spread.

"Too dangerous," he answered tersely.

The doctor, misunderstanding his reasons, shouted in his face.

"If you won't, I will."

Before the doctor could move Melville gripped his arm so tightly that he winced.

"You bloody will not!"

The imputation of cowardice had so incensed Melville that only ingrained discipline prevented him from punching the young doctor.

"Cut the heroics. We want you at the hospital, not in it. When there's fire we give the orders. Now get back."

The registrar, his face showing the shock of what he saw, mumbled an apology. Melville relaxed his grip and spoke more kindly.

"We all feel that way. If it's any consolation the kids in there will have died of suffocation before they had time to be burned. The flames take all the oxygen. At least it'll have been over quick for them."

During this confrontation the reporter was talking urgently into his transmitter. He stopped and made a comment to one of the leading firemen.

"Tough job!"

"Worse when the boss spreads the fire," came the unreflecting answer, followed by a suspicious question.

"Who the hell are you?"

"London Broadcasting."

"Get lost, mate. We're busy."

The reporter retreated a moment ahead of the doctor, causing Melville to spot him.

"Who's that?"

The leading fireman shrugged. "You were lucky to get out just now," he said.

Melville agreed silently. When this was finished and they were back in Greycoat Place Fire Station and he was going over the lessons to be learned from it, he would in fact have to criticize himself. He had little doubt that his rescue had made the fresh outbreak possible by disturbing the foam cover. The thought raced through his mind and was as rapidly relegated to later consideration. Forgetting the reporter, he began redirecting the hoses to hit the fire harder.

Plowden, the chief fire officer, had been around on the outer side of the wreck when he heard the shout

"We have fire." This was far trickier than the concourse side to deal with, because there had been trains at every platform when the DC-10 came down and they blocked the firemen's movements. The tremendous impact not only had squashed the coaches directly beneath, but had also knocked them sideways, derailing them and leaving them keeled over either against each other or against the platforms. Every carriage in the station had rocked on its wheels, even though they were many yards from the actual impact. Some passengers, instinctively heading for the concourse, had fought their way through the wreckage. Most had streamed out down the platforms, trying to escape up the steps to the Eccleston Road Bridge across the station, but the gates at the top of the steps had all been locked. For a few minutes the surging crowd of travelers had been in more danger from themselves than anything else, pressing the front ranks wildly up against the iron gates, while others ran confusedly farther along the platforms and would have jumped down on the lines had not Chisholm's police constables been out on Platform 14 and maintained a semblance of calm until the keys were brought. Within twenty minutes every passenger who could walk had been guided out of every train, ambulancemen were using the Eccleston Bridge entrance to reach the injured, and a casualty post had been set up on the bridge itself by a medical team from St. Stephen's Hospital in Chelsea.

Shortly afterward a huge thirty-six-ton breakdown crane, mounted on rail bogies and accompanied by two tool vans, had reached Victoria from the Stewart's Lane Depot, two miles away in south London. So had the diesel shunting engine, which could remove carriages without the lines having to be electrified again.

When the mechanical engineer in charge had presented himself to Plowden, the fire chief's demand had been simple. He had gestured at the long rows of coaches.

"How soon can you pull them clear? They're a serious fire hazard with all this kerosene around."

The engineer had scarcely needed reminding. The suburban commuter trains occupying platforms 9, 10 and 11 were elderly stock, largely constructed of wood, and they would burn easily. They had only one advantage. They were built on a solid chassis to which you could attach draglines or winches even if the superstructure were smashed to matchwood. By contrast the main line trains that had been drawn up in platforms 12 and 15, underneath the airliner's main point of impact, were new steel carriages, built of integral construction like modern automobiles. Or, as the cynic phrased it, like baked bean cans. The damaged coaches had split open and might well have to be taken away piece by piece. But at least there was not so much combustible material in them.

"We can uncouple the four-car sets at the country end and shunt them out," commented the engineer. "Some are derailed where they link with the damaged sets, but as far as I can see the buckeye couplings have all slipped OK."

Plowden grunted, remembering from a rail crash study he had once attended that the buckeye couplings were designed to disengage under any up or down stress.

"The faster you haul out of here, the happier I'll be. I want this fireground clear."

"It'll be a four-to-five-hour job, jacking the overturned ones back up onto the rails. We'll do our best."

But by the time the fire started only twenty carriages out of fifty-two had been pulled away. Blue-overalled engineers were sweating to unscrew couplings that would release more, while others labored with jacks and timber balks to right those derailed. The firemen remained appallingly obstructed, having to clamber over crazily tilted carriages to reach the farther platforms, while debris and dangling roof girders further impeded setting up the hoses. The one thing they had plenty of was water from Victoria's trunk hydrants, and Plowden was using some of it to wash the

134

kerosene down the drains that run between the platforms. Nor had he any lack of foam.

Within seconds of the outbreak Plowden confirmed over his radio that the divisional officer on the concourse should drive the fire away from the buildings. Any other action would put the Grosvenor Hotel and the neighboring streets at risk. But it meant pushing the conflagration toward the one area that definitely held survivors pinned in the older, wooden-built rolling stock and where there might still be airline survivors from the rear of the aircraft.

At the same moment as Melville was making his dangerously brave rescue attempt on the concourse side, the grim-faced chief officer was watching the first of the Fire Brigade's own casualties being brought out, scorched and overcome by flames. There had been too many firemen deep in that wreckage, painstakingly dismantling it piece by piece to find the injured, for them not to suffer casualties. It was that kind of fire. Whatever had set it off—a spark from a hacksaw or simply a hot engine half submerged in fuel which finally brought the kerosene to flash point—it was bound to be a sudden inferno. The only way firemen could safeguard their own skins in such a situation was by not attempting to save others. Plowden reckoned there were very few men in the London Fire Brigade who would even think of that alternative.

A figure in a grimed raincoat appeared at Plowden's side. It was Donaldson. He shouted in the chief officer's ear.

"The flight recorder. It'll be in the tail."

Plowden recognized him, did not need reminding of the AIB's importance. Nonetheless, his answer was uncompromising.

"People come first."

This was the question Plowden had been asking himself. When the British Airways Trident caught fire at Staines, also an appreciable time after crashing, the blaze had been extinguished in two minutes. But that was on open ground, in a field. Here there were other elements: bags of mail, roof timbers, the carriages, a

135

hundred crevices and cavities where kerosene must be lying, ready to burn. Fire could even spread to the catacomb of storerooms under the thin floor of the concourse. It would certainly run down with the kerosene into the sewers.

"Ten, fifteen minutes," shouted Plowden.

The noise and heat were overwhelming, foam hissing on hot metal, steam and smoke fouling the air. The sweat was streaming down Plowden's face, streaking the dirt, making him look older than his fifty years. Donaldson himself felt he was being roasted alive. They were forced to move back. Suddenly in the midst of the fire a blinding, fizzing white firework of flame burst out.

"Magnesium metal in the undercarriage, most likely," said Donaldson, more to himself than to Plowden. "Oh, Jesus, we've got a job on."

This fire was going to destroy so much evidence, so many clues to what had happened. Donaldson realized there was nothing he could do here. If anything, he was in the way. Better to find out whether his engineering inspector had reported in yet. He touched Plowden on the shoulder.

"Best of British luck," he shouted.

Plowden glanced around, jerked back from his renewed concentration on the fire fighting, annoyed at the interruption.

"We'll find your ruddy black box," he said dourly.

"Thanks," said Donaldson, and thrust his way past relays of firemen out of the station by the cartoon cinema, where a poster, already curling and blistering, announced a "Funtastic season of cartoon comedies." Injured firemen were being given first aid in the cinema entrance, while a photographer hovered behind, taking pictures. "To most of the public," Donaldson reflected bitterly, "that will just be entertainment, too." Abruptly he realized that this accident, more than any other he had investigated, had created two worlds. In there, amid the wreckage and the flames, enclosed by the station as securely as by the walls of a prison, a life-and-death struggle was being fought out by the firemen. In there, when they had finished, would still lie the riddle that he had to solve, the riddle of why the DC-10 had crashed, to which there could only be one correct answer, one truth, even if he never succeeded in finding it. Outside, things would be different. Public interest, expanding as rapidly as the firemen's foam, would be enveloping the whole situation, fed by endless rumor and speculation, by ministerial statements and television interviews and by the colossal sums of insurance money at stake. It would be the major spectacle Britain had to offer the world this weekend, since all the world welcomes a disaster. For a moment he wished profoundly that he was not at the center of it. Then he braced himself and walked across the Buckingham Palace Road toward the control point opposite the station in Grosvenor Gardens.

In the street it was as though the tumult of the fire had been curtained off, reducing it to a dull roar in the background, overlaid by the revving of ambulance engines and the wail of horns. Police constables were still escorting office workers away, firmly guiding them down a side street, despite their curious glances back at the scurrying stretcher-bearers and the huge writhing column of black smoke above Victoria from which an oily sediment was falling on the whole neighborhood.

As Donaldson walked along the side of the station before crossing the road to the control point in Grosvenor Gardens, he noticed a gang of three men tumble out of a small van and rush to a manhole cover on the corner. They wore blue overalls, thigh-length rubber boots, and blue-painted protective helmets like construction site workers. One began levering the square cover up from the pavement while the others fenced it off. Seeing Donaldson approaching, they called out, "Keep away, sir, keep clear."

In the same instant Donaldson felt the paving stones shiver. A thunderous belch of smoke and flame shot up the shaft in the ground, just as the workman heaved the heavy cast-iron plate out of the way. A breath of foul-smelling air wafted past. Farther along the street another cover shot up with a bang, blown clear out of its seating. Mystified, Donaldson stepped up to the gang.

"What on earth was that?" he asked.

"Kerosene's burning in the sewers, sir, near enough exploded in the galleries I reckon—and stirred up the silt, too, from the smell of it," explained the elderly weather-beaten-faced foreman. "We were checking some brickwork along in Wilton Road when the first of it came down. Got out bloody fast, I can tell you."

"Mind if I look?"

Donaldson craned his head and gazed down the narrow shaft. Rusty iron footholds stuck out from the brick.

"Eighteen feet down and a five-foot-six gallery when you're there," commented the foreman.

"Do all the drains from the station run into here?"

"I don't rightly know about what's under the station. That's the railway's responsibility. We're the City Council sewermen. But it does all run into ours at different places. And ours join the big GLC sewer. More like a river that is, pumped along at thirty knots."

Donaldon cut him short, feeling that if unchecked, he might prove as loquacious as Hamlet's gravedigger.

"But at one point everything washed out of the station will come into yours."

"That's right, sir. And with the quantity of water the firemen have been pumping down to flush that kerosene, there'll be a quantity of junk with it."

Donaldson glanced inquiringly at the man.

"All sorts of things end up in the sewer, sir. Rings, jewelry, you'd be surprised. Used to be quite a sideline finding them once. But it's dangerous. Stirs up the silt and the sewer gas. More than a few men died scratching in the old days, so it's forbidden now."

"Who would authorize it then, a search I mean?"

"The city engineer, sir. He's our boss."

Donaldson smiled. "We certainly live and learn." The familiar excitement of discovery was making his adrenaline run. And, as often was the case, he did not know why, not yet.

His thoughts were quickly forced back to immediate issues. When he reached the group of control vehicles, he saw that a big dark blue-painted trailer had been moved into position, hauled by an articulated truck cab. He recognized it as a mobile police station. With luck its facilities would include a direct link to his own Information Room. At least if they were following standard air crash procedures it would. As he approached a constable stopped him.

"Excuse me, sir. Are you on official business?"

"AIB," said Donaldson, pointing at his armband with its royal crown. The constable, who was encountering a greater number of unusual officials than he had supposed existed, let him pass grudgingly. Around the group of control vans, the air crackled with radio messages as ambulance, fire and police incident officers all kept up clipped, urgent dialogues with their headquarters. Commander Thompson was standing outside the mobile police station, talking to a man who Donaldson guessed must be another police officer although he was in a city suit.

"Has my engineering inspector checked in yet," Donaldson asked. Thompson glanced up at him.

"The duty officer inside should know," he said tightly, then checked himself and indicated the man with him. "Mr. Donaldson, this is Mr. Chance, who's the CID chief in the division. You'll be seeing him again, I expect."

"David Chance," said the chief superintendent cheerfully, and shook hands. He was a young-looking forty with a strong, jutting jaw, a black mustache and a swarthy complexion.

"Let's hope there's not much criminal to investigate," Donaldson replied, then added, "I don't need to tell you that any eyewitnesses the police can turn up will be valuable, anyone who saw the aircraft at all. They don't have to be experts. In fact, it's often better if they're not. Experts throw in too many of their own conclusions."

"We'll keep you posted," said Chance.

Thompson interrupted firmly. "Now, Mr. Donaldson, if you'll excuse us, we have a lot to discuss."

Donaldson took the hint and walked up the short stepladder into the trailer. Thompson's assistant, Sturgess, was seated at a folding table; behind were telephones and radio receivers. Donaldson explained himself and reiterated his query.

"AIB, name of McPherson. He should have checked in by now."

"If he hasn't, then he's about the only official in London who's failed to. That's why we cordoned this area off."

Sturgess consulted a log sheet on a clipboard.

"In your line we've had two American diplomats, the local airline manager, someone from Hanson's Air Accident Branch. . . ."

Hanson was the firm of undertakers who specialized in identifying and then disposing of the corpses from air crashes.

"Are they setting up a mortuary?" Donaldson asked.

"He and the commander were talking about Chelsea Barracks. If the coroner and the army agree, that is." Sturgess was still perusing his log. "McPherson. Yes, checked in about five minutes ago. Can't be far away."

Donaldson paused, wondering why McPherson had not called him on the shortwave radio transmitter all the AIB inspectors carried. Maybe he had, but the buildings had blocked the transmission. He decided to contact his office before finding his colleague.

"Have you fixed up a line to the Department of Trade yet?"

Sturgess stared at him, then picked a bright red folder marked "Metropolitan Police Major Incident Procedure" and flicked through the index doubtfully.

"That's a new one on me, sir. To be honest, we're so busy we don't have time to practice the procedures much. Major incidents don't happen that often."

"Nor air crashes in Westminster, happily. Well, take my word for it, you are supposed to provide me with communications. Can I use a line now?"

Sturgess agreed hesitantly, and a moment later Donaldson was through to his information officer.

"Thank God you've rung, Jim," he said as he heard Donaldson's voice. "There's a real panic on here. The minister's around our necks because the home secretary wants to make a statement in the House of Commons, the telex from Washington has hardly stopped, and we haven't got a sausage to give either of them. What's the gen?"

The way wartime RAF slang permeated some flying men's language annoyed Donaldson, so he replied with slight irritation.

"As you may have heard, it caught fire about"—he consulted his watch,—"about seven minutes ago, at five twenty P.M. It was a DC-10 of Atlantic Airlines. The pilot was Captain Bill Curtis." He pulled himself up. "I just happen to know the pilot was Bill Curtis. That should not be released. There was at least one seriously injured survivor."

"We know more than that here already."

"I've no doubt you do," said Donaldson tersely. "For some time yet you're going to be a lot better informed than I am. Now you can tell me something. Did the crew transmit a Mayday call, did they know what went wrong?"

"Air traffic control at Heathrow telephoned us a transcript a few minutes ago. Hang on a second. Yes. Shortly after their final course correction the crew reported a rear-engine explosion. That was at twelve miles out, near enough, and two thousand six hundred feet. The next thing they reported going out of control. By then the radar had lost them in the clutter."

"That's all?"

"Except the controller at Heathrow said the tone of voice was pretty calm on the first call, pretty confident."

"I had got as far as thinking the number two engine had failed—that's the one in the tail," Donaldson admitted. "And had caught fire." He paused. "Look, we don't want any statement put out that would prejudice our inquiry."

"The minister wants to make a statement to the House. His private office is pestering us for facts."

Donaldson swore silently to himself. His hand was being forced, and every instinct he had acquired in nearly twenty years as an investigator warned him that this was an occasion when he himself might need to force other people's hands. He made a rapid decision, realizing as he did so that it might have far-reaching consequences.

"I think the minister's statement had better refer to preliminary investigations suggesting that the cause of the accident may have been a failure of the rear-engine turbine. In answer to questions he can say that a jet engine can disintegrate and damage the airframe. Don't on any account mention the word 'explosion.' "

"Suspicions of sabotage are ruled out?"

"Correct," said Donaldson decisively, "in spite of my being able to think of a lot of people who would prefer sabotage, including the president of Atlantic Airlines. Now, more seriously, I badly need help down here. McPherson has arrived, but I could use another airframe inspector. And I'll want an emergency readout of the flight recorder jacked up."

"Our specialist's on his way. So is a press officer."

"Good. Finally, would you tactfully explain to Scotland Yard that we need a special telephone of our own? At the moment I'm borrowing one."

Suddenly Donaldson remembered something that the pressure of events had made him forget completely.

"And tell my wife," he added. "Say I'll phone her when I can."

"Will do."

Donaldson rang off with some relief, thanked Sturgess and descended from the trailer to find McPherson outside.

"Where the hell have you been?" he complained.

McPherson, a tall, gaunt-faced Scot, seemed unperturbed.

"I couldna raise you at all," he replied impassively.

Donaldson reflected that interference must have

prevented it, nodded, then walked away from the cluster of vehicles, motioning McPherson to follow.

"Mac," he said in an undertone, "I don't like this crash. Not only did the pilot report an explosion, the only survivor I know of was near the tail. He told a doctor there was 'a helluva bang.' Just before she caught fire, a few minutes ago, I'd got into the flight deck, what was left of it."

"No a nice sight, I imagine," McPherson interjected sympathetically.

"From the instruments the number two engine must have been on fire. It was throttled back. The fuel was shut off. And it had no turbine revs at all."

"None at all, you say?"

"Zero registering on the instrument panel. Even with the fuel cut off it would go on spinning for some time, wouldn't it?"

"I would have thought so. Unless it was disintegrating." McPherson scratched his chin in puzzlement. "And that would be unusual at low power on the approach, verry unusual." McPherson slurred the word "very," emphasizing it.

"Could have been a bird strike," said Donaldson, "only that would be unusual at around three thousand feet, too."

McPherson laughed.

"That bloody great beast of a turbofan could ingest a dozen birds and not notice them. Just throw them out the back end plucked and roasted."

"The sooner we find number two engine the better. I'm fairly certain it broke free on impact and was carried forward by its own weight into the wall of the hotel. An awful lot of people from the minister down are asking us questions, Mac. That engine holds most of the answers."

"So it was an engine failure?" cut in a voice.

The two men were so absorbed that they had failed to notice the approach of a short, slightly fat man with a press armband around the sleeve of his brown velvet jacket. Donaldson jackknifed around to face the intruder.

143

"I said no such thing," he snapped. "Who are you anyway?"

The journalist stood his ground.

"Sam Eckhardt, *Sunday Post*," he replied blandly. "I take it you are Mr. Donaldson, the accident inspector."

"I am. But it is far too early to make any statement about this crash."

"With respect," said Eckhardt, oil in his voice, "you have this moment made one. 'That engine holds the answers,' you said. May I ask which engine?"

"You may ask," interrupted McPherson vehemently, "but you'll no get an answer." He scowled. "Bloody reporters."

Eckhardt smiled, though there was a hard glint in his eyes. He was used to this. The essential thing was to keep sources of information talking. "If you want newspapers to read, then you must allow us to write them," he remarked equably.

McPherson's face reddened with anger. Donaldson held up his hand for silence. He himself bought the *Sunday Post* regularly; he knew Eckhardt's name well. But that was irrelevant.

"Don't get excited, Mac," he said quietly. "We all have a job to do. Now, Mr. Eckhardt, when we have something to say, we will make a statement. We will do so as soon as we can. In the meantime, may I remind you that many hundreds of lives and many millions of pounds are involved in this crash? Great harm could be done by publishing the wrong conclusion about it. Particularly in a reputable paper like yours."

"Just as a favor, make a statement on Saturday, will you? We Sunday paper men have to live."

It was a cheap witticism, and Donaldson had difficulty choking back the retort that Eckhardt, with his fleshy flace and trousers tight over his belly, looked as though he lived pretty well. Instead, he gave a straight answer.

"As it happens, that is possible. Assuming we find the flight recorder quickly, we could have an uncalibrated readout of the tape by Saturday—"

An explosion inside the station, clearly audible, interrupted him. They all spun toward it, but could see nothing more than the same swirling black smoke, funneling up into a new, almost cloudless blue sky.

"Fuel tank, maybe," commented McPherson.

"That fire's going to play hell with the evidence," Donaldson muttered. At this rate charred bodies and molten metal were all that would be left. The thought preoccupied him.

"Are there any survivors?" demanded Eckhardt.

"I know of one," Donaldson answered automatically, then realized he had said enough already. "Now look, as I said, just now, we all have a job to do. That includes us."

Reluctantly Eckhardt accepted the dismissal and edged away, then paused to scribble in a notebook.

Donaldson turned to McPherson.

"Mac," he said tersely, "get in there as soon as you can. I want a word with that airline manager. He ought to be producing accurate passenger lists and loading sheets, not sightseeing."

"Some of our best friends are airline managers," said McPherson sententiously. He had a doleful, offbeat sense of humor.

"Don't remind me," Donaldson replied, as they parted.

Eckhardt watched the two investigators go and then made the error of asking a police constable where to find the press telephone. Despite his protests and explanations, he found himself being firmly, almost forcibly, escorted across the forecourt of the station to Neathouse Place, the small side street designated by Thompson as the press center. The constable saw him through a gap in a line of flashing yellow lights, between which white tape was strung up as demarcation line to keep the ambulance route down Wilton Road clear, and departed.

"Welcome to the pen," joked a voice Eckhardt knew. It was a radio commentator standing by a smart black-painted London taxi with darkened windows, a prominent aerial on the roof and the words "BBC Radio News" neatly lettered on the door.

"Anything happening over there?" asked the commentator.

"Not much," said Eckhardt guardedly.

"The buggers won't let us inside the station. They'll have to soon. The TV boys are going mad."

He jerked a thumb at two large green-painted vans parked a little farther down the road. A camera crew on top of one was filming casualties being brought out to ambulances opposite.

"OK, so there's a fire," said the commentator bitterly. "We need to see it."

Eckhardt nodded agreement and devoted a minute to sizing up the scene. Within Neathouse Place, which passed underneath the middle of an office block as an ancient right-of-way, a crowd of reporters were besieging two police spokesmen, shouting questions, jostling and pushing. This was not the way that Eckhardt did business. Only a promise from the news editor that he would have a full page, probably two, kept for him exclusively in the paper had persuaded him to take on the assignment. What he needed now was a telephone and some privacy. He was thinking this when he realized that he was on familiar ground, or rather at the back of it. A girl he occasionally took out worked for a magazine in this very office block. He forced his way through the crowd and out at the far side, into the wide Vauxhall Bridge Road. This was the open end of the "pen," and he was soon around the corner and bounding energetically up the steps into the foyer and the lifts. The commissionaire was preparing to leave but challenged him nonetheless. Because of the IRA bombs, he had strict orders to let no strangers pass.

"Is Miss Carslake here?" asked Eckhardt.

The man said he thought so, dialed on the internal phone, announced Eckhardt's arrival, then handed the phone to the reporter.

"Gilly, darling, can you spare a moment?" Eckhardt was at his smoothest.

"Come upstairs," she said. The stairs led to the

twelfth floor. It was exactly as he remembered. Her room was at the back of the building and had a commanding view of Victoria Station. He could not resist crossing straight to the big plate glass window.

"It's both fantastic and terrifying," she said. "I was sitting here when the plane crashed. I thought the end of the world had come; it sounded exactly as though it was going to hit us." She shuddered. "It must be terrible down there. Thank God they seem to be putting the fire out."

She was right. Although dense smoke was still billowing up from the shattered roof, there were no flames visible. Eckhardt noted the time. 5:31 P.M. Then her humorous voice cut in on his thoughts.

"Well, so that's what brings you to the offices of *Lady Beautiful*. I feared it wasn't little me you wanted to see."

Eckhardt turned and faced her, raising his arms theatrically as if to embrace her. It was not difficult to pretend to be attracted to Gilly Carslake. She was tall, blond, with a figure that curved appealingly in all the right places and an attractive wide mouth with a ready smile. Eckhardt had first met her when he took her out for dinner after a cocktail party, and it had never since occurred to him to wonder what went on inside her head, even though he knew she was the assistant editor on a leading fashion journal. It was enough that she was good company and admired his own established success.

"Sweetie, for once you see me baffled. Downstairs it's impossible. Every free lance in London is milling about chasing for copy. By rights I should have been following up that Israeli terrorist story in Paris. Then the news editor hijacked me for this. A lot of crap about needing the paper's best writer."

Gilly smiled. When it came to sheer, unembarrassed conceit Sam Eckhardt was hard to equal. At the same time she found his self-assurance attractive.

"It is a big story, you must admit. And?" She let the question hang delicately.

"Is there any way I could use your office temporarily? Until Saturday. As a bolt hole and a place to telephone." Eckhardt squeezed her hand affectionately. "Officially or unofficially. Do I slip fifty quid to the man at reception, or to you, or what?" His light-hearted tone hardened. "And I must get a photographer in here."

"That won't be a scoop, I'm afraid. The roof's crawling with photographers already."

Eckhardt's ebullience subsided fractionally.

"I'll try," said Gilly decisively, moving to the door. "The editor can't have left yet. I'll ask her. Better to be on the level."

"Can I use your phone?"

"Lucky for you I have an outside line." She vanished, closing the door softly behind her.

Eckhardt wasted no time. He rang the *Sunday Post* news editor, confirmed that this had to be the worst disaster in London since the 1940 German blitz, demanded that all the cuttings on DC-10 accidents be researched, especially problems with its engines, and explained that with luck he had secured an office overlooking the scene, not to mention an eyewitness of the crash. The news editor was impressed, as Eckhardt meant him to be. He lacked the foreign editor's experience of the journalist's steamrollering technique. Nonetheless, he expected to hand out some guidance of the sort he customarily gave home reporters.

"Make a point of interviewing the crash experts," he said.

"I've this moment come from talking to the accident inspector. He promised me a statement on Saturday." Eckhardt's exaggerations were always skillfully close to the truth.

"Get it tomorrow if you can, Sam. We want a center page story on this away tomorrow night; we'll keep the front page for genuine Saturday news."

"That's what I'm saying, it will be Saturday's news. They haven't even found the flight recorder yet. Anything else?"

"Nothing much. AP says the airline's president is flying across tonight. Oh, yes, there's a message from

148

the Libyan Embassy. Would you ring Ahmed soonest? But you'll have to forget that Paris story for the time being."

"OK," said Eckhardt. "I'll be in tomorrow afternoon to hammer out the center page."

He put down the receiver, pondered briefly, then dialed the Libyan Embassy. After the usual delay, the diplomat came on the line.

"Ahmed," said Eckhardt, not waiting to hear what the other man wanted, "I am very tied up. The Israelis are going to have to wait."

"You mean the air crash?" The Libyan's tone was suave and soft as always. "I know, my friend. You are covering it."

"Yes." Eckhardt was momentarily surprised; then he realized the news editor must have told him.

"That is a terrible accident. Are there any survivors?"

"At least one." Eckhardt recounted what he knew.

"I believe an old friend of mine was on that plane. It would be of the greatest assistance to me to know as much as possible about this disaster."

"What is your friend's name?"

As the Libyan was explaining that his friend was traveling incognito and might have used one of several names, Gilly came back, unnoticed by Eckhardt, who was leaning on the edge of the desk, watching the activity below the window as he talked.

"I will do what I can, Ahmed, but I can promise nothing. I'll call you tomorrow."

Her return caught him unawares.

"I'm not certain you can call him from here," she said, making him jump. "The editor's gone. I'll have to ask in the morning. But come along and we'll hope for the best."

"You are a honey." Eckhardt recovered himself immediately, put down the telephone and took her hand and kissed it ceremoniously.

She replied with a mock curtsy and then asked idly, "Wasn't that the man who helped you with the Paris story? Didn't you tell me it was an Arab?"

Eckhardt felt a faint prickling of the skin, a warning that something was amiss. He had a highly developed feel for the drift of the most innocuous conversations. On reflection, perhaps he *had* mentioned the source of his Israeli story when he took her out for a jubilant dinner on his return from Paris last Saturday. He had felt like having an appreciative audience, and she had certainly been one. That she had now heard the name hardly mattered . . . and yet. Eckhardt's rule was never to divulge his source except to his editor, and then only under pressure. He must have drunk too much last Saturday.

"Did I?" he said, deliberately not answering her question and promptly changing the subject. "Look, love, there are more pressing things on hand. Do you by any miracle own a radio?"

"By a miracle, I do." She reached into a drawer and produced a pocket-sized transistor, flicking it on with her finger. A newscaster's voice blared out, reverberating tinnily.

"You are listening to LBC, where news comes first. The time five thirty-five. And now, live from the scene of the tragic Victoria air crash, another special report in our round-the-block coverage of London's worst disaster since the blitz."

A more urgent, dramatically breathless voice came in, speaking against considerable background noise. "This is Vic Newton on Victoria Station. As firemen douse the catastrophic fire that inexplicably engulfed the Atlantic Airlines DC-10 an hour after its death dive onto rush-hour crowds of rail commuters, I am here among rescue workers witnessing the unbelievable carnage. Beside me a doctor pumps morphine into what must be the last survivor, a man saved by the heroism of two firemen, hauled half dead from the flames. I hear his heart rending cry 'My wife and children are still there.' Then he faints. Ambulance-men sprint to bear him away and I follow."

The voice of the station announcer cut back in.

"As Vic Newton traced the tragedy of one victim, officials counted two hundred seriously injured already rushed to the hospital and sixty-two dead before the fire broke out—not counting the hundreds of airline passengers who must have perished in the crash. And now back again to Vic Newton at Victoria."

Again the quiet of the studio was abruptly replaced by a cacophony of noise, magnified by the reporter's microphone.

"Vic Newton, Victoria. Now I have followed the last survivor to the temporary dressing station on the station concourse, where teams of doctors and nurses toil over lines of injured. They say the man I saw saved is in deep shock, legs burned. It's touch-and-go if he can live. A Catholic priest in long black cassock stained with blood kneels beside the man, giving last unction. As he smooths the ointment from a tiny pot onto his forehead, the man passes out totally, merciful morphine taking him away. Whether he will live, no one knows. This is Vic Newton, Independent Radio News, Victoria."

"Heard enough?" asked Gilly. Eckhardt grunted, and she switched it off. "You've got your work cut out to beat those boys, Mr. Eckhardt," she observed coolly. "And this is Gillian Carslake, editor person, telling you so."

Eckhardt frowned. He disliked being made fun of, and more he resented the truth in her remark. To obtain a news beat on this story was going to be exceptionally difficult. Somehow he would have to find an exclusive angle, one that was alone.

"Stop being flip," he said rudely, "and tell me what you saw."

"Seriously, do you think I ought to make a statement to the police? As an eyewitness. They must want eyewitnesses."

"Tell me first." He pulled out his little notebook.

"Well, when I heard that awful grinding, roaring noise, I ran to the window. The plane was huge. It can't have passed more than fifty yards away. It had a big engine in the tail which seemed to be on fire, and pieces were falling off the tail, it looked as though quite big pieces were missing. . . ."

At home in Epson, Jane Donaldson had spent a disordered day. After her husband had left for the city she had sat down and attempted to weigh up the pros and cons of moving to America. Having recovered from her immediate emotional reaction against being uprooted, she had started to calculate. Seventy-five thousand dollars a year did sound like a colossal amount of money. She telephoned the bank and asked about exchange rates. It really was forty thousand pounds a year, more than four times Jim's present earnings. Her enthusiasm cooled a little when the bank manager told her that the Inland Revenue would rake back at least two-thirds of it.

"Oh, but it's in America," she said. "We'd be living there."

"Tax rates are a lot lower in the United States. How low exactly I don't know." He was getting out of his depth, though he left no doubt in her mind that from what he had heard they would be comfortably off on such a salary.

It was from then on the day fell apart. She wandered around their cramped modern home, thinking about the larger, more gracious Edwardian houses near the Downs, realizing how unattainable they were on Jim's salary. She thought of the increased demands that educating the girls would make on their resources, of luxuries forfeited and unpleasant domestic economies. By the afternoon she not only had convinced herself that her husband had accidentally found the proverbial pot of gold at the end of the rainbow, but was desperate to question him on a mass of details, like the cost of schools and clothes and food and holidays in America. The bank manager had warned her to take these into account, but she had no idea how to. By teatime she had relapsed into a dreamy contemplation of future comforts. It was only through force of habit that she switched on the television to watch the news at six.

The air crash was the lead item, totally eclipsing all other events. She watched horrified and fascinated at the same time, though secure in the knowledge that

Jim could not possibly be involved, not when he was still tidying up another investigation.

The phone in the hall rang. Reluctantly she left the television. It was the information officer from the department on the line.

"Mrs. Donaldson? I'm so sorry I couldn't telephone before. You heard about the crash at Victoria? Your husband is there. He asked me to ring you."

Jane felt the breath leave her body. "But he can't be. He's only just back from America."

"He was the duty PI, Mrs. Donaldson. I'm sure he'll ring you himself as soon as he can."

She replaced the receiver, dazed. How could they do this to her? How could they! She went back into the sitting room, switched the TV off and poured herself a stiff drink, her anger gradually mounting. This was once too often, she told herself. She was damned if she would stand for it. For Jim hadn't been back twenty-four hours yet.

Commander Thompson was planning his next moves. There was little he could do inside Victoria Station until the blaze was completely extinguished. So long as it lasted, the "fireground" was the Fire Brigade's responsibility and theirs alone. Without a fire there could be, and sometimes was, friction over which service was *primus inter pares,* as the old Latin expression put it. Logically, Thompson felt, the police should have overall control of any disaster situation because they were responsible for public order and the preservation of life. But in a typically British way, the relationship between the emergency services was largely undefined. While the Fire Brigade was controlled by the Greater London Council, as was the Ambulance Service, the Metropolitan Police depended on the GLC for finance, and their direction was entirely in the hands of its commissioner. Even the government, in the shape of the home secretary, could not give orders to the commissioner, only advise him or request his force's assistance. This independence, unrealized by the average British citizen, was a major bulwark of democracy. And at the same time the lack of police power over other official agencies was, too. Thompson recognized both these aspects of his job and that, at this immediate moment, he was going to control the multitude of interests involved in this crash as much by strength of personality as by legal right.

Just how rapidly the pressures of the outside world were mounting was evidenced by the requests and queries coming into the mobile police station. Going over them quickly with Sturgess, Thompson was amazed. The last fifteen minutes had seen calls from the airline's insurance brokers, from two more embassies, the Israeli and the Italian, both of whom believed citizens of their countries had been on board, from the Social Services Department of the Westminster City Council, the city engineer, from the home secretary's office.

"I've had the Department of Trade on the blower again, too," remarked Sturgess equably. "Did you realize that the guy in the raincoat, Donaldson, was God in disguise? Well, he is. For the record, he has power to require anybody to make a statement, to impound anything he thinks fit, to go anywhere and to penalize anyone who interferes with him."

"Sounds worse than a coroner."

"On a par, and incidentally, that's another one who's been on. The Coroner's Office want to discuss the mortuary."

"We'd better have a briefing," said Thompson. "Now."

"I've taken the precaution of asking the key people to assemble."

Sturgess allowed himself a smile. After a year with him he knew the commander's habits fairly well. One that Thompson had never lost dated back to his marine commando days. He would call in all the subordinates concerned with an operation, listen to them summarize their own problems, then issue his orders.

"Bring them in," said Thompson, "what are you wasting time for?"

As Sturgess rose and went to the caravan door, Thompson reflected that this was as much a battle as any military one, a battle against death, destruction, and disorder; a fight to bring a key part of a great city back under control. It could only succeed if he coordinated it as firmly as a general commanding his troops.

As eight people, led by Chisholm, the railway police chief superintendent, and including a woman in a green uniform, filed in through the narrow doorway, the figure of the Fire Brigade's incident officer appeared, too.

"Fire is surrounded, sir," he announced.

Thompson checked the time, it was 5:29 P.M., then welcomed his small audience, standing cramped around the table.

"We'll have to keep this short, ladies and gentlemen," he said. "It sounds as though the fire's been contained." He nodded to the ambulance officer. "The injured come first. How is your side of it going?"

"The situation's desperate but not serious, as one of my men used to say. We've close on sixty ambulances from all over London involved now. In the last hour and five minutes since we started, that is." He consulted a sheaf of notes in his hand. "We've taken two hundred and twenty-one casualties away. But there are almost that number lying out on the eastern station concourse and the Ebury Bridge end of the platforms waiting to be moved. That's serious, except there are seven medical teams here now dealing with them. What is desperate is finding beds to send them to. And then actually driving them there through the rush-hour traffic."

"Didn't we clear routes to the three designated hospitals?" Thompson queried.

"Commander." The ambulanceman spoke with heavy emphasis. It was extraordinary how everyone assumed that because London had a bevy of famous teaching hospitals, those same hospitals would have empty beds. That had been one of the lessons of the Moorgate tube train disaster, when the hospitals had not been adequately warned of the numbers they would be expected to accept. "Commander," he repeated, "the Westminster, St. George's and St. Thomas' were full twenty minutes ago. None could clear more than fifty beds, and considering St. George's is officially no longer accepting casualties, we were lucky to get any in there at all. I've just spoken to our control at Waterloo, and the current batch will fill up St. Stephen's, the Middlesex and Guy's, even allowing that we're already transferring their less ill patients to other places. And even to St. Stephen's in the Fulham Road, the round trip is taking nearly twenty-five minutes in this traffic. Control have had to designate hospitals as far away as the London in the East End and the West Middlesex out at Isleworth. The driving's a nightmare, especially with the worst injured being brought out last. It's going to be more than half an hour now before we get some of the major surgery cases through the doors of a hospital, let alone on the operating table."

Thompson turned to a large street map which Sturgess had contrived to hang up. He could see the ambulanceman's point. To reach Isleworth meant the ambulance drivers were heading down the Great West Road along with a mass of homeward-bound commuters, while going east along the Mile End Road to the London Hospital would be as bad.

"Colin," he said, "call the Operations Room and ask if the other divisions can clear routes to these hospitals. Give my inspector the details," he said to the ambulanceman and turned to Chisholm, the railway police chief superintendent, whose height was forcing him to stoop uncomfortably under the low roof of the caravan. "Peter, what are your problems?" Then before Chisholm could reply, he added, "Once this fire is out, you're going to have one hell of a lot more dead bodies to cope with. Not to mention lost property. Have you enough men?"

"We've brought in British Transport police from Waterloo, Charing Cross, Paddington and several other stations. London Transport have sent men, too. I've ninety-eight all told. They have got plenty on their hands, though. All the entrances to the station are being manned. We've been able to go on working on the east side in spite of the fire. The snag is space.

156

As you've heard"—Chisholm glanced at the ambulance officer—"the concourse is fully taken up with casualties. So are the bars and buffets on that side. I've allocated the Eastern Booking Hall to railway passengers' luggage, stuff we can be sure is railway luggage, that is. The problem is mortuary space. At present we're using the cab road that runs up between platforms Seven and Eight and screening it off with portable notice boards. I reckon we'll need another temporary mortuary over the other side. Up along Platform Seventeen would do. That could be screened off easily. Even before the fire the corpses were no sight for the squeamish."

A quiet, educated voice cut in. "As the commander knows, Atlantic Airlines have retained me to deal with the identification and repatriation of the victims from the aircraft. My staff are already bringing two thousand polyurethane recovery bags. I would be happy to help with the railway dead also."

"For Christ's sake," Chisholm burst out, "there aren't going to be two thousand corpses."

The man who had spoken, a slightly built man, soberly dressed in a gray suit, held out his hand to Chisholm.

"Forgive me, I should have introduced myself. Peter Danman of Hanson's. With respect, Chief Superintendent, not all the bodies will be intact. I speak from experience."

"Mr. Denman," said Thompson decisively. "I'd be glad if for the moment you deal with all the victims."

"I have asked the London District Headquarters for mortuary space in either Wellington or Chelsea Barracks."

"You settle the details and keep me informed." Thompson set that matter aside crisply and addressed another man in ordinary clothes. This was the City of Westminster's social services director.

"You've opened an emergency rest center?"

"We have, Commander, and with the help of our friends here"—he indicated the blue-uniformed Salvation Army Captain, a Red Cross official and the WRVS

157

lady—"we should be able to cope. We could be accommodating as many as two thousand people tonight, what with guests evacuated from the hotel, stranded railway passengers, children who've lost their parents and others."

The Salvation Army captain chipped in. "We've taken over two hundred into the Buckingham Gate hostel already. Not hospital cases, but not fit to go home either. Suffering from mild shock, most of them."

Thompson thought for a moment, then spoke to the lady, whom he had met on various occasions before. "What have you brought along, Mrs. Dean?"

"The regional office have sent two vans down. We have masses of tea, sandwiches, blankets."

"I would prefer you to see to the firemen and other rescue workers. There are a good five hundred around now. They'll be at it all night, and they'll need food and hot drinks."

The lady, organizer of thirty unpaid spare-time workers for the Women's Royal Voluntary Service in the Westminster, was just starting to ask what more was needed when the fire officer reappeared at the doorway.

"Fire out, sir."

"Thank you," replied Thompson calmly, then spoke to the group.

"I won't keep you any longer. There's enough to do. Please remember that the main casualty bureau is at Scotland Yard, where they've opened the Operations Room. The deputy assistant commissioner will be in control there now. It is essential to keep lists, not only of casualties, but of every person you accommodate, if possible of everyone you give treatment to. We're going to have a list of missing persons as long as Buckingham Palace Road. Every old lady in Britain who thinks her granddaughter might have been on a train to Brighton will be ringing up, and there are going to be more than a few people genuinely unaccounted for. Please keep Inspector Sturgess here informed."

As the group filed out, he caught Chisholm by the arm. "I should like to go around the station with you,

Peter," he said. "We're going to have to let the press in now."

"There are pickup points and power for the TV round on Platform One. They use them for state occasions, but they're a long way from the wreckage."

"That's the TV's problem, not ours," said Thompson shortly. "I'm concerned with keeping them out of the Fire Brigade's way."

As the men stood poised to leave, the sergeant operating the radio called out, "Half a tick, sir. Important message coming up."

He finished scribbling on a pad, then tore off the sheet of paper and handed it across to Sturgess, who read it out.

"Home secretary and police commissioner expected arrive Victoria six twenty P.M. No special arrangements required."

Thompson and Chisholm looked at each other and simultaneously broke into laughter.

"Well, Colin," said Thompson, "what are you waiting for! You'd better start not making those arrangements."

He stepped down out of the caravan. Overhead a helicopter circled, the insistent clacking of its rotor blades adding to the noise as fire appliances revved up their engines and more ambulances braked to a halt, joining a queue of vehicles picking up casualties. As the two men crossed the forecourt to enter the station the police press officer hurried across from Neathouse Place.

"It's all hell in there, sir," he exclaimed. "There must be a hundred and fifty reporters waiting and a dozen film crews."

"Tell them the home secretary and the commissioner will be here at six and they can watch as we show them what's going on."

"Suppose we cordon off the corner of the main concourse where the arch leads through from the eastern side," suggested Chisholm. "Restrict them to a small area there."

"If you don't, they'll be all over the place," said

159

the press officer. "Look at them!" He pointed upward to the neighboring buildings. Photographers were clearly visible up on the parapets and roofs overlooking the station. "They're on Terminal House; they're everywhere."

"So much for evacuating the office workers," commented Thompson bitterly, then added resignedly, "You two had better work out the access for the press as fast as you can. Then allow them in beforehand. They'll need to film the brass arriving." Despite the annoyance the press caused him, Thompson had a basic understanding of their requirements. "And no arc lights without the Fire Brigade's consent," he added. Then he separated from Chisholm and the press officer and made his own way into the station from the forecourt, thinking about where precisely he might take the minister.

Even Thompson's wide experience did not prepare him for the interior of the station. He had seen fires before, and he knew the kind of inferno that a carpet factory or a timber store can become. He had seen dead and wounded before, too—more of them on the beat in the East End of London when he was a constable, in fact, than during his time as a commando. The elimination of rivals was a standard occurrence in East End gang warfare, and Thompson had often acted the part of a male nurse at the London Hospital, pushing a badly carved-up criminal through the casualty department in a wheelchair in case the man tried to escape. Nonetheless, when a railway police constable let him through the gates on to the Chatham side concourse, the scene took his breath away. Ranged across the black tarmac were rows of injured, some lying on stretchers, some on the ground: four rows, with a medical team working its way along each in the gloom of the unlit interior. Drifting smoke obscured the roof, keeping out the daylight; presumably the fire risk precluded using electric lights. Everything was smutted and dirty, while the makeshift nature of the whole arrangement reminded him of an old print he had once seen of Florence Nightingale toiling among lines of wounded at Scutari in the Crimean War. As he watched, a young doctor realized that one casualty had died, briefly felt for a pulse in the wrist in vain, gently examined the eyes, then drew a blanket over the corpse's head and quickly wrote out a death certificate which he tied to the body. A moment later two ambulance men bore the stretcher away. Thompson saw that the corpse's feet, protruding from beneath the blanket, were burned. He stopped across and asked where the senior medical officer was.

"I thought we'd saved that one," the doctor murmured. "I really thought we had."

"The SMO," Thompson repeated quietly. "Oh. In the buffet place, I expect. He's set up an office there."

Thompson walked around to the buffet, with its plastic counter and stool, where less than two hours ago travelers had been consuming tea and coffee. The senior medical officer, dressed in a white coat, was with another ambulance officer. Over to one side a constable sat at one of the small tables, a casualty logbook in front of him, in which he had been recording details of people given immediate first aid and then discharged. The doctor glanced up as Thompson entered.

"How's it going?" Thompson asked.

"Not much for your man to do, unhappily. Nearly all the injuries we're treating now are serious, a lot of skull fractures. Some die before we can get them to an ambulance."

"I saw one," said Thompson. "By the way, the home secretary is due in a few minutes."

"It's his colleague, the health minister, I'd like a few quiet words with," said the senior doctor vehemently. "The ambulance service is magnificent, simply magnificent. But we just do not have the hospital facilities in central London to cope with this scale of disaster. The Health Service is too overloaded, permanently overloaded. Not to mention overworked and underpaid."

"It's true," added the ambulance officer. "We've just

heard the control at Waterloo arranging transfers of patients to Crawley in order to clear beds in London hospitals. Crawley in Sussex! Thirty-odd miles away."

"And meanwhile," said the doctor, "cases needing immediate surgery are lying out there on the ground, waiting. You know something, Commander, I was a registrar at the Westminster during the blitz. We used to accept eighty to a hundred major casualities a night then, every night, night after night. As soon as they'd been patched up, we discharged them. And it was all done without any fuss—"

A young doctor appeared in the doorway, interrupting him.

"Excuse me, sir. We're had a bad one brought out. Ruptured spleen, I think. Could you come and have a look?"

The senior medical officer rose and hurried out, throwing a parting sally back over his shoulder.

"Give my apologies to the home secretary. Tell him we're a trifle busy."

Thompson reflected that the hospital consultants showed little sign of losing their long-standing antipathy to the government. He reckoned that if he bothered to make the calculations, which he never did, he would find himself working as long hours and probably for less pay. Certainly, the coming weekend was going to be yet another duty one, without much sleep either. He shrugged and then strode out to visit the mortuary, leaving the documentation constable, who had been watching him, wondering what exactly went on inside the boss' head.

The temporary mortuary, hidden by screens bearing cheerful posters advertising "Goldenrail Holidays" and seaside resorts, was curiously less gruesome than the casualty clearing area. The corpses lay on stretchers covered in a variety of blankets, which Thompson guessed had come from as wide a variety of organizations as their colors. Two WRVS girls were setting down another bundle as he reached the trestle table where a sergeant and a constable were writing up a casualty book. The sergeant stood up.

"We're trying to label each body, sir, but there are only fifty labels in these incident boxes." He pointed to a black plywood container, full of an assortment of notebooks, pads of forms, cards, pens, pencils, string, and maps.

"You name it and it's in the box, but not enough, sir. We're on the last of the labels now."

Thompson picked one up. It was simple enough. The front had spaces for the date, time, place found, name and address of the casualty and a signature, while the back was ruled in lines for a list of property found on the person.

"Nip across to Imspector Sturgess in the caravan. If he hasn't any more, then get railway luggage labels and use them."

"Yes, sir."

"There's a firm of undertakers who specialize in air crashes setting up a full-scale mortuary. They should be moving this lot out during the night with luck, before the rest of the world wakes up in the morning."

The sergeant saluted and then, as Thompson moved off, murmured morbidly to the constable, "Only hope I'm never a passenger who ends up as a railway parcel."

"Express freight to heaven," said the constable with a show of cynicism. In fact, his mouth was still bitter from the vomit that had welled up inside him as he had checked the possessions on a badly mutilated corpse.

"More like hell in here," replied the sergeant, who liked to have the last word.

Finally, Thompson passed through the arch between the two parts of the station. He found Chisholm, deep in discussion with Plowden, the chief fire officer. A dozen or so railway police were cordoning off an area near the arch with portable barriers and white tapes. Beyond them the wreck was so totally changed by the fire that Thompson simply stood and stared at it for a full half minute. Where before objects had been recognizable, if twisted and torn, as girders, or pieces of fuselage, now there was a charred mass of molten metal, all collapsed inward on itself at what had obviously been the center of the blaze. Over to the left, on the platforms where the tail end of the aircraft had fallen, the destruction was less. Swaths of foam lying over it, slowly dissipating, testified to the effectiveness of this method of fire fighting. From what he could see, the forward end of the plane, up against the hotel and the side of the station, was also little affected.

"That center section's where most of the fuel lay. Nothing could have saved it," commented Plowden, reading his thoughts. "Nor my men." His voice was savage. "I lost two dead and three badly burned in the eighteen minutes the fire lasted. If there's a devil in creation, that's the kind of work he gets up to."

He pushed his big white helmet back on his head and wiped the sweat off his face.

"It's going to be a foul job bringing the bodies out, too," he said. "There's hardly enough left of some of them to put on a stretcher."

"That firm Hanson's have brought two thousand polyurethane bags down. Do you want some of my men to help?" asked Thompson.

"I'd appreciate that."

At this moment Donaldson came up to them and spoke to Plowden. "I have a fair idea where the flight recorder must be. Can you spare the men to hack it out yet?"

"There may still be a few people trapped in the carriages who are alive, ones who were away from the fire." Plowden thought for a second. "All right. I've enough men. You can have Melville and his two crews again."

"Have you any clues to why the aircraft came down yet?" Thompson asked, mindful of the inevitable reporters' questions that he would be facing soon.

"Not really," said Donaldson, "and in any case I shall be extremely reluctant to commit myself until we have the readout from the flight recorder, and, of course, the cockpit voice recorder. Incidentally, I suppose you do know that some radio news bulletins are claiming the pilot reported an explosion on board."

"Christ alive," exclaimed Thompson, shaken out of his normal self-control. "I did not. Thank the Lord you told me."

"Hold hard, Commander. Don't start jumping to the same conclusions as the press. A turbine blade fracture followed by disintegration of the engine could feel like an explosion to the pilot. Remember he's a full hundred and fifty feet in front of that rear engine. He can't hear it. What happens is that he feels the shock in the controls and sees violent indications of trouble on the engine instruments."

As Donaldson was talking, his engineering inspector, McPherson, joined them and said quietly, "Could I have a word with you in private, Jim?"

Donaldson excused himself, giving a parting caution to Thompson. "No matter what pressure is put on us, we have a completely open mind as to causes until we have firm evidence. That's one reason why I try to avoid speaking to pressmen myself."

Donaldson followed McPherson a short distance away and stopped. "Well, Mac, what have you found?"

All the canny Scot in McPherson's nature had come to the surface. He whispered to Donaldson like a conspirator, despite the clamorous noise all around.

"Jim," he said, "I think you should have a wee look at that number two engine with me. It's had a blade fracture all right. And it's been on fire. But when it broke free, most of the jet pipe went with it, and there are some very strange holes in it indeed. If it weren't an impossibility, I'd have said that there'd been an explosion outside the engine as well as inside."

Chapter Six

News of the crash reached America in a matter of minutes. From Shellmex House in London, the chief inspector of accidents telexed brief details to the National Transportation Safety Board in Federal Office Building 10 on Independence Avenue in Washington only moments after the air traffic controllers at Heathrow had confirmed that the aircraft concerned was Atlantic Airlines flight 260. Simultaneously, the deputy inspector telephoned the Federal Aviation Authority's representative in London, Colonel Harrison Daly, U.S. Air Force (Ret.), at the American Embassy. Thus it was barely midday in Washington when Daly's call came through to the FAA building where copies of the telex message already were being circulated. Daly was told that accident investigators from both the FAA and the Safety Board were to leave that evening on the Pan Am flight direct to London from Dulles Airport. Under the terms of the Chicago Convention, representatives from both the state of registry of the crashed aircraft and the state of manufacture are always invited to participate in the inquiry, though its overall direction rests with the authorities of the country where the accident occurs. In other words, the British would run the show. But Daly's final words to his Washington office were prophetic: "Send the best guys you can. There's going to be one helluva sensitive situation here."

Simultaneously cables and telex messages were landing in other parts of the United States. At the McDonnell Douglas plant near Los Angeles, where the intensive publicity given by the British press to the DC-10 disaster outside Paris in 1974 still rankled, technicians were ordered to fly to Britain. On Wall Street all airline shares dropped, and Atlantic Airlines' own stock plummeted ten points in as many minutes and continued to slide until the close of business. Meanwhile, airline insurance brokers hastily checked to see what proportion of the DC-10's value was reinsured with the London Market—the hull alone carried a twenty-million-dollar tag. Under the Montreal Agreement, passenger liability compensation was limited to seventy-five thousand dollars per person, including legal fees. But should negligence by the airline be proved in court, individual litigation could easily jack the insurance payout to the hundred-million-dollar level—or beyond. By midafternoon the New York brokers realized that with British Rail claims for property and passenger deaths thrown in, they could be facing the highest claims in airline history.

Hugh Johnson had just stepped out of the elevator and pushed open the glass doors of his outer office when a secretary ran up to him.

"Mr. Johnson, Mr. Johnson, something terrible has happened, just terrible. The Blue Ribbon crashed. . . ."

Johnson hadn't been through the mill from pilot to president for nothing.

"OK, honey," he said. "Calm down." In times of crisis he called all women that. "Let's have the facts."

She handed him the telex with its brief details.

"We've been keeping a line to London open, Mr. Johnson."

"Let's have it then."

For a while Johnson merely listened as the London manager, speaking from the town office in Regent Street to which he had returned at Donaldson's insistence, explained what was known, concluding with

168

the dismal news that the wreck was on fire. At this point Johnson interrupted.

"I'll be on Pan Am two tonight. Book a suite at the Connaught for five, six days. And a couple of other rooms, too. Yeah, I'll have at least one engineer and one airframe man along. Meet us at Heathrow. Have all the data with you, right. And the local papers. No. *Times, Telegraph,* those ones, plus the *International Herald Tribune*. No, sir." Johnson's tone was emphatic. "The best public relations man in the goddamn universe is no good at a time like this. And don't you make any statement whatsoever to anyone till I come. Understood?"

Johnson slammed the phone down, saying to himself, "Crazy bum, trying to tell me those aren't local papers."

Then he called his personal secretary on the intercom.

"Honey, book three seats on Pan Am's flight two tonight. Tell Walker to roust out the two best engine and airframe technicians we have. Call my wife and ask her to pack me enough clothes for a week." He had a sudden thought. After this he was going to need that guy Donaldson more than ever. Donaldson had a wife who might need persuading. His own wife could help. "Tell her she ought to come, too. If she agrees, fix a fourth seat. And before you do any of that, call Bill Curtis' wife and see if she's going to be home this afternoon. Don't tell her anything. Say I'll be out around her way and will drop in."

Bill Curtis had been his copilot and chief pilot. Above all, he had been his friend. A man didn't have many such close associates in a lifetime, and the least he could do was break the evil tidings to Bill Curtis' widow himself. Pan Am two took off at 7 P.M. There was just time to visit her, collect his wife and baggage and catch the flight.

In London, in the residential districts near Victoria, it seemed as though the seesaw wailing of the two-tone horns on ambulances and police cars would never stop.

Thursday evening was the most intensely social one of the week in a city which, for all the nation's problems, had by no means lost the art of enjoying itself. But this Thursday was different. Westminster, Pimlico and Belgravia were totally cordoned off, the streets clear of all traffic except emergency vehicles. Buses as well as cars were banned; at Victoria and St. James's Park underground stations, the trains were running without stopping. Thousands of city workers were walking home.

The British government minister ultimately responsible for such a catastrophe was the home secretary, one of the most senior members of the Cabinet. However, news of the aircraft crash and its disruptive effects had reached him more than an hour after it happened. The afternoon and evening's speaking time in the House of Commons was scheduled for a debate on penal reform for which he was the government's leading speaker and, when word of the crash reached his staff, he had barely started. They dared not interrupt. Only after he had finished and sat down again on the worn red leather of the front bench, his fellow ministers applauding his oration, did one of the House of Commons' celebrated badge messengers, dignified in a black tailcoat with the thick gold chain and badge of his office heavy against his starched white shirtfront, walk quickly down between the crowded rows of benches to hand him a folded note. A moment later, a worried look on his normally benign face, the home secretary rose to leave, whispering to the leader of the House, "A bad crash at Victoria. I shall have to go. I can make a personal report to the House when I return."

At the door to the chamber he found his private secretary waiting.

"There's a police car outside, sir. The commissioner will meet us at Scotland Yard."

They hurried through the high-ceilinged Gothic corridors with their statues of statesmen in heroic attitudes and reached New Scotland Yard in two and a half minutes.

"That was quick," commented the home secretary to the driver. He made a point of always saying something friendly to underlings. Every workingman had a vote.

"You should see the rest of London, sir. It's chocca. Worse than New Year's Eve in Piccadilly Circus."

It was not long before the home secretary understood why. He was taken up in the elevator to the first floor, then hurried along a bare passage to the Operations Room, adjacent to the Information Room where the first news of the crash had been received. The Operations Room was activated only for major emergencies. It had been constructed after a riot outside the American Embassy in Grosvenor Square in 1968 had come close to overwhelming the police force's capabilities.

The room reminded the home secretary of a movie in which some mastermind sat on a raised crescent-shaped platform giving orders to subordinates while watching the world outside on a bank of television screens. In truth the "mastermind" was the Deputy Assistant Commissioner Operations, who was standing explaining something to the commissioner when the home secretary entered. Both men moved down to greet him.

"You haven't wasted any time going into action."

The deputy answered. "The duty inspector opened the room up immediately he heard about the crash, sir. Very sensibly. This is one of the worst incidents we've had." He pointed to the far corner where a group of policewomen were busy answering telephones and sorting cards into an indexing system. "The casualty bureau lines are pretty well jammed with calls. At the rate they're coming in, I'll be surprised if we end up with less than a thousand recorded casualties. Come and have a look, sir."

He led the way past curving rows of desks with each official's position neatly identified by a small placard—"Catering Liaison Officer," "CID Liaison Officer," "Assistant Staff Officer," and many others—until they reached the women constables.

"The girls have more feel for dealing with relatives than men do. They complete the cards from information coming in. Pink for the casualties, white for every inquiry made about a casualty, green for next of kin."

"And the girls have to match them up?" the home secretary asked.

"That's right, sir," said one. "And if Moorgate was anything to go by we'll have up to half a dozen inquiries for every casualty. Let alone the hoax calls."

"I remember those. Such people are sick in their minds."

"We had the first just now. As soon as the inquiry number was put out on the telly. A man who asked endless questions, gave a cackle of laughter, said, 'Ever been had?' and rang off. Sick or not, I wish I could lay my hands on him."

"Can you trace the calls?"

"We trace the bomb hoax ones," interjected the deputy, "but we're too busy for these."

"I should like a briefing on the whole situation," said the home secretary decisively, "then I should like to visit Victoria."

The two police chiefs exchanged a quick glance.

"They're barely finished fighting the fire, Minister," said the commissioner. "If we could delay until—"

Picking up his cue, the deputy indicated one of the television screens, showing an indistinct picture of the burning station from above.

"You see what it's like, sir. That's from a helicopter. We've chartered two extra helicopters from Battersea and mounted a small TV camera in one. It's proving fairly successful, especially for the traffic control."

"How is the rest of London being affected?"

The deputy pointed to the screens again.

"Those are some of the traffic pressure points. Virtually the whole of central London is severely congested, but it's worst to the west. We're trying to keep routes clear for the ambulances going that way. The ambulance control at Waterloo are having a hell of a time."

A staff officer rose from his place in front of the platform and approached the deputy.

172

"Excuse me, sir. I've got Inspector Sturgess on the line from the control point. They're having trouble with the bus station. Access to both it and the British Airways terminal had to be closed off. Is it OK to allocate them Chelsea Bridge Road for loading?"

The deputy consulted a map.

"So far as I'm concerned, yes. One moment. Tell him the home secretary and the commissioner will be coming at. . . ." He hesitated and turned inquiringly to his superiors. "In twenty minutes?"

Reluctantly the home secretary nodded agreement. The sooner he returned to the penal reform debate, the better. He had already been away from it half an hour.

At the mobile police station in Grosvenor Gardens, the bus station official waited impatiently. Having successfully argued his way through the inner barriers, he was growing more indignant by the minute. As soon as Sturgess put down the phone he burst out.

"I've thirteen hundred passengers stranded. Thirteen hundred and forty-two at the last count. The cafeterias and waiting rooms are overflowing. If you won't let us run buses then you can look after them. I can't be responsible."

"We're allocating you a loading area in Chelsea Bridge Road, outside the cordon."

"And how are the passengers going to get there?" demanded the official irately.

Sturgess' patience snapped.

"Walk. You're bloody lucky the plane didn't land on you. Take a look at the railway station and then tell me you've got problems!"

"This is outrageous."

Realizing that he had just done the one thing a police officer should never do—lose his composure—Sturgess paused. When he spoke again it was with stony politeness.

"We are very busy," he said. "The most we can do is detail half a serial of policemen to escort your pas-

173

sengers. That's two sergeants and ten men." They were his only reserve at the moment, standing waiting by their "pixie," as the police called a minibus.

Sturgess went to the door of the caravan, looked around and called out, "Sergeant Smith. Take half a serial with this gentleman and clear the bus station passengers to Chelsea Bridge Road, please."

Sullenly the official left.

"Some people are enough to make a saint blow his halo," muttered Sturgess to no one in particular, then realized that a well-dressed swarthy-faced man was standing in front of him.

"Commander Thompson?"

"The commander is busy, I'm afraid. I am his assistant."

"My name is Allom, first secretary at the Israeli Embassy." The man reached into his inside coat pocket and pulled out a blue diplomatic certificate of identity. Sturgess quickly compared the photograph inside with its bearer and handed the card back.

"What can I do for you, Mr. Allom?"

"One of our diplomats was traveling on the aircraft. Maier." He spelled out the name. "Ben Maier."

"There's not much hope, I'm afraid. I understand there were no survivors from the front of the plane, and that's where the first-class compartment was."

"Ours is not a rich country. We always travel economy."

There was neither rebuke nor humor on Allom's face. He spoke flatly, yet somehow impressively. It occurred to Sturgess that this man was tougher than the usual run of diplomats. He motioned the Israeli up the steps into the caravan. "You can speak to the Scotland Yard casualty bureau direct from here. I believe two passengers from the rear part did survive."

"Thank you. Naturally we are concerned for his life or, if he is dead, for his body and possessions."

"You'll have to ask the commander about that," said Sturgess. "However, he's waiting for the home secretary to arrive. He'll be tied up for some time."

Inside Victoria Station, the effects of the fire were forcing Jim Donaldson to reassess his objectives. What had been a recognizable aircraft fuselage after the crash was now reduced to a blackened skeleton, deep in whitish aluminum ash. The only parts of the DC-10 to survive the fire were the forward cabin, which had broken off from the main length of the fuselage in the crash, and the tail, which had done the same and was perched grotesquely in the station roof.

Gazing at the charred wreckage, still smoking although everything was slimy with the fire fighters' foam, Donaldson guessed what must have happened during the fire. The intense flames had seared through the cabin roof, immediately turning the fuselage into an open-ended cylinder, a chimney up which the blaze roared as though in a blast furnace. Because the rear end was highest, the fire had swept away from the nose section toward the tail, which bore deep scorch marks as evidence. But the foam had been spurted all around quickly enough to hood the fire in. It was the center part of the plane that had burned most savagely. Seats, carpets, lockers, the interior furnishings which designers call "falsework," all had been consumed, and with it the bodies trapped inside.

Even now the heat made the wreckage unapproachable, and the stench was overpowering.

Donaldson stood on the concourse, so depressed he was heedless of the firemen and rescue workers milling past him. Before the fire, most of the DC-10's two hundred and ten thousand component parts and forty miles of wiring had been identifiable, sheared or twisted perhaps, yet complete enough for an investigator to deduce a great deal from them. In particular they would have revealed any failures in the electrical circuits or in the complex systems of rods, cables and hydraulic jacks that operated the aircraft's flying controls. Some of the cables and the fittings at the end of the hollow control rods might still survive. But overall the fire had severely complicated his job. As he methodically wrote down his observations he decided that he ought to now limit any further damage by well-meaning rescue teams and, above all, recover the flight recorder. His airframe assistant had brought diagrammatic drawings of the DC-10's construction. These showed the flight recorder housed close to the frame of the rear cargo door on the port side, within the pressurized hull, though very close to the tail. The cockpit voice recorder, which monitored the crew's conversations, was there, too. Finding these boxes was going to be a difficult and dirty task. It was, however, one that he preferred to undertake himself. He pulled on his yellow plastic overalls and went in search of the chief fire officer.

Plowden had established a vantage point for himself in the corner of the British Caledonian Air Terminal, on the other side of the wreck. Perched up on steel supports above platforms 15 and 16, it had been a glass-walled one-story structure nestling beneath the station roof. Now all the glass was shattered, leaving the offices exposed with desks and telephones still intact, looking curiously out of place, as though an earthquake had left them miraculously untouched. Plowden was standing at the corner, a conspicuous figure in his heavy serge uniform and white helmet. Donaldson shouted up to him.

"Can you spare a moment?"

"Come on up."

Donaldson trotted up the escalator, feeling unbalanced because it was not moving, and joined Plowden. Looking down at this side of the wreck, at the derailed carriages and the confusion of debris on the platforms, he realized the fire had radically changed more tasks than just his own. Now it was possible for a whole range of winches, jacks, hoists, saws and oxyacetylene cutting tools to be brought into use. Where before firemen had labored in small teams, trying like individual craftsmen to prize out the living, now they were extracting the dead with considerable mechanical backup. The sounds that filled the air were the hammerblows and sharp cracking noises of the breaker's yard. Only in a few places where survivors might still lie entombed were the firemen taking apart the wreckage with extreme caution, bringing out the bodies under the direction of the senior medical officer. Finally, there was the most grisly change of all. The dark gray plastic sacks provided by Hanson's were being put to use, bulging with the shapes of what had been limbs and torsos and labeled with the part of the wreck in which they had been found. Freshly arrived squads of soldiers, guardsmen from the London duties battalion, were humping these sacks onto army trucks for removal to the mortuary hastily set up in tents at Chelsea Barracks. The loading of the trucks was hidden from the public and the press by canvas screens.

"The boys are getting their teeth into the job now," said Plowden, jabbing a finger at the men laboring below.

"Rough handling could damage my airplane!" yelled Donaldson above the din.

The unintended humor hit Plowden like a steam hammer, smashing the accumulated tension of the past three hours. He let forth a great bellow of laughter.

"Damage your airplane! Have you seen it recently? That's a good one, that's a bloody good one."

"You can laugh." Donaldson was unamused. "I have to transport every single damn fragment of that DC-10 down to Farnborough and piece it together again on a hangar floor."

A jolting, clanging crash obliterated the last of Donaldson's words. Railway engineers had succeeded in winching two compacted coaches apart before lifting them back onto the tracks. But Plowden caught the word "Farnborough" and guessed the rest. The Royal Aircraft Experimental Establishment at Farnborough in Hampshire was where the remains of aircraft were usually taken for examination after fatal accidents.

"Understood," he replied. "I've warned my crews to take care."

"And the railway engineers, if you're controlling them."

"For a while yet. Until we have the last body out. Could be Saturday. The nose of the plane is a solid mass, like sardines in a tin."

"I know." Donaldson needed little reminding. Then an idea occured to him, and he turned to face Plowden. "Can you do me a favor?"

"Go ahead."

"Can Melville be seconded to me?"

Plowden was surprised. He did not know that earlier his divisional officer had lent Melville to the accident inspector.

"Melville has responsibilities," he said cautiously.

"Listen, Chief Officer. As I told you before, I have to find the flight recorder. I may also have to hunt for other things I don't necessarily want the world to know I'm interested in. If your Fire Brigade is going to be here another day and a half, the best person to help me with recovery would be a fireman."

Plowden considered this. He would be lucky if he saw his own bed tonight. But he looked after his men better than himself.

"I've had to call in reliefs for some crews already," he said. "A fire as hot as this takes all the stuffing out of a man in minutes. Melville's only human."

"He understands what I'm after," insisted Donaldson.

"How come?"

Donaldson explained, and Plowden relented.

"All right. I'll have him report to you. But I've an idea he's on duty again tomorrow. If that's the case, he must have a rest period tonight. That's an order."

"Thank you," said Donaldson simply, and hurried away down the escalator. His next target was the railway engineer. He found him directing efforts to extricate the coaches on platforms 14 and 15, almost beneath the air terminal. He introduced himself and then came straight to the point.

"I'm worried about damaging what's left of the aircraft," he said.

The engineer looked at him in amazement.

"I'm serious," said Donaldson. "I have to salvage every bit I can, and as intact as possible."

The engineer pointed down the platform. The crumpled, but unburned forward section of the DC-10, perhaps fifty feet long, lay, supported partly by the hotel wall, partly by the carriages on which it had fallen. Furthermore, the impact had made the train at Platform 14 keel over sideways, so that it was derailed and leaning against the train next to it.

"We'll have to jack up that section of the plane before we can winch those coaches out," he said. "Not that we can start properly until the firemen give the OK. Apparently there are a lot of corpses in that end."

"Can you get a crane in first to remove the fuselage?" suggested Donaldson.

"Pretty well impossible, I'm afraid. We have to clear a track for the cranes, and as they're steam-operated and burn coal, we can't bring them in until there's absolutely no fire risk. At a guess it'll be twenty-four hours before we get one in. Meanwhile, we'll use our heavy hydraulic jacks."

A familiar unsparing voice interrupted them. It was Mick Melville, the sweat running down his face, his thick uniform tunic sodden. He wiped his face with the back of his hand.

"The chief sent me across," he said impatiently. "What's the problem this time?"

The fireman's tone took Donaldson aback, until he realized that it was due to tiredness, not hostility.

"The flight recorder. It'll be in the plane's tail and that's a good forty or fifty feet up in the roof."

"Is that the thing they call the black box?" asked Melville, his curiosity aroused.

"Correct. Only it's painted dayglo orange or possibly red."

"Let's get around there," said Melville decisively.

Accompanied by the engineer, they made their way to the concourse, where firemen were extricating more savagely burned corpses from the wreck and onto the end of platforms 9 and 10. Above them the airliner's huge tail, itself as large as an old DC-3 transport plane, hung in the girders, held up by the solid brick wall between the two railway stations. The fuselage of the DC-10 had broken apart ahead of the horizontal tail, and they could see the inside of what had been the extreme end of the rear cabin.

"Like looking into a house when a wall's collapsed," commented Melvile.

"Must have cracked just ahead of the rear pressure bulkhead," said Donaldson reflectively. "Probably when the rear engine broke free."

He gazed up at it and thought he could distinguish the frame of the cargo door in its underside. "There's a good chance that the recorders are there."

"What we need," said Melville, "is a hydraulic platform. Like they use for cleaning streetlamps from. Only ours are stronger."

"You'll risk it sinking into the tarmac," said the engineer.

"I'll chance that. The question is, can we bring it here at all? It doesn't need much clearance when it's wound down."

"You could bring it in the cab road on the Chatham side and then through the arch."

"Right," said Melville. "We better find some men to clear all this debris and cut away the ticket barriers."

The buckled wrought-iron gates between the concourse and the platform would be an obstacle.

"How long will it take?" asked Donaldson, checking the time. It was 6:11 P.M. by his watch.

"Could be an hour, could be more. There's a lot of junk in the way."

There was indeed. Although these two platforms were clear of the main wreck, they had been showered with boxes and cases from the rear hold and with pieces of roof.

"You find a gang of workmen," Melville told the engineer. "I'm going to call up control to send the gear."

The two men went off, and Donaldson began photographing and sketching the position of the tail. As he did so he began to realize that more of the wide horizontal surfaces of the tail seemed to be missing

180

than he would have expected—in particular, parts of the trailing edge and the elevators.

Punctually at 6:20 P.M. a procession of black saloon cars drew up in the station forecourt. Policemen stepped forward to open the doors and Thompson came briskly to attention and saluted. On both sides photographers swarmed around recognizing the home secretary's schoolmasterish appearance and thick gray hair, flashbulbs flickering as fast as gunfire. A Cabinet minister was good copy. Better yet, he was accompanied by his junior minister, the secretary of state for aviation, who was often imprudently outspoken.

"You've a job on your hands, Commander. A dreadful business."

The home secretary knew Thompson already and shook hands warmly.

"Have you met the secretary of state for aviation? He joined us at Scotland Yard."

Before he could reply one of the reporters shouted, "Will you make a statement, Minister?"

"Gentlemen, gentlemen," Thompson intervened reprovingly, aware that every word and every gesture of the ensuing minutes would be mercilessly exposed on film and in print.

The home secretary raised his hand for silence. "I will talk to the press when I've had a chance to see for myself. Lead on, Commander."

As they emerged onto the concourse, close to the taped-off area arranged by Chisholm for reporters, the home secretary stopped, blinking as though unable to believe the scene was real.

"Good God," he whispered. "Is that what happens?"

Straight ahead of them two firemen were carrying a dark shape on a stretcher. As the official party arrived a television crew had beamed a powerful light onto the scene, abruptly revealing what the previous dimness had hidden. The shape was the legless trunk of a body, charred by the fire, recognizable more by the remnant of an arm hanging from it than anything else.

181

As the home secretary gasped, Thompson muttered, "Excuse me, sir," and leaped across to the TV crew.

"Stop," he commanded furiously. "You cannot show that. You cannot let relatives see that. Stop."

Reluctantly the cameraman turned away and focused on the VIPs instead.

"Thank you, gentlemen," said Thompson, irony mixed thickly with anger in his voice, and walked back, reflecting instantly that this had been exactly the kind of outburst he was schooling young Colin to avoid. But the home secretary welcomed the action, albeit in too quiet a voice for the reporters to hear.

"Quite right, Commander. There are things the public should not see. Let us hope the news editors have a better sense of discretion."

As the commissioner added his approval the home secretary gazed at the wreckage, into which the firemen were cutting further and further.

"Appalling, truly appalling," he exclaimed. His horror was not feigned for the cameras. Though a shrewd politician, he was also a humane man, and the briefing he had received on the way had not prepared him for such bloody destruction. There always was a difference between the calm appraisal the police made of any event, and the drama that a journalist—or a politican—would see in it. But it needed no sense of the theatrical to see this disaster in the starkest terms.

"I should like to talk to some of the rescue workers," he said shortly, and launched into the routine of asking questions that would both show the government's concern and furnish him with further detail for his House of Commons statement. With officials trailing behind, he was introduced by Chief Fire Officer Plowden to several firemen, listened sympathetically to the tired and sweaty crews' account of the fire, and finally asked Plowden himself, "Do you think you will find any more survivors?"

"Unlucky number or not," said Plowden, "thirteen is the number we've found living since the fire, and they were in railway coaches well away from it. No, Minister, I'm afraid the hope is remote."

In the course of half an hour he did the rounds of doctors and ambulancemen, thanking volunteers from the St. John Ambulance Brigade and the Red Cross, congratulating the WRVS for their continuous supply of tea and sandwiches to the firemen and police, learning that all the casualties would have been found hospital beds by 7 P.M. or earlier, taking a quick look at the temporary mortuary.

"The full-scale one is being set up in Chelsea Barracks," Thompson explained.

Finally, Donaldson was located and ordered to abandon his investigations temporarily.

"Not to beat about the bush, Mr. Donaldson, do you know what caused the crash?"

"It's impossible to say at so early a stage, sir. There is evidence of the rear engine having failed and caught fire. . . ."

"For what reason?"

Donaldson appealed indirectly to his own boss, the chief inspector of accidents, who was among the covey of attendant officials.

"I'm sure my chief inspector would agree," he said steadily, "that it would be most unwise to comment until a readout from the flight recorder has been studied."

It was as near a straight rebuke as a civil servant can give a minister. The secretary of state, a young rising star of his party, quickly interposed. This was an unique opportunity to promote his own views about the siting of airports.

"Whatever the outcome of the investigations," he said sententiously, "this crash is basically the price Londoners are forced to pay for the approach path to Heathrow passing over the city. It is the price the many have to pay for the convenience of the few who fly."

In the background the reporters scribbled in their notebooks, straining to hear the conversation against the continuous noise of salvage work.

"Forget the polemics, John."

The home secretary silenced his junior minister and turned to the chief inspector.

"Well?"

The chief inspector chose his words carefully.

"No risk is one hundred percent avoidable, Minister. But the chances of an accident are appreciably less during the approach, at low power, and under radar control, than during the steep climb after takeoff. As you know, the takeoff patterns avoid the city. The very high safety standards of most airlines, all operating multiengined aircraft, made a crash such as this unlikely. Most unlikely. But unfortunately not impossible."

Donaldson listened appreciatively. Statistically the average citizen was in far greater peril of being killed by a passing car than by an aircraft. It was the luck of the devil that Aerospace had been allotted a secretary of state who saw more political advantage in restricting flying than in promoting it.

The home secretary consulted a fob watch, drawing it from his waistcoat pocket.

"Ten to seven. I must be getting back to the House. I suppose I had better say a few words to the press first."

Thompson waved the reporters forward.

"The minister hasn't much time, gentlemen, so keep your questions short, please."

The press surged forward, jockeying for position, photographers holding cameras above their heads for a better shot. With difficulty Thompson persuaded them into a half circle. The home secretary stepped forward, bathed in fierce white light from the arc lamps that had been allowed in. A dozen microphones were thrust out toward him.

"First of all," he said, almost shouting to be heard, "we should all recognize the superb work being done by the firemen, the police, the ambulancemen and all the voluntary services"—he held up a piece of paper that Thompson had given him—"and I have here a message of sympathy from Her Majesty the Queen to the bereaved and the injured. I shall be reading the full text to the House of Commons shortly, and it will then be released."

A babble of voices started up the moment he paused. He raised his hand in protest.

"Please. . . ."

The fraction of silence that followed was cut into by the same rasping Australian who had earlier floored Thompson with a question.

"Atlantic Airlines have had two major crashes in the last year. This makes three. Sounds like a damn lousy safety record. Any comment?"

There was a sudden, total hush; then the other reporters broke into a buzz of whispering. Donaldson paled; whoever that Australian was, the bastard had done his homework. The home secretary turned aside to the chief inspector.

"Is that correct?"

Perplexed, the chief inspector looked at Donaldson. Immediately everyone else did the same, aware of a sudden spark of tension between the two officials.

"You fellers must know," yelled the Australian.

Donaldson gritted his teeth, excruciated by what must inevitably follow. If ever he had known a moment when the truth would do harm, this was it. A press witch-hunt could prejudice his whole relationship with the American accident inspectors, let alone with the airline, just when he would most need their cooperation. Why could not the bloody politicians keep their noses out of investigations?

"It is correct, Minister," he said. "One at Tampa in Florida and the second last month in the sea off Bermuda."

He had spoken so quietly that only a few of the reporters at the front heard. Immediately a jabbering of questions broke out among them.

"What did he say, Jack?"

"Was that Bermuda?"

During these few seconds of excitement the home secretary came to a conclusion. His horror at what he had seen was genuine, and there was a grain of logic in the undersecretary of state's view, quite a bit of logic. Above all, there was a need for the government to be seen to act swiftly after such a catastrophe. He had intended merely to announce the official inquiry, which of course Donaldson had already begun. Now he would go further. Once again he raised his hand for silence.

"I understand that our friend here is right." He gave a faint acknowledgment to the Australian whom the arc lights' glare prevented him from seeing. "An official inquiry into the crash has been instituted, and a report will be published in due course. Meanwhile, the public have a right to further assurances. Many thousands of homes lie beneath the approach path to Heathrow. We cannot allow the appalling loss of life and destruction that we all witness here to be repeated. Both I and the secretary of state for aerospace and shipping have the highest confidence in the air traffic control system at Heathrow and the experts who man it. They are among the finest in the world. But in the last resort the safety of an aircraft depends on the experience of its pilots and the quality of its maintenance. In addition to the accident inquiry, the government will institute an immediate investigation of the safety records of all airlines using British airports. If any fail to meet our standards or refuse to cooperate we shall unhesitatingly ban them. The ghastly tragedy here today is proof enough that we cannot condone rogue operators."

He emphasized the last words, allowed a second for them to sink in and then concluded with a totally political declaration which he would reiterate later to the House of Commons.

"Small independent airlines have a role, a limited one in the government's view, but only—and I repeat, only—if they maintain the same exacting standards as the state corporation."

"And make the same losses?" called out a reporter.

It was an ill-judged remark, and the home secretary seized on it.

"The loss we cannot afford is the terrible loss of life here today. Now, if you will forgive me. . . ."

He retreated from the microphones and, disregarding a volley of further questions, turned his back on the press and shook hands with the officials. As he thanked Donaldson he remarked, "That Australian blighter nearly upset the applecart, didn't he? Too bright by half. Lucky you knew the facts."

"Nearly!" Donaldson thought as he watched the VIPs leave, escorted by Thompson. "Bloody totally. And when the truth comes out that wily old fool will eat his words without even noticing he's swallowed them." It was not often that Donaldson felt unashamedly vindicative to another fellow being. Thinking of Bill Curtis, a first-class pilot, impaled and crushed on the control column, he was still repeating, "Rogue operators, Jesus wept," when he remembered that he ought to telephone his wife, Jane. This in turn reminded him that he needed to commandeer a proper office for himself and his staff. Keeping as far as possible from the press "pen," he crossed to the eastern side of the station, noticing that all but seven or eight of the injured had been removed, and searched for Chief Superintendent Chisholm. He found him outside in Hudson's Place with the ambulance officer.

"So it would be preferable to ask the army to shift the bodies?" Chisholm was saying.

"It would," the ambulance officer replied. "Even when the last of the injured are out of here in a few minutes' time, we'll still have a lot of cases to transfer between hospitals."

Donaldson listened to them with growing impatience and then interrupted with his request. Chisholm glanced at him wearily.

"All the ground-floor rooms are in use for lost property and documentation, and likely to remain so. You can have one of my police offices on the first floor."

The chief superintendent excused himself and guided Donaldson up a narrow staircase into a long high corridor.

"You've got the lighting going, too," observed Donaldson.

"This Chatham side is very little damaged," said

Chisholm. "We could have run emergency generators from the start. It was only the fire risk that stopped us. We might even have a few trains running tomorrow, though we've a mammoth lost property hunt on our hands."

"If you find any small pieces of aircraft, you might return them to me."

Chisholm looked at Donaldson sharply, uncertain whether or not he was joking.

"I'm serious. There may have been fragments breaking off as she came down. Aluminum isn't such heavy stuff. Small bits could be lying up there in the roof gutters. I'd be grateful if you could check the whole area."

"I'm not making any promises," said Chisholm, "not until the bodies and property are accounted for." He stopped and opened a door halfway along the corridor. "Here. You can base yourself in this one."

Donaldson found himself in a big square yellow-painted room, furnished with a plain desk, chairs and a telephone. "Couldn't be better," he said warmly. "I'm most grateful."

"Ask the police officer downstairs if you want anything," Chisholm replied and was gone.

Five minutes later Donaldson was on the line to his wife. As always when there was an emergency, he found himself talking in the same tired domestic clichés. "Darling, I'm sorry. Truly. It was unavoidable. Yes, I know I only got back yesterday. But I was on duty and if you're on duty, well, you are on duty."

He needed no explanation of Jane's state of mind. Since the call from the department warning her that he was on an accident, she would have been fretting around the house, unable to decide what to do next: pouring herself a drink, going to the kitchen and wondering whether or not to start cooking supper, wandering back to the sitting room, generally working herself into a state. She had sounded flustered when she answered and it left him ashamed.

"Why the hell can't they put someone else on?" she suddenly demanded.

"I wish to God they had."

"No, you don't. You love it. You love the drama and being at the center of everything. What about me? Where do I fit in?"

Donaldson bit back a reply. She sounded distraught. He temporized.

"I promise you, if I could duck out of this investigation I would."

"It's all very well saying that." There was a sharpness in her voice which he had seldom heard before. "Listen, Jim Donaldson, I've had enough of this. You come home after three weeks away and spring the idea of moving to America on me. Then in two shakes of a duck's tail you're off again. You yourself said it all needed thinking about. Well, it does! I've thought a lot about the idea. I want to know a lot more. Will you please behave like a normal husband for once and come home?" She was standing in the hall, talking on the phone extension on the table by the stairs. Somehow standing up made her feel more aggressive. "I repeat, will you please come home? I need to talk to you."

Reluctantly, Donaldson realized that he would have to comply, even though there could hardly be a worse moment to disappear from the scene of the crash.

"Jane," he said, trying to convince her, "we haven't located the flight recorder yet. We should find it in the next couple of hours. As soon as the recorder is safely on its way to the lab I can knock off for the night. I suppose the Waterloo trains will be running as usual. It's just after seven now. Unless I ring again, I'll be on the nine forty-two."

"Can't you catch an earlier one?"

"No, no, I can't. Everyone else is going to be here all night. And tomorrow night probably. Please be sensible, Jane."

"Don't you dare miss it."

If Jim Donaldson had been the kind of man who enjoyed dramas, he might have spat back at her. As it was he said, as gently as he could, "Jane, my love, I promise to be on the nine forty-two. Meet me at the station."

At much the same time as Donaldson resumed his search for the flight recorder, Saul Horovitz, the deceptively sleepy-eyed counselor at the Israeli delegation to the United Nations in New York, took a call from the London embassy. Most other diplomats were still at lunch. Horovitz had been too busy to eat. The pressures of preparing for the next day's Security Council meeting were unyielding. The documents Ben Maier was carrying would be crucial evidence supporting the Israeli case, which Saul was having to prepare on the basis of coded telegraphic summaries. A set of photocopies sent conventionally by diplomatic courier would not arrive until the next day's diplomatic pouch. The instant Saul heard there was a London call he guessed that something had gone wrong. His colleague across the Atlantic spoke guardedly, but the import was clear.

"If there is any hope of survivors, telephone again as soon as possible. I assume the cargo will not arrive in time."

"Even when it is found there will be the usual formalities."

Saul understood the implications. When the luggage and personal effects had been identified, the British customs officials would examine them. Who could tell the difference between diplomatic and ordinary baggage? The mere fact that the embassy was making inquiries would arouse interest. So even after Ben Maier's briefcase had been found, it would be surprising if it was not "lost" a day or two longer to allow the British intelligence service to photograph the contents. Saul pondered, elbows on his desk. Somehow the Security Council debate would have to be postponed. He rose and walked down the corridor to the head of the delegation's room. Fortunately the ambassador had not departed for lunch either. Saul explained everything and then suggested, "Could we ask the Americans to press for an adjournment of the debate until

Monday? At least we shall have copies of the documents by then."

The ambassador frowned. He was a new arrival. Horovitz had far longer experience of the United Nations.

"I suppose we should be refused if we asked for an adjournment ourselves."

"We should, Ambassador. We can expect the vote in the Security Council to go against introducing this resolution into the General Assembly. Only the Americans could obtain a postponement."

Of the five permanent members of the Security Council, two—the United Kingdom and the United States—could be expected to vote against the resolution. France would probably abstain. The Soviet Union and China would vote in favor. Neither these nor the votes of the countries representing the other regions of the world could pass a resolution if one permanent member was against it. Horovitz was well versed in the mechanics of Security Council meetings.

"Would the British help us?" queried the ambassador.

"By voting, yes. In seeking an adjournment, possibly not."

"And which other countries have asked to speak?"

"Both the Saudi Arabian and Mauritanian delegates have declared an interest. It will be the usual charade."

Horovitz was a realist. Speeches at Security Council meetings were set piece affairs, often abusive, always predetermined. What really influenced voting was the preliminary discussions in the corridors and offices of the huge building. Immense effort went into the canvassing of votes.

"I shall visit the American delegation immediately," said the ambassador. "One other thing worries me." He pressed his stubby fingertips together, the strong calloused fingers of a soldier who had risen through the ranks to general before he became a diplomat. "About the copies I am less happy."

"The photocopies made at the Hakirya will be perfect. We should have to circulate copies to the fifteen Security Council members in any case."

"Their authenticity will be challenged. Inevitably. The Arabs would claim the originals were a forgery. But there is always a feel about genuine documents. You, Saul, you are a man of culture, a man of the city and civilization. You would know if a porcelain cup or a painting had the quality of its period. Me, I have the instinct for the scraps of paper captured in a battle, markings on maps, the notes for briefings, and the way a fighting man folds these things to thrust them in his pocket. The guerrilla plans will ring true in that way. We must be able to show the originals."

The ambassador, reverting as he often did to his army ways, crashed his thick fist down on the desk.

"Tell London they must be recovered. And we must secure an adjournment of the debate. Now while I arrange to visit the American ambassador, you go and break the news to Ben Maier's wife."

"I am waiting to hear from London if there are any survivors."

An idea occurred to the ambassador.

"Saul," he said, "I am a brutal, unfeeling soldier. . . ." Saul Horovitz waited, his expression displaying suitably attentive interest. "Suppose we sent Connie Maier to London. Could a bereaved and tearful widow extract Ben's belongings from the British more easily than the embassy?"

Saul blinked and hesitated, for once embarrassed.

"Ambassador, I had the same thought. I have since dismissed it. The couple were only married two years ago. She has only been to Israel once, to meet her in-laws, and she is only half Jewish and wholly American. Her loyalties are to Ben, not us. Furthermore, she is a clearheaded, determined, wealthy girl. If she decides to see how and where he died she will. Maybe in London they can enlist her help. But my advice to her as a friend would be not to go. Only anguish can result. It will be like tearing the nerves out of living flesh. I could not ask her to do that."

"She's a doctor, a pathologist. Doesn't she spend

her working life examining corpses that have been fished out of the East River?"

"It would be a grave mistake."

The ambassador capitulated.

"Handle it your way, Saul. You are the diplomat."

If it was a gibe, Horovitz disregarded the implication. In his own office he read a telex from London that there were two survivors, both from the economy class, neither identified. Forty minutes later a delegation chauffeur deposited him at Bellevue's bleak entrance driveway. The hospital was doing good business, Saul reflected. There was a queue at the reception desk, and the main hall was jammed. He decided to find his own way along the coldly efficient gray-green-painted passages to the Pathology Department and was almost there when he recognized something familiar about a white-coated doctor standing conferring with two others ahead of him.

"Connie," he called.

"Why, Saul, whatever are you doing here?"

"Don't tell me we have a voluntary patient," cracked one of the others, a man. But the joke died as he saw Connie's expression change.

"Saul, has something happened?"

Horovitz glanced meaningfully at the two doctors, who discreetly moved away, and against the background of the hospital's continual movement, of patients being wheeled past on stretchers and nurses hurrying with heels tapping on the floor in staccato urgency, he outlined the little he knew. To his relief and slight surprise, she listened almost as calmly as if a totally strange patient were under discussion. Only a tiny quivering around the mouth revealed her agony.

"You said there were two survivors?"

"So far that is all we know of. We do not know their names."

"Out of maybe three hundred?"

"Thereabouts. If the plane was full, I suppose so."

"That's a one in a one hundred and fifty chance. Saul, I have to go there, go to London. If it was one in a ten thousand chance I'd go. He might not live very long." Her voice trembled.

Saul stepped forward, arms outstretched, but she pushed him gently away, shook back the tears and held his hand.

"Take me home, will you, so I can pack. Hold on while I tell the department."

She let his hand fall and hurried off. Not until they were in the limousine's back seat did she cry.

"I've had this premonition, Saul. Ever since Ben phoned me on Tuesday, and even more since you called me about the further delay yesterday."

Saul Horovitz's body slouched exactly as it was, one arm protectively around Connie Maier's shoulder, but his brain reacted as though a gun had been fired.

"Ben phoned?"

"Of course." She was indignant. "To say he would be coming on El Al from London Thursday. Today. Ben always phoned me if he was going to be late, even half an hour. This was the longest we've been apart since we married."

It was a rule that Israeli diplomats never spoke of their travel plans on an open telephone line. Some rules were made to be disregarded. Not that one. The difficulty, Saul reflected, was that whereas Israel was at war, America was not and Connie was not. You had to be an Israeli to comprehend the nature of the struggle for the nation's existence. He could not expect Connie to understand fully, not when the last outright military conflict had been back in 1973. But Ben!

"He's a good husband," he managed to say.

"The best I have."

It was a brave attempt at humor, and it nearly made her cry again. So she turned to practicalities. "Keep busy on the small things and you'll forget the big problems." That used to be her advice to patients before she specialized. Now it was time for a dose of her own motto. Activity would restore her self-confidence.

194

"While I throw some clothes into a case, would you book me on the first flight to England?"

When they reached her apartment in Tudor City he did so. The first flight they could hope to catch was Pan Am's flight two.

"Economy is full," he reported to her. "Can you afford first?"

"No, but my credit card can."

By the time Saul drove her out to Kennedy Airport Connie was dry-eyed and motivated by the driving aim of finding the man she loved.

After he left her, Saul returned to his office and drafted a short telegram to Tel Aviv and London for encoding. It said simply that he suspected a security leak over Ben Maier's airline bookings and that he would begin investigating.

Afternoon in New York coincides with evening in London. As Connie Maier, Hugh Johnson and a stream of officials, journalists, insurance men and technicians were inundating the airlines with last-minute transatlantic bookings, Jim Donaldson was forty feet up in the Victoria Station roof. The Fire Brigade's hydraulic lift had not been easy to maneuver into position. But now its base was firmly jacked up. Even so, its six-by-four-foot platform swayed slightly, and it could not be raised right into the roof. There were too many obstructions. Melville had to support himself on a sagging roof catwalk as he cut into the hull of the plane. The problem was that hitting the roof had squashed the underside. Comparatively speaking, the frame around the rear cargo door was solid, and on one side of it was a huge circular alloy frame which gave the fuselage its shape and strength. But the stresses of flight are very different from those of a crash. The frame had collapsed as the fuselage broke apart forward of it, leaving the heavy cargo door hanging on a single hinge from the fractured top of the frame. The door was buckled, and to work on the side frame meant removing it. Detaching the hinge would have allowed the door to fall. It took Melville, Donaldson and another fireman half an hour to secure ropes to the curved hatch, cut it free and lower it to the ground.

When this was done, Melville surveyed the frame.

"You did say these boxes of yours are inside here, sir?" he queried.

Donaldson consulted the diagram and craned his head up to look at Melville, sitting straddled on a girder, his head and shoulders inside the wreckage.

"Should be," he said.

"There's a disgusting stench here," commented Melville. His eyes were streaming, and he felt as though he were going to choke.

Donaldson examined the diagram again. "The chemical tank for the rear toilets must have burst. It was located in the back of the hold."

"Trust my luck," shouted Melville. A moment later he called down, "Hey, would the boxes be inside a panel?"

"Possibly," said Donaldson. "There's probably a sign in red. They'd be fixed to a spar or a bulkhead with metal straps?"

Melville was using the shaft of his axe to hammer at a section of bent metal behind the frame.

"I think I've found them," he said excitedly. "Painted red themselves, are they?"

"Red or orange."

"I'll have to cut the panel away. Pass up the saw, will you?"

As the other fireman held out the compressed-air-driven tool, Donaldson hauled himself up onto the catwalk and edged his way along to see what Melville was doing. Deprived of the comforting floor of the hydraulic platform, he suddenly realized how precarious Melville's perch on the girder was. The damaged catwalk felt insecure enough. Far below he saw railwaymen winching out one of the last carriages. He shuffled along closer to Melville. The smell of the toilet chemical was rank and foul. His eyes began to water. Half choking, he said, "Be careful. Remember they're both wired up, but the leads unplug."

Grasping the girder, he tried to get alongside Melville, who was using the saw, its blade screeching on the metal.

"Let me get them out," he shouted above the noise. He was instinctively frightened of the recorders' being damaged, even though he knew their outer cases were made to withstand immense heat and impact.

Melville switched the saw off for a second and half turned. "Better if I finish the job, sir," he said curtly. "I'll hand them out to you."

Five minutes later he released the first and passed it back. Donaldson examined it. The dayglo paint was streaked with muck. The leads hung loose. But it appeared to be all right.

"Thank Christ for that," he exclaimed, noticing that it was made by Sunstrand.

"I'll have the other one out in a tick," said Melville.

While he was waiting Donaldson made an effort to survey the elevator surfaces of the tail plane. To his annoyance his view was more obstructed than it had been from directly underneath at ground level. Nonetheless, he could confirm his general impression that the tail plane might have been damaged before the crash. To check this in detail would mean climbing among girders strewn with small lengths of metal and pieces of glass. It would be a time-consuming business. He decided to leave that to his airframe assistant. Obtaining a readout of the recorders was more important.

Ten minutes later he was safely back on the ground, clutching one box while Melville carried the other.

"So that's what the famous black box is like," said Melville. "I've often read about it."

"The best witness we'll ever have to what happened," Donaldson replied. "Thanks to your efforts." He hesitated. "When do you come off duty?"

Melville glanced at his watch and grinned. "Two hours ago," he said. "Six o'clock. We do two days and then two nights. This was my second day. I come on again at six P.M. tomorrow."

Donaldson remembered Plowden's order about rest periods. "What happens now?" he asked.

"I go back to Greycoat Place, write a report on the actions my watch carried out and try to find a train home." He jerked his head toward the platforms and added, "Something tells me it won't be running from here tonight."

"If you can help me again tomorrow evening I'd be grateful. The chief fire officer has agreed."

"See you at six, then," said Melville cheerfully.

Donaldson thanked him again, and cradling the two recorders, hurried off toward the mobile police station to ask for a car. He had staff standing by at the Data Center to transcribe the tapes and had been worried in case the flight recorder was of the type that used a wire and took days to calibrate. Mercifully the Sunstrand did not. Furthermore, although it might have to be sent to the United States for its final analysis, the Data Center had recently acquired the equipment to make a readout from the Sunstrand's kind of tape. Within twelve hours he would have reasonably accurate information on a host of parameters: all the changes that had taken place throughout the DC-10's flight from Paris and their times, its speed, height, headings, the G forces exerted on it, the angles at which its wings had banked, the degrees its nose had pitched up and down, the thrust the engines were developing, even the operation of the autopilot. From these, given patience and hours of painstaking examination, they could build a diagrammatic picture of the flight. Finally the cockpit voice recorder would reveal what the crew said to each other at the critical moments. Tie these in with conclusions from eyewitnesses' accounts, and he would have a fair idea of where to search for the causes of the crash and would know whether McPherson's theory about the rear engine was likely to be right or wrong.

In fact, Donaldson reflected as he walked, all he would lack was time. His department normally insisted on being allowed nine months to prepare for the kind of public inquiry the home secretary had announced.

But if the home secretary's remarks to the press were anything to go by, that politician would be demanding answers this very weekend. So would Atlantic Airlines. Unless the whole business was amazingly clear-cut, he was going to be forced into a lot of stonewalling against intensive outside pressure. As he reached the police trailer he was pounced on by Colin Sturgess.

"There's a very persistent young lady waiting. Says she saw the aircraft as it came down."

"Has she made a statement?"

Usually the police took statements and he sifted through them to see which would be worth following up.

"Not yet."

"I'll see her shortly. What's more urgent is for a car to run these two boxes out to the CI Data Center at Farnborough. As fast as possible."

"We've a patrol car standing by," said Sturgess, pleased to have anticipated this request. "One of your staff arrived a moment ago too, a Mr. Hearn. He's waiting at the corner with the car."

This was excellent news. Dick Hearn was the department's flight recorder boffin. Donaldson soon found him.

"That was quick work," remarked Hearn appreciatively. Flight recorders were not always located so promptly after an accident.

"Take care of them," sand Donaldson. "Phone me if they yield anything spectacular."

As the car pulled away, he regretted saying that. He had forgotten about his promise to Jane. Damn. Dick Hearn was bound to ring when he wasn't here. Dismissing it from his mind, he returned to the trailer. There was a more substantial favor that he wanted from the police.

"Listen," he said. "We have a major problem over evidence. I am fairly certain that some parts of the aircraft became detached before it crashed. I've already asked Chief Superintendent Chisholm to search the area of the station. Unfortunately bits could have fallen some way back along its flight path."

"Let's have a look at the map, sir." Sturgess stood up and pointed to the big illuminated map of London. "Whereabouts do you think?"

"I'm going to ask the Heathrow air traffic control for as exact a plot of the aircraft's track over London as they can manage," Donaldson replied. "They have the courses they ordered the DC-10 to steer. They'll probably gauge its track accurately to within a quarter of a mile either side. There could be debris three to four miles back along it."

"The commander will love that," exclaimed Sturgess. "Oh, boy, two square miles of streets and gardens to search!"

"Not forgetting the Thames," said Donaldson emphatically. "This is vital, Inspector Sturgess, completely crucial."

"What is?" Commander Thompson was standing at the trailer door.

Donaldson reiterated his request, then, weighing his words, went on, "Commander, please don't misunderstand me, but there are indications that this accident might be due to some form of sabotage. It could be. We should neither of us exclude the possibility." He saw Thompson stiffen and continued in less formal terms. "We're going flat out to discover. Anything that came off the plane will provide clues."

"That's a considerable job, just when I want my patch back to normal."

"It might be advisable to keep the traffic cordon on Westminster and Pimlico until the area has been searched."

Thompson did not like the implicit order.

"There are other factors, Mr. Donaldson. Friday is a working day. You're asking us to paralyze a whole bunch of ministries, the Westminster City Council, all the big office buildings along Victoria Street, countless shops."

Donaldson stepped across to the large-scale map, picked up a pencil and roughed out two lines on it.

"Like a slice of cheese," he remarked, unperturbed by Thompson's controlled annoyance. "A segment west from here to the Houses of Parliament with Westminster and Lambeth bridges at the thick end of the wedge. Mark you, that's a guess. It might be safer to make the wedge extend farther south to the Tate Gallery. I appreciate there would be problems cordoning off streets on the far side of the river."

As Thompson choked back an angry retort, Sturgess interposed, diplomatically breaking the tension building up so unexpectedly between the two men.

"Surely, sir," he said quickly to Thompson, "in many respects it's easier to search the streets by night. We could ask 'L' Division to do the same across the river in Lambeth and Southwark."

"We'll do what we can," decided Thompson. "No promises."

Donaldson thanked him and turned to Sturgess. "Where did you say the eyewitness was?"

"Waiting around the back with a constable."

After Donaldson had gone Thompson swore under his breath. "Did I hear you say that man was God earlier on, Colin? Not in this division he isn't. That was a sensible suggestion of yours, though. Get weaving on it."

Standing with a policeman behind the trailer, her expression apprehensive and shifting her weight nervously from one elegant foot to the other, was a tall, strikingly pretty blonde.

"And I get paid for this, too," thought Donaldson, introducing himself. It was his practice to treat witnesses as though he were meeting them socially, eschewing anything that smacked of interrogation. The less inhibited they felt, the more likely they were to mention the trivial details which often revealed more than the obvious salient facts. His handling of evidence was one of several keys to Donaldson's success.

"My name is Gilly Carslake," said the girl. "I work in an office overlooking the station."

"And you saw the crash."

"I thought it was going to hit us!"

She bit her lip, afraid of sounding too excitable.

The constable had his notebook out and stubby pencil poised.

"I could do with a cup of coffee. Let's go and find one."

He dismissed the policeman with a brief "Thank you, Constable" and motioned Gilly away.

"Everything around here's closed, you know," she said.

"I have a highly secret arrangement with the WRVS," said Donaldson cheerfully. "They'll fix us up."

One of the WRVS large green vans had been moved into the station forecourt. Two women in vivid scarlet aprons with the initials WRVS on them in bold green letters were busily handing paper cups of tea and sandwiches from the back of the van to a fire crew enjoying a temporary break.

"Can you spare us a couple?"

The senior woman appraised Donaldson's yellow overalls and dirt-streaked face, contrasting incongruously with the neatly dressed girl, then recognized him.

"Oh, it's you. I must say you're the strangest pair of rescue workers I've seen yet."

"Actually, I'm a journalist," said Gilly innocently.

"Don't talk to me about press." The woman spoke vehemently. "They're a pack of jackals, just scavengers."

Donaldson concealed his own surprise. "This one's on our side."

"Oh." The woman was slightly mollified. "Well, here's your tea anyway."

Donaldson took the cups and, walking gingerly to avoid spilling the liquid, guided Gilly to his recently established office. Once there he asked casually, "I suppose this isn't an unusually enterprising way of interviewing me?"

"No, no, not at all. The sort of disasters I write about are when two women wear the same dress! I'm assistant editor on a women's magazine. It was because a reporter friend was so interested that I came back again after I'd gone home. Luckily I only live in Chelsea."

Sipping his tea, Donaldson began asking questions and making occasional notes.

"These pieces that seemed to be missing, could you show me where they were?" He swiftly sketched the tail of a DC-10 and pointed at the rudder.

"This upright fin above the engine. What about that?"

"Well, it looked sort of ragged. I mean, shouldn't it have straight edges? But it was the flat part nearest me that actually had pieces coming off. I could see them fluttering in the wind. It was all torn and, well, ragged too, only more so." She broke off. "Oh, I'm sorry, I am hopeless. I don't know any of the right words."

"Don't worry. Go on. This is just what I want."

He coaxed away her shyness. People who knew nothing about aircraft, and so had no bright ideas about the causes of a crash, were invariably the most reliable witnesses. He jabbed the pencil at his drawing.

"The flat part is the tail plane with hinged elevators on the trailing edge. Was the damage there or on the forward edge?"

"Definitely at the back. I could see where bits had broken off."

Donaldson continued making sketches probing the aircraft's attitude, whether the wings were level, how bad the fire was. Finally, he asked, still sounding casual, "By the way, who was the journalist friend?"

"Sam Eckhardt of the *Sunday Post,* do you know him?"

"Curiously enough, we have met," said Donaldson noncommittally, remembering his earlier refusal to make a statement to Eckhardt and wondering what such an attractive girl saw in him.

"What does he make of it?"

Gilly smiled confidentially.

"He has a theory about a bomb. At the moment he's going around the hospitals trying to find out if some important Arab was killed or not."

"Sounds a trifle wild."

"I suppose I shouldn't have told you really."

"I won't split on you. Scout's honor." He raised his right hand. "Thank you very much. Please let me know if you think of anything else."

He almost added, "Or if your boyfriend does," but thought better of it.

"My office is on the twelfth floor if you do need me," said Gilly, rising to her feet.

The brief talk to Gilly Carslake shook Donaldson to the very core. Several hundred eyewitnesses could be expected to answer the police's appeal. How many would prove as useful as she? How many would reveal such potential dynamite? Or be as pleasant to interview? He checked his watch. It was already 8:50 P.M. He ought to be on his way. Hastily he pulled off the plastic overalls and dumped them on a chair, pulled on his own clothes, washed as best he could in the adjoining lavatory and returned to the Chatham side concourse.

Across by the cab roadway he could see the burly figure of Chisholm, apparently directing the clearance of bodies from there. All the living casualties had vanished, although there was one medical team still on hand. He exchanged a quick word with them.

"There can't be many more alive," said the doctor. "We're just hanging on in hope."

Donaldson wished him and the nurses good-night and reluctantly left the station. There were a hundred things he ought to be doing rather than going home. The streets were almost deserted. Outside the ring there were no empty taxis to be found, and there were long queues of people at the bus stops in Parliament Square. So he walked on across Westminster Bridge. The day was dying under a clear sky, streaking the western horizon with red and gold. An airliner descending toward Heathrow passed overhead, a dark silhouette, the underside of its wings catching the last roseate light. Like all pilots, he could never resist watching an aircraft in flight, and he paused on the bridge until it disappeared into the sunset. This started him thinking again about the crash. What possible combination of troubles could have caused it? In spite of his worries about Jane, he was still abstracted when the suburban train deposited him at Epsom Downs station an hour later.

Jane Donaldson was standing by the barrier, a spring coat concealing one of her prettiest dresses. She had decided that the most practical way to put her husband in the mood to discuss the future was to provide a well-cooked elegant dinner, albeit a late one, and to explain her *volteface* calmly. She had drunk a couple of stiff whiskies to fortify herself as she prepared the meal.

The sight of her husband, visibly tired, went to her heart. Much as he infuriated her sometimes, she was fond of him, and it was not out of character for her to play the loving wife. She kissed him and put an arm comfortingly around his waist, guiding him to the car.

"Darling, you look absolutely whacked."

"It's one of the worst crashes I've seen. And there are things about it that don't add up, even at this stage."

"Never mind. Come home and have a hot bath and you'll find something special waiting for you afterwards. You haven't eaten, have you?"

"A cup of tea from the WRVS. Those girls and the Salvation Army are marvels, you know. The volunteers are the one good thing about an accident."

In her relief that he was still unfed, she did not mind his being so preoccupied with the scene he had just left.

As she parked the car outside the front door he touched her hand gently. "Jane, I shall have to be back there first thing. The early train."

"Darling," she spoke with firm cheerfulness, "don't worry. I'll drive you up. We'll start ahead of the rush."

Lying in the bath, steam eddying around him, Jim Donaldson felt he could breathe again. Whatever it

205

was Jane had to say, she was obviously determined not to make a drama out of it. Like many men with analytical brains, whose subconscious burrows through toward solutions while other routine work is being dealt with, he often failed to interpret his wife's seemingly illogical emotions. He could not provide the immediate, intuitive reaction that she needed in a crisis. The result was that their arguments left him as physically wrung out as they left her uncomforted.

When he came downstairs she had lit candles in the dining room. A small jug of dry martinis, jingling with ice, stood ready. She knew he had acquired a taste for them during his American sojourns.

"I'm one or two ahead of you, I'm afraid," she said, pouring a drink into a glass that she had chilled in the refrigerator. "As we have to be up early, I thought we'd eat almost straight away."

Feeling the cold glass in his hand, Donaldson smiled. "You're spoiling me. I don't know why, but you certainly are."

Jane decided that the moment had come for her revelation. She refilled her own glass and raised it high for a toast.

"Here's to our new life in America," she said.

Donaldson stared at her, the martini untasted.

"What did you say?"

"Here's to America! Darling, I've changed my mind. I do want us to go."

She tossed down her own whisky, then saw bewilderment in her husband's face. "What's the matter, Jim? Aren't you pleased? I thought you'd be over the moon." Irritation at his obtuseness began to undermine her good temper. "Don't waste your drink, darling. I made it specially."

Mechanically Donaldson raised his glass, aware that yet again things were going wrong. He made an effort, smiled back at her and tried to sound reassuring.

"I'm just surprised, that's all. Last night you said you didn't want to start all over again."

"Darling, that's exactly what I do want to do. Even

if they have to adapt themselves, it'll give the children a far better future." She spoke excitedly. "I've decided to back you up, to do what's best for all of us."

Despite the benefit of a relaxing bath, Donaldson was bewildered. Only last night she had been in tears because he spoke of possibly going to America. Now she not only had changed her mind completely, but was making it appear that he himself had made a firm decision. He pulled up a chair and sat down.

"This is a bit sudden, isn't it?" he said weakly.

"You're always saying that the middle class has had it." Jane's voice became harsher. "Aren't you? Of course you are. It's your theme song that there's nothing to look forward to in Britain except higher taxes and less freedom."

She was exaggerating. He strove to temporize. "To a point."

"Jim, seventy-five thousand dollars is forty thousand pounds, isn't it?"

"Near enough. More if the pound goes on falling."

"Are you ever going to earn that here?" It was a rhetorical question. She did not wait for an answer. "Never in a million years! And even if you did, three-quarters of it would go in tax. Tell me, Jim, what are tax rates in America?"

"I don't know exactly. I suppose about a third on that salary. It depends on what business expenses are allowable."

"So we'd be hugely better off." Jane was triumphant. "And what allowable expenses do you get against tax as a civil servant?" She laughed scornfully. "None!"

Donaldson was still struggling. There was something she didn't know, and he had to explain it. But she was in full flow, and nothing was going to stop her.

"Darling, you're over forty. I'm thirty-five. We want to be together more. The children need you. I need you. This is a fantastic opportunity."

"There are problems."

"Whatever they are, we can face them together. Anyway, who has problems on an income like that?"

"Darling," he said, "did you see the news tonight?"

"Yes, a bit. The phone rang while I was watching."

"Did you hear the name of the airline?"

"I think so. I don't know. Why?"

"The aircraft was the one I flew back from New York on. The airline is Atlantic, the one that offered me the job. When I told you on the phone that I wished someone else was the investigator, I meant it. They asked me to come and be their safety officer. I'm checking out their safety all right—from the other side of the fence."

"Johnson's offered you the job, that's all there is to it. Why, there's even a cable from him saying he wants to see you."

She wasn't going to let some silly scruple ruin her future. She ran back into the hall, picked up the Western Union cablegram from the table, and brought it back.

"Here! Doesn't this mean he wants you?"

Donaldson read the message asking him to contact Johnson at the Connaught Hotel.

Jane looked at him, her eyes blazing. "That job is yours, Jim Donaldson. If you'll only have the guts to take it."

"Jane, be reasonable, please. Since he sent this the home secretary has lambasted his airline. Tomorrow's newspapers will crucify him. Unless the minister retracts, the only person who can clear the airline's name is me, and I can't."

"Why not?" Jane was determined not to give way to her husband's pigheadedness.

Donaldson sighed. As usual, she refused to understand what his job involved. He would have to explain. Patiently he tried.

"It may be weeks before I've established the cause. I'm not allowed to comment publicly before the report comes out. You know as well as I do that the report can take nine months. Anyway, the accident may prove to be Atlantic's fault. Meanwhile, Johnson's passenger traffic will be hit, his stock market quotation will slump. It's his third bad crash in a year. He's going to want his name cleared now, immediately, and I'm not going to be able to help him. But he'll see me as the one man who can, and I'm going to have to stonewall. I told you, I'm on the fence as far as Atlantic is concerned and Johnson's not going to like it."

But Jane Donaldson was not listening. On this occasion she had no intention of yielding to what was obviously a series of excuses.

"I don't think you care a damn about me," she exploded. "Or your children. The dinner's in the oven, I'm going to bed."

She burst into tears and ran upstairs, sobbing. Donaldson stood still, afraid to follow her. In the kitchen dinner began to burn, filling the room with smoke.

Chapter Seven

At the Farnborough Data Center three technicians were patiently decoding the information on the flight recorders, painstakingly recreating the only accounts there would ever be of what happened aboard Atlantic Airlines' flight 260. No living person anywhere, no observer on the ground, not even the air traffic controller who had listened to the second pilot's last radio transmissions, would ever be able to speak with the same authority as would the tapes from the doomed aircraft. The two automatons were voices from the grave.

Dick Hearn, who had brought them down to the Data Center, longtime specialist though he was in their interpretation, invariably became tense and nervous during the process of unscrambling their information. Each tape presented different problems, and it would be a rash man who stated categorically which one was more important than the other.

The flight recorder, on which much of the development work had been done at the Royal Aircraft Establishment at Farnborough Airfield, spelled out the aircraft's height, speed, course, engine power and various other "parameters" of performance, revealing what had happened mechanically in amazing detail. But it is the crew that tells the machines what to do, and their reasons for doing so would emerge from the cockpit voice recorder, an innovation to which some pilots had objected as an invasion of privacy. The age-old wish "If only walls could speak" was made reality by the four microphones positioned on the flight deck which fed their separate clues into the DC-10's cockpit voice recorder. Hearn knew that one microphone would have listened throughout the flight to Captain Bill Curtis, another to his second pilot, a third to the engineer seated at the wide instrument console behind them, while a fourth "area microphone" would have picked up remarks exchanged by all three, plus a multitude of other sounds: engine noise, the clunk of the nose-wheel retracting into its bay underneath the floor after takeoff, the stewardess' chat as she brought in coffee, the rustle of maps, the grinding whir as the flaps were lowered on the approach to landing. Then, Hearn presumed, there would be the blare of warning horns when the engine blew up, Curtis' crucial orders, the terrible crunch of the impact—and sudden silence. All this and more would be on the tape, unless it had malfunctioned or been damaged.

Hearn arrived at the Data Center shortly after 9 P.M. It was a small building on a new industrial estate just outside the perimeter fence of the airfield. Although the Royal Aircraft Establishment was next door the center was a completely separate, commercial concern, and for this reason Hearn had to supervise the readout process. It was not unknown for complex legal actions to hinge on allegations that a flight recorder had been tampered with. Consequently he would have to certify officially that the machines had not been out of his sight from the time Donaldson handed them over right through to the making of master copies of the tapes.

His police car had reached the sprawling town of Farnborough in record time, and in spite of his own excitement at possibly unraveling the mystery of the crash, Hearn could not rush the process. Helped by the waiting computer operators, he carried the two rectangular boxes, still grimy and rank-smelling, straight to a laboratory for examination and photographing.

"Where on earth have these been?" one of the men demanded.

"The lavatory chemical tank in the rear cargo hold burst," Hearn replied tersely. "Let's get on with the visual inspection. This will take all night as it is."

They checked the physical condition of the boxes, noted the serial numbers, jotted down the amount of tape run as shown by a computer in a tiny window and photographed both recorders from various angles.

"Very little damaged, considering," Hearn remarked happily. "I reckon we can unscrew the covers."

Gently they opened up the flight recorder.

The chief computer operator grunted, peering down at the thin metal tape running between the recording heads inside.

"Looks OK. Do you want to play it back through its own heads or fit it onto our rig?"

"On yours," Hearn said. "I'm not taking any chances with this one." It was perfectly feasible to connect up the recorder and use it. But if there was any unseen damage to the heads, you risked affecting the tape.

As the technician prized out the tiny reel Hearn crossed two fingers of his left hand for a second. There, in that thin filament, must lie some of the reasons why at least four hundred lives and ten million pounds' worth of airplane had been lost.

"We'll make the master copy first," he ordered, "then copy it again and put it through the computer."

"What speed do you want it at? The tape's two-thirds used, roughly."

Hearn pondered. That meant there could be the record of twenty or more flights on this tape. The Sunstrand flight recorder ran two hundred hours and would only be taken out and played back if there had been an unexplained malfunction in the aircraft. Otherwise it stayed in place until the tape was finished, or almost. Eventually the whole of this one would have to be processed and examined. But the immediate concern was the DC-10's last journey. How long was a normal London to Paris sector? Fifty minutes or an hour at most. To be safe, he had better check it from the moment the engines had been started up at Orly.

"I'll have the last hour and a half. You can run it at fifteen times."

The tape could be played at the speed of its original recording, at fifteen times normal or one hundred times normal. Fifteen was acceptable if the tape was undamaged.

The operator carefully fitted the tape up onto the rig that would make a master copy on a big reel. He was skillful, but inevitably winding it back and adjusting it took a little while.

"I reckon this will be the quickest part of the night's work," he commented gloomily, looking at the electric clock on the laboratory wall. It was already after 10 P.M. "OK?"

"Go ahead," Hearn said, tense in spite of himself as the runthrough began with a faint humming sound and the reels spun faster. Six minutes later the tape was finished. At least it had not broken. After a brief check the operator announced that nothing appeared to have gone wrong.

"Thank Christ for that," said Hearn, relieved.

Next they went through the more complicated process of simultaneously making a further working copy from the master and producing a digital readout through the computer. While Hearn sealed the original tape against any possible interference, the operator took the master across to the computer console. The two tall steel cabinets housing the computer stood beside a large teletype keyboard, into which he typed his requirements: first the Sunstrand code, which would select the correct computer program; next the "parameters" which they wanted extracted from the tape—the aircraft's speed, height, power settings, rate of descent and so on. He tapped out the order in which these were required and the reply speed. As he did so, it all flashed up on a television type screen above the keyboard for checking.

The clock crept around to a quarter past midnight. Hearn waited impatiently for the technician to press the button that would begin the readout. The ease with which the computer untangled the complexities of the tape never failed to fascinate him. Indeed, the way the flight recorder itself operated was something of a miracle. It took sixty-four readings a second, sampling each parameter in turn and converting it into a digital "word"—which is to say a word made up exclusively of ones and zeros. So the complete tape held a swift succession of these "words" all on a single track. The computer would separate them out and print each of the many parameters separately on a wide sheet of graph paper. Although the result would be incomprehensible to a layman and would have to undergo further conversion before Donaldson could show it to an outside authority, anything peculiar about the parameters would hit an expert in the eye at once.

As the reels turned and the printed readout began emerging from the teletype machine, Hearn could hardly restrain himself from reaching out for it. At length the subdued noise ceased and the technician neatly severed the long coil of graph paper, handing it over with a brief "There you are, sir. Stage two complete."

Hearn held it in both hands, slowly sifting it through his fingers and puzzling over it as a professor might decipher the hieroglyphics on some ancient scroll. He read the termination of activity after Bill Curtis had taxied up to the terminal at Orly on completion of the flight in from New York and London, the same uneventful flight that had brought Donaldson home. He read the preliminaries of departure the next day, the climb out, the cruise, the descent over southeast England. He saw how the DC-10 had leveled out and made various changes of heading. The tiny lines of the digital printout all went either up one square on the paper or along one square, like a child's game. Suddenly, as he neared the end of the coil of paper, these jerky lines all dipped vertically away from their main direction, aberrating violently for a short space.

"Quite some dropout you've got there," commented the technician, who had moved around to watch.

"There is at that," said Hearn, "there certainly is. No ordinary turbulence caused that."

Rapidly he surveyed the short remainder of the paper, saw greater and greater increases in the engine settings and the airspeed accompanied by rapid loss of height, culminating in a total dropout at the very end of the recording. He made some hasty calculations. The first dropout was approximately fifty-six seconds before the final one.

"Something bloody powerful rocked the aircraft there," he muttered. "That was the moment when things went wrong all right."

He turned to the chief technician.

"Later on tonight we'll have to plot this into engineering units. But before that I'd like to hear what's on the cockpit tape. Will you get the studio tape deck ready while I make a phone call?"

Hearn hurried to one of the offices, found a telephone with an outside line and spent a harassing twenty minutes trying to reach Donaldson at Victoria. Eventually the railway police managed to locate McPherson.

"Jim's no around at the moment," said the Scot lugubriously. "He had tae go hame. He has a wee spot of domestic bother apparently."

"Look, Mac. We've just had a look at the raw data. If there wasn't an explosion on that aircraft, then I'm a Dutchman. There's wild dropout on the tape fifty-six seconds before the crash."

"I'm inclined to that opinion myself."

"Will you tell Jim when he's back?"

"When he is," said McPherson sourly.

"Tell him I'll be along with both readouts as soon as I can in the morning."

Hearn rang off and returned to the laboratories, where he watched two copies made of the cockpit voice recorder tape and then played one back. There was a lot of background noise, and the technician frowned as he listened.

"We're not so lucky with this one. It'll need a lot of filtering."

"Do you get double overtime for night work on weekends?" asked Hearn.

"We get reasonable overtime pay." The man was cautious.

"Then you won't mind spending a few hours on this one, will you?" said Hearn cheerfully. "Ideally I'd like a version with basically just the voices. And have both it and the unfiltered one put on Phillips cassettes for Mr. Donaldson. Do you think you can manage a transcipt of the last two minutes as well?"

"It'll be pretty rough. I'm making no promise."

"Well, do your best. I'm going around to the RAE for a spot of kip. I'll be back after breakfast. From now on you don't need me anyway."

"It's all right for some," murmured one of the assistant technicians.

"And better for others," replied Hearn tartly. "At least you boys get overtime. We accident inspectors can do twenty-four hours a day, seven days a week, without earning a penny more."

When he left the Data Center it was 1:48 A.M. on Friday.

As Pan American World Airways' flight two from New York to London passed high over the Irish Sea, flying east into the cloudless dawn of what promised to be a fine, warm day, Hugh Johnson forced himself to swallow some grapefruit and coffee. Not that the meal which the stewardesses in the first class offered him was unappetizing. But as ever on these subsonic overnight flights to Europe, you were served both dinner and breakfast in the space of six hours. He ate now only because he had a grueling day ahead after a sleepless night. To Johnson a man's domestic surroundings, where he fed, slept and made love, were important insofar as they improved his work, or detracted from it, and no further. He reckoned he himself would need someone he could confide in on this trip, so when his wife had declined to accompany him, he had employed unashamed bribery to persuade his daughter, Sharon, to come instead.

"You can have a whirl around Europe after," he had suggested cajolingly, "buy some clothes, have some fun. London is pretty nice in the spring, too."

Johnson had been glad Sharon had come the moment they stepped aboard the 747 at Kennedy. Almost the first person he had seen across the wide cabin was Connie Maier, her face set, her long black hair falling on a black dress. He had been momentarily confused, recognizing her face, but foxed by encountering her in unfamiliar surroundings. Theirs was only a nodding acquaintance. He knew her father better. Then he remembered seeing Connie the previous Sunday at the Westchester Country Club when he was entertaining Donaldson at lunch. It felt like a year ago. All this flashed through his mind as he walked down the airliner's aisle, and as rapidly his instinct had told him what he did not yet know. Being a man who faced life squarely, he had squeezed his way across to her straightaway.

"Why, Connie," he had exclaimed, "what takes you to London?" She had gazed up at him, uncertain of her emotions.

"Ben was in your DC-10," she replied, biting her lip. "Evidently he transferred to it. He was supposed to fly El Al."

"We don't know what happened yet."

"Ben has to be alive, he just has to be alive. I heard there were two survivors. Mr. Johnson, Ben has to be one of them!"

"I pray he is, Connie. I do. This crash is a terrible thing for all of us."

"He's my life, he's what I wake up for and come home for. He's got to be one of those two."

Johnson had perched on the armrest and briefly put a hand on her shoulder.

"If there's anything I can do, Connie, you say."

She had been perplexed, angry, holding back tears. Here was the one man who ought to know something. But even he did not.

"What I don't understand is why Ben changed flights. No one knows. Israeli diplomats always fly El

Al, always. There is one from Paris today. Why the hurry, why the transfer? Oh, why, oh, why, oh, why? He could be safe and with me at the apartment now, instead of. . . ."

Johnson had squeezed her arm momentarily, then risen as a stewardess asked him to return to his own seat.

"Anything I can do," he had repeated lamely.

Her reply was forceful, her voice brimming with subdued fury.

"Help me find Ben. That's what you can do."

This doleful exchange had colored the whole journey for Johnson.

Once they were airborne and at cruising altitude, he had been invited forward to the flight deck where the captain had offered his condolences.

"Bill Curtis was a damn good flier. Everyone respected him."

"Thanks," Johnson had said, "and the DC-10 is a damn fine airplane. There's something wrong about this crash, and that's why I'm going across."

He was touched by the captain's thoughtfulness. Pan Am was his adversary in the business, and it showed the good side of the aviation world that they were giving him every assistance. However, he recognized the bad side waiting for him back in the cabin in the shape of a lean sharp-faced man seated farther back. It was Falkender, an attorney whose specialty was obtaining maximum compensation for air crash victims. Whether he was famous or notorious depended on whether or not he was on your side. To Johnson's relief, the lawyer pretended not to notice him.

Nonetheless, Falkender's very presence on the plane contributed further to Johnson's sleepless night. What had the passengers' compensation figure been on the Turkish airlines DC-10 crash? He recalled a figure of a million five hundred thousand for the death of one Britisher and his wife. Maybe Connie Maier wouldn't win so much for losing Ben and his future earnings. But the tab for a whiz kid executive in a big American corporation, with a wife and three children, and earning around two hundred thousand a year, could reach five million. All Atlantic Airlines advertising had promoted the Blue Ribbon as the executive's choice in transatlantic flying. Falkender could be pursuing the biggest aviation insurance claim ever. The thought was still in the forefront of his mind as flight two began its descent into Heathrow, well on time for its scheduled 7:40 A.M. landing.

"You know, honey," he said to his daughter, "that guy Falkender must see a real killing in this one."

"So? The insurance pays, doesn't it?" Sharon was puzzled.

"It does. And if a reputable law firm were sitting in Falkender's place I wouldn't be so worried. Sure, if negligence was proven they'd take us to the cleaners. But not in the same way."

"I just don't understand."

"Falkender operates on a percentage of the damages he obtains for his clients and his way of maximizing the claim is by building up a climate of public opinion against the airline. He doesn't wait for official findings or inquiries. He assumes the airline must be guilty, so he tries his cases in the press. If we overbooked a flight to Miami five years ago he'll make headlines with it. He'll scream about every last detail of every hazardous situation we've ever been involved in. And with two fatal crashes in the past year he won't have any problem persuading the media to print what he wants either."

"That's terrible. Can't you stop him?"

"Sharon, honey, the only thing that will spike that guy's guns is conclusive proof that the crash was not our fault. If it wasn't."

He lapsed into gloomy silence, adding a moment later, "This is what I wanted that guy Donaldson to prevent."

"Maybe he can help. He's in London, isn't he?" suggested Sharon.

"I cabled him. But he's a government official there, honey."

"Couldn't he still advise you? Privately, I mean. He must know what's going on."

Johnson grinned, his mood momentarily lightened, and stroked his daughter's cheek gently with a forefinger.

"You work on that, honey, if I'm busy. Remember, Atlantic isn't just an airline. It's the roof over our heads, and food and clothing." He touched Sharon's cheek again. "It's our life."

"I'm not stupid," she said, delighted to be actively involved, "even if I am your daughter."

For the brief remainder of the flight, Johnson felt almost cheerful. At heart he was a buccaneer, a man who seized what life offered and never took no for an answer. The more Sharon showed herself to be a chip off the old block, the better he was pleased. Nonetheless, he was tense with the same gut-chewing excitement that he used to experience on bombing missions over Italy during the war, when he saw the flak coming up, bursting in white puffs all over the sky in front of him, and knew he had to fly straight and level through it to hit his target. He still had the feeling as they passed through the tedium of the customs clearance and were met in the Terminal 3 building at Heathrow by the local Atlantic manager.

"The documentation is in the office upstairs. Do you want to go there, sir?" the man asked.

"No. let's get right on to the crash site."

The manager guided them past the benches crowded with Asians waiting for arriving relatives, as Terminal 3 always was toward the end of the week, and paused to introduce Johnson to the ground hostess at the Atlantic counter in the hall, with its illuminated airlines sign.

"We're still having people come here with inquiries," the manager explained.

Johnson thanked the girl for her work, then indicated his impatience to be off. Once they were in the waiting limousine, he demanded the local papers.

"They don't make pleasant reading, I'm afraid, sir."

"Let's have them," said Johnson sharply.

The huge banner · headlines of the *Daily Express* reared up at him.

THOUSAND CASUALTIES IN LONDON AIR CRASH
Minister attacks "Rogue Operators"

Swiftly Johnson flipped through the others. All had variations of the theme. "WORST EVER AIR CRASH" and "AIR CRASH INFERNO" were two. All quoted the home secretary's remarks and Atlantic's accident record.

"Who the hell is this home secretary?" roared Johnson. "How come we're condemned before there's evidence? What kind of a setup is this for Christ's sake?"

Then before the manager could utter a word, Johnson noticed a photograph. It showed Donaldson holding the flight recorder and the caption beneath read "Accident Inspector finds 'black box' clue to horror crash."

"Is Jim Donaldson investigating it?" Johnson demanded.

The manager nodded. "He's in charge. Do you know him, sir?"

Johnson swore. "Do I . . . Yes, I do!"

Sharon had seldom seen her father so disturbed.

"Is that good or bad?" she asked.

"I don't know, honey. I just don't know. But I sure as hell want to see the readout from that flight recorder."

Jim Donaldson was in his kitchen of his Epsom home, grilling bacon, sausages and a tomato. Carefully he broke two eggs into a frying pan, basted them, then assembled the whole meal onto a warm plate, and consumed it with a rapidity that did little justice to its preparation. It was always the same when he had an early start. He wanted something good inside him, and equally he was impatient to be off. Nor did he usually rouse his wife when she had no need to be out of bed. However, this morning she had been ahead of him. As he gulped down his coffee she appeared at the kitchen door, wearing a crisp blue linen dress and her favorite pearl earrings.

"I'm ready when you are, dear," she said evenly.

Donaldson glanced at her, surprised. He was feeling guilty about the previous evening's catastrophe and had half expected that she would have decided not to drive him to Victoria after all.

"You beat me to it," he said with forced lightness. "Coffee?"

"Just a sip."

Before he could move, she walked over to the kitchen table and poured out half a cup from the percolator, then stepped back briefly to catch sight of herself in a little gilt-framed mirror that hung between a rack of herb jars and the wall cupboards. The mirror was an admission that she spent much of her day in the kitchen.

"You're looking pretty good," he commented, still uncertain of her mood.

She smiled. It was true. She had taken a lot of trouble over her appearance while he was feeding himself. Her face bore no sign of the previous evening's tears. What her husband did not know was Jane Donaldson was now totally committed to forcing a change in their way of life. True, it had been partly in deference to her that he had left the air force and joined the Accidents Branch. That was when their first baby was born, and Jane had argued for firmer roots than the continual postings of service life allowed. This time she was really going to bulldoze him whether he liked it or not, and she sensed that Johnson's arrival would give her the opportunity to do so. Somehow or other she would make sure there was no breach between Johnson and her husband. More than that, if necessary, she would engineer things so that her husband became committed to Atlantic Airlines.

"It's your future as much as his," she had told herself as she lay in bed after the quarrel. "You've spent too many years moping around the house when he's away and then getting overwrought and tearful when he's back. You stick up for your rights, my girl."

Forgetting that it was she who had chosen their house at Epsom, she had convinced herself that it was time he went where she wanted. And quite suddenly what she wanted was the good life that America seemed to offer, to break out of this suburban environment with its middle-class worries about rising school fees and rising train fares and whether you could afford a holiday this year because the pound had fallen again. She did not understand why sterling was always falling. Nor why a government that created more civil servants with one hand was set on squeezing the middle class "until the pips squeaked" with the other. She did know, now that the chance was presented to her, that she passionately wanted to live a little, to be able to indulge her whims, to feel that as you grew older you also grew richer, instead of the reverse. Wherever he was, her husband would be a hard worker, it was his nature. And she could profit more positively from this in America. She was not sure exactly what she would say when she met this man Johnson; she sensed that this was a crucial moment in his relations with her husband. She had grasped the implications of what Jim had said and, in his favorite phrase, she would have to "play it by ear." The thought made her laugh.

"What's the joke?" asked Donaldson, perplexed.

"Nothing, dear."

The reply gave him little comfort. His wife's apparent good humor seemed inexplicable, while her calling him "dear" twice in succession made him doubly uneasy.

"We ought to be off," he said. "Are you sure you want to come?"

"I'd like to see a crash for a change instead of only hearing about it. I'd like to see what pays for me and the children. Why should you have all the excitement?"

The hardness in her voice silenced Donaldson, and during the forty-minute drive Jane switched on the car radio. After traffic reports and chitchat on the coming weekend's events, there came one of the frequent early-morning news bulletins.

"The London air crash." The newscaster's phrases were staccato and urgent. "Rescue workers have given up hope of finding more survivors. The total number of dead will not be known until late today when all the bodies are recovered. So far three hundred and eighty-seven have been found, making this the worst air crash in history."

Donaldson reflected that the remaining corpses were probably those compacted in the DC 10's nose. Then he stiffened apprehensively at the newscaster's next sentence.

"Evidence from radio hams, who heard the pilot's last words, suggests that the plane may have been sabotaged."

Donaldson leaned forward and turned up the volume.

"The pilot reported an explosion in the rear engine. He then cried, 'We're going out of control.' Seconds later, the final words 'We're hitting now.' An official inquiry is already under way but Department of Trade officials refuse to confirm or deny the sabotage theory."

Donaldson switched off the radio.

"Jesus, what a mess."

"Was there a bomb?" asked Jane, resolutely keeping her eyes on the road ahead as she drove.

"There must have been an explosion of some kind."

"Well, then," said Jane, in her most practical tone, "if there was an explosion it would have to be a bomb, wouldn't it?"

Donaldson wondered whether to bore her with the technicalities of turbine compressor blade failures and their effects. Unless you had a clear mental picture of the turbine, its short, stubby blades sticking out around its circumference almost as thickly as quills on a hedgehog, with the whole thing spinning inside the engine casing at maybe two thousand revs a minute, it was hard to understand the violent effects of a blade breaking. Only one piece of toughened steel could strip off many of the other blades and cause the engine to disintegrate in seconds. But Jane was far from mechanically minded.

"If something damaged the engine," he replied slowly, "it could come apart almost explosively. But that explanation doesn't ring true to me. It's difficult to think of what could have caused a real explosion except some sort of bomb or warhead."

In his present state of uncertainty, this was more than he would have said to anyone outside his own team of investigators. He would have been horrified had he known it was giving his wife an idea of what she might say to Johnson.

"I thought so," she said triumphantly, thinking how Johnson must react to such a theory. "Do you know something, Jim? I'm not always as silly as you think!"

"Anyway," said Donaldson, relieved at escaping from the subject, "if it was sabotage, we'll find out pretty soon."

Although they reached the approach to Chelsea Bridge before 8 A.M. the traffic was already almost stationary. Temporary roadsigns warned of diversions at Buckingham Palace Road. Evidently the inner cordon was still in operation. Equally clearly, many commuters had failed to heed the broadcast warnings to avoid the Victoria area and were hoping, like Donaldson himself, that an early start would enable them to get through. A double line of vehicles stretched as far as they could see, and the sidewalks were crowded with pedestrians.

"You'd better drop me off and I'll walk," suggested Donaldson as his wife inched the car forward across the bridge.

"No. I've got this far. I'm going on. Haven't they given you a pass or something?"

It took them twenty minutes to cover the next five hundred yards. At the junction where he wanted to turn right the street was blocked by red-and-white-painted trestle barriers and tripods with flashing yellow lights. He produced the black-bound official card bearing his photograph which identified him as an inspector appointed by the minister under the provisions of the Air Navigation Acts, and one of the constables lifted the barrier aside so that they could drive through.

Behind them someone less privileged tooted his horn in annoyance. The road up behind Chelsea Barracks seemed strangely empty.

"There's not much to see," complained Jane, as they passed the British Airways Terminal.

It was true. Apart from eight fire engines lined up by the side of the railway station near the cartoon cinema entrance and a khaki-painted army truck with a group of soldiers in fatigues, the most unusual aspect of the scene was the absence of traffic. That and the large number of policemen, one of whom directed them into a side street to park as they neared the control point.

"It's all inside the railway station buildings," Donaldson explained. "Frankly, that's not a place for sightseers."

Jane bridled, then after a brief argument declared, as though the idea had only that moment occurred to her, "At least I could meet your famous Mr. Johnson."

Donaldson saw a way to sidetrack his wife's unexpected and unwelcome interest in his job.

"Didn't the cable say he would be staying at the Connaught and was bringing his wife over? Even if he comes straight here, she is bound to check in at the hotel. Why not wait for her there and introduce yourself?"

He could hardly have made a suggestion that fitted her intentions better. She made a reluctant show of submission.

"Suppose he isn't there? How can I contact you again?"

"You can always leave a message with the department. Otherwise I'll phone you around teatime," he said and quickly kissed her good-bye.

In Grosvenor Gardens, Colonel Daly, the local American representative of the FAA, was standing outside the police trailer.

"Hi there, Jim," he called out in his amiable drawl. "I was hoping you might show up soon. Hugh Johnson of Atlantic should be here any time. Understand he's driving straight from Heathrow. And not only that," Daly went on, "seems your police have found a few pieces of airplane around the streets."

"Have they?" said Donaldson sharply, excusing himself and hurrying up the steps into the trailer. Colin Sturgess was seated inside, bleary-eyed. Commander Thompson was standing. Both had obviously been on duty all night, and Donaldson felt more than a touch of embarrassment.

"I'm sorry, but we had a spot of domestic trouble last night." The admission hurt. "How goes it?"

"I'm transferring to Rochester Row shortly. I've just come from there," said Thompson. "Chisholm's sorting out the lost property. Apparently the railway engineers have cleared a lot of junk away. I've not had time to see for myself. What with lost children, stranded passengers, angry residents, sightseers, the Coroner's Office, and the press, we've had a night to remember. As if the crash wasn't bad enough, the chaos it brought with it is damn near unbelievable. We've also been hunting for your wreckage."

"I'm truly grateful."

"It's lucky we practice the callup of men into the center of the metropolis occasionally," Thompson remarked wryly. He felt strongly that Donaldson should have kept himself available during the search. "The deputy assistant commissioner drafted almost a quarter of the force on to it. If you count both last night's shift and this morning's, we've had close on five thousand men out. The trouble is that they can't easily tell what is part of an airplane and what isn't. The commander of 'L' Division says he's got a load of assorted scrap piling up at his headquarters across the river in Brixton. A few small bits have been found in Westminster and taken to Rochester Row."

"You will have recorded where you found them all?"

"I imagine so. Certainly the collators at each police station have had orders to do so." Thompson's tone was cold. Then, seeing puzzlement on Donaldson's face, he explained. "The home beat men work to instructions from a collator, an experienced sergeant or constable. Though I say it myself, it's not a bad system."

"So long as we can make an accurate plot of the wreckage trail, I'll be happy."

"I think I can promise that. What we could not do is leave the evidence lying on the street. It's essential to reduce the cordon and start the traffic moving again."

"In fact, sir," Sturgess chipped in, "two largish pieces have been left *in situ*. One's on a school playground and the other in the front garden of a house. Both in Lambeth. They're being guarded until you arrive."

Donaldson's lean face colored. He rubbed one forefinger along the side of his nose, as though soothing away an itch.

"One of the patrol cars can drive you there," Thompson offered, thankful that his own wife had simply commiserated with his being caught by an emergency yet again, letting him get on with the job unworried. To his experienced eye the investigator looked like a man with a lot on his mind and who had enjoyed precious little sleep in spite of going home.

As Donaldson left the trailer he motioned to Daly to accompany him.

"Come along, Colonel. This could be more rewarding than waiting for Hugh Johnson."

Daly followed obediently, wondering why such a quiet, undemonstrative man was speaking so acidly this morning. Then he murmured, "What the hell," to himself and began humming "We're Off to See the Wizard!" as they walked to the white-painted police car. He had done enough standing around.

After they had gone, Thompson gave Sturgess a quick look, one of those almost intuitive exchanges that become possible when people have worked together closely for a long time.

"He could have had a rougher night than we did," said Sturgess.

"Much what I was thinking."

"We could always offer him a bed at Rochester Row. It's nice and quiet in the cells."

Thompson laughed.

"No comment. I haven't met his wife." His tone changed. "Now, my lad, are they ready for us at Rochester Row?"

"They've cleared a couple of rooms for the airline passengers' personal effects and an office for you. But I think we may have underestimated the sheer volume of the luggage. According to the airline, there are four hundred and three suitcases and bags. That's without the freight the plane was carrying. Customs want the whole lot under guard."

"How about using the Military Police building opposite?"

"I'll ask the army. At least it should be secure."

"That could be important," said Thompson abruptly. "There's a lot at stake in this accident, Colin. It may not be only wife trouble that's worrying Donaldson."

"Talking of troubles, sir. We've still got that Palestinian demo on Sunday. Should we have it called off?"

Thompson reflected.

"If Westminister isn't back to normal by then, the commissioner will want to know the reason why. It's not his policy to cancel demonstrations. No. The poor bloody constables will just have to suffer another extra stint. At least they'll get time and a half and another day off in lieu. What else?"

"Documentation is about the worst thing. We're going to end up with enough paperwork to fill a pantechnicon. There've been over eleven hundred injured treated or sent to hospital, about half that number accommodated either by the Social Services or the Salvation Army. Operations says they're jammed solid with calls from relatives, and the Israeli diplomat was here again asking about a passenger called Maier. Incidentally, his wife is flying in from New York."

"He could be alive."

"If not, she could have an unpleasant wait." Sturgess checked the entries on his log. "So far Hanson's has identified only twenty-eight dead who are definitely from the plane. Their man Denman reckons it could be three to four weeks before they finish. That reminds me, sir. The ambulance control officer wants a word."

"What's the problem?"

"He wants to move his Land Rover to the forecourt."

"Give him a shout."

As Sturgess left to fetch the man, Thompson reflected that the handling of this whole incident was entering a fresh phase. While he himself had been shaving, snatching a hasty breakfast and making plans at Rochester Row, the implications of the new day had evidently begun to hit the rescuers on the scene. Dawn always had that effect if you had been working all night. During the darkness you labored on to finish the previous day's task, countering tiredness by an automatonlike determination to reach the set objective. But first light changed everything. However gritty-eyed and sweaty you felt, the routine morning actions of washing and eating, coupled with the rising of the sun, somehow transformed everything, forcing you to think again about what you were doing. Thompson was unalterably a "morning person," and this was the time when his responses were sharpest, even after no sleep.

The ambulance officer, who had taken over only an hour or so earlier, immediately reinforced Thompson's desire to close operations in on the railway station itself.

"It's been eight hours since the last living casualty was brought out," he said. "The chances of finding any more must be pretty slim. The medical teams have all gone. I'm cutting the attendance down to a single vehicle. To be frank, Commander, we've too many demands on our services to be able to help with the dead."

Thompson assented.

"Fair enough. I gather you want to move into the forecourt. Make it the bus station part, would you? That's where this trailer will be going. The main carriageway's going to be needed for low loaders removing the aircraft wreckage."

The ambulance officer agreed and was about to leave the trailer again when Thompson remembered that sometime this morning he was going to have to give another press conference. Judging from yesterday's bitter experience, it would be wise to have a reserve of unassailable facts to hand.

"By the way," he asked, "exactly how many casualties did you lift to hospital from here altogether?"

"I thought you might want to know." The ambulance officer smiled and flipped open a small notebook. "The answer is that the London Ambulance Service have taken three hundred and sixty-two seriously injured and six hundred and five with minor injuries. The St. John Ambulance Brigade took fifty-six serious and ninety-two minor. That makes four hundred and eighteen serious and six hundred and ninety-seven minor. But of course, it isn't the total admitted by hospitals. Another sixty-three found their own way there. It always happens. Someone receives cuts and abrasions or is in shock. He can still walk. So his first instinct is to get clear of the accident. Half an hour later he's wandering around, not knowing where he is, and a taxi driver or a passerby brings him in. Quite a few were with the Red Cross and the Salvation Army until it became clear that they needed hospital treatment. So the total to date is one thousand one hundred and seventy-eight. That includes three firemen."

"For the record," interjected Sturgess, "the number of homeless and others not sent to hospital whom the Social Services, the Salvation Army and the Red Cross cared for overnight is more than two thousand. Names are still being sent in to the Casualty Bureau. Bodies recovered up to eight A.M. totaled three hundred and seven approximately."

"Approximately?" queried Thompson. "Surely to God they've either extracted three hundred and seven or they haven't!"

"The ninety-eight from the trains are certain enough, sir. But the aircraft corpses were dismembered."

The ambulance officer looked disturbed.

"That's hardly for public consumption, surely?"

"No!" said Thompson emphatically. "It is not. Make a note of all those figures for me, please, Colin. And forget about 'approximate.' The press are having enough of a field day as it is."

"I'll do that right away. You'll need some facts for the lord mayor of Westminster. He's expected at eleven. His Council officers have given us a lot of help."

"Damn the VIPs," said Thompson tersely. "Yes. I'll be here."

When the ambulanceman had gone, he pulled up one of the folding chairs and spoke quietly to Sturgess.

"Whatever else happens, Colin, it's important that we don't lose sight of our priorities. Now that the immediate lifesaving and the fire are over, we're going to be inundated with officials. Some of them matter. Like the coroner, who's responsible in law for determining the cause of all the deaths. Help him. Others are not so important. Every ruddy civil servant who can think of an excuse will be along here, from the girl who sticks on stamps in the employment exchange upwards. You'll be surprised. Be polite, but don't let them distract you. Our job is to safeguard life and property and restore law and order. In other words, to bring our patch back to normal. When we've done that there'll still be a long haul of clearing up and investigations ahead. For the public it'll be a weekend wonder; for us it could be three months' hard grind. Whatever anyone tells you, there are no shortcuts in police work."

Sturgess listened attentively. Why, he wondered, did these fatherly bouts of instruction always come when he was dog tired? His fatigue must have communicated itself to Thompson, who changed his tone abruptly.

"When are we likely to complete the street search?"

"Midday at the present rate."

"I'd like you to stay on duty until we've reduced the cordon to the immediate area round the station. Then you can cut off and get some sleep. We're going to need you fresh and clearheaded at the weekend."

A constable appeared at the trailer door.

"Excuse me, sir. There's a gentleman here insists on seeing you."

"Who is it?" barked Thompson.

In answer an unmistakable American voice cut in.

"My name's Johnson. I own Atlantic Airlines."

Thompson stepped outside and found himself confronted by the tall, solidly built frame of the airline president. The policeman edged uncomfortably to one side, still reluctant to allow the intruder past.

"That's all right." Thompson dismissed the constable. He was adept at interpreting faces, and saw from the firm set of Johnson's mouth and the steady eyes that this man was likely to be what he claimed.

"Thompson," he said, shaking hands. "I'm the local police commander." There seemed little point in mentioning "A" Division to a foreigner. "So you owned the aircraft?"

"I and a few thousand stockholders. What's more, the pilot was one of my oldest friends."

"I'm sorry."

"I'd like to inspect the wreckage." Johnson gestured over his shoulder. "Brought a couple of my technical boys across with me."

Thompson sensed that Johnson was trying to bulldoze him, and inwardly he cursed at Donaldson's departure. He was unfamiliar with the international protocol on occasions like this, but there could be no doubt from the home secretary's remarks the previous evening that the airline was the subject of an inquiry, which in turn meant that its representatives could conceivably have an interest in tampering with the evidence. He weighed this thought against his personal appraisal of Johnson and decided to temporize.

"Unfortunately," he said politely, "the senior accident investigator has been called away for a while."

Johnson's temper began to kindle.

"Listen, Commander, we've come from New York just as fast as we could. We don't want to waste any time. Believe me, the pilot of that plane was not, repeat not, accident prone."

"Surely no one's suggesting that he was."

"Oh, yes, they are," Johnson replied heatedly. "Every damn newspaper here is gunning for him and us both. Not to mention that home secretary guy. I tell you, we want to see what happened to our aircraft."

"I would prefer that you wait until the accident inspector returns."

In spite of knowing that an airline in a foreign crash situation is automatically represented by its own embassy officials and has little standing in its own right, the frustration of being barred from his objective after so long a journey overcame Johnson. He was also accustomed to steamrollering recalcitrant officials.

"You mean you want to watch us being crucified?" he almost shouted. "What kind of setup is this?"

"One that I am in charge of," snapped Thompson. "And while we're on the subject, you might like to know that clearing up your mess has already needed the efforts of several thousand people, quite apart from its cost in lives. Now, you can either wait quietly, or you can leave."

Johnson flushed. He had fast been developing a suspicion that the British had it in for him. Thompson's words reminded him of the traditional image of the London "bobby," fair-minded and impartial. Maybe there was some truth in the legend.

"This accident is pretty bad news for us, Commander. I apologize."

"Frayed tempers are something we try to avoid, Mr. Johnson. There's enough potential friction in this situation as it is."

Thompson spoke matter-of-factly, without rancor. He was certainly different from the average New York precinct captain, Johnson reflected, and his next remark took the airline president totally by surprise.

"As it happens," he said, "I was going across to the station. You can come with me if you like, although"—he indicated the technicians—"it will have to be you alone."

To Thompson the crash appeared transformed since

he had last visited it during the night. Fire hoses were still laid out, flat and inert, across the station concourse. The wreckage still lay blackened and tangled in the roof and across the platforms, in places glistening where the fierce heat had left only silvery white ash and runnels of molten aluminum. The foam used to fight the fire had dried up, while the firemen themselves were still cutting into the forward fuselage of the DC-10 in search of bodies. But it was obvious that order had been brought out of chaos. There was a sense of control and purpose in the way groups of people were working. Railway engineers were systematically lifting away girders and fixing props under what remained of the roof. All the train coaches except those directly beneath the aircraft's impact had gone. Chisholm's railway police were methodically recovering the remaining pieces of luggage and personal property that had survived the fire. Even the TV crews in the press enclosure appeared to have calmed down and were lounging by their cameras, gossiping and waiting for action exciting enough to film. Above all, it was now possible to see clearly within the station. Bright sunlight was slanting down through the shattered roof spans, vividly illuminating random parts of the rescue work and intensifying the drama of the whole scene.

Johnson gazed at all this, dumbfounded, shaking his head in disbelief.

"What a hell of a way to end," he said huskily. "You know something, Commander? That ship was my dream, the transatlantic service that would put us on the map." He drew in his breath sharply. "It's done that all right."

"Things are not as bad as they were yesterday."

The policeman's attempt at consolation failed.

"We were in a different league yesterday," said Johnson bitterly. "A different world." He turned away. "I guess I'll wait for Donaldson. He is the investigator, isn't he?"

If Thompson was surprised he did not show it.

"That's right." Then, observing that the reporters

had noticed them, he advised, "You'll do best to stay over at the trailer, away from the press."

He felt a lot of sympathy for Johnson at this moment.

When the airline chief had gone he went in search of Chisholm to discuss the secure keeping of the lost property. He found the chief superintendent in his office on the east side of the station, poring over a large diagram of the platforms with the area manager and another railway official. Chisholm straightened up, an action which his great height made significant in itself, worth a dozen normal salutations.

"This is our divisional civil engineer. The area manager you've met, I believe."

Thompson shook hands, recognizing the manager as the one who had been suffering from shock the previous afternoon immediately after the crash. He still looked pale.

"How did you get on with the Salvation Army?"

"To tell you the truth, I can't remember much. They took me to a hostel near here and put me to bed. I had a job persuading them to let me out this morning."

Thompson was unsurprised. If the hospitals had not been swamped with serious casualities, this man would be in a ward now.

"The funny thing is," said the manager, "this isn't the first time that a plane's crashed on Victoria."

Thompson expressed scant interest. He was more concerned with the present.

"Yes, a Heinkel 111 was shot down here during the war. The crew were all killed, I think."

"We were discussing how soon we can get a train service running again," interjected Chisholm kindly, prompting the manager, who made a noticeable effort to collect his thoughts.

"We're in direct touch with the traffic control at Croydon," he said. "They tell me parts of the line are electrified again. We could start leading trains from Eccleston Bridge." He looked at Chisholm. "Can the passengers walk through this side?"

"Once all the bodies are out. Tomorrow they could But there'll be no booking office facilities here. The Eastern Booking Hall's completely full of baggage our own casualty bureau for relatives of passengers is operating from the headquarters offices on the first floor. There's a serious shortage of space."

The manager agreed, weakly passing a hand across his forehead.

"What I need to know," Thompson demanded, "is how long the station is going to stay out of action."

"I reckon we could be running better than fifty percent of the normal service by Monday morning," said the engineer. "If we work from Eccleston Bridge, that is, and if we confine ourselves to restoring the main line services first, diverting the suburbans into London Bridge as we're doing today. But it will be two or three weeks before even temporary repairs to the roof are finished."

"How about the underground?" Thompson asked.

"Virtually unaffected. The Victoria Line passes beneath platforms Five and Six, but so deep that it's as safe as an air-raid shelter. The District and Circle lines run more or less below the bus terminus in the forecourt. The London Transport engineers are checking the tunnel roofs for cracks. So far they're not too worried. They've simply told drivers to take it slowly through this section; otherwise things are back to normal. Except, of course, that no trains are stopping here on any of the underground lines until you say they can."

Thompson leaned over and surveyed the station plan. Looking up at Chisholm, he said tentatively, "We could open up the Victoria Street entrance to the underground, I suppose."

"So long as the forecourt is kept clear of sightseers. Enough have found their way through the cordon as it is." Chisholm's broad face with its battered nose, the souvenir of many Saturday afternoons on the rugger field, clouded angrily. "They pretend to be relatives, railwaymen, journalists—bloody anything. You'd hardly credit the way they behave. All for a gawp and a cheap thrill."

"We need to allow traffic along Victoria Street before the rush hour starts, even though Buckingham Palace Road will have to stay closed," declared Thompson. "Apparently the snarl-ups along the Embankment and at Hyde Park Corner have been phenomenal. Will you tell London Transport they can reopen the underground this afternoon? But the bus station will be closed for several days. Our various press officers had better put out statements, too. Now, about the luggage and lost property. . . ." Chisholm was about to explain that the customs officers were concerned about any possible mixup of railway luggage with airline baggage that inevitably had not been customs-cleared when a knock on the door interrupted them. A constable entered and looked inquiringly at Chisholm.

"Is the engineer here, sir? The fire officer is asking for him."

"That's me," said the engineer, and followed the constable out, leaving Chisholm and Thompson to their discussion.

On the main concourse one of the divisional fire officers was standing with a group of firemen, several surprisingly boyish under their high black helmets, all eyeing a savagely burned section of the wreck that was partly suspended in the sagging roof girders. Donaldson's assistant airframe inspector was pointing at it and talking to them.

"This was the forward area of the economy-class cabin, with the forward cargo hold beneath its floor." He jabbed his index finger at the confused jumble of metal at platform level, in which blackened shapes of what had been cargo containers were visible.

"They're so heavy they must have contributed to the breakup of the fuselage here."

Farther back the massive transverse spars of the wings, largely stripped naked of their aluminum covering by the fire, were still lodged firmly in the roof. So was the center section of the fuselage, also burned through to a skeleton of ribs and spars. But this part had one end straddling a railway carriage and the other cocked up at a crazy angle, apparently held up by one of the thirty-foot-high cast-iron Corinthian columns which supported the roof girders and which ran in a line between platforms Thirteen and Fourteen.

"What I want to know," demanded the divisional officer, noticing the engineer's arrival, "is whether that pillar is going to hold. I don't want the whole bloody lot coming down on top of my men."

"These old structures can take a remarkable amount of stress before they collapse."

The engineer moved in closer, hampered by tangles of wire, charred seats and other debris. He gazed at the ghostly shell of the plane's body. Its most solid remnant was the floor.

Having made his inspection, he stepped back.

"The column has fractured slightly. On the other hand, that lot can't weigh so much. The problem is removing it."

"We've got to," said the divisional officer bluntly. "Until we do we can't fetch the last bodies out of that coach."

"We can jack it up a few feet, pack it with timber."

"Can't we bring a crane in?" asked the airframe inspector. "That's the obvious answer."

"Not over the concourse," replied the engineer. "The absolute weight limit is two tons. There's a regular catacomb of storage chambers and passages under here. You'd be surprised." He gazed thoughtfully at the jungle of twisted metal in front of him. It was true that they needed a crane. On the other hand, his men were already making progress in propping up the roof, working toward the center of the damage.

"I reckon we can insert more temporary props under the main lines of girders, then cut away enough of the roof to bring in one of the railway cranes to Platform Fourteen and hoist the wreckage away."

"How long?" demanded the divisional officer.

"We could probably fix the supports during the day.

Cutting the roof away"—he frowned—"up to three days. It all depends."

The divisional officer swung around toward the nose of the aircraft, lodged in the side of the Grosvenor Hotel. It too had broken off, but the gaping end that faced them was less burned.

"And is that hotel wall going to hold?"

"It's not as bad as it seems. Most of the force must have been taken by the extension with the lounge and lavatories in it. The main hotel wall is a good twenty feet further back, and it's as solid as they come. There'll be no major collapse."

"Then concentrate on shoring up this part, will you, and we'll try to cut our way further in." The divisional officer turned to his subordinates.

"You heard the message, boys. Take it slow and sure. When there are no more lives to be saved there's no sense risking our own. See if you can tackle that last coach from its ends."

Meanwhile, Donaldson and Colonel Daly had reached the school in Lambeth, close behind the grounds of the ancient red-brick Archbishop's Palace and not far from the Thames. Lying on the tarmaced playground, guarded from a growing crowd of inquisitive children by two stolid constables, was a large section of aluminum-covered structure, jagged at one end and crumpled where it had hit the hard ground. A proportion of the sheet aluminum skin had peeled back, springing the rivets and revealing spars.

"Is it part of the wing, sir?" asked one of the constables as he moved aside.

Daly examined it.

"Parts of an elevator from off the horizontal stabilizer, I guess."

"The tail of a big aircraft is actually larger than the wing of a small one," Donaldson explained to the constable. "This one had a seventy-one-foot span."

He and Daly knelt and spent ten minutes examining the find, while the children chattered and giggled excitedly in a ring around them.

"There are some odd penetrations in this, ver odd," remarked Donaldson, very lightly touching a irregular series of roughly V-shaped holes in the skin

"One theory is a rear-engine turbine failure, cor rect?" asked Daly. "From what I recall that turbin sits above and foward of the elevator. It wouldn't be easy for blades to break through the casing and dam age it. For one thing there's quite a space between th turbine and the casing."

"Much what I was thinking," agreed Donaldson

He glanced up at the policeman. "How far away is the other bit that fell in a garden?"

"Hardly a couple of hundred yards, sir."

Five minutes later they were facing an irate middle aged woman at the front door of a small terraced home.

"It's all very well this 'We are assisting in investigating the cause of an accident' lark. It's all very well I tell you. I could have been killed. If I hadn't been out at the bingo I could have been hanging out the washing and been killed."

Eventually her tirade ended, and she allowed them through the narrow linoleumed hall and out by the back door into an ill-kept garden with a clothesline. Partially buried in a flower bed was another, though smaller, section of the same elevator. Donaldson carefully photographed it.

"Perhaps we should take this away with us if the lady doesn't mind."

"Mind!" she shrilled. "I should bloody well think not. You take it away just as fast as you please. That could have killed me, that could."

As they gingerly lifted it out of the soil Donaldson noticed a fragment of metal lodged in the torn aluminum skin. Very carefully he removed it.

"If that's a piece of turbine blade, then I'm the President of the United States," said Daly.

"I'd rather have the power plant experts make sure, nonetheless," replied Donaldson quietly, wrapping the ragged sliver of metal in a clean handkerchief tissue and putting it in his pocket. "Spectographic analysis will tell us its composition sure enough."

As they carried the segment of elevator out through the narrow hall the woman pursued them, carpet slippers slapping the lino.

"What about damages then? Trampling all over the garden, messing up the 'all. Nothing won't ever grow there again." As they emerged through the front door she attacked the policemen. "Call yourselves coppers. I could have been killed and a fat lot you'd care. Compensation, that's what I want."

"Here, love," said Donaldson, groping in his hip pocket with his free hand and pulling out a pound note, "have a bingo session on us."

After they had escaped, and arranged for the recovery of the other section, the police car ferried them back toward Victoria. As they crossed Lambeth Bridge the driver remarked, "They're dragging the river for you, too."

Donaldson asked him to stop, and all three men clambered out and stood on the parapet of the bridge. It was low water, and the river was reduced to a channel between glistening, slimy banks of mud, littered with chunks of wood and other debris. A short distance away, toward Westminster Bridge, two river police launches were stemming the combination of current and ebbing tide. Men in black oilskins were hauling on what appeared to be a net from one launch, and Donaldson thought he saw a diver's helmet in the murky water close to the other boat.

"We can ask how they're getting on if you like," offered the driver proudly. "They can talk to any police car. In fact, they can even link up with a constable's personal radio through Scotland Yard."

"That's not a bad idea," said Donaldson. He squinted into the sunlight looking back across the bridge, then turned and gazed in the other direction toward Victoria.

"Tell them there's a strong likelihood of finding wreckage between these two bridges, most probably nearer this one."

The driver returned to the car, and they could hear the radio small talk begin.

"It appears to me," said Donaldson cautiously to Daly, "that there must have been an airframe failure in flight simultaneously with the engine failure."

"Agreed," said Daly, leaning on the parapet, watching the river, "and something damn sudden caused it. Mind if I advance a line of thought? I've seen those kind of penetrations before—and in the horizontal tail surfaces at that."

"You have?"

"All but identical. In the tail of a Phantom shot down by a missile in Vietnam."

Donaldson whistled. He was not given to making dramatic exclamations of any kind. But this tallied with an idea that had already occurred to him and that he had dismissed as too improbable to pursue without the justification of evidence.

"Curiously enough, when McPherson located the rear engine yesterday, he suggested there were signs of an explosion having damaged the jet pipe."

"This Phantom," Daly went on, "got itself hit by a heat-seeking missile. Caused a darn lot of damage to the jet pipe, too. But that wasn't why it crashed. It came down because the explosion tore great chunks off the stabilizers, so they quit providing aerodynamic balance and the airplane pitched nosedown into a dive. There was no way the pilot could recover."

"It's a feasible scenario," Donaldson admitted. "With a plane the size of a DC-10 it could take a few seconds for the slipstream to tear off enough damaged tail plane skin to affect longitudinal stability. That would square with the first radio call not reporting a loss of control."

"Right," exclaimed Daly.

The screaming whine of a British Airways Trident passing overhead interrupted them. Both men looked up. In the bright sun every detail of the plane was visible.

"On a day like this," Daly shouted, "you couldn't hardly miss."

"Higher than it seems, though. Should have around three thousand feet at this point," said Donaldson as the noise died down.

"Less from the top of one of those towers." Daly pointed at the near horizon of the south bank. "The Sam 7s in Vietnam were reckoned to have fifteen hundred meters range as I recall. That leaves more than five hundred meters in hand," he pondered. "Sure, the slant range would be more. Still, I guess it's possible."

Donaldson swung around and faced him.

"If you're right, this investigation is going to broaden out pretty dramatically. I imagine the flight recorder readout will do a lot to either prove or disprove your theory. If it provides confirmation then the police are going to be busy with something more than controlling the traffic and coordinating the rescue. They'll have a terrorist to catch, and they may well want us to keep our mouths shut until they've found him."

Daly winced.

"That could be tough on Johnson. He needs to clear his name real bad."

"Colonel, it's not my style to stand on ceremony. I'm running this investigation. Officially I could insist that you don't divulge details of the accident even to your own government. You'd demand the same of me if our roles were reversed. But I'd rather just ask you as a friend to keep it under wraps as long as you can."

"It's a bastard for Johnson, and he has friends in high places."

"I don't care if he has a hot line to heaven," said Donaldson emphatically. "He'll just have to sweat it out for the time being."

The driver came back from the car, interrupting them.

"No luck yet, sir. The diver's carrying on until half an hour after low water."

"Let's go then," said Donaldson.

In the car Donaldson continued.

"I think you ought to know that recently Johnson offered me a job. As yet I've neither accepted or declined. Nor will I until this is over."

245

Daly grinned.

"Boy, you could have problems. If you want the job, that is."

"Believe me, that is irrelevant. Totally. I have a reputation and I'm not tarnishing it. As far as possible I shall insist he obeys protocol and deals with you."

"I'll do what I can."

"Thanks," said Donaldson, relaxing a little. "I'm grateful."

The confrontation was not long delayed. As the two men stepped out of the police car at Victoria, Johnson hurried forward from the control area and greeted them. He was clearly having difficulty suppressing his impatience at having had to wait.

"Hello, Jim. I'm sorry we had to meet again in these circumstances," he began.

"So am I," said Donaldson with feeling. "I really am."

"No point in bucking fences. Have you any idea what went wrong? First I heard there was an engine fire; now your local radio station's talking about sabotage." Johnson spoke with earnest intensity, his shrewd eyes fixed on the investigator. "I have a serious need to know. This crash could break my airline."

Donaldson counted to three, methodically steadying himself, and then spoke with a controlled formality.

"Mr. Johnson, I appreciate your dilemma. I will be happy if you can give my technical teams advice and help when needed. But it never has been my practice to reveal evidence from major accidents at so early a stage."

"Have you read your own newspapers, Donaldson? I have to refute that crap. I have to say something."

"Mr. Johnson, your accredited representative here is Colonel Daly. I am employed by the British government."

"The government with that home secretary guy in it? Jesus wept!"

Daly intervened tactfully.

"Jim Donaldson has a job to do. We have to let him do it his way. This is his country."

At this moment Colin Sturgess appeared from the trailer.

"Your assistant has just arrived from the Data Center at Farnborough, sir."

"I'm sorry. I must go." Donaldson felt that whatever his principles, he was somehow behaving like a heel. He had no time to consider whether Johnson's whole approach might not have been designed to make him feel just that. As he moved away Johnson turned to his fellow American.

"Listen, Colonel. We have a national interest to protect. . . ."

At the trailer Hearn was waiting, his eyes redrimmed despite the sleep he had snatched at the RAE's officers' mess.

"I tried to contact you around midnight," he began.

"Mac told me. I'm sorry."

Donaldson was slowly becoming more and more angry with himself for having allowed Jane to drag him away from his job at such a crucial time. How the hell could a man explain to his juniors that his wife was tearing him apart? Perhaps they knew anyway.

"We had a snag with the cockpit voice recorder tape. Otherwise I'd have been back earlier."

He handed over the flight recorder readout, now printed with scales of height, speed and the rest expressed in feet, knots and other conventional forms—engineering units as the trade called them. Donaldson whistled when he saw the dropout fifty-six seconds before the crash.

"No wonder you rang," he commented.

"Listen to this then," said Hearn, producing a cassette recorder and switching it on. "This is roughly the same period of time on the flight deck."

Out of a lot of background interference there came a distinct, though distant-sounding, explosion, followed by the insistent bleeping of the engine fire warning. There were muttered remarks, scarcely audible, then loud and clear the second pilot's voice.

"Mayday, Mayday, Mayday. Atlantic two six zero rear-engine explosion."

Sturgess listened, fascinated as the variety of sounds increased. This was a new world to him.

"That's increased engine power, I presume," said Hearn.

Then came a shout.

"Help me, son, let's get hold of this bastard."

With a sense of shock, Donaldson recognized Bill Curtis' voice. Something would have had to be very wrong indeed for Bill Curtis to shout. He was the sort of man who seldom, if ever, raised his voice. The welter of noise grew, obscuring fragmented remarks by the crew until there came Curtis' last transmission to the Heathrow Air Traffic control.

"We're hitting now."

There was a rending, thundering roar, then a colossal bang that made the tape recorder itself vibrate, then total silence.

"It's a damn nuisance that American regulations don't require the individual mikes to pick up everything each crew member says," commented Hearn. "In this kind of situation there is far too much being picked up by the area microphone. They've a tape on the filter bank now trying to sort the voices out."

"Nonetheless," said Donaldson, "that confirms what we thought."

He looked at Sturgess.

"It's time you brought the CID in. This investigation is entering a different league, a different league altogether."

"I ought to consult the commander first. Unfortunately he's with the lord mayor at the moment."

"Well, buttonhole him as soon as he's free, will you?"

Donaldson turned back to Hearn and pulled the fragment of metal from the tail plane out of his pocket.

"In the meantime, you can take this down to the RAE for urgent spectographic analysis. We want to know if it could be a chunk of turbine blade, or of a missile warhead casing, or whatever. Ring through the result. And you can tell them that the first load of tinware should be arriving this afternoon, so they'd better finish clearing a hangar for it."

As Hearn left, Donaldson sat down on one of the folding chairs, wiped his forehead and grinned at the inspector.

"Yes. As our American friends would say, 'This is a different ball game.' And so long as they don't know it is, everything will be fine. I suppose you have this kind of drama every day in the police force?"

"No," said Sturgess, "only on weekends."

Chapter Eight

Connie Maier's arrival in London had been less obtrusive than Johnson's. While he had been fretting in the queues to show his passport and collect his baggage at Heathrow, she had been discreetly met at the arrival gate by one of the Israeli Embassy staff and taken through with diplomatic privileges.

"My car is outside," the young diplomat had explained. "You are to stay with the Alloms, and we will go there now."

"But we must go straight to the hospital!"

She had been desperate to find Ben, knowing that if he had escaped death his injuries might be critical.

"Unfortunately it is not so simple, Mrs. Maier. There are nearly a thousand casualties, and they have been distributed among twelve or thirteen hospitals. At this moment, Mr. Allom is making further inquiries."

Sensing the logic in his words, Connie sat back in her seat, and their drive into the city was slow. Where the M4 motorway narrows to two lanes and rises on to an elevated section to pass through the suburb of Chiswick, there was a two-mile-long traffic jam.

"I suppose this is the rush hour?" Connie had asked, her frustration building up at this delay after the speed of the flight from New York.

"It's often bad at this time. These Londoners start

work late!" the young man had explained. "But today it must be the effects of the crash as well. I heard on the radio that the police are keeping a large area closed."

It had been nearly ten before they reached the old but spacious mansion flat that the Alloms rented in Kensington. During the ride Connie had been becoming more and more apprehensive. It was a race against time, and every second lost was a defeat. Delays always spelled bad news to her, yet the friendly welcome she received from Jakov Allom's cheerful, bustling wife, Judith, lessened her inner tensions a little. Because Jakov was still out making inquiries, she had been persuaded to wash, change and accept coffee and cake.

Shortly after eleven Jakov returned, a worried expression clouding his strong features. After greeting Connie, he came straight to the point, speaking calmly in his accented English.

"It is worse than I could have imagined. To obtain information by telephone is impossible. The special inquiry lines are occupied all the time. It is the same with the hospitals. Every hospital had its own casualty bureau, and their telephone exchanges are all engaged. Only with the aid of a police officer did I find out two things. First, no one is a hundred percent certain who of the critically injured are from the trains and who from the plane. Of about eleven hundred and fifty casualties, four hundred and twenty are seriously hurt."

Following Judith's hospitality, Connie was composed again after the stress of the trip. Calmly, she put into words what Jakov had hesitated to say himself.

"Ben had to be among the seriously hurt. The human body just can't absorb that kind of impact and escape with cuts and bruises—at least only by a miracle."

"You are a brave girl. I am glad you understand." Allom paused. "I am glad because the second thing I learned was that so far Ben's name is not on any list. He may not be dead," he added hastily. "The dead are included on the police's coordinated record. But naturally the unidentified survivors are all among the badly injured, the ones who are unconscious or cannot talk."

"Where are they?"

"Five different hospitals. That is, the unidentified men are distributed between five. There are unidentified women and children in many more. The nearest to here is St. Stephen's in Chelsea."

Connie was already on her feet.

"What are we waiting for? Let's go. Excuse me, Judith. You've been very kind. But we can't lose any time."

St. Stephen's Hospital appears deceptively small when viewed from the Fulham Road. Its modern low-built Accident and Emergency Department distracts the eye both from the new six-story block beyond it and from the drab Victorian brick edifices that house the old wards. Jakov Allom hesitated at the "no parking" sign as he drove through the gates by the A and E reception.

"Take a doctor's space," commanded Connie. "After all, I am one."

Back in an atmosphere she understood, from that moment she took control. She led the way in through the glass doors, past a cluster of people sitting in the vinyl-floored accident waiting area and spoke briskly to the receptionist. "My name is Dr. Maier. I come from Bellevue Hospital in New York. Could I speak to the doctor in charge?"

To back up the request, she extracted a visiting card from her handbag. The girl gave it to a nurse, who walked around to an office off the waiting area. A moment later the nurse beckoned Connie and Jakov in.

The room was tiny. Standing by the document-littered desk were two doctors, a man and a woman, both in long white coats. The man, who looked worn out, stepped forward and shook hands, more clinically than warmly.

"I'm the consultant in charge. This is the registrar on duty. Dr. Morton. What can we do for you?"

Connie explained her mission, concluding, "I know you're being pestered by relatives. Nonetheless, I hope you can help me. It is my husband."

"The Health Service has its faults." The consultant smiled briefly. "Happily failing to assist doctors from overseas isn't one of them. Anything we can do, we will. The snag is that being a general hospital, we usually pass specialist cases on to others. We still have about thirty casualties from the air crash, but we've already tranferred the head injuries to the Atkinson Morley, the chest injuries to the Brompton and the burns to Roehampton. Quite a number were very badly burned."

"Our search is widening," remarked Allom glumly.

"Unfortunately most of the staff who were on duty yesterday are off now," continued the consultant. "We had a mobile team in action at Victoria twenty-seven minutes after the crash, and we were still doing emergency theater work here at three o'clock this morning. So I've sent them all home. However, Dr. Morton can take you around the wards."

The woman doctor, a fair-haired girl of about Connie's own age, moved toward the door.

"I'll be glad. The police and ambulance control officers are still here; it won't take long to check any possibilities.

She led Connie and Jakov across the waiting area. "We had to spill over into accommodation we don't normally use. We've got tea and sandwiches going for relatives in the nursing school. The police are in the medical records office." She ushered Connie into a small room where an inspector and a sergeant were seated at a table with a stack of record forms, compiling an index. At Dr. Morton's request the sergeant flipped through it.

"No one with the name of Maier, I'm afraid, Doctor."

"How about unidentified?" asked Connie. "Male."

"There's only one." He read from a form. 'Face —round. Hair—black. Complexion—dark. Nose— straight. Teeth—good. Number M. A. 3."

"Let's go see him."

After further checking, Dr. Morton led them down a long corridor and up a wide staircase.

"Even with five hundred and twenty beds we seldom have any empty. By transferring patients we managed to clear two wards, one of the old ones and Nell Gwynne here," she explained.

They came to a large area divided into small eight bed wards, supervised from a central "station" of desks and filing cabinets.

"I believe you have Major Accident Three here," inquired Dr. Morton.

The ward sister, neat in pale blue dress and white starched cap, glanced dubiously at Connie and Jakov.

"M.A. Three is in a critical condition," she said hesitantly.

"It's all right. I'm a doctor," said Connie firmly, then turned to Jakov. "You'd better wait."

Allom looked at her with admiration, she was so calm. The ward sister took Connie and the woman doctor to one of the wards, with its steel-framed beds and wide windows.

"He had to go straight to theater when they brought him," said the sister. "He was in a terrible mess. We took out his ruptured spleen, but he also has compound fractures of the tib and fib in both legs, fractured pelvis and head injuries. Been unconscious throughout, luckily for him. Seems he was in his shirt sleeves so there was no wallet or anything to identify him by. We think he may have been in the plane itself."

Connie listened with her heart racing. The dreadful injuries were consistent with the violent deceleration of an air crash. Men often took their jackets off during a flight. This was indeed likely to be one of the survivors of the DC-10.

The three women came to the foot of a bed, beside which on top of a locker was a gray plastic bag containing M.A. 3's personal belongings. The bag lay limp, almost empty, seeming to mirror the condition of the pathetic figure between the sheets. His head was encircled with bandages, obscuring most of his face. Connie steeled herself and stepped forward. Only the eyes and nose of the patient were visible in the white cotton cocoon. She bent over for a moment, then stood back.

"No," she said, her voice dead, "he's not Ben." She took a deep breath. "I'm glad it isn't."

"He can't last," said the sister quietly. "It'll be better if he never comes to."

Connie squared her shoulders and went briskly out again to the "station," shaking her head at Jakov. At the door she thanked the sister and turned to Dr. Morton.

"If he was Major Accident Three, there must have been numbers one and two."

"Let's consult the ambulance officer," agreed Dr. Morton.

She led Connie downstairs again, talking spasmodically to relieve the tension.

"We've had a lot of experience with bombs—we had the victims from nine last year—but a really major incident overstretches everything. We can't keep fifty beds empty just in case!"

Connie forced herself to reply sympathetically, but she was thinking only that she and Jakov could have a long day ahead of them. The ambulance officer confirmed the impression.

"That's right," he explained. "We transferred M.A. One to the Atkinson Morley and M.A. Two to Roehampton." He checked his records. "Both last night."

"Can you remember them?" demanded Connie.

"The one with the head injuries was middle-aged, late middle-aged. We had him on a spinal board. The one with burned legs was thirtyish."

"How far is Roehampton?"

The ambulanceman pursed his lips. "Four, five miles. Takes us from ten to fifteen minutes with the bell and lights going."

"We can beat that!" Jakov simulated a cheerfulness he could not feel. "If I am to be your chauffeur, I shall earn my keep."

Connie smiled halfheartedly and turned to shake Dr. Morton's hand warmly.

"Thank you very much, Doctor."

Outside in the car she said simply, "Ben has to be somewhere. If that man could survive, so could he."

"We'll find him, Connie," answered Jakov. "I promise we will."

Mohammed Khadir slept late. He had chosen his room in Earls Court because it was in a rabbit warren of a house, grossly overcrowded with its sixteen "flatlets," set in a road of similar houses and buried in an area teeming with cheap hotels. It was next to impossible for London's understrength police force to monitor transients effectively. Kamal, the more sophisticated of the two, disliked living even temporarily in such sordid surroundings and had made tentative efforts to clean the place up. Mohammed scorned these. If he had to sleep on stones in the desert during an operation—so be it. And if the cause demanded that he lived for a while as the impoverished England lived—so be it also. He treated his room exactly as previous tenants had—with uncaring neglect. On the stained carpet lay scattered late editions of the previous evening's papers, headlines proclaiming the disaster he had caused. On the table, remnants of tandouri chicken they brought ready spiced and cooked from one of the local Pakistani shops seeped grease through a paper plate. Beside it stood a quarter full bottle of cheap red wine.

Eventually the light beating through the thin cotton curtains woke Khadir. He rolled over, broke wind, cursed the taste that the cheap wine had left in his mouth, then pulled on his trousers and went to the bathroom on the landing. As he reached it the telephone rang. Cursing again, he came back and lifted the instrument. A cautious voice asked for Kamal.

"He is asleep."

"Is that the friend of Abu Youssouf?"

"It is Mohammed, fool."

There was a silence, a click and the diplomat called

Ahmed came on the line. Mohammed recognized his accent. In rapid Arabic he ordered the two terrorists to come at once to the embassy. As he replaced the receiver Mohammed cursed for a third time. These Libyans assumed too much authority. This diplomat was merely a postbox for movements like his own Abu Youssouf 73. Today's victors were himself and Kamal, achieving real revenge for Israeli aggression. They had consented to remain in England until witnesses confirmed that Maier was dead and the documents destroyed. Now to be roused in this way was intolerable.

At midday the two Arabs arrived at the embassy in Prince's Gate. Mohammed was unshaven and rebellious. Kamal, faithful in small ways to his middle-class origins, was more presentable in clean jeans and a flowered shirt. The diplomat welcomed them curtly in the foyer of the embassy and set about belaboring them once they had penetrated to the quiet of his back room office.

"So you think you are heroes! You are wrong. You have failed! Several passengers survived. Possibly even Maier himself. Much of the baggage is in the hands of the police. Your mission is incomplete."

Mohammed stared back at the diplomat insolently.

"Could you have done better yourself? Did we not shoot down the aircraft? Did it not catch fire? I do not believe there can be survivors! We should be claiming the credit for a victory over Israel, not skulking here in a foreign city."

The diplomat stared at the two terrorists.

"While you two sleep," he said contemptuously, "others work." He tapped a folder of telegrams on his desk. "In New York the Americans have obtained an adjournment of the Security Council meeting until Monday. Why do you suppose they do that? The wife of the Israeli courier Maier has arrived in London. Why? I will tell you why, you boneheads. It must be because the Israelis hope to recover the documents this weekend. It is the only possible reason. You must get them first. These are the orders from your brothers of Abu Youssouf."

"And your airline pilot who directed us. Will he finish the job also?"

The diplomat raised his hands in protest. It had been impracticable to prevent the pilot from resuming his normal schedule, even though he was employed by their national airline.

"His further absence would have aroused harmful comment. In any case he aided you; he did not direct you."

Kamal interrupted. "We are wasting time," he said brusquely. "Revenge is good, Mohammed. If the Jew Maier is dead, we shall have revenged Argenteuil. But that raid should never have been possible. Our brothers in Paris were too lax. That publicity was embarrassing enough. We cannot afford to fail again."

"I see you have more understanding," commented the diplomat, thinking to himself what amateurs these two were at the game of politics.

"Listen, my friend," he went on, "if the cause of this air crash is discovered the PLO will deny any involvement. Egypt, Saudi Arabia and others will deplore the loss of life. It will be the end of financial support for Abu Youssouf 73. Two failures in as many weeks! Pouf."

Kamal nodded and spoke to Mohammed. "He is right." He turned back to the diplomat. "What do you suggest?"

The diplomat told them.

"And you will check on the details?"

"Naturally. I have my informants."

When Gilly Carslake's office phone rang she was making yet another effort to resolve two problems simultaneously. The first centered on writing a caption for a "filler" article about furnishing small bedsitting rooms. A photograph the magazine had brought from abroad showed a room so narrow that it was filled completely by the bed. From the ceiling above hung a thick woven strap. Did you swing yourself into bed by hanging on this strap, or when you pulled on it, did the bed itself swing up against the wall to make more living space, or what? Gilly could hardly write a caption that simply disregarded the thing. It was too prominent, hanging down from the ceiling in the middle of the picture. It could not be airbrushed away. What on earth was it for? Her second problem was that constant disturbance caused by Eckhardt. He was using her magazine table to write on, in theory polishing the story he would deliver to the *Sunday Post* by teatime, in reality pacing up and down, pausing to gaze out of the window at the wreckage in the station roof and the teams of blue boiler-suited men slowly cutting it away, stopping to try dramatic phrases out on her—in short ruining any chance she had of completing her own work. She lifted the phone, answering distractedly.

"Oh, yes, hang on a moment. I'll fetch him."

Holding one palm over the mouthpiece, she called out to Eckhardt. "Hey, genius. It's your Arab friend again."

Grumbling Eckhardt rose from his chair and took the call, leaning on the edge of Gilly's desk. He listened impatiently for half a minute and then interrupted.

"Much as I wish you well, Ahmed, I am dreadfully busy at this moment in time. Why don't you ask one of your tame MPs? There are four or five parliamentary questions on the crash down for answer this afternoon."

A greater degree of irritation crept into his voice as the Libyan pressed him for information.

"I told you that the operation is now being controlled from Rochester Row and everything is being taken there. Of course not the bodies. They're using tents and barracks rooms in Chelsea. Yes, there is a lot of speculation about sabotage."

Suddenly Eckhardt became exasperated.

"Ahmed, my friend, I was grateful for the lead you gave me on the Israeli commando story in Paris. Most grateful. I imagine it helped you, too. That's fine. But the paper pays me for writing fact, or as near as I can get to it. Your idea won't wash. All right, thank you for telling me. I appreciate your thoughtfulness. Good-bye."

He slammed down the instrument.

"Temper, temper," said Gilly reprovingly. "You're not at home, you know. I don't want my telephone broken, thank you."

"Crazy Arabs."

"Whatever made me think you liked them?" Gilly teased him. "Could it be something you said?"

Eckhardt disregarded her sarcasm.

"Trying to persuade me the Israelis sabotaged the aircraft because an important Arab was on board! An American aircraft going to New York, where most of Israel's support comes from. Crazy."

Annoyed at the way he was disrupting her work, Gilly could not resist baiting him. He really was unbearably self-important.

"You mean," she exclaimed, her blue eyes wide, accenting her words like an actress, "you really mean that your love affair with Islam is over?"

Ridicule was the only weapon guaranteed to injure Eckhardt's professional vanity. With silky deftness he began gathering up the draft of his article and his notebooks and fitting them into a slim leather briefcase.

"Time for me to return to Fleet Street," he said, "especially as my welcome here appears to be running out."

He eyed the photographs, proofs and layouts on Gilly's desk.

"Fortunate for the public that some of us write about the world as it really is," he remarked, and was gone. Sam Eckhardt was accustomed to having the last word, both in print and in private.

Soon afterward the telephone buzzed again. This time it was Donaldson, speaking from Thompson's temporary office at Rochester Row.

"At last. You're a difficult young lady to get through to."

"Not always," said Gilly. "What can I do for you?"

"Quite simple really. You remember the horizontal tail of the airplane? I drew it on a pad last night."

"Yes."

"Think very carefully. It sticks out on both sides of the airplane below the upright fin. Was it most damaged on the far side or the near side?"

"On the far side, I think."

"And the wing nearest you was lower than the other."

"Definitely. I'm quite certain of that."

"Thank you very much. I mean that. You're a great help. If anything else at all comes to mind, ring me. I'm speaking from Rochester Row Police Station. You can always leave a message here or at Victoria."

Pleased for more reasons than she could have analyzed, Gilly returned to wondering how the magazine's readers might react to strap-hanging bedtimes.

At Rochester Row, Donaldson and Daly were facing Thompson and David Chance, the burly detective chief superintendent of "A" Division. Spread out on the table between them was a long piece of graph paper with a variety of wavering lines running across it at differing angles. It was the readout from the flight recorder, expressed in engineering units, which had been brought up from Farnborough. Unlike the earlier digital version, this version bore notations of the airliner's speed, height and other parameters in knots, feet and other more familiar measurements. After recounting his conversation with Gilly, Donaldson continued his analysis of the readout.

"What she saw tallies with this and with the sections of the elevator found in Lambeth. The aircraft was in a steepening dive to starboard."

He pointed to the extreme right of the graph, where all the lines veered wildly and ended.

"That's the impact point when all the parameter traces became aberrant. Altitude nil with the line curving back up to level flight at three thousand feet forty-three seconds earlier. During that time the airspeed had risen from one hundred eighty knots to nearly two hundred forty knots. Compass heading was two hundred sixty degrees at three thousand feet but veered to the right and was two hundred eighty-one at impact. There was forward pitch, some starboard bank —as the girl confirmed. The auto pilot was disengaged, considerable increase in engine thrust suggests they were trying to maintain height."

"Amazing," said Thompson. "It tells you all that?"

"It's uncalibrated, of course. So the readings could be slightly wrong, two or three knots of airspeed, a degree in the heading. That's why we never allow others to see it. Errors can easily cause misinterpretations."

"Darn little room for doubt on this one, though," Daly commented. "You can see to within a couple of seconds when hell broke loose."

"The G trace shows it too," Donaldson agreed. He indicated a line that ran at a constant level on the graph, but with incessant tiny waverings. At forty-three seconds before impact there was a sudden wide oscillation.

"See that, Commander. That was a change in the G forces when something momentarily rocked her in midair."

"Such as the explosion of a missile," said Daly.

"You're not serious," Thompson exclaimed. "You mean a terrorist shot the plane down? It's impossible."

Thompson studied the graph, almost expecting some spectacular message to rise up from it and illuminate his growing confusion. He had some understanding of graphs. He could see what had been pointed out clearly enough, but those wavering lines did not speak to him as they spoke to Donaldson and Daly.

"Impossible," declared Chance, "our security experts believe that anyone taking a potshot at an airliner would have to do so close to the airport."

"It ain't necessarily so," said Daly cheerfully. Quoting the appropriate lines from songs always amused him.

"For Christ's sake, Colonel," Thompson burst out,

"this is no joke. If you're right, we're the first victims of a completely new technique in terrorism."

"Not exactly. President Amin sent a team of Palestinians to shoot down a plane near Nairobi. Luckily the Kenyans caught them before they could try."

Thompson was still not convinced. The idea of launching the Metropolitan Police on a wild-goose chase, with huge attendant publicity, horrified him. "If this crash was caused by a missile," he said slowly, "we have a major manhunt on our hands, a really full-scale CID operation." He looked at the accident investigator. "Do you honestly believe this is what happened?"

Donaldson was more cautious than Daly.

"Until a forensic expert has examined the wreckage, we can't be one hundred percent sure," he said. "But I think it probable that the aircraft was shot down."

"Most crimes have a cause."

"That is more a matter for you than us."

"Gentlemen," Daly interrupted, "I'm damn sure it was a missile. Let me make a suggestion. From this readout we can plot exactly where the aircraft was at forty-three seconds before impact. Right? Why don't we do it?"

"I have already requested the information," said Donaldson quietly. "I hope to have the result late tonight or early Saturday. It's a complicated calculation even with the computer."

Daly was impressed.

"That's great. Then we can plot the possible trajectories of a missile to that point."

"Given further time."

Now it was Thompson's turn to interrupt.

"Time is precisely what we lack. Surely the roof of a tower block is the only place that would provide the field of fire for a missile? There aren't so many tower blocks."

He cast his mind back to the tactics of his commando days, before ground-to-air missiles were invented.

"It must be like setting up a machine-gun post. You need a good view."

"True," Daly admitted, "And London is no rival to New York in respect of high-rise buildings."

"We would only need to search in an arc behind the forty-three-second point," put in Donaldson excitedly. "Why not use a helicopter?"

"As it happens," said Thompson, not wanting all his thinking done for him by outsiders, "we carried out a survey recently on the use of helicopters in fire situations. All the tower blocks are charted. The question will be what to look for."

Daly leaned forward, gesturing with his hands. On this subject he was a real expert.

"Most missiles leave a signature, Commander, some kind of scorch or burn. In a field the grass would be flattened in a pattern. Maybe they even hid the launcher tube someplace, who knows?"

Thompson felt that events were acquiring a momentum of their own, threatening to run out of control. In the twenty hours since the DC-10 came down, there had been discernible progress in bringing London back to normal, especially this morning. Although a mountain of minor problems had still to be demolished, his own interim report would be on the police commissioner's desk by Monday morning. Now the possibility of terrorism would introduce a host of new and unpredictable considerations.

"Frankly," he said, "I'd be happier if we knew of a motive. There would have to have been somebody, or something, of great importance on board. We'll have to investigate that at once. Meanwhile, I want rock-solid confirmation of your theory. The kind of proof that would stand cross-examination in a court of law. There's too much at stake to risk making fools of ourselves!"

"There's one other thing." Chance confronted the two aviation experts squarely across the table. "These theories must be kept strictly to ourselves. No leak at all. We have to stiffen controls at ports and airports.

We have to check out known terrorist groups in London. All of them, from the anarchists to the IRA."

Donaldson was gently rubbing the side of his nose with his forefinger. He was apprehensive about Daly's reactions.

"I have warned Colonel Daly to expect a request for secrecy," he said quickly.

Daly frowned. His position vis-à-vis Johnson was delicate, and the airline president had not minced words during their earlier conversation. Johnson had deployed every argument—from protecting American national honor to a straight threat that if Daly didn't play the game his way, then Daly would soon be out of a job. To the colonel's credit he had stalled, but he worried how much longer he could continue to do so and, indeed, how far it was desirable to from an American point of view.

"A helluva lot of money and prestige hangs on this crash not being Atlantic Airlines' fault," he said, looking straight back across the big table at Chance. "Johnson deserves any break we can give him."

"What about the gunmen?" asked Chance bitterly, remembering how much of the IRA's money came from New York. "We're getting the terrorists licked here, at least, we were. We don't want to hand them anything, not anything at all. I suppose you don't know about that kind of problem in New York."

"I just happen to live here in London," replied Daly coolly. "I also reckon that pretty soon pressures from New York and Washington for information are going to become overwhelming. I'm none too sure that if when that happens I can continue riding shotgun for British interests. It's not what I'm paid to do." His tone became tougher. "God damn it, your own radio stations are carrying reports of sabotage right now."

Thompson intervened. The time had come for a little diplomacy.

"Time is always the enemy. At least give us tomorrow, Colonel. By then it may all be in the government's hands anyway, if what you say is right. And if a terrorist is involved."

"By 'government,' do you mean the home secretary?"

"He would be the responsible minister," said Thompson carefully.

Daly grinned happily. "OK, I'll buy that. He's the one guy I *would* like to see landed with this problem. Those well-chosen remarks of his are headline news in the States, too. I guess politicians are the cross all four of us have to bear."

Daly's dig at the home secretary relaxed the atmosphere of the meeting. Donaldson smiled and left the ugly nineteenth-century police building for the quarter-mile walk back to Victoria. He wanted to see how his team was progressing. To his surprise the red double-decker buses characteristic of London were moving along the Vauxhall Bridge Road, although it was still closed to ordinary traffic, while barriers sealed off all the small streets between it and the railway station. Neathouse Place had been abandoned as a press center and was occupied only by a couple of police cars. As he turned the corner, Donaldson realized that he was outside Chestergate House, where Gilly Carslake had her office. On the spur of the moment he was tempted to drop in, to see her eyewitness view of the station for himself. He got as far as the foyer, where the clock on the wall reminded him that it was well into lunchtime, 1:13 P.M. to be exact. She was bound to be out. To the surprise of the commissionaire, he turned around and left as abruptly as he had entered.

Wilton Road was also barricaded off, but Donaldson showed his pass and was allowed through. Along the side of the station, where last night ambulances had queued to collect casualties, there was now only a single vehicle, presumably standing by in case a rescue worker was injured. Down in Hudson's Place two black police lorries were being loaded with an assortment of baggage, much of it charred and obviously demanding careful handling. He kept an eye open for Chisholm and found the tall chief superintendent a moment later.

"That's the bulk of the airline luggage disposed of,"

Chisholm remarked. "Even the containerized cargo was slightly burned. The hand luggage is trickier. A lot of it is badly damaged, and how do you tell whether handbags and briefcases belonged to an airline or a train passenger? That's to say if it has no airline tag."

Donaldson commiserated with him. "I suppose the contents should help. Passports, credit cards, that sort of thing."

"Not always. It's a hell of a job, listing every item in every suitcase and handbag. That's the trouble about police work. You're accountable for anything you touch. It could take us another three days."

"If you find any drugs or firearms, you might let me know."

"Never fear." Chisholm laughed. "The customs are busy ferreting out possible contraband. The way they're going about things they'd find a hidden whisky miniature."

Donaldson wondered how much he should tell Chisholm. Deciding that the chief superintendent had little "need to know," he merely said guardedly, "Surprising items can be useful evidence for me. Especially the condition things are in and the places they were picked up."

Chisholm nodded. "We're labeling all the personal belongings with a note of where they were located in the wreckage."

"Did your men find anything on the roof?" Donaldson asked.

"They did. A few pieces, which have been handed over to your assistant."

"I must see how my teams are getting on. We could be removing some of the tinwork later today."

Chisholm looked at him inquiringly.

"The remains that we're not interested in, like aluminum covering the wings, metal definitely not associated with the failure. There should be some RAF vehicles coming from 71 Maintenance Unit to collect it."

"That reminds me," said Chisholm. "There have

been quite a few messages. Your ministry's after you, and from the sound of it, so is your wife."

Resignedly Donaldson went to the office upstairs. McPherson was there, scribbling on a pad.

"I'm glad you're back, Jim, the ruddy department's been ringing every half an hour. Could you not speak to them?"

"What's the problem this time?"

"It's these parliamentary questions. The secretary of state has three down for answer this afternoon, and the poor fool doesn't know what to say!"

Donaldson checked his watch. 2 P.M. already. He would have to forget about lunch. He rang the department, reminded them with some acerbity that he could not comment on possible sabotage and suggested that in the unprecedented event of the minister's being tongue-tied, he could always say that this was one of the widest-ranging air accident investigations ever initiated in Britain. He could tell the House of Commons that separate teams were being constituted to examine the DC-10's maintenance, its structure, its power plant, its systems, the human factors potentially affecting its crew and the way in which it was operated by Atlantic Airlines.

McPherson listened enchanted. He was a fundamentally rebellious man himself.

"That's what I like to hear, Jimmy boy," he enthused. "Let them have it amidships."

"More seriously, Mac, how soon can you recover that rear engine?"

"It's all of four tons, man. And the firemen are still cutting bodies out of the fuselage close by."

"Fix a hoist and get it down to Farnborough as soon as you can, will you? I badly want to know what happened inside that engine."

When McPherson had gone, Donaldson dealt with the other messages, rang the Connaught Hotel and asked them to tell Jane that he was on his way, then descended again to inspect the clearance of the wreck.

The undamaged Chatham side of the station was like the rear area of a battlefield. Although the absence of trains at the platforms and staff at the barriers gave it an unreal appearance, the concourse was a hive of activity. Boiler-suited workmen were carrying joists and steel struts through to the crash side, a variety of newly arrived officials were making notes, and in the midst of it, standing on the cab roadway where the temporary mortuary had been, were two huge RAF flatbed trailer trucks. An RAF flight lieutenant, incongruously smart in service dress, was supervising as workmen in khaki overalls carried "tinwork" through the arch from the wreck. Donaldson spoke briefly to the officer and walked through to the main concourse. One of the Fire Brigade's divisional officers was by the demolished remains of the bookstall. Donaldson crossed to him.

"Mr. Plowden's gone, I presume?"

"Yes, we've cut back our attendance considerably, though the job's proving more of a pig than we expected. We had hoped to have the last bodies out before the shifts change again at six. There's not much chance of that."

A few yards away firemen were patiently hacking away at the tilted remains of what had been the economy-class cabin. Donaldson watched as soldiers took away yet another gray plastic sack of human remains, pausing to allow a constable to label it. Police photographers were hovering behind the firemen, recording each newly exposed corpse, while he recognized Denman compiling a chart of their positions. There was a stranger with Denman also taking notes.

"Who is the other man?" he asked.

"Coroner's officer," answered the fireman. "We've half the world here worrying about where things have been found."

"Saves work in the end."

"Doesn't make it any easier on my lads."

"So when do you reckon to be out of here?" Donaldson asked.

"I wouldn't like to say. There's still the nose of the plane to deal with. When it comes to death you just have to work all the way through."

Donaldson remembered Melville, mentioned his being due on duty at 6 P.M. and the need for his help, then made his way back to look for more remnants of the tail. This in turn required him to find a senior railway engineer and ask that as little further damage as possible should be done to the tail plane.

The assistant chief mechanical engineer whom he eventually buttonholed reacted unenthusiastically.

"We're running a railway, sir. Not a scrap collecting competition. Two hundred thousand passengers a day pass through here normally. We need Victoria back in service."

"I realize that," said Donaldson. "And indeed I'm responsible for the removal of the whole aircraft."

"I reckon we can push the wreckage through the front of the station," said the engineer. "Clear the platforms and push the junk out toward the forecourt."

Donaldson's eyes blazed. He imagined bulldozers thrusting twisted metal into piles as though it were valueless.

"Emphatically not! It may seem like scrap to you. But the cause of this accident is not yet known. Even tiny items can provide clues. The whole aircraft has to be reassembled down at Farnborough. In particular we want every single fragment of the tail that we can find. We still have to make an exhaustive search of this area. It could be Tuesday or Wednesday before I'm satisfied."

The engineer's face flushed angrily. "The public must come first. We've got to have trains running again by Monday. And before then the station structure has to be made safe. There's a lot of shoring up necessary."

Donaldson glanced around. As he did so he realized that in the welter of other considerations there was something he had overlooked: the size of the exits. At the moment the RAF teams were having no problem transferring the initial batches of tinwork through the arch to the Chatham side where the low loaders were parked. But they were taking only small sections. The larger parts of the aircraft would never pass through, unless they were cut up to an extent he wanted to avoid. When you came to examine Victoria, recent rebuilding had narrowed down all the ways into the station except along the railway tracks themselves.

"The normal exits are too small anyway," he commented. "I have to dismember the wreckage as little as possible."

"In fact," the engineer replied thoughtfully, "the logical way to cope is to take it out on bogie bolsters. They're our equivalent of your flatbed trucks, with much the same limitations I imagine. They can take cargo up to thirteen feet high and ten feet wide."

"And they can go to Farnborough Station?"

"I don't see why not. What's more, we can use railway cranes to load them."

"That would certainly help."

"We'll start just as soon as I can bring the cranes and the bolsters in," declared the engineer, relieved.

Donaldson turned to face him. "You must understand," he said. "You can't rush this. . . . You can work quickly, but you can't rush. The police and the customs also have an interest. We'll have to discuss it with Mr. Chisholm. You just have to allow this kind of job the time it takes."

By the time Donaldson had explained, cajoled and finally insisted on what he wanted, it was after 3 P.M. Walking up toward Buckingham Palace, past groups of gossiping sightseers at every closed-off street junction, he did not reach the Connaught Hotel in Mayfair until nearly half past. The fine weather had begun to change, and the sky was overcast. It would probably rain before long.

The Connaught is one of London's most elegant hotels, much beloved of the more sophisticated visiting American film directors, actors and publishers. Hugh Johnson liked to stay here because if his guests thought they had seen a familiar face across the dining room, the explanation was always simple—they had. The real surprise was that no one made a fuss about the famous. When in good humor Johnson felt that if the world were completely perfect, the Connaught would be situated in Boston or New York.

However, by the time Donaldson trotted up the steps and into the small oak-paneled lobby, his disheveled appearance causing the hall porters mild astonishment, Johnson was pacing restlessly up and down. Jane and Sharon were sitting chatting in armchairs a yard or two away, bulging shopping bags attesting to their own day's activity. To a casual observer they could have been two socialites, cool, independent, enjoying a spree. A columnist's aphorism flashed through Donaldson's mind. "Any woman is twenty percent more desirable without her husband." If that was true, today's markup would be nearer fifty percent. He apologized briefly to Johnson, then went to greet his wife.

"Where have you been, darling?" she cried. "You look like a chimney sweep."

"You can't move down there without getting filthy. Be a love and order some tea while I have a wash."

While he was gone Sharon called out to her father. "Daddy, for Pete's sake come and sit down. You're making us both nervous."

Reluctantly he obeyed, but he could barely restrain himself when Donaldson returned.

"Listen, Jim, this whole town's buzzing with sabotage rumors. Come clean with us, will you? What's the truth?"

Before Donaldson could answer, a waiter appeared with a teapot, cups, bread and butter, jam, and cakes. There was a strained silence as he arranged these ingredients of English afternoon tea on the table between them. It was Jane who reopened the conversation with theatrical emphasis.

"Darling, Mr. Johnson is under dreadful pressure. Reporters keep telephoning the hotel and coming around. Already he's had horrible calls from people threatening him."

"Some language, believe me," Johnson cut in.

"I don't understand what gets into people," said Sharon.

Embarrassed, Donaldson gazed at the spotless white tablecloth. He thought of the grimy chaos he had just left and the fireman's clumsily phrased words, "When it comes to death you just have to work all the way through."

Jane continued, climaxing her argument.

"Airplanes don't just fall out of the sky, darling. That's what you've always said yourself. All Mr. Johnson needs is a statement that it could be sabotage. That would see him through until things calm down."

"In law sabotage also constitutes negligence by the operator. He's expected to take precautions."

"As I remarked this morning, Donaldson, let's not buck our fences." Johnson's clipped accent was harsh. "Am I right that you think this accident could be due to some kind of explosion or warhead?"

Donaldson drew in his breath sharply and glanced at Jane, but she busied herself pouring tea, pretending not to notice.

"I want to know what that readout revealed. Don't try to kid me either, I know you've examined it."

Donaldson sat up, warning bells sounding in his mind. He could reliably expect that what he said now would be leaked to the press. Johnson had obviously been cross-examining Jane. With so much at stake he would not be scrupulous. Indeed there was something suspicious about the way Jane had backed up Johnson.

"The flight records show that your aircraft went into a steepening dive from which it was impossible to recover," said Donaldson. "There is no conclusive evidence as to the reason, and I am not prepared to release the tape until it has been sent back to Sunstrand for a fully calibrated readout free of transducer error."

"Is that all you'll say?"

"As I said earlier, if you want technical information you will have to ask Colonel Daly."

"Whom you've successfully suborned," Johnson stormed.

Other people in the hotel were beginning to watch them. To Donaldson's surprise and embarrassment this did not appear to worry Jane. She intervened again, speaking with slow insistence, though her tone was brittle.

"Jim Donaldson," she rasped, "may I ask whose side you are on? Are you on our side or not?"

His face coloring, Donaldson looked at his wife.

"My dear," he began gently, "I am on no one's side. I cannot be—"

She did not wait for him to finish.

"Yes, you can," she insisted angrily. "You can most certainly. You can be on my side, your children's side. I want to go to America. I want you to take this job. Now will you or will you not do as I ask and give Mr. Johnson the statement he needs?" Briefly her tone softened, and she pleaded, "Please, Jim. Do something for me for once."

Donaldson stood up. He was trembling slightly, but his voice remained steady.

"I wish you could understand that I must be impartial," he said. "I cannot, I will not take sides, even for you."

Jane rose to her feet, flushed and furious, spitting out the words.

"To hell with you and your principles, to hell with your scientific detachment and your impossible high-mindedness. Go and sleep with your principles tonight if you're so fond of them."

Donaldson did not reply. He simply picked up his raincoat from the chair he had left it on and walked out of the hotel. After he had gone, Jane sat down again, blew her nose and sipped some tea.

"He is the most stubborn man I've ever met," she said bitterly. "Without exception."

By late afternoon Connie Maier and Jakov Allom reached the ninth hospital at which unidentified victims of the crash were being cared for. It was the Westminster. When they presented themselves at the Accident and Emergency Department there was some hesitation over Connie's now smoothly rehearsed request. After a brief interval a dark-suited man appeared, introduced himself as an assistant administrator and began systematically querying Connie's medical credentials. Eventually he came to a decision.

"There are a large number of relatives waiting for information. We've allocated the consultant's dining room to them. I'm afraid you'll have to take your turn."

"In the States we'd certainly go out of our way to assist a fellow doctor."

"To be blunt, we can't take everyone at their face value."

Allom stepped forward, pulling out his diplomatic identity card.

"The embassy will vouch for her."

"What is this all about?" demanded Connie. "Why shouldn't I be on the level?" She was tired and overwrought from the long day's ordeal.

"We've suffered the attentions of one fake doctor already, examining casualties at Victoria and giving press statements. It was twelve hours before we spotted him." The administrator almost snorted. "A failed first-year medical student who had picked up an armband with doctor on it."

"Will you listen?" cut in Connie irately. "That's not my bag. I may be bending the rules, but I've come a long way, and all I'm after is identifying one man. Don't you have a disposal officer here, someone with a casualty list?"

Abashed at Connie's robust attack, he relented and fetched a young doctor.

"I was the registrar with the first mobile team," the doctor explained. "By chance, the one man I helped rescue myself is here."

"Our mystery case," added a senior nurse, holding a clipboard with long lists attached to it. "The only clue to his identity was a visiting card, and the airline says nobody of that name was on board."

"He had very severe abdominal injuries," the doctor went on. "He's in intensive care. The only time he spoke he sounded like an American."

"May I visit him?" Connie's throat was dry. She thought they must be able to hear her heart pumping.

The administrator indicated agreement, and the young registrar escorted her up to the wards. For the ninth time Connie found herself being introduced to a ward sister and shown down a row of patients to an inert form beneath hospital blankets. She felt dazed, and the sister, noticing her unsteadiness, guided her elbow, but she shook herself free, and steeled herself to move alongside the bed and examine the man's face. For the ninth time the features she gazed down at were not her husband's. She stepped back, her eyes dull at the extinction of hope.

"No," she said wearily. "It's not Ben."

The young registrar led her away out of the ward and down to where Allom was waiting.

"It was scarcely a survivable crash," said the registrar hesitantly, running his fingers through his tousled hair, uncertain how much to say.

"Tell me." Connie stood erect in the hallway, pale, but controlled.

"There was one place where the plane's back seemed to have broken, throwing a few of the passengers out. That man was one. Only very, very few of the injured could have come from the aircraft."

"And the fire."

"I think the impact would have killed the others long before the fire."

"Thank you," said Connie. "Thank you very much. I wouldn't like to think of Ben suffering."

As she and Allom returned to the car she held his arm. "Thank you too, Jakov. You've been marvelous. I'm glad I came."

"A good wife could not do otherwise. I know the ambassador would like to see you, if you feel strong enough."

Connie assented, and Allom drove her to the Israeli Embassy in Kensington Palace Gardens, escorting her through the myriad security checks that protect the house. They had to speak into a microphone under television surveillance at the outer gate, and when the main door was finally opened, its thick steel bolts slid back with a solid clunk like a strong room grille. From across the street a policeman in a cubicle watched them. Even though she was accustomed to the checks at the UN offices, Connie was impressed.

"We are at war," commented Allom simply.

Inside, they were taken through the pillared hall and up the wide staircase to the ambassador's office. After conventional greetings, Allom related their day-long fruitless search.

"Then we must assume that Ben was killed?" queried the ambassador. "I am deeply sorry, Mrs. Maier, you will be in all our prayers."

A flicker of unspoken communication passed between him and Allom, barely more than a look, and he leaned forward in his chair, delicately placing his fingertips together, weighing his words.

"May I call you Connie?"

"Please."

"This may come as a shock to you, Connie. I think you should know that your husband was carrying documents of the greatest importance. His return from Jerusalem was delayed because of them. He stopped over in Paris to collect more."

"I guessed there was something like this," said Connie slowly. "Ben was normally so, well, dependable. He wasn't the kind who's always changing plans. Go on."

"We do not know if it was bad luck that his plane crashed"—the ambassador's dark eyes were fixed on hers—"or not."

"You mean . . . sabotage, somebody trying to kill him?" Connie's voice was rising. "You mean they'd . . . it's not possible."

The ambassador spread his hands in a gesture of uncertainty.

"With terrorists, anything is possible. But we cannot wait to find out. We must recover those documents urgently. Of course, we can apply through diplomatic channels. That will be a slow process. We need them in New York by Monday. Effectively we have two days only. As Ben's wife, seeking his personal possessions, you could perhaps retrieve them more easily than we can. Now that you are here, will you help us?"

Connie's head was swimming. The enormity of destroying a whole aircraft full of people, of killing her husband, of anyone doing that deliberately, overwhelmed her. Through a mist she replied.

"Yes, I will, of course I will."

"I am glad," said the ambassador. "Thank you."

Mick Melville checked in at the Greycoat Place Fire Station shortly before 6 P.M., one of two thousand firemen coming on duty in London as two thousand others finished an eight-hour shift. After the routine of returning to the fire station the previous evening to shed his heavy, sodden uniform and clean up, it had then taken him twice the usual time to find a train home to Purley. Instead of riding the pump, bells clanging, other traffic giving way to him, he had been abruptly projected back among the throng of ordinary commuters, waiting hours for trains because so many services had been disrupted by Victoria's closure. When he had finally reached home his wife, Patsy, had taken one look at him, brewed up a hot rum toddy with lemon and packed him off to bed. He had slept a solid ten hours. Today she had cooked him a huge lunch, pork chops with all the trimmings, and kept her questions to a minimum.

"Are you through with that air crash yet?"

"The character investigating it wants me back tonight." He had swallowed a mouthful of roast potato, licked his lips appreciatively and reassured her. "Don't worry, love. The worst is over."

However, when he and his crew reached the Victoria forecourt, their huge Dennis fire pump refueled, cleaned, and replenished with foam, he was grabbed by the divisional officer and told to forget Donaldson.

"Here, Mick, you're the man I need. It was you brought the pilot out yesterday, wasn't it?"

"That's right." Instantly Melville was keyed up. Those minutes spent hacking through into the gory sandwich of the cockpit would remain vivid in his memory all his life.

"The crews we've got coming on are mostly fresh. They need direction. Take them over, will you? There's an obstruction to fetching the last bodies out."

"Come on, lads"—Melville gestured to his own men —"bring the cutting gear."

"Watch out for kerosene," warned the officer. "There's still some around."

Melville led the way across the concourse, stepping over hoses, crowbars and other impedimenta of rescue. He noticed that the appearance of the wreck had changed substantially. Temporary girders, wedged with planking, reared up from the tarmac floor, supporting the damaged roof. Teams of RAF technicians in dirt-splashed khaki overalls were prizing free sections of the plane's fuselage and wings. Like ants scavenging the carcass of a dead bird, they and other salvage workers were slowly detaching and removing the wreckage, segment by segment. The station resounded to hammering, the screeching whir of saws, the rattling clunk of chains being pulled taut by winches and cranes. The Brighton side had been transformed into a gigantic workshop.

Melville absorbed all this, rapidly dismissing it when his attention focused on his own objective. Where the aircraft had rammed at first-floor level into the Grosvenor Hotel's gallery lounge, cratering the walls, stood an extraordinary structure. Great timber balks had been brought in to shore up the brickwork, so that firemen could safely work on scaffolding platforms around the plane's nose. What was going on below was concealed by temporary screening and guarded by railway police, presumably to prevent the TV cameras from filming it. There were still at least thirty-five reporters in the "pen." Their restless attentiveness to every movement on the concourse trumpeted their interest in whatever was hidden.

A fire crew coming off duty emerged as Melville approached, their grim expressions telling more than words.

"Makes you believe in the devil, that does," muttered one.

Melville swarmed up one of the ladders and found the departing officer. "What's the situation?"

The officer pointed to the hollow shell of fuselage, its sides wedged into the brickwork, within which firemen were cutting like miners at a tunnel coalface, save that the colors here were the torn and blood-spattered interior decor of the airliner's cabin.

"Looks like a bulkhead broke loose and shot forward," said the officer to Melville. "That's what's blocking us."

Melville took over, directing some men to try to cut their way back from the flight deck into the cabin. As the minutes passed he began to understand what he was dealing with.

Along most of the DC-10's length there were cargo holds below the passenger cabins. But the forward hold contained a galley for the stewardesses to prepare meals in, from which two narrow elevators rose to the cabin above, concealed in a wide bulkhead which also divided the first class from the economy class. Underneath the galley, lower down still, was the plane's huge nosewheel assembly, a solid concentration of heavy metal. Tremendous forces had been released when the aircraft crashed. The seemingly strong fuselage had been crushed like an eggshell in a child's fist. The nosewheel had been punched up into the galley, and in turn, the galley was squashed into the cabin floor, which also had buckled upward. In the same instant the deceleration of the plane's hitting the wall had made the passengers' seats tear free from their mountings, sending both seats and people hurtling forward. And from behind, like a ram compressing the carnage, had come the bulkhead containing the elevators.

The way Melville realized all this was to give him nightmares for weeks to come. He watched a fireman wielding a compressed-air-driven hacksaw, when suddenly the hacksaw blade ran red.

"Stop," he yelled.

The fireman switched off the power, saw the blood, retched and muttered, "Christ alive, what's in there?"

Twenty minutes later, gingerly using chisels, they

had cut away enough to know that it was an elevator and that a stewardess had been inside it, presumably trying to escape from the galley as the plane crashed.

Later, when they had managed to hack the bulkhead away and started taking out the last bodies from what had been the first-class cabin, Melville turned to the leading fireman, his voice choking.

"Maybe she was lucky."

The passengers in the front had nearly all lost their feet above the ankles, brutally severed by the metal frames of the seats in front of them. Some had lost arms; some had been decapitated. Piece by piece these terrible remnants, often held together only by blood-soaked clothing, were brought out and handed down to be put in bags and labeled. A tarpaulin had been spread over the tarmac where this was being done, and great dark wet patches on it testified to the horror of the operation.

On the way back to Victoria from the Connaught, Donaldson felt faintly dizzy, so he stopped for some tea at the WRVS canteen van that was still parked in the forecourt.

"You look half dead," sympathized the scarlet-aproned woman running it.

"Tell me," he asked. "What does a man do when he's quarreled with his wife and he thinks it's her fault?"

"Oh!" She laughed. "My husband always stays the night at his club and has a good sleep. He's absurdly traditional. He comes back the next day."

"Thanks," said Donaldson, cheering up. "I'll recommend you for a medal."

Then he unexpectedly found himself detained, first by the county surveyor, who was charting both the wreck and the overall damage to buildings, and next by a representative of the insurers. Yet again he was asked if the accident could have involved sabotage.

"The hull alone is marked at twenty million dollars," the man explained. "The lawyers reckon the airline could be sued for up to a hundred million by the families and the rebuilding of the station won't exactly be cheap. Over seventy percent of the insurance is on the London market."

Donaldson laughed. "Ironic that they did a face-lift on the station only a year ago because British rail couldn't afford to rebuild." He paused. "I'm afraid that's the only comment I'm prepared to make."

"Can we start salvaging wreckage?"

"Emphatically not." Donaldson blazed up momentarily. "I want nothing touched, and frankly I'd rather you kept away until all the bodies have been cleared."

"We're under severe pressure from the airline. . . ."

"I'm sure you are," snapped Donaldson. "Try coming back next week."

Having delivered this snub, he walked off to find Melville. The fireman had completely forgotten about the original assignment.

"Sorry, sir," Melville called down from the scaffolding, "this had to come first."

He waved agreement to Melville and went to ask the divisional officer for another crew to help him continue his examination of the tail. The huge assembly, normally standing as high as a house, was still perched grotesquely in the roof girders. He had given strict orders for it not to be touched. It was dusk before Donaldson and his airframe inspector had seen all they needed. Wearily he departed, took a taxi to the RAF Club in Piccadilly and telephoned his wife. Their conversation was short and painful.

"I don't know if I even want to see you," she said. "Not if I can't come first in your life."

Exasperated and tired, he let fly at her. "I believe you've deliberately helped fix Johnson's mind on the sabotage theory. What on earth do you think you're playing at!"

She gave a little gasp, there was a click, and he realized she had rung off. It cost him an effort of will not to dial the number again immediately.

"That evens up the score," he told himself. "I walked out of the Connaught, and she's put the phone down on me. Now let's leave things to cool down a bit."

Fearful of weakening, he left the booth and went upstairs to the television room. He was curious to see what the reporters were making of the crash.

As he entered the dimly lit room, Donaldson thought he heard a voice he knew. With a shock he realized that the face on the screen was Johnson's. Whether the colors were heightened by the medium or by makeup, and precisely why the camera emphasized certain facial features rather than others, Donaldson did not know. What hit him was that Johnson came across as the archetypal lean-jawed, weather-beaten, plain-spoken American. And some plain speaking was what he was treating the interviewer to. A moment later Donaldson understood why. The third man on the program was Falkender, the attorney; the fourth was a parliamentarian noted for his vituperative attacks on private enterprise, Enoch Andrews, the Honorable Member for Mid-Fife.

"You British," Johnson was exclaiming, "are famous for your sense of fair play. Right? A man is innocent until he's proved guilty. Right? Yet your government has condemned my airline out of hand. So far as I can see, the whole of Britain has. Without waiting for evidence."

Tension was rising in the studio. The interviewer tried to restore the balance.

"It *is* unfortunate that the representative of the insurers was unable to join us here."

"The insurers wouldn't dare," cut in Falkender quickly. "Not with the size claims they're in for."

"Surely international treaties limit those claims, too," suggested the interviewer, glancing hastily at the research notes compiled for him beforehand. "What about the Warsaw Convention and the Montreal Agreement? Doesn't 'Montreal,' as airline people call it, set a limit of seventy-five thousand dollars?"

"No, sir," declared Falkender roundly. "Not so far as Americans are concerned. To quote one of our leading aviation lawyers, Mr. Stuart Speiser, 'This treaty in effect inflicts foreign economic and moral standards upon American citizens in their hour of greatest suffering for the benefit of airlines which collect their handsome fares in American money.' "

Johnson bristled. He knew the quotation from Speiser's standard work all too well. But before he could reply Andrews saw an opportunity and seized it.

"Unhappily," he said sententiously, "there is another law for the British. The infamously inadequate Fatal Accidents Act of 1846, even as amended by the Law Reform Act of 1934, puts the value of a British life at a piddling seven hundred and fifty pounds."

Andrews leaned forward, the camera following him in close-up. "That, Mr. Johnson, is one reason why Members of Parliament like myself are so concerned about this terrible crash."

"In my view British families affected by this disaster could sue in New York," chipped in Falkender, neatly plugging his own mission.

Andrews was not to be deterred. He poked forward his weasely head, with its sandy hair and prominent ears, as though he were sniffing for a kill. "We cannot afford low standards, Mr. Johnson. As the home secretary said, we cannot afford 'rogue operators.' "

The camera panned across to Johnson.

"But what if it is sabotage," demanded Johnson, "which I have strong reason to believe it is?"

Andrews flicked his fingers contemptuously, as though brushing away an insect. "Speculation is no substitute for facts. The facts are that a dreadful tragedy has occurred."

"Let me tell you something," said Johnson angrily. "I came on this program for one reason only. To defend my airline because we're having a raw deal. When that happens a man in my position has more than a right to speak out. He has a duty. I have a duty to myself and the good name of American aviation. Let me tell you something, Mr. Andrews, I've just had a close look at the passenger list of my Blue Ribbon flight. And to hell with diplomatic protocol. I'm going to tell you what's on it. The names of three men plenty of people would have good reason to want dead."

Even watching from the back of the room in the RAF Club, Donaldson could see the pallor creep over Andrews' freckled face. He hunched as though Johnson had threatened him with physical assault. It was Falkender who answered, timing his thrust perfectly to fill the gasping pause.

"Isn't that a trifle melodramatic, Mr. Johnson? And even if it were true, failure to safeguard an aircraft against sabotage still constitutes negligence."

But Johnson had done his homework, and seeing Andrews falter, he followed up ruthlessly.

"Can you deny that this city has already seen the attempted assassination of a Jordanian ambassador, letter bombs sent to prominent Jews and countless Irish killings? Can you deny that?"

Andrews shook his head. He was regretting being on this program.

"There were important citizens fitting all those three categories aboard my aircraft, sir." Johnson managed to instill unbounded contempt into the last word. "Maybe you'll mention that in your next parliamentary question to the home secretary?"

The interviewer, responding to worried signals from the producer's control box, intervened and terminated the program with a string of platitudinous thanks.

In the RAF club television room there was a general stirring and whispering.

"Wiped the floor with that bugger Andrews, didn't he?" remarked one listener.

"And with me," said Donaldson, rising to leave and go to bed.

Chapter Nine

As Londoners breakfasted on Saturday morning, lazily aware that the day's business consisted of nothing more strenuous than shopping, sport and watching the weekend television programs, a white police car left Rochester Row for the Battersea heliport on the south bank of the Thames. Inside were three men, a forensic expert from the Ministry of Defense, David Chance, the CID chief superintendent of "A" Division, and Donaldson. They carried with them the calculations made at the Data Center, showing the approximate point above south London where the DC-10 experienced its unknown explosion. The car made a slight detour to drop off Donaldson at Victoria before speeding down to the Embankment.

"You're in for a bumpy ride, I'm afraid," he commented as they left him.

Donaldson was right. The weather had changed. A strong northwesterly had brought low clouds racing across the sky with an occasional spattering of rain. On arrival at the heliport the two men sheltered in the tiny terminal building beside the landing pad and briefed their pilot. They were being deliberately vague about the purpose of their flight. Chance displayed a map of central London jabbing his finger at an arc of roughly a half-mile width extending south of the river in Southwark.

"We want to take a close look at every high-rise block in that area. Can you land on a roof?"

"Pretty dicey with most buildings, sir," said the pilot doubtfully. "That's what the fire survey showed. They nearly all have water tanks or lift machinery or ventilation ducts."

"You could winch me down, though," suggested the forensic expert.

"No winch on our Bell 47s I'm afraid, sir. Or on the Enstrom. Probably the nearest choppers with a winching capability are with Bristow's at Redhill. The best I can offer is a rope."

Chance swore. "We can't afford to wait. Fix a rope."

Ten minutes later the glossily painted helicopter, its doors removed, was flying along the river. As it turned right over Bankside, once the site of Shakespeare's Globe Theater, across the water from the majestic bulk of St. Paul's Cathedral, the CID officer remarked over the intercom, "Only seven at most."

Compared to the forest of towers in the City north of the Thames, south London had few. Chance gave a cheerful thumbs-up sign. Although he and Commander Thompson had both been up most of the night, he was invigorated by any form of chase or action. He liked events to move fast, and a year ago he had been commended for bravery in tackling an armed burglar.

"Let's get on with it," he said over the intercom, and ordered the pilot to hover briefly over each high-rise building in turn.

From the ground the buildings all appeared to have flat roofs. But it was surprising how cluttered their tops really were. Only two appeared to offer the view, the space and the concealment behind a parapet, which a clandestine missile firing would have needed. After a quick consultation, the two men plumped for the tallest, contacted the patrol car collaborating with them and gingerly readied themselves to descend the rope. It was not going to be easy. A television aerial obstructed the pilot's maneuvering. Gusts of wind rocked the helicopter. Chance went first, swaying as he clutched the rope, hair and clothing whipped by the rotor's down draft. Far below in the street a barrow boy paused to watch, until the patrol car roared up and he decided prudently to move on.

When the helicopter whirled away, blades clattering, to hover close by, the forensic expert stood quite still and looked carefully around.

"These small missiles scarcely leave any ground signature," he explained. "The main rocket ignites a good fifteen feet from the launcher and incidentally doesn't make a vapor trail either, except in extremely humid conditions. Still, the initial propellant may have deposited some trace of powder."

They discovered empty beer cans and rubbish in a corner and various stains on the roofing.

"We can't ignore them, I suppose," muttered the forensic expert, kneeling down to make an examination. Fifteen minutes later he rose to his feet. "No go, I'm afraid." He indicated the horizon, with Big Ben distinctive in the distance. "The firer would have had to face west because the missile would follow the aircraft. So any mark from the launcher would have been behind him and away from the parapet. Nothing much worse than an illicit picnic's been going on up here."

Chance raised his hand high and signaled the helicopter to return. The pilot edged in above them, the rope dangling.

"I'd forgotten we might have to climb up again," said Chance ruefully. However, he managed it with remarkable agility, scrambling on hands and knees through the helicopter's door space and then pulling his companion up after him.

"Haven't gone up a rope for years," panted the expert, as Chance hauled him over the sill. "Glad we aren't escaping from a fire!"

Minutes later they were lowering themselves down onto the next tower, not far from Southwark Bridge. Again the pilot hovered a few yards away, while people in the streets craned their heads back to watch.

"Let's hope this is the one," shouted the expert. "I'm not sure I could do that again."

Making deductions based on the airliner's track on the Thursday, he selected a part of the roof to search. But it was Chance who found the first clue— a scrap of the thick water-resistant protective paper in which the missile had been wrapped. Whoever had been here had not cleared up thoroughly enough. By the time the helicopter returned the forensic expert had also found what he was seeking on the bitumen of the roof covering. Down at ground level local police had routed out the keyholder from his home and were opening the main entrance doors.

Breakfast in the Alloms' flat was proving a cheerless meal. The evening before, Judith, warmhearted and hospitable, had hustled Connie off to bed early, persuading her to take a sleeping pill as well. Indeed Connie had required little persuading. A night spent crossing the Atlantic, jet lag and the searingly emotional trail around the hospitals combined to leave her bone tired. She had slept late, waking relaxed and a little muzzy. But within moments she had been seized by fear; her insides turned over and she felt sick. She reared up in bed, almost screaming. A second later she remembered what was wrong: she had not found Ben. She sank back and clenched her fists, knowing that she would not give up searching. Then she got up and dressed purposefully.

"Never mind what I said yesterday," she insisted as they all sat in the large kitchen and Judith brewed more coffee. "As far as I'm concerned Ben's alive until it's proven otherwise."

Jakov Allom sighed to himself. He was convinced that Ben could not have survived and now wanted to concentrate on retrieving the vital documents. Though himself an affectionate husband, Allom was a realist. The dead should wait for the living, and the living Israel needed Ben Maier's briefcase, not his body.

Connie misinterpreted Jakov's silence.

"Visiting mortuaries is no kind of fun," she went on. "But at least I'm accustomed to them. I guess I can take it."

"Then I will make the arrangements." Allom went to telephone, returning twenty minutes later somewhat agitated.

"I am so sorry. It is terribly complicated. The mortuary is organized by a specialist firm retained by the airliner. I spoke to the head office. First, they said it is their policy never to allow relatives into the mortuary after an air crash. When I argued they said it was a matter for the police. They could not authorize." As he recounted what had clearly been a verbal battle, Allom's command of English grammar began to slip. "I argued more. They said in any case less than forty bodies have been positive identified. No Maier is among them. It is very strange. I was thinking the police ask relatives to make formal identifications after accidents."

"Maybe not after air crashes."

Connie sat puzzled for a few moments. Then the long-nurtured reaction of a strong-minded woman, used to getting her way, came to the surface.

"Listen, Jakov," she said firmly. "No disrespect to you. None at all. But would you mind if I call the U.S. Embassy? After all, I was born an American citizen. They'll have some centralized organization going for relatives by now."

Allom could not object. This woman had the determination that builds nations, the grit Israel herself could use.

Connie discovered that the embassy had a counselor service operating on a twenty-four-hour basis, and had done so since half an hour after the crash.

"A number of next of kin have arrived," the vice-consul on duty told her. "And we've a load of telex and cable messages. Most people are waiting for the British to come up with information and we're telexing back for details. Dental histories and such. You're the first we've had wanting to go right in there. I'll see what I can do."

Connie waited impatiently for another half hour, for an hour. Shortly before 11 A.M. the vice-consul rang back apologetically.

"I'm afraid, Mrs. Maier, you'll have to ask the police. Not only is there strict security. They feel, well, it could be a pretty upsetting experience for anyone." The vice-consul circled around the direct phrases that he might have used. "I have to warn you that few of the corpses are, well, easily recognizable. I really would advise against visiting the mortuary, Mrs. Maier."

Connie replaced the telephone.

"Jakov," she called. "Who was that helpful policeman you met? Let's go find him."

While the helicopter was flying over Southwark, Donaldson had begun catching up on his own team's progress at Victoria. In contrast to the previous morning, he was feeling alert and vigorous. He had half expected to be woken in the middle of the night by a call from Jane, but no peremptory buzzing from the night porter had disturbed his slumber. He had risen at seven, shaved and descended to make a swift survey of the morning papers as he munched toast and marmalade in the dining room.

The crash again dominated the headlines, this time with a mixture of casualty figures and speculation deriving from Johnson's outburst on television. The number of bodies retrieved had evidently reached four hundred. Along with an assortment of interviews with people who had narrowly escaped death were photographs of the wreck, of lost children reunited with their parents and, not surprisingly, of Johnson himself.

Donaldson could not restrain a smile as he skipped through the sabotage theories. Each paper's air correspondent had his own idea, though there was a certain consensus about a possible bomb in the DC-10's rear toilets. However, no newspaper had any theories about a missile.

Thanking his maker for small mercies, Donaldson had gulped down his coffee and then taken a taxi to Rochester Row, hopeful that the flight path calculations would have arrived. They had, together with a note confirming an earlier message that spectographic analysis of the fragment he had found in the tail suggested that it was relatively impure, unstressed metal that had been fractured by blast. It emphatically was not any part of a turbine blade.

Now, as the police car drove him back to Victoria, Donaldson felt he had been living with the turmoil in the station for a week at least. It was hard to believe that the disaster was still only forty hours old, albeit entering its third calendar day. Apart from the distraction of Jane's unexpected moods, the pressure of events had absorbed him totally. It was always the same with major accidents. The moment when brainpower began to dominate what had happened, instead of vice versa, was as slow in arriving as the catastrophe was fast. But, unlike Commander Thompson, he never would control events. His life was spent analyzing the reasons for them. It struck him that perhaps what Jane really objected to was the fact that he dealt entirely in the unexpected. She could never tell her friends in advance what he was going to be investigating, or when, or where, and with every emergency he vanished from ordinary domestic routine.

Coming back to immediate questions, he reflected that he was a long way from mastering the causes of this crash, even if a missile did prove to have been basically responsible. For all he knew a partial disintegration of the rear engine could have also damaged the tail. The control cables that operated the elevators could have been severed. Equally Bill Curtis himself could have had heart failure as the emergency developed and taken the wrong corrective action. Heart failure was an element in a surprising percentage of airline accidents and Curtis was a good fifty years old. Every possible contributory factor would have to be examined and either exonerated or judged responsible.

When Donaldson stepped out of the car at Victoria he saw that the new day had brought its changes. Where there had been a long line of fire appliances in Buckingham Palace Road, now there were only four. The one remaining ambulance had gone. Significantly so had the khaki-painted army trucks, and he guessed that the last bodies must have been recovered. Another of the RAF's sixty-foot-long low loaders was parked by the cartoon cinema, the kind jocularly known as a "Queen Mary" because of its size. On it was one battered but recognizable aircraft engine, mounted in a protective cradle. As he walked through the entrance into the station, he almost bumped into McPherson, directing the transfer of another engine out to the low loader. The engine itself lay on wooden balks on top of two ordinary luggage trolleys, which were cracking under the weight in spite of the wood spreading the loads. In the roadway sweating workmen busied themselves around a big Scammell truck with a crane mounted on it.

"We got the bastard out at last, Jim," announced McPherson, wiping his forehead with a hairy forearm. His hands were black with oil and soot.

"There's your rear engine for you," he went on caustically, "and further forward than I trust I'll ever see one again. It must have hit the building like a steam hammer. It's been a right pig digging out. In fact, we could never hae done it wi'out a rare bit of kit these railway boys own. Have you seen that Lukas jack affair?"

Donaldson nodded. He remembered watching one raising part of the cargo hold the day before. McPherson glanced around.

"It's a miracle that thing. Lifted this lump like a baby while the man stood playing with the keyboard like a toy organ. Not that we didn't have a hell of a time swinging it across on to those damn fool trolleys. Had to use two sets of block and tackle. You know, Jim, moving stuff out of here's not going to be so easy."

"I'm fixing for us to use railway wagons," said Donaldson, but his eyes were on the engine. None of the enormous round intake cowling remained. That most characteristic feature of the DC-10's silhouette must be lying in fragments on the platforms. The engine was like the kernel of a nut. Outside were the cowlings; at the heart was the near solid hunk of elaborately

294

machined turbines which delivered the power. At the front of the engine was a huge fan, more than a man's height in diameter, which in flight swirled air back to the two stages of high-pressure compressor. Donaldson noted that the fan's thirty-eight massive blades had been violently bent back and the ring protecting them torn off. Behind it was a long casing that hid the turbine compressors and the annular combustion chamber. Severed pipes, coils of wire and mangled auxiliary components hung around the casing's circumference, all scarred by fire.

"It's a bloody great engine, it is," remarked McPherson, admiration strong in his voice. "The manufacturer's manual arrived last night. One inch less than nine feet in maximum diameter. And one inch more than sixteen feet long. Forty-one thousand pounds of thrust on takeoff. A bloody fine engine."

"Well," said Donaldson practically, "no doubt when it's been taken apart at Farnborough we'll know roughly how much thrust it was delivering when it hit."

McPherson pointed at the way the fan blades were bent and broken. "At first glance I'd guess it was no more than windmilling. And it's most certainly been on fire in the air. I've an idea that one of the turbines broke up."

"Are you sure?" asked Donaldson, "As well as being hit by flying metal from the outside?"

"I'm not certain, mind. But I'll bet you a tanner to five pound that when she's opened up they'll find deposits of alloy downstream from the second turbine and the turbine itself'll be stripped clean as a whistle. There'll be not a blade on it, that's my opinion."

"Could it have been an explosive disintegration?"

McPherson glanced at Donaldson warily, a cunning expression on his dirt-smeared face.

"If it's explanations for those bloody reporters you're seeking, then that's one you could get away with."

Donaldson's thoughts were racing. Keeping their theories secret was going to be extremely difficult. "Are the manufacturers sending a technical advisor to help you?" he asked. The complexity of the power plant was such that the investigation team would need a specialist familiar with its precise type.

"Aye," McPherson admitted grudgingly, "a man's arrived from Frankfurt, and he'll be waiting at Farnborough."

"Well, be nice to him," said Donaldson. McPherson was apt to resent rival experts. "And don't let him see anything that could lead him to guess what we think has happened. All right?"

"You're joking!"

"I am not, Mac. We have to keep this under wraps, so stall him, take him out to lunch. Anything you like. OK?"

Donaldson moved away, leaving McPherson dolefully shaking his head, and began checking the progress made in removing the wings and fuselage. The team of mechanics had been expanded today. Technicians from both his own ministry's establishments and from the RAF were painstakingly marking each piece of debris with its location in the wreckage. Removing it all would be a mammoth task, involving a multiplicity of decisions: where precisely to dismember unmanageably large sections; how to extricate them from the roof girders which railway engineers were busily cutting away in some places and supporting in others; how to raise the starboard engine from its burial place in the lavatory beneath the remains of the bookstall when no crane could be brought onto the concourse. They would be lucky if they got it all out by next Wednesday, as he had told the railway engineers they might.

Nearby the airframe inspector detailed to assist him was making a chart of the wreck, showing the exact distribution of the debris. The chart would be a key document at the eventual public inquiry and would be published. Donaldson was discussing it when to his surprise he saw the chief fire officer bearing down on them.

"I didn't expect to see you here, Mr. Plowden."

Plowden was in the everyday uniform of the Fire Service, a conventional black tunic and a peaked hat with a shield-shaped enameled badge based on London's coat of arms. He shook hands with Donaldson, as if being out of fire-fighting gear restored formality to his working relationships. But the way he spoke was as terse and unsparing as ever.

"When I've been in charge of a fireground I check it out myself. There's a lot of worry in this business. I wouldn't want anyone else held responsible for what I've handled."

Plowden gestured at the last four fire crews, who were rolling up hoses and taking away the tripodlike fixed ground monitors that had held them.

"We're putting the hoses up. There's no fire risk worth speaking of anymore. All the unburned kerosene was washed down into the drains yesterday. Ordinary water's the cure for that. It was cutting out the bodies that held us up."

"When did you find the last one?"

"Three hours ago. Soon after dawn. It's all yours now."

Donaldson gazed at the wreck. He recalled Melville's efforts: saving life from the flames; cutting through to the corpses of the crew; searching in the still hot metal for the flight recorder.

"There is one thing," he said.

Plowden glanced at him sharply, anticipating further demands on his permanently overcommitted resources.

"I'd like to see Melville's devotion to duty recognized."

"Oh." There was relief in Plowden's voice. "Oh, yes. He's a good lad, Mick Melville. Between ourselves I've ordered him around to headquarters this afternoon to tell him so."

"I'm glad. If anyone deserves a medal out of this, he does."

"I may yet recommend it," grunted Plowden, who considered awards were the Fire Brigade's business, not outsiders'. He shook hands again before rejoining his men.

As the "Queen Mary" low loader rumbled down the M3 motorway to the Farnborough exit, bearing the two battered aircraft engines cradled in steel and timber frames, McPherson sat up front in the cab. The roaring motor effectively blocked conversation with the driver, so he silently pondered the effects that an external explosion might have on a turbine, something of which he had no experience to date. Was it the explosion or the crash that had severed the fuel lines? If the former, then the rear engine could have suffered a flameout. Basically a jet burns fuel mixed with air inside a combustion chamber. The air expands colossally and then is shot out backward, pushing the aircraft forward. If deprived of fuel, the flame goes out and the engine ceases to produce power, though its finely balanced turbines will continue windmilling. Was this engine burning *and* turning, or only turning? Either way its outside was certainly on fire. Then again, had internal disintegration sent slivers of turbine blade slicing like shrapnel through the casing and into the adjacent tail plane?

McPherson was jolted out of his unpleasing reverie as the truck swung off the motorway and headed for the drab lines of streets and shops that had turned Farnborough from a village into a sprawling town with a growing complement of light industries and a world-famous name as the host of the biennial international air show. A few minutes later the driver eased the low loader through the main gate of the Royal Aircraft Establishment, the security guard checking them in. The RAE looked what it was—a place that had grown according to need. Hangars, workshops and offices were spread out around one side of the airfield, but the overall impression was misleading. Nothing proclaimed the fact that eight thousand people worked here, more than fourteen hundred of them scientists. The whole place was a classic piece of British understatement, and it always tickled McPherson's sense of humor that the only permanent monument to the successes of the past was a small tree, standing gaunt and leafless near the ancient black painted corrugated iron sheds that had housed the original army balloon factory in 1905 and which now were the airfield fire station. The tree was leafless for the very good reason that it was fashioned of metal, a commemorative replica of the stunted growth to which S. F. Cody used to tether the crude biplane he built here and in which he made the first officially recognized powered flight in the British Isles in October 1908.

The low loader ground past this curious monument in second gear and, obeying traffic light before crossing the end of the main runway, followed the perimeter track around the large white hangar where the stress tests on the Concorde supersonic airliner had been carried out, then went on behind the raised terraces where aircraft manufacturers set up their stands during the air show. After another half mile the driver stopped at hangar T-49, the graveyard of the airfield, the place where the structures department would lay out the remains of the Atlantic Airlines DC-10.

A group of men were waiting with a mobile crane standing by. McPherson noticed that the concrete hardstanding at the side of the hangar was completely taken up with the wreckage of a variety of aircraft. He climbed down from the cab, and one of the four accident investigators based at Farnborough stepped forward to greet him.

"How are you, Mac? Long time no see."

"Good to see you again." McPherson shook hands with his colleague, then jerked a thumb at the wrecked planes on the concrete. "You've cleared some space for us, I see."

"Correct. We had to move several others out to make room."

McPherson drew the man aside.

"Why not show me the hangar for a wee moment?"

Mystified, the investigator led him through the door and into the high hangar, its floor dark with oil stains. Rows of bright lights hung suspended among its green-painted roof girders. Completely empty, save for various trestle tables and lightweight metal frames, the interior looked huge. Eventually the pieces of the DC-

10's fuselage would be mounted on the metal frames and the innumerable small components of its mechanical and electrical systems would be laid out on white oilcloth sheets on the tables. Already a blackboard stood at one side with the DC-10's details chalked on it. It would take weeks, possibly months, to sort out all the wreckage into precise order, nor could it be removed until the public inquiry was over. Then some parts would be sent to the United States, if the airline or the manufacturers wanted them, while the bulk was handed over to the insurers for sale as scrap.

"The last time we cleared this place out was for the Trident. The DC-10's a much larger aircraft. I reckon it'll be a tight squeeze," commented the Farnborough investigator, walking over to a table and picking up a plastic model of a DC-10. "We had the boys make up a kit as usual to give us the proportions. We'll certainly need to stagger the layout of the wings."

"Well," said McPherson, "that's not my problem, thank the Lord. Anyway, you may not need to bother yourself too much with the wings. The reason I wanted to talk to you in private, laddie, is that we may have a 'first' on our hands. For the moment there's a bit of trade secrecy about the fact." In RAE jargon, any type of accident they had never encountered before was called a "first."

After McPherson had explained the probable background to the crash the investigator demanded firmly, "And what about the man from General Electric? He's flown in from Frankfurt. The reputation of the CF6 engine's at stake, and he's raring to open up these. He's already pointed out quite forcefully that the CF6 is flying on four types of wide-bodied aircraft with a large number of airlines. The reason he's in Germany is that Lufthansa chose it for their 747s. As he said just now, a lot of guys in a lot of countries are going to be curious about what's on that truck. It's going to be difficult to stall him."

McPherson rubbed his chin, feeling the bristles and wondering how and where he could shave. He felt as unwashed as indeed he was. The effects of laboring all night were beginning to tell on him.

"You're right at that. Any decent engineer will spot there's something odd about the damage soon enough. We'd best go and telephone Jim or the department—and do you keep a razor in your office by any chance?"

The briefing rooms on the first floor of Rochester Police Station had been commandeered for coordinating lists of airline baggage, where a number of constables were laboriously establishing the names of the owners with the aid of a passenger manifest and two customs officers. The second floor was buzzing with CID men. Radio and news reports that the rescue operation was being "masterminded" from here had created a rush of telephone calls, some genuine, some hoaxes. Outside in the street a small group of photographers and reporters waited by the entrance trying to snatch interviews from anyone who went in or out.

On the top floor Thompson, Donaldson and David Chance were in conference, while Sturgess made notes.

"So the evidence is conclusive?" Chance was asking. "From this moment on we're definitely hunting a terrorist?"

"Checking back," Donaldson replied, "what have we got? Penetrations in the aircraft's tail surfaces. A fragment of metal which spectrographic analysis reveals is not from a compressor blade or any other known component of a DC-10, so is presumably a shrapnel fragment. Crew reports of an explosion. Flight recorder showing a violent tremor. Unusual penetrations in the jet pipe and casing of the rear engine. The forensic expert's opinion that some form of missile or rocket has recently been fired from a tower block in Southwark. Of course," said Donaldson dryly, "these things could all be unconnected. No one has seen a missile."

"We suspect several have been brought into Britain in the diplomatic bags of an Arab state," said Chance.

"Surely the real question," Thompson interrupted, "is whether this was a random shot at an airliner, one that happened to be passing, as if were. Or whether this DC-10 was a specific target."

Suddenly Thompson wondered if he was talking nonsense. He was exhausted. No sleep on Thursday night had been followed by yesterday's preoccupations with restoring order, with the homeless, relatives, sight-seers, VIP's, officials. He had made more snap decisions in those twenty-four hours than he normally needed to make in two months. Then last night there had come a flurry of Home Office and Scotland Yard concern after Johnson's allegations on TV, adding new dimensions of uncertainty to the situation. If Johnson was right, and Donaldson's suspicions well founded, then somewhere in the wreckage lay the objective of the attack on the aircraft. In consequence he had little time for sleep last night either. Hours of debate in airless offices over cups of coffee while other people chain-smoked had left him feeling stale and dry. Being a nonsmoker himself made things worse. Despite a bath, he still felt that if there were some way of lifting out his inflamed eye-balls, he would find the sockets full of sand. The moment of self-doubt passed as Chance questioned the accident inspector.

"Given that we know the plane was shot down, do you think the airline president's allegations on television last night were more than guesswork?"

Donaldson hesitated, rubbing the side of his nose gently with one finger as he often did when embarrassed. If the banner headlines in this morning's papers were to be believed, it was the question all Britain was asking. And only he knew that it was his own unthinking remark to his wife, which had been relayed to Johnson or his daughter, Sharon, that might have triggered the sensational statement.

"I'm not sure," he replied slowly. "I suspect that he took the existing press rumors about sabotage, had his staff make a careful check of the passenger list and decided he had enough ammunition to give the home secretary a run for his money. Johnson's had a pretty raw deal. Even discounting what we know, he's had a rough ride from a nation allegedly dedicated to fair play."

"The home secretary's remarks landed us all in the can," Thompson admitted, "but this is far worse. You've seen the reporters outside. Scotland Yard's Press Office is besieged. It's like Thursday all over again." He rubbed his eyes wearily. "There's going to be one hell of a lot of public interest in this story."

"I've already had demands from my department for guidance," said Donaldson. "And I have to be at the secretary of state's office at two this afternoon."

Now it was David Chance's turn to speak.

"Irrespective of political considerations, what we have here is a straightforward crime," he argued resolutely. "We have a few facts. I've a large number of men ferreting for more. Don't forget we do have one advantage. All the speculation is about sabotage, which most of the papers seem to think means a bomb smuggled on the plane at Paris. We must do nothing to alter that impression. Even so the TV interview may well have alarmed the terrorists, unless they've skipped the country. We must keep our mouths shut for at least another day."

"David's right," Thompson declared. "It all hinges on what, or who, they were after."

As he spoke there was a tap on the door. A constable entered.

"Excuse the interruption, Commander. There's a Miss Carslake wanting to see Mr. Donaldson."

Donaldson excused himself and followed Sturgess downstairs. Waiting in a tiny interview room off the hall was Gilly, sitting on an upright wooden chair at a plain table.

"This is my first experience of police stations," she confided after the constable had gone. "It's all rather unnerving." She glanced at the bare walls and sparse furniture. "I feel halfway to a cell already."

"Never mind. I'll bail you out," said Donaldson kindly. "What brought you here?"

"I saw that discussion program on telly last night."

Gilly was diffident, twisting a silk scarf in her fingers. "And, well. . . ."

"And?"

"It's probably nothing. Please don't think me an idiot. It reminded me of something Sam Eckhardt said yesterday."

"Go on."

"He was having another interminable phone conversation with his Arab friends when he got annoyed and rang off. He told me they were crazy. They were trying to persuade him that the Israelis had sabotaged the aircraft because an important Arab was on board. He was quite annoyed."

"And then?"

"He walked out. He didn't like my teasing him about the Arabs. For some reason he always takes the Arab side in arguments."

Donaldson's thoughts were racing. However, his final question revealed nothing of his excitement.

"Will he be using your office today?"

"He can't unless I'm there, and frankly I've had enough of him. He just uses people all the time."

"I didn't take to him much myself." Donaldson remembered the journalist's well-fed face and his velvet jacket, incongruous among the rescue workers. "Anyway, thank you. You're the most valuable witness to come forward yet."

Gilly relaxed. In an obscure way she felt she had been betraying confidences. The manner in which Donaldson received them reassured her.

She beamed at him, a wide, generous smile. "I'm glad. Really. Now I can go shopping and forget that wretched man."

Donaldson grinned, thinking to himself that it was all too long since he had talked to a happy girl like this.

"Unfortunately I'm in a meeting, or I'd offer you coffee. But please keep in touch," he said lightly, ushered her out and almost ran back upstairs.

"That was quick," remarked Thompson. "We thought if it was the same blonde as yesterday we might not see you for a while!"

Donaldson was uncertain whether to laugh or not. He was very self-conscious about his relationship with women. But rather than disregard the policemen's smiles, he replied in the same vein.

"I would have been tempted if she hadn't told me something interesting."

After he had recounted it, Thompson and Chance looked at each other. The two men had been working together for over three years, and the commander had developed a respect for his subordinate's ability to sense when a person or a situation was "bent."

"Are you thinking what I'm thinking, Dave?" asked Thompson.

"Either this reporter fellow is keeping an eye on things for more people than just his editor or the Arabs are taking an unusual interest in this incident?"

"Both." He turned to Sturgess. "You had an Arab making inquiries about passengers, didn't you."

"Yes. And the Israelis, too. There was one very persistent Israeli diplomat." Sturgess paused. "There's also the Palestinian demo this afternoon."

"Christ alive," Thompson exclaimed. "So there is. What with control being delegated to another commander, I'd put it out of my mind. I'll be forgetting my own mother next."

He sat still for a moment, scratching his chin in a contemplative way.

"I can tell you one thing," said Sturgess. "There were no Arab names on the DC-10's passenger list. If there was an important Arab on board, as this journalist Eckhardt was told, he was incognito."

Thompson stopped his scratching abruptly, and Chance whistled.

"That's not conclusive," commented Donaldson. "Important people often travel under false names. A surprising number of airline crashes include a mystery passenger."

"If we're looking for who shot this plane down," said Chance emphatically, "my money's on the Arabs. And I think we ought to talk to the Israelis."

Now memories of what had been going on before the

crash engulfed Thompson's mind. As he recalled his discussions with Sturgess about handling the demonstration, suddenly the dribbles of information they had discussed at Cannon Row, in the eternity ago of Thursday morning, fitted together in a different pattern.

"We've made a cobblers," he said to Chance. "Not that anyone could blame us. Those two agitators whom Special Branch reported entering the country weren't here for the demo. Or the Cup Final. Or the beer."

"Luckily," said Chance. "I don't think Special Branch have forgotten them. The last I heard they were making pretty intensive inquiries."

"Gloucester Road's the place," suggested Sturgess, "or Earls Court. The area's stiff with them. I know. I live there."

Chance was about to remind the inspector that the Special Branch had substantial reference files on undesirable aliens when there was a knock at the door and the constable reappeared.

"Sorry to disturb you again, sir. But there's another lady downstairs."

This announcement precipitated a roar of laughter from all four men, bewildering the constable, who was not accustomed to bringing the house down with an opening remark. "She wants Inspector Sturgess, sir," he said stolidly.

"Oh, she'll have to wait her turn if she wants *him*," said Thompson, still laughing. "Off you go, Colin."

As Sturgess left, Chance turned back to Donaldson. "In your experience why does anyone try to blow up an aircraft?"

"Generally speaking, there are only two reasons for aircraft being sabotaged. To kill someone. Or to destroy something. All the cases I've known boiled down to one or the other. A husband wants to kill his wife to get the insurance, subversives want to kill a politician —that's presumably what happened to the Middle East Airlines Boeing that came down in Saudi Arabia. The second kind often wants just to destroy an aircraft for the publicity. Like the men with the bazooka at Orly. No one's even sure which airliner they were aiming at."

306

"Terrorism is certainly indiscriminate," agreed Chance. "Could our lot have meant to shoot down a completely different plane?".

"On a clear day and with the aircraft at least four miles apart as they come in, it doesn't sound likely. Though possibly all this terrorist wanted was to bring down a wide-bodied jet just to show his organization could do it."

"In which case," Chance reflected, "it's odd that they haven't claimed responsibility. They've staged their stunt. Why not get the credit? It can only be because the job is in some way unfinished."

As the CID man spoke an idea took shape in Donaldson's head.

"This journalist Eckhardt," he said. "Rather foolishly I told him I might have something by this morning. I've no doubt he'll turn up demanding his interview. If you think he has a connection with the Arabs, I could pass him on to you."

"Good idea," interjected Thompson enthusiastically. "We might wheedle something out of him."

"Or feed him a line," suggested Chance. "We could use a line to the terrorists." He clicked his tongue in irritation. "If they are Arabs."

"Eckhardt will probably come around midday," said Donaldson. "He said he had to file his story early."

As Donaldson spoke Colin Sturgess reentered the room and addressed himself to Thompson.

"It's the wife of the Israeli who was in the plane. Mrs. Maier. There's a man with her, the diplomat who visited me a couple of times in the trailer."

"Have they been to the casualty bureau?"

"No joy there, apparently. They want your permission to go to the mortuary. They want to try to find her husband's body. She's desperate to know whether he really is dead or not."

For the second time in less than fifteen minutes an unexpected statement produced an instantaneous effect on the three senior officers. This time, instead of laughter, there was silence. Thompson broke it.

"She must be a very determined woman," he said

slowly. "I wouldn't want to go there searching for what was left of my spouse. Nor of anyone I liked."

"She is a doctor," Sturgess explained, "a pathologist, apparently."

"We ought to find out more about her husband," said Chance. "As quick as we can." He grunted. "I suppose the diplomat could refuse to be interviewed."

Thompson tapped the table with his fingernails. "I have a notion that a little old-world courtesy might pay dividends. I think I will escort Mrs. Maier myself."

He rose from the table, pulled his tunic straight, reached for his peaked hat with the impressive silver braid on its rim and nodded good-bye to Donaldson.

"Tell that man Eckhardt I'd like to see him." He motioned to Sturgess. "You'd better come with me, Colin."

No one having given Thompson any description of Connie Maier, he was surprised when he descended the stairs and found a striking, young woman with cool, intelligent eyes. He had subconsciously expected someone temperamental and foreign-looking. She introduced herself and Jakov Allom in a firm voice.

"I came all the way from the States to find out if my husband was alive. As we can't find that out, I want to know positively if he's dead."

Only as she spoke did Thompson recognize the strained tautness that he had heard and seen so often before in relatives of the injured. Whether they were emotional or self-controlled, whether they were men or women, that feeling was always there, a tension liable to crack and splinter unexpectedly at any time. Indeed, if he had not spotted it in Connie, he would have begun to doubt her credentials. As it was, she had a remarkable grip on herself, and he wondered how well she could sustain it. Not easily in a mortuary, he thought.

"Forgive my asking when you last contacted our central casualty bureau," he asked gently, automatically adjusting his manner to the occasion.

"What time did you call them, Jakov?"

"About nine o'clock. Possibly a few minutes later."

"And after that I called the embassy," said Connie, pressing her point. "The U.S. Embassy, I mean. Their relatives bureau had no trace. I guess the only way left is to go see if I can identify his body."

"It could be a distressing experience, even for a doctor," said Thompson, "and some more identifications will have been made in the last two or three hours. I would rather you checked with the casualty bureau again."

"But it's so hard to get through to them!" Connie's voice was rising.

"We're here to help, Dr. Maier. Luckily I was about to leave for the Commissioner's office. It's not usual to allow relatives access to the bureau. For one thing it's in the Operations Room. But I might persuade them to make an exception." Thompson could become quite fatherly when faced by a person in trouble. It would have been a hard-hearted man who did not respond to Connie's plea, and his instinctive feeling that her husband might have been the target of a terrorist attack increased his sympathy for her. "Our business is to help people," he reiterated.

He led them out to the car, where his driver, Bert, was waiting.

"A slight squash, I'm afraid," he apologized as Bert opened the front door for Connie and he, Sturgess and Allom got into the back.

On the way he talked casually about his job.

"The first duty of our police force is to protect life and property. It always has been, and I hope it always will be." He emphasized the word "property."

Allom hesitated, then picked up the cue that Thompson had deliberately provided.

"There is also the question of Ben's belongings. Naturally as he was traveling on official business he was entitled to diplomatic privileges. Our embassy had made a request to your Foreign Office for the baggage."

Thompson displayed only an appropriate modicum of interest. He had cast a fly over Allom, and the Israeli had seemingly risen to it, confirming the impression that his function was more than merely giving the woman moral support. At the same time the contents of diplomatic luggage were not Thompson's legitimate concern.

"What did it look like?" he asked.

"The silly thing is," Connie replied in slight confusion, "I don't know. He probably took the Gucci one I gave him for Christmas."

"The briefcase, you mean," asked Sturgess, guessing.

"Oh, yes, the briefcase," said Allom. "Unlike you, we do not issue our diplomats with anything standard." He smiled faintly. "No royal cipher and regulation black hide for us. That would be a little, how shall I say, obvious."

At this moment Bert turned into the front entrance of New Scotland Yard, leaving Connie with the last word.

"Anyway," she declared passionately, "our first priority is to find my husband."

Leaving Sturgess in the foyer to look after the two, Thompson disappeared upstairs, returning a few minutes later.

"The deputy commissioner in charge agrees. But only for Dr. Maier. Fortunately the Operations Room's function is virtually over; otherwise you could not have visited it." He spoke to Sturgess. "Colin, take care of Mrs. Maier, will you?" As Sturgess led Connie to the elevator, Thompson turned to Allom. "I would appreciate a word with you while she's gone. You might be able to help me."

Stepping out of the elevator at the first floor, Sturgess led Connie down a long passage which reminded her of a hospital with its pale paint and vinyl flooring. When she saw a laden trolley she exclaimed, "What's that?"

"The Information Room's in there on the left. That's their major incident trolley. Everything from first-aid kits to megaphones. Here we are."

He ushered her through a door on the right, almost opposite, and into the large, brightly lit Operations

Room, with its curving rows of desk space and the control dais for the commissioner behind them. A small group of officers in their shirt sleeves were talking quietly. Over the other side things were busier.

"That's the casualty bureau," said Sturgess, guiding her around behind the dais.

Women police were seated at tables sorting out cards of various colors, supervised by several sergeants, both male and female. Long rows of card index boxes stood on other tables at the side, evidently arranged alphabetically, while half a dozen girls were manning telephones, all of them in use. Sturgess introduced Connie to a woman sergeant in a neat white blouse and black skirt.

"I begin to understand the problem," said Connie.

"It's the worst I've ever known," said the sergeant. "We took nearly two thousand calls yesterday, and there'd have been more if we could have handled them. We've cards for over eleven hundred and fifty injured and four hundred and twenty-eight dead. Now what was the name, dear?"

"Maier." Connie spelled it out. "His given name was Benjamin." She felt odd giving it in full. He had always been plain Ben to her.

"That rings a bell," said the sergeant. She crossed the room and began systematically going through the card index boxes, coming back with a large white card.

"Are you Mrs. Constance Maier?" she asked kindly.

Connie nodded.

"You inquired before?"

"Yes."

The sergeant displayed the card, her face sympathetic.

"This white card records your inquiry. We have his name from the airline passenger list, too. Care of the Israeli Embassy, is that right?"

Connie struggled to see the card clearly. A mist seemed to be creeping across her vision. Through the blur she saw there were two columns, one headed "IN-QUIRY RE" and the other "PERSON MAKING INQUIRY." She saw Ben's name under one and her own under the other. "This is all wrong," she thought. "I fill in forms about other people, not them about me. It's I who am the doctor. How did I lose control?"

The sergeant's voice jolted her back to attentiveness, though the woman spoke far from harshly.

"There ought to be a pink card to match up with this, one our phone operators compile from information sent from the hospital or mortuary. Sometimes with foreigners Christian names and surnames get transposed. But there's nothing under Benjamin as a surname either. He must be among the 'Unidentifieds.' There are still one hundred and eighty-seven dead on the cards with particulars but no names. It was the fire."

"May I see?" asked Connie, surreptitiously dabbing at her eyes with a tissue.

The sergeant shook her head dubiously, then relented and fetched one from another index tray, carefully marking its place. She handed it to Connie. This pink card had two columns as well, for "identified" and "unidentified," with numerous boxes to be filled in. Connie stared at it. There was a cross in the box marked "DEAD." The space headed "STATE OF BODY" was ticked against "SLIGHTLY DISFIGURED." There was a list of basic physical characteristics, familiar to her professionally, which had also featured on the white card: "Sex—Male. Build—Heavy. Marks—Appendix scar left side. Dress—gray flannel suit, black shoes, brown socks." Connie skipped the rest.

"Honestly, love," said the sergeant. "I couldn't swear to recognize my best friend from one of those. Not unless I knew what she was wearing, or she had some really distinctive jewelry or a scar. When the details are exact, we can match them up, staple the two together and inform the next of kin. Often something quite small confirms it, like labels on a shirt. Or eventually the dental charts. The real identification's done at the mortuary. Don't think I'm being unhelpful, but the details on your white card aren't all that complete, are they?"

Connie picked up Ben's white card again, forcing

herself to concentrate. Had she provided these details? No, the embassy must have. Well, they weren't inaccurate. Ben was thirty-four, height five feet ten inches, eyes brown, complexion dark, nose straight. But the spaces for distinguishing marks, dress and jewelry were all blank.

"The policewoman who marries these cards up says she has at least seven who could fit that description," said the sergeant.

"Could I please see them?"

"That's one I gave you. I'll ask her to sort out the others. It may take a minute or two, though."

"I'll wait," said Connie. She sat watching a telephonist respond to the flashing lights, answer a call, patiently write down information on a log sheet, pass it to a colleague and take the next call. Someone brought around cardboard cups of tea on a tin tray. Gratefully, she took one and drank a little, but found she had no stomach for the sweet, strong brew.

On another floor, Commander Thompson was in conference with the Deputy Assistant Commissioner "A" Operations, who had been directing the overall response to the crash. It was he who had allocated police reinforcements when Thompson had asked for them, and now he and Thompson had been joined by the DAC "C" Operations, who dealt with crime, and by the commander in charge of the antiterrorist squad.

Thompson recapitulated the morning's events, starting with the helicopter search and ending with the conversation he had just had with Allom.

"The diplomat was very guarded at first. Until I told him we thought the rumors of sabotage could have some foundation. Then he came clean." Thompson paused momentarily. "Their man Maier who was on the plane was carrying Palestinian plans captured by Israeli commandos in Paris last week."

"The Argenteuil raid!" exclaimed the antiterrorist squad commander. "By God, that does add up. From what I've heard of Palestinian guerrilla groups they'd go all out for revenge. Killing a few hundred other people en route wouldn't worry them. This must have been a Palestinian job."

"It occurred to us," said Thompson, "that they might also have been trying to destroy the plans or perhaps recover them. Assuming the gang is still in London, it might be possible to tempt them into another try . . . if we can make them believe the plans survived." He outlined his ideas about Eckhardt.

After further discussion they agreed to reactivate the Operations Room fully during the Palestinian demonstration at 3 P.M. Also, they would scrutinize the details of both the passengers in the aircraft and every possible inquiry about them. Eckhardt was to be put under surveillance. All the baggage recovered from the wreckage was to be searched, as well as the wreckage itself. Eventually the two crime officers left, and the DAC "A" Operations began questioning Thompson on his progress with the aftereffects of the crash on "A" Division.

"We mustn't forget that restoring Westminster to normal is the main aim."

"I haven't, sir," said Thompson, a hint of asperity in his voice. "As far as we're concerned, by tomorrow it should be over except for the paperwork. Westminster City Council have coped with most of the homeless. A lot were foreign visitors who should have caught trains to the Continent. They've been fixed up. The sad cases are the children whose parents are missing. We're trying to help find relatives through local police stations. And we're putting out press appeals."

"The casualty bureau can take that over. It'll be operational for a few weeks yet, I imagine. What about the station?"

"We'll still need alternative loading points for the London Transport buses. The forecourt can't be reopened yet. Otherwise it's a domestic problem for the railways. And for the accident inspector, of course. We've had trouble with sightseers today, but that won't last beyond the weekend. There's so little to see from outside."

Their conversation was interrupted apologetically by Sturgess, who had come up from the casualty bureau.

"Mrs. Maier hasn't had much luck. She's even been through the cards herself. There are four or five that could conceivably be her husband. She's insisting on going to the mortuary."

"Perhaps you could take her, Colin. Let me know what she finds and whatever makes the diplomat with her excited."

"Is this the woman whose husband might have been a target?" asked the DAC "A."

"Yes," said Thompson, "unless there was someone else among the two hundred and sixty-four people on board."

"Someone ought to keep an eye on her," said the DAC "A" sharply. "She might be next on the list."

"The Israeli with her seems pretty switched on," said Sturgess. "I wouldn't be surprised if he was armed."

The DAC "A" grunted.

"Don't let her come to any harm while she's with you, Inspector. Get a gun yourself."

Donaldson found no lack of things to occupy him when he got back to Victoria just before midday. Indeed the way events were developing made the CID's problems minor issues to him. He was immediately spotted by reporters and surrounded. They shouted questions and thrust microphones towards him.

"Can you confirm sabotage?"

"Was it a bomb?"

Repeating, "No comment, I'm sorry, no comment at this stage," he escaped with the aid of two policemen. Upstairs on his desk a pile of messages testified further to the whirlwind that Johnson's broadcast had raised. Never before had Donaldson been responsible for investigating an accident on which political controversy had centered, although he had been on the sidelines of the Munich disaster many years ago. A BEA airliner had crashed as it took off in slush and snow, killing the

Manchester United football team. The official German report that accused the captain of failing to have ice removed from the plane's wings had, it emerged years later, been accepted only because the German authorities had suppressed eyewitness evidence both that there was no ice and that uncleared slush on the runway was sufficient to prevent the plane from gaining flying speed. As that affair had developed, growing ever more bitter, Donaldson had resolved never to become involved in the suppression of evidence himself, a vow that the message from Daly at the American Embassy now brought back to mind. He rang the embassy. Daly sounded as though he were losing his habitual cool detachment.

"Am I glad you called, Jim. This place is a madhouse. When old man Johnson isn't pounding on the door, I have the FAA in Washington on the line, and when it's not them, it's the media."

"I can sympathize," replied Donaldson. "I'm ordered to report to my minister this afternoon."

"Listen, Jim. There's no way I can hold out on this. Do you realize how much pressure a guy like Johnson can exert when he wants to? Everyone from the ambassador down is besieged. We have senators and congressmen making person-to-person calls, the telex machine looks set to run out of ticker tape, and I'm told the cipher clerks are having leave canceled."

"I take the point, Colonel," said Donaldson reluctantly. "More than that, I shall make it to the minister when I see him. You appreciate I can only advise him. This whole business is being jacked up to a political level that it's beyond me to control."

"Likewise," said Daly. "As things are, you'll understand that I have had to brief the ambassador."

Donaldson sighed. "I understand."

"Incidentally," Daly continued, "you sure have made some kind of a hit with Johnson."

"I have?"

"Yeah. One minute he thinks you're Benedict Arnold, and the next he's wishing you were on his payroll, not someone else's."

"I had to walk out on him yesterday."

"So I heard. I think he may feel somewhat guilty, too. Seems he contributed to some kind of a bust-up with your wife, if you forgive my mentioning it."

The reminder of Jane and his own domestic chaos wearied Donaldson.

"I'd rather you didn't spread that around," he said. "I'll keep you posted on the other things."

He rang off and sat for a few seconds with his face in his hands. The one person from whom there had been no message was Jane. Was she sulking at home, or walking out on him, or what? He could not guess. He felt completely out of contact with her, aware only that something new and unpleasant was intruding on what he always imagined was a happy and workable relationship. There was no point in ringing her; she would only ask when he was coming home, and until he had seen the minister he would have no idea.

Then he remembered Eckhardt, dismissed Jane from his thoughts and went to warn the police downstairs that there was one journalist they should allow through.

Sam Eckhardt arrived around midday, as Donaldson had forecast, tracking down the first-floor office and entering before his cursory knock was answered. It was not his policy to wait for an answer. Half the art of interviewing lay in confronting one's quarry with enough decisiveness to thwart a refusal.

"Didn't think you'd forget a promise," Eckhardt declared, smiling ingratiatingly. "Do you mind if I sit down?"

"Be my guest," said Donaldson. He had been too busy making notes for his meeting with the minister to plan exactly what he would say. However, he was clear that he should give a minimum of information and then suggest Eckhardt call on Commander Thompson.

"What can I do for you?" he said.

"Tell me," asked Eckhardt, unblinkingly direct, "what *did* cause this crash? Sabotage? Engine failure? What?"

"Is this off the record?"

"Naturally, if you say so. Some quotes would be helpful, of course."

"You'll have to ask the minister for those," said Donaldson, reflecting that the more pressure they put on the minister at this stage, the better. "However, I can show you something I intend to show him." He pushed a fat limp-bound manual across the table. It was open at two pages of photographs of jet engine compressors. "That's what happens when an engine disintegrates. As the book says, it can cause major damage and often fire. In fact, it's not unlike a localized explosion."

Eckhardt pushed the book back.

"I'm no technician," he said. "You mean the pilot could have thought it was an explosion. That it was not sabotage."

"I can only leave you to draw your own conclusions, I'm afraid," said Donaldson. "You can say that we are investigating the possibility."

"Is the wreckage being searched?"

"Exhaustively. If there had been a bomb, incidentally, we should find slivers of metals in the seats—and indeed in the passengers' bodies."

"What happens to things you find?"

"Normal procedure," said Donaldson. "Airframe to Farnborough, bodies to the mortuary under direction of the coroner, baggage guarded by the police."

"At Rochester Row?" queried Eckhardt.

The question provided an ideal opening. Donaldson seized it.

"Why not go along there and ask for an interview with Commander Thompson? He's the man you ought to see."

"I thought he loathed journalists." It was typical of Eckhardt's vanity that he did not refer to himself as a reporter.

"You can say I sent you if it's any help."

In spite of being given this lead, Eckhardt thanked Donaldson with a noticeable lack of warmth. No sabotage was no news, and he had little taste for explaining the technicalities of aircraft engines to *Sunday Post* readers. At the door he fired a final question.

"Surely most of the baggage was burned?"

"No," said Donaldson levelly. "A lot was thrown out when the aircraft broke up. Unhappily luggage survives a crash better than people."

As he said it, he wondered whether his exact words would reach the terrorists. Possibly Thompson would say something more memorable. As the door closed he forced himself to forget about this, just as he had forgotten Jane, and bent over the papers on the desk.

Twenty minutes later Sam Eckhardt was seated in the third-floor office at Rochester Row, congratulating himself on obtaining an interview with Thompson so easily. This exclusive could be the salvation of his story. The commander sat at a wide desk, set across the corner of the room. Normally it was the Rochester Row chief superintendent's, but he had obligingly vacated it for his superior.

"Was it sabotage?" Eckhardt asked. "Was there a bomb in the toilets at the rear?" It was part of his method to put the same question to every informant. The variations in the answers often gave him useful clues.

"Not so far as we know," said Thompson.

"The tail section did break off, though?"

Thompson wondered precisely what kind of remark would elicit the lead he wanted. He and Chance had agreed there would be two objectives in this interview. First to obtain confirmation of the Libyan Embassy's interest in the disaster and secondly to feed Eckhardt a line about the recovery of baggage which he would pass on and which might provoke direct Arab inquiries here at Rochester Row. If they thought there was a lot of unidentified luggage, they might simply come and claim what they wanted. It was a long shot. But it might work. He leaned forward across the desk. "Could I put a question to you, Mr. Eckhardt? Why *should* anyone blow up this flight?"

Eckhardt smiled noncommittally.

"Come on," said Thompson flatteringly, "we all read

your piece last Sunday about the Israeli commandos in Paris. You probably know more about this kind of thing than I do."

"I was told there had been an important Arab on board," said Eckhardt. "And that certain people wanted him dead. However, there were no Arabs on the passenger list."

He does his homework, thought Thompson, and said aloud, "We've had inquiries from several Arab embassies. Maybe there's something in it. He could have been traveling under a false name."

"That's true." There was a definite sharpening in Eckhardt's interest. He made some notes.

"Strickly off the record," said Thompson, "there was what you'd call a 'mystery passenger.' An Arab from his appearances. We're trying to track down his identity through the personal possessions we've recovered."

"I had heard a lot survived."

"I've two teams cataloguing it all now," said Thompson. "Downstairs."

"The devil you have," Eckhardt exclaimed. "Can I quote you on that?"

"If you want to." Thompson reckoned that the Arabs would read the papers avidly tomorrow morning. "I'm supervising the checking myself. I would prefer you didn't quote me on the unidentified passenger, though."

Eckhardt was beaming. He had the guts of a story with exclusive quotes into the bargain. No bomb in the plane, but an incognito VIP and baggage searching. He rose to his feet, pocketing his notebook.

"Thank you, Commander."

"I'd better see you down," said Thompson. "We don't want you being arrested on the way out, do we?"

As they shook hands in the hall, Thompson wondered whether his ploy would work. There was one thing he had omitted to tell the journalist: the baggage itself was all being opened in the Military Police building across the road, not in this one.

After leaving Rochester Row, Eckhardt walked up to Victoria Street to find a taxi. Passing a call box, he stopped and telephoned the Libyan Embassy. If possible, he wanted some quotes about the incognito Arab.

"Ahmed," he said excitedly, "you told me an important Arab was on the crashed plane. Who was he?"

"My friend, much as I would like to assist you, it is not in your interest to reveal his name yet."

"It's only a matter of time. The police know about him and are checking all the passengers' baggage to establish his identity."

"You say they are checking . . . it was not burned in the fire?"

"At Rochester Row Police Station," said Eckhardt impatiently. "Do me a favor, Ahmed. Who was the VIP?"

"I am sorry. I cannot tell you. Perhaps tomorrow."

"The *Sunday Post* goes to bed tonight. I need the facts now."

"I can only say we are convinced this crash was caused by Israeli saboteurs."

Eckhardt rang off in disgust. He could not understand how such an intelligent man could try to feed him such an obvious propaganda line.

Eckhardt's information was relayed to the two gunmen immediately. At the Earls Court house Kamal was squatting on the stained threadbare carpet, fitting together the parts of a crude, yet proven type of bomb. Spread out on a sheet of newspaper were two small slabs of plastic explosive, a detonator, a high-powered flashlight battery and a cheap watch with a Mickey Mouse face. Methodically Kamal pushed the thin metal detonator into the soft explosive, then fitted both into a cardboard box, making holes in the lid for wires. Using black masking tape he secured the battery to the outside of the box and arranged the wires to the detonator. One wire had a clip that would finally be attached to the battery's positive terminal. The other ran to the detonator via the watch, from which he had removed the glass and the hour hand. The wire was fixed to the minute hand with a tiny blob of liquid solder. Kamal glanced up at Mohammed, who was sitting on the bed cleaning a pistol with an oily rag.

"At what time was it set for?"

"It will be close to four thirty P.M. How can one be exact?"

Kamal grinned. "So long as we make the adjustment less than one hour before, it will be well."

He bent over the Mickey Mouse watch again and attached a second wire to the face with Plasticine. When the minute hand reached the half hour it would make contact with this wire, otherwise insulated by the Plasticine, completing the circuit between the battery and the detonator. He taped the watch's bright red plastic straps tightly to the top of the box. It lay there looking like some crazy joke, with its wires and the battery, a surrealist depiction of a bomb displaying its insides for all to see. Kamal was a talented engineer, and it amused him that something so apparently ludicrous would also be so lethal. He wanted it that way for two reasons. First so that anyone who found it would know at once what it was and call the police. Secondly so that the mechanism was quickly and easily accessible. Finally, he placed the whole contrivance inside a shopping bag emblazoned with the words "Finest Foods Store Taking Away Specialty" and packed tissue paper carefully on top for concealment.

"It is ready," he announced.

Mohammed Khadir grunted. His mind was on other things. He held up the 9mm Makarov pistol, barely more than six inches long.

"I desire to take the Skorpion," he said truculently.

"For the love of Allah, how can you conceal a submachine gun? Have you not seen the police activity today?"

Mohammed rose and went to the wardrobe cupboard, where he kept a small arsenal in a cheap canvas grip. He pulled out a compact gun, with a short stubby barrel and a wire stock folded forward over it.

"It is a machine pistol. Not a submachine gun," insisted Khadir stubbornly. "Those Czechs made it for close-quarters fighting." His instruction at Odessa had taught him to like the Skorpion, and it had a wicked, ugly look about it. "Automatic fire could be useful. That Makarov, what is it good for? Shooting mice?"

Kamal shook his head in despair. They had argued half the night over this operation.

"So it is small, too. But not small enough. It must appear that we are empty-handed. Mohammed, my friend, what about a grenade? That and the Makarov. Both can be hidden in the pockets of a raincoat."

"And this afternoon the sun will shine!"

"I tell you, the British would wear raincoats in the desert. It is their national costume."

Grudgingly Mohammed agreed. He regarded London as his territory and increasingly resented Kamal's intrusion upon it.

"I will take the hand grenade," he said. "Next there is the question of the car."

At the two big marquees pitched on the parade ground in Chelsea Barracks, the coroner felt that order had at least been imposed upon the arrangements for the dead. He himself was struggling against fatigue. Since he had hurried to the crash from his Coroner's Court offices in Horseferry Road, less than a half a mile from Victoria Station, to assess the scale of the casualties, he had slept only four hours. As Her Majesty's coroner for Inner West London it was his duty to investigate "any violent, unnatural or sudden death" for which the cause was unknown. A lawyer by training and independent of both local and central government, he was answerable only to the highest crown law officer in the land, the lord chancellor. The verdict of his inquest into the cause of death, arrived at with the assistance of a jury of between seven and eleven people, would be an official pronouncement of legal significance. The inquest could rule whether a husband and wife, killed in the same accident, had died simultaneously, or one before the other: a decision on which substantial inheritance claims might hinge, and tax claims, too. At the other extreme the verdict could lead to presecutions for murder. No bodies could be returned to their families for burial without the coroner's consent.

More immediately, the coroner had been responsible for finding a place to put the corpses. The Westminster Mortuary, to which some had been sent initially, could take seventy. His own in Sheepcote Lane, Battersea, about the same number, while a disused cleaning station next door to it could be pressed into service. But in total these would have accommodated only half the four hundred victims. When he realized the scale of the disaster, the coroner had readily agreed to Denman's suggestion of asking the army for the use of Chelsea Barracks. From the moment the tents were ready he had put aside his dignity and himself shifted tables, screens and corpses, turning the helpers available into a coherent organization.

At ten o'clock this morning the coroner had escaped back to his court for long enough to go through the formalities of opening the inquest and to issue a brief press release. He would hold only one inquest into all the deaths, the basic cause being the same. But although he could presume this he could not complete the proceedings on that presumption. His inquest would be adjourned until the public inquiry into the crash was complete, possibly for as long as nine months in fact. So he had not delayed in returning to the barracks again, where the khaki-colored marquees were attracting a crowd of sightseers who peered though the iron railings and periodically had to be ordered back by the police constables and guardsmen at the gate. As the coroner drove in, the sentry snapping to attention, he decided to ask for canvas screens along the railings. There seemed no end to the morbid curiosity of the public. He parked his car and walked across to the first tent, murmuring a thank-you to the two police cadets keeping watch on the entrance as they pulled open the flaps for him.

There could be no disguising the smell of death inside, the sickly sweet odor of it. Nor could partitions conceal the grimness of the work. Along one side of the tent lay the most recently recovered bodies, still in their torn, stained clothing, though decently concealed by the opaque grayish polythene body bags that contained them, each bag prominently labeled with a number attached to a sort of pocket roughly above the chest of the victim. In the middle of the tent stood eleven tables, each with three or four white-coated figures busy at it, while technicians made notes. On these tables the corpses were examined and the autopsies carried out. After completion of the autopsies the bags were zipped up again around the naked bodies and they were carried through to the other tent, where Hanson's team embalmed them and prepared caskets.

Four pathologists from the Royal Air Force, veterans of many aviation disasters, had been joined by eight from London hospitals for the work. Operating a shift system, dissecting and examining day and night, they were striving to complete this essential groundwork as fast as possible. Nonetheless, it would take up to two weeks. Although on average one autopsy took only an hour and yielded the technical detail both for identification and for the death certificate, the pathologists had to sleep and eat. Fatigue was always the enemy of accuracy and accuracy was crucial. Now Denman found a mistake, though not of his own team's making. He approached the coroner.

"I'm afraid there's been an error somewhere, sir. We've two number one seventeens. We only discovered it after we had completed identification and were marking it up on the list."

"Let's have a look," said the coroner wearily. He had made a bet with himself that this would happen. On the evening of the crash the police had been numbering corpses laid out in the railway station and at the same time others had been taken to the Westminster Mortuary. Together they crossed the tent to another screened-off section where the secretariat was collating the paperwork. His own coroner's officers, police constables posted to him for a tour of duty, several of Denman's assistants and a number of policewomen constituted the secretariat.

"There are two autopsy forms for one seventeen"—

Denman held up the long blue sheets of paper—"and only one body."

"With luck it will be either seventeen or eleven," said the coroner. "You'll have to go over the bodies. If this ever happens again, I shall start the numbering at one thousand."

Denman expressed agreement.

"You can't work nonstop for a day and a half without starting to make mistakes, sir."

The coroner nodded. That was about the size of it. Everyone was overtired.

"How are things otherwise?"

"A fair stream of dental histories have been coming in on the telex to our offices. Most of the passengers were American, and the response from New York is very quick. Atlantic Airlines obviously have an efficient relatives bureau running there, and our managing director flew out yesterday to advise them. The troubles really center on the seventy-one seriously burned bodies. They're almost totally carbonized."

Shrunken black lumps that had been living people were something new to the coroner. He had never dealt with an air crash before.

"Then," Denman went on, "there was a group of French ladies on some kind of cultural tour to New York. They were all together, and a lot of them are badly mutilated. As you know, a woman keeps everything personal in her handbag. The handbags got thrown all over the shop. What's more, this group included two sisters who often wore each other's clothes."

The coroner's officer who was in charge of the secretariat, a large cheerful constable who was sweating in spite of the air conditioning that had been installed, interrupted politely.

"Excuse me, sir. The Irish Embassy's after us again and the Israelis are insisting on sending someone down to make an identification."

Sudden irritation overwhelmed the coroner.

"Damn the Irish. Can't they understand that we don't even know which their nationals were yet? How the devil can we release the bodies?

"They won't take 'no' for an answer, sir."

"Ring Mr. Smythson at the Home Office, will you, and ask him to get them off our backs. Why are the Israelis upset?"

"They had a diplomat on board, sir. Name of Maier. Benjamin Maier. His wife wants to identify him. The message said Commander Thompson's agreeable if you are."

The coroner turned to Denman.

"My principle is to avoid allowing relatives in the mortuary if I can. What do you usually do?"

"Exactly the same, sir. If it's inescapable, we could screen off a small area in the other tent, clean up the body and show it there if we think we've identified it."

"We could do without this kind of extra pressure," the coroner said angrily. "You'd better start checking up on this man Maier."

Twenty minutes later Colin Sturgess arrived, tactfully asked Connie and Allom to remain outside in the police car and presented himself at the secretariat. In spite of the training period he had spent in a hospital when he himself was a young police cadet, and in spite of being no stranger to mortuaries, the mammoth "butcher shop" unnerved him. The coroner's officer directed him through to the second tent. Here the scene was subtly different. This was the end of the production line. Corpses that had been finished with by the pathologists lay on the ground in their thick polythene bags, waiting to be lifted onto tables and embalmed by two teams of men in white coats. Down the far side of the tent stood rows of coffins. The strong smell of chemicals stung Sturgess' eyes and made them water. Denman saw him enter and straightened up from examining a body. Sturgess noticed that the body bag unzipped along its length, so the entire contents could be examined. The bags lay close together in rows, their bulky contents only vague gray shapes, to which this open one made a startling contrast. The pallor of the corpse's flesh and the appalling lacerations on the limbs made a sudden surge of vomit rise in his throat. He swallowed and said huskily to Denman, "Is that Maier?"

"One of three possibles."

"We can't let her see them. I'd go berserk if I saw my girlfriend like that."

"I'm glad you understand. Seeing a victim has been known to give a relative a heart attack."

"What on earth made you go in for this?"

"We've been in it since the 1930s," said Denman. "There's a lot at stake in an air crash, and the identification and repatriation of the dead is quite a specialized business." He gestured toward the caskets. "Different countries have different regulations. Victims always have to be in zinc-lined caskets under IATA regulations, but the Italians insist on inch and a half thick timber with dovetailed joints as well. By knowing the rules we save the families a lot of agony and delay, and they never even see a bill. The insurers pay us." Denman's tone became brisker. "We mustn't waste time. These three men who could be Maier were all without their jackets—it must have been warm in the aircraft—so we've no wallets, passports or credit cards to help us. Maier's dental records haven't landed yet either. However, there was an Israeli banknote in the trouser hip pocket of one. If I can talk to the widow, I can possibly establish identity for certain. I just need a few minutes longer on the characteristics."

"I'll hang on," said Sturgess. He was slowly becoming acclimatized to this clinically macabre scene. Fiercely bright lights hung on wires between the tent poles, and there was a continual low whirring throb from air-conditioning units, supported on makeshift stands against the tent's window openings. For a moment he watched the embalming process. Two men appeared to be draining blood from a corpse. Hesitantly he asked what was going on.

"Simple really," said the white-coated senior embalmer, who spoke with the clipped assurance of a demonstrator in a laboratory. "Takes about an hour and a half. First we remove the corrupt parts. The blood, that's a corrupt part. Drain it out therefore. In-

328

ject the arteries with fluid, like my friend is doing." He pointed at a pair of five-gallon plastic containers on an adjacent counter. "Inject the solution of formalin. Colored pink, that is, to avoid confusion with other fluids. Now this," he went on, picking up a large hypodermic, "this fluid is the strong stuff for the body cavities. This we will inject into the thorax and abdomen." He jabbed the long thick needle toward the rib cage of the corpse, and Sturgess involuntarily shuddered. "These fluids," the man continued firmly, "solidify the body. Their internal application preserves it for an indefinite duration of time."

"Completely different technique from the ancient Egyptians, if you're interested," cut in Denman's voice. "They practiced external embalming."

"More effective, this is," continued the embalmer stoutly.

Sturgess had a sudden vision of him, off duty, studying Egyptian mummies in the British Museum.

"Otherwise we'd have to fix up refrigeration until the coroner releases the bodies, which could be weeks. Even in a city it would be hard to find a cold store."

"Wouldn't want to know, would they, sir?" responded the embalmer loyally.

"Come on," said Denman abruptly, "let's get Mrs. Maier over with. Thank you, Mr. Jones." As they walked out he added. "You might not think it, but coping with the relatives is by far the trickiest part. That's why Mr. Geoffrey has gone to the States. It's not so easy to make rules for the living."

Sturgess noted that he referred to the managing director by his Christian name, prefaced by "Mr." That was one hallmark of a contented, traditional family firm, even in a union-dominated Britain. Together they went to fetch Connie.

Loath though she was to admit it, Connie felt terrible waiting in the car. No amount of determined hope could eradicate the feeling that she had reached the end of her search. The military trucks, parked in a line near the far tent, the police cars and the ominously familiar plain vans, all contributed to undermining what little confidence she had left. Ben had narrowly escaped death when his jeep ran over a mine in the 1967 war. He was a reserve lieutenant, and the war had erupted within weeks of his graduating from New York University and returning home. She remembered a letter he wrote describing the incident, joking about junior lieutenants being the most expendable rank in the army, and that being the obvious reason for his survival. Now, unaccountably, she felt that this alien barracks must have claimed him. For some moments she had a clear vision of Ben during these earlier periods of his life, although she had not witnessed them. She also saw herself going through the tortuous journeying that had brought her to this place, as if observing another person. Then the illusion faded, and she sharply told herself to fight off the apprehension and the tiredness for a little longer.

By the time Sturgess came back to the car with Denman she was clearheaded again. But Allom held her arm as they led her to a room in the barrack block that had been allocated for interviewing.

Seeing the strain of worry in her face, Denman made his questions gentle, delicately drawing her out. She described the suits she knew Ben had packed for his trip, his shoes, his ties. All the time Denman avoided being specific, knowing the effects autosuggestion could have. If you showed a widow a shattered watch, the implication was that it had belonged to her husband and she would collapse in tears, only later admitting that she had never seen it before and assumed it had been acquired during the trip. When he had built up a picture of Ben's possessions Denman turned to his health. Had he been ill recently?

"He had mild bronchitis last week." Connie forced herself to think clinically about her husband, something she had never done before. "He had scars on his right knee and elbow. Those were from 1967. His blood group was A positive." Desperately she tried to recall such of her husband's ailments as might have left traces that an autopsy would reveal. "He was absurdly fit, despite all the desk work." Then suddenly the depersonalization began again. Ben lay before her, naked, and she was examining him, detached, professional. In a distant voice she continued, "He had curly hair on his chest, he was circumcised, of course, the knee scars I mentioned." She could see nothing on his feet. She rolled him over. "A lesion on the right shoulder, a mole. . . ." Her head was swimming. What was she doing, what was she talking about? She gazed at the tiny brown mole on his back, so familiar, somehow so personal. The acute visual image dissolved. Her voice faltered, and she stopped, near to tears. Allom reached out and held her hand.

"I think you have told me enough, Mrs. Maier," said Denman quickly, glancing at his notes. He would have to go back to check because he had deliberately left the official autopsy report in the mortuary rather than risk her catching sight of it, but he was already certain. Mild bronchitis tallied with the mucus found in the respiratory tract; he recalled the scar on the shoulder; the clothing fitted some she had described. He rose to leave.

"Wait," said Connie urgently. "I forgot. There was the gold ring I gave him, inscribed with our initials inside. He wore it on the second finger of his left hand. He never took it off. Never."

Denman stopped short, embarrassed. When Maier's possessions were eventually handed over she would want the ring. It would not be among them, and for a good reason. He could save a lot of emotional upset by explaining its absence now.

"I'm afraid there is no trace of a ring. Unfortunately the valuables were removed from some of the victims by police after the crash. It must have been accidentally lost. There was frightful confusion on the station."

It sounded like a lame excuse. He hoped she would accept it, and he was carefully avoiding any mention of viewing the corpse.

"I suppose you will know it's Ben anyway," she said, fighting back the tears.

"Connie," said Allom, still holding her hand, leaning forward beside her and turning his head to look her squarely in the eyes. "Connie, my dear, there will be no purpose in your seeing Ben. You above all people know that. You, a doctor and a pathologist yourself."

He felt her hand relax a little, as if in relief. "You could be right, Jakov. I think you're right. Ben wasn't like other people. I couldn't treat him as a . . . as an object. You go. I'll just wait."

"That is wise. I will view the body," Allom said.

Denman and Sturgess exchanged glances.

"He has the commander's permission," said Sturgess.

"If you absolutely insist," said Denman to Allom, "then I will have the body made available."

"I do insist," said Allom with quiet forcefulness.

Some ten minutes later the three men stood in a screened-off part of the tent, gazing at the corpse. Its face and legs were seriously disfigured, and white bandages had been hastily wrapped over most of the forehead and over the left hand and wrist.

"Why those," asked Allom, "when he is dead?"

"We try to lessen the shock of seeing the worst injuries."

"It is Maier. I have no doubt." Allom's tone was hard. There was the same toughness about his manner which Sturgess had observed before. "Remove the bandages on the wrist, please."

There could be no mistaking that this was an order. Sturgess nodded assent, and reluctantly the assistant who had brought in the body obeyed. Slowly he unwound the fabric, the men watching in silence. As it came free Sturgess saw with horror that much of the hand had been violently torn off, completely wrenching away two fingers. Tendons and scraps of flesh hung from what had been the back of the hand.

"Now you understand about the ring," said Denman coldly. He had tried to shield them from this unpleasantness, and he was angry at being overruled.

"Now I understand other things," said Allom evenly.

Chapter Ten

THE SEWER FOREMAN prized up a manhole cover in the Victoria Station forecourt and prepared to descend the sixteen-foot shaft that led to the labyrinth of brick-lined tunnels beneath the city. He was going to check that the remnants of the aircraft's kerosene, washed down in the drains by the Fire Brigade, had dispersed. It ought to have run through the local sewer into the main Greater London Council sewer under Wilton Road, a wide river of effluent, pump-driven, which flowed at thirty knots to an outfall miles away on the Thames estuary. The river authorities had been warned, although by then the fuel would be so thinned out as to constitute no danger. Here, under Westminster, it could possibly catch fire, as it had briefly soon after the crash.

A small crowd of sightseers watched from behind the police barriers as the foreman and his two maintenance men put on overalls and thigh-length waders. The two crewmen laid down a metal frame bearing two black oxygen bottles and began unreeling a rubber pipe as the foreman clamped his blue safety helmet on his head, an electric torch clipped to the front of it over his forehead. Finally, he connected a celluloid-fronted mask to the oxygen pipe. One of the other men did the same. The third would stay aboveground to control the oxygen and summon help if necessary.

Although their only communication would be a thin line that could be jerked as a distress signal he had a direct radio link to the engineer's department in the City Hall.

"Ready, Joe?" asked the foreman of the older, leather-faced veteran accompanying him.

Joe grinned behind his mask and took the emergency line. The foreman lowered himself into the square hole and clambered down, his studded soles grating on the rusty iron rungs set in the brickwork. At the bottom he paused, tightened a length of cotton waste that he wound like a scarf around his neck and stooped low to enter the tunnel.

There were two hundred thirty miles of sewers under the streets of Westminster, mostly constructed in the mid-nineteenth century, all meticulously brick-lined. They linked with other boroughs' systems, and you could walk through to Hampstead if you knew the way.

With the light from his torch wavering on the brickwork, the foreman left the shaft and entered the sewer. Its ceiling was arched, like a church window, and his hunched shoulders occasionally brushed the sides, which were moist and mildewy. The tunnel stretched away into darkness, distant sounds echoing from it, distorted and mysterious. The floor was concave, and he walked along the center, his boots splashing in the sewage and squelching on soft lumps of muck. The effluent was mostly water—bath water, washing-up water, rainwater—and it diluted most other things except fat and some chemicals. He knew that when he came below the fish restaurant on the corner of Terminus Place there would be chunks of dirty white cooking fat sticking to the sides, while the fumes from the chemicals that the dry cleaner's shop discharged would be acrid and choking. All sorts of things turned up in a sewer—rings, watches, teaspoons. Salvaging them used to be one of the sewerman's perks, "scratching" it was called. But the search stirred up the sludge and released the sewer gas. Many a man had been overcome and lost his life scratching, so it was officially banned.

After a few feet the foreman paused. He could hear the low throbbing of a pump. Suddenly a torrent of clear water pulsed out of a wide pipe in the side of the brickwork ahead of him and cascaded down the sewer in a torrent. It was icy cold water from a subterranean stream, which seeped into the Victoria underground station and was collected by pumps and blown out in a two-minute spasm every ten minutes. The foreman waded on through it, sticking his elbows out sideways to help his balance. He passed slowly around a corner and on to the junction with the bigger five-foot-six-inch-high sewer underneath Wilton Road. It was a relief to be able to stretch up to nearly his full height. He paused, removing the torch from his helmet and flashing it around. Three rats were caught in the beam and scurried away. There were signs of burning high up on the brickwork here, where the kerosene had flared up on Thursday. But the flow carried no signs of the fuel now. Nor could he smell kerosene vapor or anything more than the usual rank odor of the tunnels.

"Seems clear enough, Joe," he said over his shoulder to his assistant. "You check left a few yards, and I'll go right. Remember that investigator asked us to keep an eye out for debris, too."

The foreman nodded and moved into the main sewer to let the older man past. They separated briefly. Five yards farther on the foreman almost stumbled as he felt something hard beneath his boot. Investigation revealed a shard of thin metal. The foreman shook the muck off it, shoved it in his pocket and trudged on. A moment later he trod on another object. Steadying himself, he explored for whatever it was with one foot, careful lest he overbalance, then reached down, feeling in the water with his rubber-gloved right hand. His fingers touched another piece of metal. He gripped it and slowly pulled it out. With the free hand he shone the torch on his find and whistled in surprise. Dripping slime was a handcuff with a few inches of broken chain hanging from it.

"Joe," he called, his voice echoing into the darkness, "come and have a look-see here."

For reasons of safety sewermen never strayed beyond shouting distance from each other. Joe turned back, the water swishing against his boots as he walked.

"Well, I'm jiggered," he said. "I've seen a lot of odd things down here, but never handcuffs. It'll be Charles the First's head next."

On the way back the foreman washed their find in the gush of water from the underground station. Finally, in the strong daylight at street level they examined it more closely.

"Anything peculiar strike you about that?" asked old Joe quizzically, a grin lurking on his lined face.

"Can't say it does," said the foreman. The handcuff was somehow less bulky than ones he had seen in films, but otherwise. . . . "Needed some force to snap that chain," he suggested. "Whoever broke it must have been a hefty chap."

Joe's grin surfaced, wide and mischievous, revealing tobacco brown teeth.

"You've missed the point, Guv." He took the handcuff and pulled at it. "See. Locked tight. Shut like a clam. The point, where's your hefty friend's hand gone? Or was he Houdini?"

The foreman paled.

"I hadn't thought of that. Here, we'd better fetch a copper."

Ten miles south of Victoria the regional officials of British Rail were holding an emergency meeting at their headquarters, Southern House, a modern office block in Croydon. With no secretaries or staff around, the building seemed lifeless and strange. However, a commissionaire did duty on Saturdays, and he had fetched beer and sandwiches for the gathering, which included Chief Superintendent Chisholm. The last time Chisholm had been called on to advise such a conference was after the Hither Green derailment in 1967.

"To sum up," the divisional civil engineer was saying, "it'll be a good six to seven weeks before temporary repairs to the roof and platforms are complete."

The strong voice of the planning manager cut in.

"Gentlemen," he demanded, "can we run a full service again on Monday if we do this?"

There was a general murmur as people deliberated snags.

"If the Chatham side concourse and booking halls are clear, yes," said the traffic manager.

"Will they be, Chief Superintendent?"

Chisholm had prepared himself for this question.

"We can move the lost property to Waterloo. It ought to go there anyway. We can screen off the arch between the two sides and the underground access to the Brighton side."

"That's settled then."

"How about the long term?" demanded the engineer. "I can't see repairs costing less than a million pounds, one and a half million possibly. At that rate we might as well go the whole hog."

There was a buzz of interest around the table. Everyone knew what he was referring to. It was the major development plan, an ambitious scheme for a new hotel, offices and a conference center over the platforms. It was a way of turning the immensely valuable land on which Victoria stood into more of a revenue-yielding asset for the city. Earlier plans had been shelved because of the government's refusal to invest the capital. Instead a "face-lift" had been finished in 1975, which improved the station interior without in any way adding to its revenue-earning potential. It had been a halfhearted political compromise of the sort that bedeviled the managers of all Britain's nationalized industries. Now the DC-10 accident had seriously damaged the roof, the key to redevelopment above the tracks.

"This crash could be a godsend," argued the engineer.

337

"You're assuming the airliner's insurers will pay," asked the planning manager a trifle caustically. British Rail carried no external insurance; it underwrote its own risks.

"Even if they didn't," went on the engineer doggedly, "what about the government? We would never have got the face-lift if the IRA hadn't blown up the booking office. Let's ask them now, before we've made too much progress with repairs."

"Major policy decisions are a matter for the Railways Board," said the planning manager stiffly. "Not for us."

As he went on to recapitulate more immediate arrangements the commissionaire came in and sidled down the room to Chisholm.

"Excuse me, sir. Phone call, urgent. They want you back at Victoria."

The train service from East Croydon to Victoria is fast and frequent. Half an hour later Chisholm was back in his own office. The sewer foreman, one of his own sergeants and Colin Sturgess were waiting for him. The foreman recounted his tale for the fifth time as they all stood around the table on which the thin handcuff and length of chain had been placed, carefully protected by a clean sheet of tissue paper.

"It'll have to go for forensic examination," remarked Sturgess. "Could it be connected with the crash?"

"Could have been washed down the drains easy," said the foreman. "It's not so heavy, is it? When the firemen were flushing away that kerosene they didn't half use a lot of water, caused a real surge in the sewers they did, worse than a storm. More concentrated than a storm, see."

Chisholm was only half listening. He was leaning on the edge of the table, his massive body stooping as he examined the find. He knew he had seen something like this before. Suddenly he remembered. There had been a diplomatic courier boarding the night ferry for Paris one February when Heathrow had been fog-bound and flights were canceled. The courier had a diplomatic pouch held to his wrist with a sort of handcuff and a chain.

"It's a diplomatic courier's," he exclaimed. "Was there one on the plane?"

"Christ alive," said Sturgess excitedly. "Yes, there was. I saw his corpse this morning. That's why he lost his left hand!"

"So somewhere there's a missing diplomatic bag or pouch," said Chisholm slowly, mystified at the intensity of Sturgess' reaction. The cause of the crash had not been revealed to him.

"No, no!" Sturgess almost shouted, then restrained himself, remembering that he was addressing a senior officer. "No, sir," he said more quietly. "We're looking for an unmarked briefcase. With a few links of chain still on the handle. Unless the handle also broke."

Chisholm glanced at Sturgess, gruffly accepting that this was something he did not need to know more about. "I take it the recovery of the item is urgent."

"The commander would appreciate its being found."

"You don't want us to go back and look for the hand, then," asked old Joe disappointedly. He had a taste for the macabre.

Chisholm shook his head.

"As the briefcase may be at Rochester Row I think I'll be getting back there," said Sturgess. "Will you look here as well, sir?"

"Naturally."

As Chisholm gave the orders to his sergeant it occurred to him that there was one place they had probably not searched before.

Lunch at the Alloms' apartment was another gloomy occasion. Jakov had gone straight on to the embassy after bringing Connie back from the mortuary, leaving the two women to eat alone. Connie had been so upset that she barely touched her food; she seemed to withdraw into herself, shutting out her surroundings and making only the briefest replies to questions. Afterward Judith managed to persuade her to rest on the living room sofa. She lay there, her head propped on several cushions, her eyes wide open and staring at the ceiling. Her hostess kept quiet and pretended to read a book, like a watchful nurse by a patient's bedside.

Abruptly, Connie sat upright and swung her legs off the sofa. Startled, though trying not to show it, Judith glanced up from the book.

"I have to go home," said Connie, her voice tense. "There's nothing to stay here for, nothing I can do. It's all over with. It's all finished. I have to get back."

From the moment when Jakov had walked back to the police car and told her simply, "It is Ben," a whirlpool of emotions overwhelmed her. She had seen Ben as she had loved him, shyly presenting her with primroses from a wood, shaking a martini for the first guests of their married life, affectionately kissing her shoulder when she wore a lowcut evening gown. And she had also seen Ben as she had never known him in more bizarre sequences of imagined action: thrown from his jeep when the mine blew up, his khaki-clad body curving through the air to crunch on its shoulder among the stones; futilely tightening his seat belt as the aircraft plunged over Westminster; lying bloodsoaked on a stretcher. Somehow the war had claimed him, and this, in turn, led to a shocked reconsideration of facts she thought she had accepted. Ben belonged to another country, to another people, to another tradition. Living in New York, you imagined you knew about being Jewish. Sitting opposite Judith, pecking at a salad, Connie remembered that being an Israeli was something more, very much more. It was fighting for existence in a hostile land and pioneering beneath a cruel sun. When that fight had mysteriously taken her husband it had at the same instant severed her own ties with Israel. She might visit his parents, but she would never live there. As from far away she heard Judith speak.

"I think I understand. America is where you belong. Neither here nor in our country."

"Oh, Judith, how does it happen? Why? One moment I was married, happy, loving. The next . . . nothing."

Judith moved across to sit beside her on the sofa, seeing that at last she was breaking down, as break down she must. In Judith's family there was no dishonor in weeping.

"We didn't even have the baby. . . . We planned to have a baby. Later. When we moved somewhere else and I had no job. Now there's nothing at all of him left."

Judith put an arm around her, and suddenly Connie turned and buried her face, sobbing.

When Jakov returned Judith had led Connie off to lie down in her bedroom, to cry until she was exhausted and could sleep.

"We have sent a diplomatic note demanding Ben's effects," said Jakov. "And privately we have given one last piece of information to the police. Apparently Ben was nervous of losing the documents. He insisted on attaching the briefcase to his wrist. It is not normal for our couriers. The Paris embassy had difficulty finding a suitable chain."

"So the police are searching now?" asked Judith. Jakov nodded. "I am glad. If you had asked Connie for more help I should have forbidden it. She must go home to America."

"If it was I who had died I know you would stay."

"That would be different," said Judith with finality. "I am Israeli."

Punctually at 2 P.M. Jim Donaldson presented himself at the Department of Trade's head office in Victoria Street. Like most ministerial empires, the department spilled over into many other buildings, and its implacable growth had been marked by various changes of name. As far as Donaldson was concerned all they meant was that his ultimate political boss suffered from an enforced split personality under the title of Secretary of State for Aerospace and Shipping. They might have added Parking Meters while they were about it, he reflected bitterly. At least the minister would understand those. There had been precious little evidence of his understanding aviation during his term of office. Donaldson's thoughts in the elevator were clear, if bitter. He intended—no matter what the reason for this summons—to pursue the strongest line a civil servant could with his minister. He was going to advise that the cause of the accident be revealed and he would record that advice in writing. He was desperately afraid that the minister would either not comprehend the series of incredibly fast disintegrations that had sent the DC-10 out of control or, worse still, would seize on the engine failure part of that sequence and pervert it into a justification for his own and the home secretary's ill-judged remarks. It would not be the first time that a minister had chosen to disregard the expert advice of an accident investigator and accept a politically more comfortable solution.

To Donaldson's relief his departmental head, the chief accident inspector, was already there when he was ushered through to the inner office. The secretary of state did not rise to his feet or shake hands. He merely waved brusquely to an upright chair in front of the huge desk. He was a year younger than Donaldson, a bright boy of the party with plenty of doctrinaire pamphlets to his credit, but little actual experience in wielding power. One of his axioms was that civil servants invariably connived to the intentions of political masters. In consequence he was abrasive to the point of rudeness.

"Now," he said, "I want the facts from the horse's mouth. All right? We're under heavy pressure. It was our intention to make a statement to the House at question time on Monday. We may not be able to wait that long." He made a petulant gesture at the morning papers, neatly arranged on a side table. "Irresponsible reporting isn't helping either. Was it sabotage?"

"You bloody hypocrite," thought Donaldson, "when only yesterday your own irresponsible comments created the headlines!" Nonetheless, he kept his temper.

"I'm satisfied that it was not sabotage in the accepted

342

sense. My belief is that the aircraft was shot down."

The minister looked at him coldly, as though addressing an official accused of misconduct.

"So the chief inspector informs us. If that is likely to remain your opinion, perhaps you'd explain it."

It was as though the minister were deliberately trying to pick a quarrel. Out of the corner of his eye Donaldson saw concern mounting on the chief inspector's face. There was a moment's silence during which the near insult hung unanswered between the three men; then Donaldson produced the ICAO manual which he had shown Eckhardt earlier.

"I will put this in layman's terms as far as possible, sir," he said, contempt audible in his voice. Making swift sketches and referring to photographs in the manual, he outlined the probable sequence of events from the missile's explosion to the progressive destruction of the tail surfaces and the crash.

"Technically there was also an explosion in the rear engine then?"

"Yes, Minister," said Donaldson stonily. "But not one that can in any way be attributed to either the airline's or the manufacturer's negligence." Evidently the minister had grasped the technicalities. Equally clearly he was nettled.

"Such an unprecedented occurrence hardly invalidates the home secretary's strictures on the operational standards of some airlines."

Donaldson sat still, wondering how this arrogant politician was going to make the case appear to fit his predetermined theories.

"I suppose the crew did take the correct action in response to the emergency?" asked the minister with unpleasant emphasis. "No possibility of drink, drugs or disease affecting them?"

With unexpected perception he had thrust straight through to one area of doubt.

"The pathologists' autopsy reports on the crew members are not yet available. They will be much more exhaustive than any carried out on the passengers."

"And the actions taken by the pilot? Was he at fault?"

Donaldson hesitated. It would take many weeks' analysis of the recorder readouts before the crew's action could be determined. More important, it was the investigator's job to find out why an accident had happened, not whose fault it was. The dividing line could be thin. But it was there.

"Minister," he said firmly, careful to employ the exact wording of an official memorandum, "the assessment of blame or responsibility is not included among the duties of the accident investigation authority." He watched the minister stiffen at this second rebuke and swiftly continued. "It is my view that damage to the airframe caused the aircraft to enter a dive from which it was not possible to recover. My advice is that a statement should be made as soon as possible about the missile. Maintaining the imputation of negligence will cause grave damage to the airline and to our relationship with the American authorities."

"When I want your advice, Mr. Donaldson, I'll ask for it. Did the crew take the correct action or did they not?"

"The bastard," thought Donaldson, "he wants to pin it on the dead in order to save his own face."

Mercifully the chief inspector interrupted. "It's impossible to reconstruct all the crew's actions, Minister. We do know from their radio calls that they appreciated the emergency."

"But not immediately, judging from the transcript you showed me."

"Everything happens very fast in an accident, in fractions of seconds. Strictly speaking, sir, it isn't within our brief to pass judgment."

Somehow the chief inspector managed to take the sting out of defending his subordinate by speaking in an almost offhand way. "We may never know what went on in the pilot's mind or everything that was said between the crew members. Unfortunately the American cockpit voice recorder systems rely on a single-area microphone to pick up flight deck conversation.

The individual mikes only record remarks made on the intercom or actually transmitted. As you know, sir, it's normally quite quiet in the cockpit of a jet. But when things are going wrong there can be a lot of other noises. So far it's proved impossible to distinguish the flight engineer's voice at all, yet he must have spoken to the captain when they lost an engine. That's the advantage of our system. It picks up everything. Except their thoughts, of course."

The minister smiled and ran a hand through his lank hair as he always did when he recognized an expedient path out of a tricky situation. Watching the two men, Donaldson realized that the way the chief inspector had provided a legitimate minor grouse against the Americans to replace tht previous unfounded accusations was brilliant. Much as he would like to have seen the politician's face rubbed in the dirt, Donaldson had to admit that this was a better solution. The minister spoke again, this time quite warmly.

"In the circumstances," he said with no trace of embarrassment, "I feel we ought to be honest with the Americans over the basic cause of this crash. Subject to certain riders, of course. The public inquiry, postmortems and so on."

"I strongly recommend that, sir," replied the chief inspector.

"Then it remains only to consult the home secretary. Would you gentlemen mind coming with me? We shall need your help in drafting the press release."

Together the three men walked the short distance across Victoria Street and along Storey's Gate to the massive stone edifice that housed the Home Office and underneath which Churchill once had his wartime headquarters. Donaldson and the chief inspector waited with other officials in an anteroom, while the secretary of state went in to see the home secretary.

"This is as good a chance as any to have a word in your ear, Jim," said the chief inspector, leading him into a quiet corner. "You're going to have to learn to be a trifle more tactful with our political masters, even if they do get up your nose. I was afraid you'd queer your pitch completely just now."

"I don't like hearing the truth distorted. He can jump in the lake as far as I'm concerned."

"No, he cannot, Jim, my boy."

"I'm not with you, I'm afraid." Donaldson rubbed his nose gently as though to soothe away his fatigue. "As long as I stick to the facts and don't fiddle the expenses he can't touch me."

"He can refuse to accept a recommendation I'm making. You may not know that my deputy is resigning to go to Australia. I'm recommending your promotion to replace him."

Donaldson stared at the chief inspector, genuinely amazed and feeling increasingly confused.

"That's very kind of you," he muttered.

"You did a good job on that 707 near Washington. You've done some fine deductive reasoning in the last twenty-four hours. They will never admit it"—the chief inspector nodded toward the door through which the secretary of state had disappeared—"but you've saved their bacon. The fact that they made charlies of themselves will be completely forgotten when this news breaks, and what's more, they'll take the credit for having solved the mystery so quickly." He paused, puzzled by Donaldson's expression. "What's the matter? You don't look exactly overjoyed."

Donaldson sat down heavily on the nearest chair. What would have been fantastically good news only two weeks ago somehow lost its glitter when it meant making an immediate decision on Johnson's offer, with the attendant complication of Jane's fervent desire to go to America. Provided, of course, that Johnson's offer held.

"To be honest, I'm pretty well bushed. The last thing I expected out of this was promotion."

"Well, it's yours if you want it," said the chief inspector, still disconcerted. "Your wife should be pleased at any rate. More money and fewer absences."

While Donaldson was trying to frame a more enthusiastic reply, there was a sudden stir among the other officials. The private secretary to the home secretary came across the room.

"They've decided on an immediate announcement. They want a draft in ten minutes. No mention of Arabs or Israelis, and we're to warn the police commissioner."

Mohammed Khadir argued with Kamal over the details of their operation to recapture the documents up to the moment they left Earls Court in the early afternoon. He was despondent and irritable. Friday's self-assured anger with the Libyan diplomat had faded with the understanding that after waiting many months in London to be called upon, he had failed in his mission. To key himself up for action again was not as easy as it was for Kamal, freshly arrived and psychologically in better shape. Kamal's plan was subtle and complicated.

"Do not worry," he told Mohammed. "Once we have the case, everything will fall into place. The price we shall ask is trifling: papers that are of no importance to Britain and an air passage to Tripoli. The British will not refuse. It is an external affair, a matter between Arab and Jew. That will be their excuse."

"What if we do not succeed?"

"We escape to the crowd of demonstrators," said Kamal confidently. "We become two among many. Even if we are arrested they will release us. Did they not release Leila? Their leaders are scared of offending the Arab world, my friend. We are buying Britain house by house and farm by farm. If we remove our money the pound collapses. If we cancel our contracts their businesses become bankrupt. Their government is in debt to us beyond imagination."

"I hope this has been explained to the police," said Mohammed sourly.

"It is time to go." Kamal ignored the snub. Taking the bomb in the carrier bag and the weapons they needed, they went down to the street.

The car they had bought for the operation was

old. A pale blue Triumph convertible with bucket seats, the passenger's one of which was loose on its mounting. The bodywork was rusting and the engine noisy. It was what the motor trade called a "banger" and the formalities connected with its purchase had been nominal: seventy one-pound notes laid on the dealer's counter and a transfer of ownership form which Kamal had completed in a false name.

"You're in luck, mate," the man had remarked. "It's taxed to the end of the month."

Kamal had smiled. The car had only one journey to perform.

The cloudy weather continued, a damp sweat on the pavements testifying to occasional drizzle, while a sharp wind whipped around the street corners. The hot sunshine of a week ago seemed gone forever. When the two Arabs parked the Triumph in Horse Guards Avenue and walked to the top of Whitehall they realized that the rain had diminished the turnout for the demonstration. At the most only five hundred people were gathered near the foot of Nelson's column. A few dozen banners and placards swayed above their heads in the wind, bearing slogans in Arabic and English. Only one group appeared organized, a solid phalanx of young men and women whose bold red and orange banners proclaimed they were International Socialists. Their disciplined chant was audible across the square.

"Israel OUT, Israel OUT, Israel OUT, OUT, OUT!"

As Kamal and Mohammed crossed to Trafalgar Square the leaders gave a signal and the cry changed.

"Arabs IN, Arabs IN, Arabs IN, IN, IN!"

Undeterred, tourists threw food to the pigeons and were snapped by roving street photographers. Perhaps twenty uniformed policemen stood at various points, while a dark blue control van with an observation turret in its roof was parked on King Charles' island by the equestrian statue.

"Is this the demonstration?" asked Mohammed incredulously.

A flicker of doubt assailed Kamal. In Beirut such a cause would bring out thousands of marchers and end in a battle. Here the spectators seemed more likely to die of cold and boredom. He soon found the man he was looking for and held a brief conference.

"It is agreed," he said finally. "Four thirty will be the time, when the marchers are outside the Parliament."

A quarter of an hour late, at 3:14 P.M. the first speaker rose from his seat on an improvised wooden platform alongside one of the great bronze lions that flank Nelson's column and began a peroration on the history of Israeli aggression and the disinheritance of the Palestinians in Gaza. He was introduced by Enoch Andrews, the Honorable Member of Parliament for Mid-Fife. The International Socialists stopped chanting and listened with obedient enthusiasm.

At the police control van, the commander allocated to replace Thompson commented to an inspector, "Looks like a damp squib to me. Still, we'd best hold a reserve serial by the Houses of Parliament. Hardly worth a Saturday afternoon, is it?"

The moment Enoch Andrews started his speech on the platform in Trafalgar Square, the home secretary's statement hit Fleet Street. Aided by another official, the duty press officer at the Home Office telephoned Reuters, the Associated Press, the main newspapers, the BBC, the Independent Television News, and the Independent Radio News. The statement he read over was very brief. Inquiries had revealed, it said, that the DC-10 crash appeared to have been due to the explosion of a surface-to-air missile. Intensive investigations were being made into its origins and the identities of those responsible.

"Sorry, old chap," the press officer repeated as he made each call. "No further comment. Nothing on the record at all. For your guidance the police have found the place it was fired from but wish to keep it secret for the time being. No, I cannot say what kind of missile it was. Sorry."

By any standards, it was a sparse press release for

so newsworthy a subject. Naturally, there was no reference to the home secretary's disparagement of Atlantic Airlines on Thursday evening, or to American concern, or to Israeli interest. The press officer had been warned to avoid any comment whatsoever on possible international implications. To make this task easier, he had not been told what they were. Nonetheless, the excitement the statement provoked was intense. By 4 P.M. the only evening newspaper to publish on Saturdays, the *Evening News,* had an edition on the streets. The story jerked out on clacking ticker tape machines in clubs and in Sunday newspaper offices, messengers hurried round the building taking tearsheets of agency material—the "snaps"—to the specialist writers involved.

At the *Sunday Post* the news editor glanced quickly at the first snap headed RUSH, swore effusively, and told his assistant, "Get Sam Eckhardt down, will you?"

On the floor above, Eckhardt was adding the final polish to his front page article. Before hurrying down, he gathered up the typescript, the top sheet neatly headed "Air crash. Eckhardt 1," all in double spacing and with two paragraphs only on each quarto page to leave the subs plenty of space. It ran to eleven pages. How the hell he would achieve a decent style typing direct into a computer, when the new technology arrived, he did not know, and he made a joke about it as he stood facing the news editor's cluttered desk.

"That's the least of your problems. What about this for Christ's sake?" The news editor flung the agency snap at Eckhardt. "What price your 'No sabotage' theory now, old man?"

Eckhardt read the brief agency message, and his face purpled. For a moment his main thought was one of relief that he had not actually handed over the sheets of copy he was holding. The news editor read his mind. It had begun to occur to the news editor that whatever praise the foreign staff might heap on this man, basically the only difference between him and a run-of-mill reporter was that he was less disciplined and far more conceited.

"Don't show me the load of crap you've brought down. Take all this." The news editor pointed to a growing pile of agency reports on police searches and expert comments. "Take it upstairs and try to write something that may match the competition. Find out who might have shot the plane down. We'll need a complete new lead for the paper by five. Meanwhile, I'll hold the center pages so a junior can edit out the worst of the howlers from your inside piece."

Not trusting himself to reply, Eckhardt leaned forward and picked up the sheaf of teleprinter slips. As he turned to go the news editor's voice, both angry and mocking, held him back. "Listen, old man. There's something you ought to know about this game by now. You can only fool some of the people some of the time."

Again Eckhardt said nothing. He made his way out of the newsroom, humiliated and shocked, affecting not to see the tittering junior reporters whose desks he passed. As he went he glanced at the later snaps. "Arab guerrillas obvious suspects" was the headline on one. By the time he reached his own office some new and very unpleasant thoughts were troubling him.

When the rush edition of the *Evening News* came out at four o'clock, inspiring the street corner paper sellers to shout "Air crash sensation, read all about it" in a way they seldom bothered to nowadays, one of the people to respond was Johnson, on his way back to the Connaught after another meeting with his lawyers. He read the headline with something approaching disbelief, then with elation. So completely by guesswork he had struck close to the truth in his broadcast the night before. At the hotel he found Sharon waiting for him.

"Take a load of this honey," he cried as excitedly as a schoolboy. "Those goddamn limeys have come clean at last."

When Sharon saw the headlines she leaped up and

351

threw her arms around his neck, hugging him in delight. Now she stood in the lounge of the Connaught, as excited as her father was.

"Does this mean they can't sue us?"

"It emphatically does," replied Johnson. "The most our insurers will have to pay is the seventy-five thousand dollars per passenger under Montreal. That attorney Falkender can set about eating his words from here on. Unless he persuades someone to sue the British government he'll be without clients. No one could pretend the accident is due to our negligence. Shooting down an airplane isn't sabotage; it's more like an act of war. Whether it can be that technically I wouldn't know yet, but it's certainly a case for the war risks insurers."

She hugged him again. "Let me read it all."

Sharon sat down and carefully went through the newspaper story. As he watched her Johnson's cheerfulness subsided. No amount of exoneration would bring Bill Curtis and the other dead back to life. Nor would the stain on Atlantic's reputation be easily eradicated. People would sympathize, yes. But they would instinctively book on another airline the next time they flew.

Sharon finished the article and faced her father. "I know you don't go much on the woman's intuition bit. But when it says all this about official inquiries, doesn't that have to be Jim Donaldson? He was pretty unhappy over that row yesterday. I could tell."

"You mean his wife's a bitch?" asked Johnson.

"No, Daddy, I do not. OK, she may be, but that's not what I mean. Donaldson didn't like what's been happening any more than you did. It was obvious. I'll bet ten dollars to a dead rat he had something to do with this home secretary guy changing his tune."

Johnson sat down in an armchair, ran a finger round his collar as though loosening it and finally admitted with some embarrassment, "You could be right, honey. You could be right at that."

"If I am, you owe him an apology."

"No man walks out on me twice. Once is the finish."

"All Jim Donaldson did," maintained Sharon firmly, "was stick to his guns. His job wouldn't allow him to comment, and so he wouldn't. And in one way you're right. His wife did act like a bitch, and I think he walked out on her more than on you. May I tell you something, Dad? You need men like that in the airline."

"I sure need a good flight safety inspector," acknowledged Johnson. As he spoke a waiter approached them and hovered politely a couple of feet away.

"Hey, fetch me a scotch on the rocks, will you? A double."

Sharon stepped forward.

"Tea," she said. "Not scotch. Tea for two."

The waiter hesitated and then disappeared.

"You win," said Johnson. "I owe him an apology."

Exactly at four Mick Melville entered the chief fire officer's room at the London Fire Brigade's headquarters on the Albert Embankment of the Thames. Plowden had summoned Melville to congratulate him. The Fire Brigade had its own awards, among the highest being the Queen's Gallantry Medal and the Queen's Commendation for Brave Conduct. It was Plowden's intention to recommend Melville and two others for the lesser award and to give them his own Chief Officer's Commendation. But it could be six months before his own commendations were presented at a ceremony at County Hall, probably together with several Royal Humane Society Certificates for rescues, and it would be a year before awards by the Queen were announced in the official *London Gazette* and the presentations were made by Her Majesty at Buckingham Palace. Thus, Plowden wanted the firemen to know immmediately that their courage and tenacity were appreciated. He interviewed Melville first.

"You did a good job, Mick," he commented after they had discussed the incident for a few minutes. "A bloody good job. Even if you were close on taking one chance too many."

The reference to his dash back into the wreck, to rescue the railway passenger whose family had remained trapped, made Melville feel an emotion akin to pain. Although it was two full days, almost to the minute, since the bells had gone down at the Greycoat Place Fire Station announcing the crash, although he was free of his heavy tunic and had washed the gritty dirt out of his hair and ears, he was still mentally fatigued from the crash. At home this morning after his night shift he had unashamedly cried from exhaustion. A doctor would have advised that the savage experience of cutting out bodies had left him suffering from delayed shock. He looked at Plowden.

"When there's someone alive in there you just drop everything," he said determinedly. "It's all you can do, isn't it?"

"I may have six thousand firemen, but I can't afford to lose a single one of them. Anyway, that's not what I asked you here to talk about."

Plowden rose to his feet, straightened up and leaned across his desk to shake hands. For the chief officer to shake hands with his own men was a rarity, an accolade in its own right. It was the measure of Plowden's leadership that he could invest a simple gesture with great significance.

"Congratulations, Mick," he said. "Well done."

"Thank you, sir," Melville replied, conscious of the honor, and then asked, "Do you know what happened to the bloke we got out from the plane?"

"He died during the night," Plowden spoke softly, aware how this could add to Melville's depression. "It wasn't a survivable crash, any more than the Trident at Staines was."

"I suppose not," said Melville dully.

After thanking the chief fire officer again, he left to walk across the river to Westminster. There would be a mound of paperwork to cope with at the fire station. Reports to be written and forms completed, all in careful undemonstrative official phrases, all with exact times and correct names. At Lambeth Bridge he saw a newspaper seller's placard: "AIR CRASH—MINISTER'S STATEMENT." He bought a copy and paused, reflecting that the time was only four twenty and he was in no hurry. He was not on duty until six. At first he could scarcely believe the story. Shot down? To a fireman the worst crime is arson. This was arson and murder, and Melville trembled as he scanned the page, fury added to the emotions already plaguing him. Then he told himself to forget the past and went on walking back to Greycoat Place.

At ten minutes past four the demonstrators began their struggling march from Trafalgar Square, with the International Socialists again chanting "ISRAEL OUT, ISRAEL OUT, ISRAEL OUT, OUT, OUT!"

In the Operations Room at New Scotland Yard the Deputy Assistant Commissioner "A" Operations watched them on the television monitors and heard the commander in the control van on King Charles' island give his orders.

"Inspectors one and two, move your men forward. Gaps of ten yards. Inspector three, man the barrier. Over."

The inspectors acknowledged, two directing their constables to string out alongside the procession at ten-yard intervals, the third sealing off the entrance to Downing Street. Out of sight near the Houses of Parliament a reserve of mounted police waited, their horses pawing the ground impatiently. The demonstrators moved very slowly down Whitehall, banners and placards swaying. It was raining again, and the Arabs among them looked dejected.

As the march began Mohammed Khadir stopped the battered Triumph on the western side of Vincent Square, ten minutes' walk from the Houses of Parliament. The square was so large you could imagine you were in the country. Two teams of schoolboys were playing cricket on the well-tended grass. Khadir parked the car as the umpire was trying to decide if the rain should stop play. Khadir did not even notice. He was making sure that this place was visible from the back of Rochester Row Police Station. He had chosen the square because Rochester Row ran parallel to its north side. The police station lay between, its front entrance on the street, its backyard opening onto the square. While Mohammed satisfied himself, Kamal opened the car's trunk and bent over it. Inside was the shopping bag with the bomb. Kamal wound the Mickey Mouse watch, set the minute hand and cautiously clipped the wire onto the battery terminal. The time was 4:16 P.M. After a final check he closed the trunk and locked it.

"Let's go," he said, adding in an undertone, "not too fast."

Casually they strolled up the side of the square and through to Rochester Row, turning left away from the police station, and went into a small café, where they bought cups of weak coffee and sat down at a table to wait.

Commander Thompson was compiling notes in the third-floor office that he had borrowed. It was a curiously shaped room with one window immediately opposite the door and another set diagonally across the corner behind the desk. From the outside this window appeared to be in a turret, which in fact was a sham. The architect who had designed the place in 1900 had allowed his fancy to run free to a mild extent, erecting mock turrets of brick at each corner and a white stone balustraded parapet along the roofline between them. Perhaps he thought a police station ought to resemble a fortress. And he had given the building only one main entrance, so any visitor had to pass within sight of the station office—the "engine room" as it was known—before he or she could reach the door leading to the stairs. These consisted of three bleak stone flights giving access to the canteen and the briefing room on the first floor, where Thompson had held his earlier conferences, the CID office on the second floor and the senior officers' room at the top.

It was quiet, for which Thompson was grateful. He was finding it increasingly hard to concentrate. His recollections of the hours immediately following the crash were becoming more and more blurred. There were endless obstacles to completing his report for the commissioner, which he was slaving over now in the hope that he could manage to take most of tomorrow off. Tomorrow was his wedding anniversary, Sunday, May 12. When he did get home, he reflected, he would hardly be able to keep awake anyway. He had been on the trot for nearly three days and two nights. As an antidote to weariness and failing memory he tried recording events in reverse, working back from the situation as it was now. A summary would be one way to start. He numbered the notes as he made them.

1. Total presumed dead 428, of whom 151 railway passengers confirmed dead, 13 aircraft crew, 264 airline passengers.

So far only three of the survivors who might have come from the plane had been identified as such. All three had died. Eleven more had turned out to be train passengers. It had to be assumed that no more airline passengers would be found among the serious casualties. He scribbled the next heading.

2. Serious casualties 418, minor casualties, 604, total 1,022.

Thompson paused again. The log Sturgess had kept revealed a discrepancy. More people had been treated by hospitals than the casualty bureau had records of. A number of the less injured must have got themselves to hospital. This reminded him that they would also have to consolidate statistics of the assistance given by voluntary services like the Salvation Army and the Red Cross. He labored on with his list.

3. Property.

Thompson stopped. God in heaven, the facts one needed. Compiling the report was almost worse than dealing with the incident, and this was only a preliminary one. Chisholm would know how many items of property had been recovered. He lifted the telephone and asked for the chief superintendent only to be told that he was on the way across. Wondering if Chisholm had located the missing briefcase led Thompson's thoughts back to the terrorists and their motiva-

357

tion. From Allom he knew that the Israelis were anxious to produce the original documents at the United Nations. But it did not necessarily follow that the terrorists thought them so damning. Probably there was more to it than Allom had disclosed. Anyway he had a hunch that his leak to Eckhardt would produce some kind of inquiry, which in turn begged the question of whether the terrorists, or their friends, knew what the briefcase looked like—or even knew the documents were in one. The Israelis themselves had only just heard that it had been chained to Maier's wrist. Thompson thought it a fair presumption that anyone asking at the Inquiry Office downstairs would try to establish ownership by describing the documents themselves. They could hardly hope to walk in and seize them, which meant effectively that they could be interviewed. It was, he reflected, a long shot. Meanwhile, the CID was combing London for suspects. David Chance was due back in a few minutes. Maybe he would have some news.

There was a knock on the door, and Chisholm entered. Thompson saw the triumph in his face before he noticed what he had brought.

"Here you are!" announced Chisholm, lifting up a brown paper package and depositing it on the desk. "We found it." He stripped off the wrapping with the aid of a pocketknife, revealing a dirt-spattered brown cowhide briefcase.

"We've gone over it for fingerprints. You can touch it."

Thompson gazed at the case. So this was the object on which someone had set so high a price that neither death nor destruction mattered. It had once been elegant. Its two combination locks were of heavy brass. So were the fittings of its handle, now twisted almost off. Almost but not completely. From one end of it hung three links of thin steel chain, the last one deformed.

"One hell of a force yanked that apart," commented Chisholm.

Indeed the underneath of the case had clearly caught on something; the leather had been gouged clean through for several inches.

"And where did you find it?" asked Thompson.

Chisholm's big features creased into a grin. 'Stupid really. I should have thought of it earlier. It was with all the stuff removed from the left luggage office by Platform Fifteen. The office is only a yard or two from where the plane's nose hit. I reckon this case must have been thrown right out, like some of the bodies were, fallen near the left luggage store and been mistaken for an item from it. Although the fire didn't reach there the place was so badly damaged that we transferred the whole lot. So I wasn't only looking for a case with a bit of chain attached, I was looking for one without a left luggage office sticker. It took less than twenty minutes—once I'd had the idea."

"Have you checked the contents?"

"Do you have the combination?" asked Chisholm pointedly. "Knowing they'll claim it's diplomatic baggage, I didn't dare force the locks."

Thompson drew in his breath sharply and swore.

"I'll have to seek advice, I suppose. Not that opening it would take an expert long." He lifted the case gently and placed it on the floor beside the desk. "Thanks," he said warmly, "thanks a lot. The commissioner will be more than pleased. Oh, by the way, can you give me the tally of property recovered?"

"I'll get back and phone you the figures," said Chisholm. "We've just about sorted it all out now. What a way to spend the weekend!"

After Chisholm had left Thompson telephoned the news through to New Scotland Yard and asked for instructions. After a short delay he was told the Home Office had to be consulted. They would ring him back. Resignedly he launched on a fresh attempt to begin his report.

"At 1616 hours, Thursday, May 9, a DC-10 aircraft of Atlantic Airlines crashed on the western or

Brighton side of Victoria Station. The first police officer on the scene was. . . ."

A cracking explosion, as violent as a thunderclap, reverberated down the street, shaking the building. The window frames rattled. There was a second or two's complete silence, as if the city were holding its breath. Then, as Thompson leaped to his feet, the police station came back to life. An alarm bell rang. There were shouts. Men ran down the stairs, their boots hammering on the flooring. Thompson rushed out to the landing, almost colliding with the inspector from the room next door.

"Sounded pretty close, sir," the inspector called out and bolted down.

It took all Thompson's self-discipline not to follow. Reminding himself that Rochester Row had a well-established routine for bombings and that there was no need for him to interfere, he returned to his desk. From outside he heard the wailing of a two-tone horn and, glancing through the window, saw a blue patrol car roar past.

On the ground floor policemen streamed out of the rear entrance into the yard that gave into Vincent Square. Horses in the stables were whinnying with fright. A sergeant, seeing from the smoke and dust where the bomb had gone off, raced back indoors to the station office and alerted the telephonists. As they put through calls to the ambulance and fire services and to Scotland Yard's Information Room, the sergeant dashed out again and around the square.

Injured schoolboys in white sweaters were lying on the grass. All the windows of the buildings opposite were shattered. Strewn in the roadway lay twisted pieces of metal that he recognized as parts of the car. A seat had been thrown up in the air and impaled itself on the railings. The rest of the Triumph had burst into flames. Three minutes later the huge red Dennis pump appliance from Greycoat Place arrived, the first ambulance hard behind it. Firemen dragged out hoses, and as they extinguished the small fire the stretcher-bearers began loading casualties.

Inside the café where Mohammed and Kamal sat pretending to drink their coffee the explosion produced momentary consternation.

"Christ," said the owner. "Another bloody bomb."

Several people ran out onto the pavement. But Vincent Square was hidden by houses, and there was nothing to be seen. They returned disappointed.

"The copshop's close enough," said one. "No need for us to worry."

Kamal and Mohammed stayed silent. After another four minutes they left and walked along Rochester Row. In the distance they could hear emergency sirens and an alarm bell. The reporters who had been waiting outside the police station had gone. Mohammed adjusted the fold of the raincoat over his arm, feeling stupid at carrying it when there was rain falling, although the grenade bulged comfortingly in its pocket.

The police station's double doors were unguarded, and they passed through, finding themselves in a narrow hall with four doors off it. Nothing indicated where any of these led, except a glass-paneled one on the left marked "Inquiries." Through it they could see a counter and a police sergeant. As they stood in the hallway, momentarily uncertain, he noticed them.

"This way," said Kamal decisively, and pushed open the door.

"The inspector Donaldson told us to come here," he announced boldly. "We have information about the air crash."

From the communications room beyond came a high-pitched chatter of radio and telephone dialogue.

"Inspector Donaldson?" queried the sergeant. "Never heard of him. Listen, friend, we're a bit busy just now. Come back another time, would you?"

"The gentleman investigating the crash of the airplane," Kamal insisted.

The sergeant remembered who Donaldson was.

"There's only the commander here at the moment," he said.

"That is the gentleman we are to see." Kamal sounded confident.

"Why didn't you say so then?" The sergeant's instinct was to tell this pair of wogs to clear off. But he knew there was an all-out search for evidence in progress. He called to the one duty constable who had not gone out to Vincent Square.

"Here, Mike, show these two upstairs, will you? And come straight down again."

In silence they followed the constable up the three flights, noting that the landings were exposed to view from the canteen and other rooms off it. Both men were on edge, surprised at the ease with which their bluff was succeeding. The constable knocked on Thompson's door.

"Come in."

"Two men about the air crash, sir."

A moment later they were facing a strong-faced man with a tired, worried expression on his face.

"This will be easy," thought Mohammed. "It is perfect. A corner office at the top of the building." He rapidly absorbed the scene. The commander behind a wide desk with an ungainly metal lamp, a telephone, his peaked hat resting on a small white-painted safe to the right, the window behind him. The door clicked shut behind them as the constable departed.

"So you have some information?" said Thompson, realizing in the same instant that his hunch had been right. What did not occur to him was that the appearance of these two Arabs so soon after the bomb explosion was no coincidence. The movement with which Mohammed pulled out the Makarov caught him unawares.

"Do not move," snapped Kamal, in the same moment reaching for his own pistol and stepping back against the wall, out of the line of sight from the main window. Mohammed moved closer to the desk. Together they covered Thompson from two angles.

Thompson did not stir. Both his hands were on the desk and he kept them there. He was unarmed, and if there was an alarm bell in this office he did not

362

know its whereabouts. "This is one for the book," he thought. "A holdup inside the station." Aloud he said coolly, "And what can I do for you two gentlemen?"

Mohammed pointed the Makarov at his head. Thompson recognized the make.

"The documents that are guarded here," demanded Mohammed, wanting to have his say. "The plans of Abu Youssouf!" In his excitement he was shouting.

"Quieter," hissed Kamal, then turned back to Thompson. "The documents can be of no interest to your country. They are important only to us. Return them and give us safe-conduct to Beirut. Either that or we kill you."

"Very dramatic," remarked Thompson, remaining absolutely still. He was rapidly sizing up the situation. From previous experience with a siege he knew there were three cardinal principles in a hostage situation: to gain time, to gain the confidence of your captors, and to persuade them that they had no hope of success. The catch on this occasion was that the terrorists' objective stood wrapped in brown paper behind his desk. He had to pray that they would neither spot the package nor ask what it contained. At least they clearly did not know what they were looking for.

"There are two problems," he remarked with an air of detachment, as though his own life were in no way at stake. Kamal reacted with immediate suspicion.

"I see no problems."

"First," said Thompson coolly, "I am expendable. If you shoot me, that's my bad luck. The government gives my widow a pension. . . ."

"The documents." Kamal began to raise his own voice. "We want the documents the Israeli was carrying."

"That is the second problem. So do we."

"What do you mean?"

"I mean that we are searching for them, too."

"That is nonsense!" cried Kamal angrily. "Do not try to deceive us. We know all the baggages are here."

Thompson paused. In spite of the danger, he felt perverse pleasure at the success of his leak to Eckhardt

—by God he would get that bastard now! But the immediate question was for how long could he spin out this conversation and when David Chance would return. A plan was forming in his mind. First he wanted to give them something to think about.

"If your Libyan friends told you the airline baggage was here," he said calmly, "they were wrong. The customs have been insisting on examining it."

The reference to the Libyans registered all right. Seeing bewilderment grow in their faces, he pressed on. "Our difficulty has been that we do not know what the Israeli was carrying. Can you describe it? Perhaps then we can do a deal."

Mohammed and Kamal exchanged glances, and Mohammed muttered something.

"You can safely talk in Arabic," suggested Thompson. "I shall not understand."

It was true, even if making the suggestion was a risk. But the more they talked, the less likely they were to act. Once they realized that he could not follow their conversation, a tiny measure of trust would be established. Later, if this became a siege, external microphones would pick up every sound in the room. Translators and psychiatrists would advise the police outside. But it would only become a siege if they began to negotiate. If.

"My friend is in favor of shooting you," said Kamal, as though announcing a proposition to a meeting.

Thompson shrugged, still being careful not to shift his hands, and looked straight at Kamal.

"If that will give him satisfaction, go ahead. It will not gain you anything. All the baggage is in another building. If you kill me there will be no possibility of you reaching it. None at all."

That was enough, Thompson decided. Let them chew it over. To his relief they began a hurried discussion, though the gun in Mohammed's hand barely wavered. Thompson sat and waited. Suddenly Mohammed's eye lit on the brown paper package, a corner of which was showing from behind the desk.

"What is that?" he demanded.

"A parcel."

"Show me."

Very slowly, very deliberately, making certain his movements did not alarm the gunmen, Thompson leaned down and lifted the loosely wrapped briefcase onto the desk.

"Take off the paper," commanded Mohammed.

Thompson began to unwrap it. There was no doubt in his mind that if they realized what it was they would shoot him and hope to escape.

Downstairs David Chance entered the building and called in at the station office. He had heard the explosion, distantly, and the wailing of the emergency vehicles' horns.

"What's up?" he inquired.

"Bomb in Vincent Square, sir. Bloody awful mess. Injured several school kids."

"Is the commander in?"

"Couple of blokes with him, sir. Information about the air crash. Arabs, they looked like."

Chance froze. There was too much happening at once. As far as he was concerned "Arabs" meant "gunmen."

"When did they come?"

"Ten or eleven minutes ago."

"Is anyone else upstairs?"

"All out in the square, I should think, sir."

To the sergeant's amazement Chance pulled out the .38 Smith and Wesson revolver that he carried in a shoulder holster under his sports coat, snapped it open, spun the chamber to check the rounds, closed the gun and cocked it. Like most police marksmen, he preferred a revolver to a pistol. It was less likely to jam.

"Come on," he said, "the constable can hold the fort. We'll go up nice and quietly. When I go in belt in after me. I'll take one, you take the other."

Leading the way, he climbed the stairs, moving fast but softly. On the top landing he tiptoed to the door and stood for a moment listening, holding a hand up for silence. Kamal's harsh voice came distinctly through the thin wood.

"Open the case. If you do not open the case we will kill you."

With a single movement Chance turned the handle and pushed the door violently. It flew back, leaving him standing in the entrance, revolver in hand. Directly ahead, by the window, he saw a young Arab in a crumpled brown suit holding a pistol, and he fired at him as he leaped forward into the room. As he did so Thompson, who had already decided which of the desk ornaments was his best weapon, threw the heavy iron lamp at Mohammed and ducked. Mohammed fired but missed, his aim upset as the lamp crashed to the floor, caught short by its cord.

The sergeant charged through the doorway as Kamal slewed around and shot at Chance, who simultaneously fired again. Both men fell, Kamal squirming on the floor, coughing blood. Chance, hit in the thigh, reached out toward the doorpost for support but overbalanced. Mohammed glanced around, neatly dodged the sergeant and decided in the same split second that the game was up. He seized the briefcase, jumped over Chance and ran pell-mell down the stairs, pursued by Thompson and the sergeant. Both men were obstructed by Chance's trying to raise himself up in the passage.

Mohammed reached the ground floor, burst through into the door into the hall and paused long enough to fumble in his raincoat pocket for the grenade. As Thompson and the sergeant came after him, he yanked out the pin and lobbed the grenade toward them.

"Get back," yelled Thompson. "Down!"

He retreated, throwing himself and the sergeant flat at the foot of the stairs. Two seconds later the grenade exploded, blowing out all the doors and showering the station office with broken glass.

Outside Mohammed sprinted along Rochester Row toward Victoria Street, Parliament Square and the safety of the crowd of demonstrators. If the organizers had fulfilled their promises, some of the marchers would have surged away from the Houses of Parliament across Parliament Square and toward Westminster Abbey. It was in one of the small streets behind the Abbey that Kamal had fixed their emergency rendezvous.

When Mick Melville heard the Vincent Square explosion he stopped instantly, but high buildings distort sounds, so he could not tell the precise direction of the bang. A moment later common sense reminded him that the best thing he could do was return to the fire station. He set off running, dodging pedestrians, cursing the innumerable obstacles of lampposts, parking meters and other so-called "street furniture." He covered the half mile to Greycoat Place in four minutes. The two appliances had gone, and the high doors stood open. Panting from the exertion, he went to the watch room and sheafed through the teletype messages. As he did so another one clacked out "FROM ADO BRIGGS AT VINCENT SQUARE BOMB FIRE SURROUNDED 1647." So that was where it was. He hurried to pull on his boots and tunic in order to set off for the square. He reckoned they would be able to use another officer.

As Melville emerged a swarthy-faced man came running full tilt out of Rochester Row, clutching a briefcase under one arm. He stopped for a fraction of a second, confused by the three converging streets ahead of him beyond the fire station. Then he continued running across Greycoat Place, a car driver hooting and braking to avoid him. Melville saw him and suddenly realized that the short black object in his right hand was a gun.

"Christ," he exclaimed, half aloud, "it's the bomber."

As Khadir passed the fire station Melville dived straight for the gun. The Arab swerved, slipped on the wet pavement and fell. As he scrambled up, Melville recovered his own balance, raised his right arm and chopped viciously down with the hard edge of his outstretched hand, slamming into Khadir's forearm just above the wrist, paralyzing the nerves and sending the Makarov flying into the roadway. Nonetheless, Khadir regained his feet, cursing in Arabic. As he straightened up Melville performed one of the first un-armed combat tricks he had ever learned. He jerked his right knee up into Khadir's groin and simultaneously thrust both thumbs hard into his eyes. As the Arab doubled up in agony, reaching for the fireman's hands, trying to pull them away, Melville drew back his right fist and thumped a punch into his solar plexus. Then, as Khadir rolled over on the pavement, winding and groaning, he kicked him hard under the chin. The Arab's head snapped back and he lay still.

A small crowd gathered as Melville picked up the Makarov and the briefcase and hauled Khadir by the coat collar into the fire station. The crowd gasped, and a woman screamed. Melville turned away from them in disgust. It was always the same in emergencies. Only one in a hundred people did anything. The rest just gawped.

Once inside Melville threw a bucket of water over Khadir and set about reviving him. When he showed signs of coming to, he tied the Arab's hands behind his back and pushed him into a sitting position against the courtyard wall, his legs stretched out in front of him. It was then that the first policeman arrived.

Reports of the bomb explosion came into the Operations Room at New Scotland Yard just as the Palestinian demo turned disorderly. To the Deputy Commissioner "A" Division it seemed probable that the two were related. He sent squad cars to Vincent Square and ordered the demonstrators to be dispersed along the Embankment. Two more serials of police were dispatched to assist the commander in charge and motorcyclists temporarily diverted traffic away from Parliament Square. Near Westminster Abbey a combination of mounted and foot police headed off the two hundred or so marchers trying to force their way toward Victoria Street. There were a few struggles as the more determined ones clashed with the police, shouting abuse and trying to hit the horses with their placards. A girl who jabbed at one of the horse's flanks with a knitting needle was nearly trampled underfoot as the animal reared. She and two men were arrested. Then the police succeeded in linking arms to form a human chain across the road, and the brief fracas was over. The marchers retreated.

At the entrance to the House of Commons the Palestinian petition was being presented to Enoch Andrews, the Honorable Member of Parliament for Mid-Fife, who was doing his best to disregard the growing disorder. A few minutes later the commander came up to him. The commander was extremely polite. Members of Parliament had to be treated with kid gloves. Nonetheless, the orders over the radio from the Operations Room were explicit. He was to bring Andrews in for questioning. Special Branch had just heard of his inquiries about Ben Maier's flight from El Al.

Andrews objected volubly.

"It would be in your own interest, sir," the commander insisted. "We have reason to believe that this demonstration has been used as a cloak for other activities, and we should like you to assist with our inquiries."

Andrews recognized the euphemistic phrase. Suspected criminals were invariably reported as "helping police with their inquiries." With an unconvincing show of willingness he agreed.

Donaldson was at Victoria Station by the cartoon cinema, watching the removal of more wreckage. The first of the bogie bolster trucks had been shunted in, and he wanted to see how successful the railway cranes would be in lifting sections of the airliner onto it. To his relief, there were few problems, despite the lack of room for maneuver. He surveyed the diminishing remains of the DC-10, with the workmen hammering and hacking at the twisted roof girders above and around it. He thought of the engineers who designed this aircraft, the skill lavished in building it, the passengers and the crew who had died in it.

"Such a bloody waste," he exclaimed angrily to himself. "Such a rotten bloody waste." If all the investigations he did in his life only prevented one accident recurring then his time would have been well spent. There would certainly have to be a tightening of security after this one, though by what means was another matter.

As he stood there a railway policeman interrupted his contemplation. "Excuse me, sir. You're wanted urgently on the phone. A Mr. Johnson."

Donaldson was surprised. He had not expected to have any further dealings with the airline president. He hurried back to the first-floor office on Hudson's Place. As usual there were several messages on the desk. One, he noticed, asked him to ring Miss Carslake and gave a London number. He picked up the telephone.

"Donaldson," he said simply.

"You're an elusive guy, Jim." Johnson's voice was as clipped and incisive as ever, though he sounded friendly. "I've had people looking for you all over."

"What can I do for you?"

"I reckon I owe you a load of thanks. That government statement has killed any possible charge of willful negligence on our part."

"I'm glad." Donaldson was uncertain what to say.

"Listen, Jim," said Johnson, trying to talk as personally as if he were face to face with the investigator. "I also owe you an apology. A downright humble apology."

"I don't think so," said Donaldson, embarrassed.

"For two reasons. First, I attacked your impartiality. That was plain stupid. An investigator who isn't impartial is no good to God or man. Second, I think I may have influenced your wife to betray your confidences. I'm sorry."

"Please forget about it." Donaldson wished he could cut off this conversation. It was only heading toward further embarrassment.

During the past twenty-four hours he had come to a firm conclusion about Johnson and Atlantic Airlines. Characteristically, he did not intend to change his mind.

"If you want that job, Jim," said Johnson, "you can name your price."

"I'm going to be fully occupied with this investigation for up to nine months. There will still be a public inquiry. There is going to be a great deal of hard work in establishing the precise sequence of events following the explosion of the missile. It'll be the biggest investigation I've ever handled. I couldn't possibly resign in the middle."

"I repeat. You can name your price. And come when you're ready."

Donaldson steeled himself. There was no avoiding the issue. "I'm very sorry. I'm afraid I can't accept."

"Uh?"

"Things have changed dramatically. I have been offered a promotion."

"Money is no obstacle." Significantly, Johnson had dropped the Christian name, and his voice was tougher.

"It's not that. Frankly, I've thought about it, and I know I'd find prevention of accidents boring. Safety inspectors end up checking the tire pressures. They live in a different world from determining why an accident really did happen. It's not my game." Donaldson hesitated. "There's something else. It may sound odd, but there's a kind of freedom working in our department that I'd hate to lose. In Atlantic Airlines, what Johnson says goes. We'd end up having the most almighty quarrel."

Johnson was taken aback. He did not like the implication that he rode roughshod over subordinates.

"You're a buccaneer at heart, Mr. Johnson," Donaldson went on, "which is just the kind of leader an independent airline needs. I wish Atlantic well. I mean that. But it's no place for me."

"You could be right," said Johnson reluctantly, uncertain whether to be pleased or angry. There was no point in wasting breath. He prepared to ring off. "It's been a pleasure knowing you. Thanks for all you've done."

"I'm glad you understand. I've no doubt we shall be meeting again. Don't judge us by our politicians."

Johnson laughed. "Nor us. And may I tell you something else. Accept a buccaneer's advice. Take a hairbrush to that wife of yours. So long."

It was somehow typical of Johnson to achieve the last word like that, Donaldson reflected, being both outrageous and friendly at once. It was also regrettably true that he would have to come to terms with Jane. In any case Johnson's suggestion wasn't his style. Thinking about it, he decided that the sooner Jane knew they were not going to America, the better. It would also enable him to say that he would be coming home tonight. If the WRVS lady's psychology was right, Jane would accept his return without comment. The phone rang. It was the police office downstairs.

"There's a lady here to see you, sir. Your wife. Shall we show her up?"

"Yes. Please do."

Donaldson had a sudden feeling that perhaps the WRVS lady was a more reasonable wife than Jane, and when Jane entered the room the suspicion was confirmed.

"So," she remarked, "this is your little hidey-hole, is it?"

She walked around, inspecting the room haughtily.

"It's bigger than my normal office, curiously enough," he said, standing up awkwardly. She showed no inclination to kiss him or make any conventional greeting. "I was about to ring you," he added.

She turned on him, her voice harsh and sarcastic. "So you decided to ring at last. That was nice of you. Very nice."

Her face was faintly flushed under her makeup. He glanced at his watch and concluded that she couldn't have been drinking. The time was only 5:30 P.M.

"We've been appallingly busy," he murmured, uncertain whether to sit down or remain standing. He sat down.

"Too busy to give your wife and family any consideration evidently." She moved across the room and perched on the corner of the desk, swinging one leg and looking contemptuously at her husband. "Of course, why should we expect any? After all, we always have come second in your life. Second to the great inspectorate. Well, what news *is* there from the fantasy world of accident investigation that kept you so very busy? All night."

"The most recent event is that Johnson rang me. He apologized and asked me to take the job."

A flicker of concern crossed her face. Donaldson noticed it. Was Johnson right? Her expression suggested that she knew she had behaved badly, that there was something to her disadvantage. In better days she used to be frank about mistakes. She had the same look now, albeit suppressed.

"What did you say?" Her question was in a more level voice. The answer clearly mattered to her. Donaldson told her. Immediately she flared up.

"So you decided not to go, did you? How lovely. How charming. You didn't think of consulting *me* by any chance? No? Of course, it's only my life and the children's you're throwing away, isn't it?"

Donaldson struggled to speak against the stream of bitter comment.

"We'll be better off when the promotion comes through."

"Oh! So it's 'we' all of a sudden now? What a pity you didn't think as 'we' earlier." Her tone became more strident. "I don't want to be married to a tuppenny ha'penny civil servant, do you hear? I don't want to go on in this lousy rut with a dull husband and a dull home. I want to live a little. *I* want some excitement for a change. For me. Do you understand that?"

Donaldson's temper was beginning to kindle. He strived to keep it in hand.

"The deputy chief inspector's job is very well paid. There's nothing tuppenny ha'penny about it."

"Then you stay with it. Stay in your office, stay wherever you like, but stay away from me."

Jane gave him a withering glance and picked up her handbag. In the doorway she loosed her final barb.

"Two can play at walking out, Jim Donaldson."

Marching down the passage, she reflected that she would call her solicitor on Monday.

Donaldson sat listening to her fading footsteps, barely able to believe that he could have misjudged her so badly. He felt alone and weary. It was lucky he hadn't given up his room at the club. It was often full over weekends.

Mechanically he began dealing with the messages on the desk. He responded to Gilly Carslake's call fourth.

"Thank the Lord you've rung," she exclaimed. "I thought you were never going to."

"What's up then?"

Donaldson pictured the tall blonde at the other end of the line, enthusiastic and friendly. He wondered what she was so excited about.

"I heard the news, about the missile I mean. Now, look, I am a journalist myself. You do remember that?"

"Naturally."

"You don't sound very understanding. Can't you see? It's a tremendous story, isn't it? I mean I was the last person to actually see the plane before it crashed. Now that it's all come out I want to, well, to be honest I want to cash in on it. Do you mind?"

Donaldson laughed in spite of his dejection. There was something about this girl, a sort of infectious naïveté that cheered him up.

"Not at all. You're not subject to the Official Secrets Act."

"That is a relief! Well then, will you help me? I've arranged to write my eyewitness account for one of the Sundays. I have to phone it in to them by seven."

"It doesn't sound as though you need much assistance!" he said dryly.

"Oh, yes, I do. I don't know what all those bits that fell off the tail were. That's how you can help me."

Donaldson hesitated. What the hell. He had nothing to lose.

"Come round straightaway," he said. "I'll take you out for a drink. I could do with one anyway."

"That'll be lovely," said Gilly breathlessly. "Thank you so much. See you soon."

Donaldson sat at the desk and rubbed the side of his nose gently with his finger. Life might have some compensations after all, he thought.

Bert, the commander's driver, eased the black saloon to a halt outside the block of mansion flats where the Alloms lived. He hopped out and opened the door for Thompson and Sturgess. As if by magic the hall porter materialized at the entrance. Hall porters, Thompson reflected, had a knack for appearing when anything interesting was happening.

"Mr. Allom's flat, sir? The third floor, sir."

The two officers went up in the elevator, and Thompson touched the bell. Allom himself appeared.

"Good evening," he said courteously. "I will fetch her."

He returned shortly with Connie Maier. She was more composed now, Sturgess noticed. Her face was carefully made up; her dark hair glistened; she was dressed for traveling.

"How are you feeling?" Sturgess asked solicitously.

"Better, thank you. It's kind of you to collect me."

"You should thank the commander." He introduced Thompson. She made a brave effort to smile.

"We began to feel a rather personal concern to see you safely to the plane, Mrs. Maier," said Thompson gravely. "There have been too many deaths in connection with"—he was about to say "your husband," but checked himself—"with this affair."

"I take it you are officially handing back the documents?" asked Allom uneasily.

"The briefcase is in the car," said Thompson. "I cannot say what it contains. It has been treated with the diplomatic privileges you demanded."

They could scarcely complain at that. In fact, it was barely an hour since the home secretary had decreed that the case should be returned and Mrs. Maier escorted to Heathrow for the first available flight to New York. In consequence there had been no time to break the combination of the briefcase's locks, simple though it must be. Thompson himself had been hard pressed to see Chance off to hospital, make arrangements at the airport and change into a clean uniform. Anyone seeing his well-pressed tunic, polished shoes and leather gloves would have found it hard to believe that he had been in a gunfight an hour and a half earlier.

Allom was considering his next move. He would have no idea whether the briefcase was the right one until it was opened.

"We cannot afford any more mistakes," he declared.

"None of us can," snapped Thompson irritatedly. "If you're not happy you had better come along, too."

"I intend to," said Allom. "I am accompanying her on the flight."

While Sturgess rode in the patrol car behind, with two armed constables, Thompson took Connie Maier and Allom in his saloon car. As they drove away, two police motorcyclists revved up and roared out ahead of them.

"Heavens," exclaimed Connie. "You're giving us the real treatment!"

"Oddly enough," said Thompson, "because my driver, Bert, is a civilian, he's not allowed to use the horn or jump the lights, even though I am the commander. That's why I asked for the outriders tonight."

"You British remain a mystery," said Allom. "After two years here I still do not understand. Now, the briefcase, please."

The armed constable in the front seat handed back the damaged brown case. Deliberately, no attempt had been made to clean it up. Connie gazed at it and felt for Allom's hand. The sight of the thing that had caused Ben's death and the whole three-day nightmare was too much for her.

"Jakov," she whispered. "It *is* the one I gave him."

She bit her lip, determined not to break down in front of these strangers but unable to say any more. Allom put an arm around her and after a little while asked gently, "Do you know how to open it?"

Memories whirled around her; she felt faint. It had

been a birthday present. What was it Ben had said? She struggled to recall his words.

"He said he would use the date of our wedding. He said he would never forget that." This was almost worse than anything, driving with these strangers and the sirens wailing in front. Driving to what? It was going to take her a long time to come to terms with Ben's death. She realized that Allom was tense beside her, waiting.

"The fourth of March, 1973." She said, "It was a Sunday."

Thompson examined the locks again. Each lock had three combination rings, making six in all. Carefully he rotated them to read 431973. The fourth day of the third month of 1973. He slid the catches sideways. Nothing moved. The hasps of the locks remained fast. As Allom watched nervously, he tried once more. Then he had an idea.

"Perhaps your husband added a naught in front of the single figures?" he suggested. "So that the fourth became zero four."

"I wouldn't know. I simply wouldn't know," said Connie, exhausted at this last element of strain.

Thompson moved the rings to 040373 and slid the catches. With a click both locks flicked open. He carefully raised the lid. Inside were several folders, labeled in Hebrew.

"Please!" demanded Allom abruptly, though he already felt relief because the folders looked familiar. Thompson shifted the case across, and Allom began checking through it. In one folder, carefully protected by transparent plastic, were the crumpled and blood-stained handwritten lists that had been captured at the café in Argenteuil. There could be no mistaking them for anything but the originals. Allom knew their appearance from photocopies. He relaxed.

"All is well," he said.

Connie gazed over his shoulder, unbelieving and tearful.

"You mean those are what Ben died for? Just a few scraps of paper? It's not possible. It can't be."

"Many people died for them," said Allom gently. "That is the way of wars."

At Heathrow they drove straight to a special parking area and were then led to the ramp for the evening 747 flight. The captain of the aircraft was waiting for them.

"Look after her," said Thompson. "Make sure she gets home safe."

"We have two security guards on board," he said. "She will."

Thompson shook hands with the formality he reserved for visiting dignitaries.

"Good-bye," he said. "I hope you'll have a happier visit here one day."

Connie tried to smile, but could not. The plane's captain and Allom helped her away into the cabin.

Thompson and Colin Sturgess stayed at the airport until the time for takeoff, two solitary figures standing on the roof, out of sight of the crowds. They watched the lumbering bulk of the 747 being pushed away from the ramp by a squat tractor, heard the whine of its engines increase as it began to taxi under its own power and finally saw it far away at the end of the runway lining up for takeoff. It seemed to gather speed very slowly. When it still seemed impossible that so huge a machine could rise from the ground, the nose came up and it took off, beginning a long climb to the west, its navigation lights winking against the pale evening sky.

"Come on, Colin," said Thompson. "Let's find our faithful Bert and go home."